"In the Night — In the Dark"

Tales of Ghosts and Less Welcome Visitors

by

ROGER JOHNSON

First edition published in 2011
© Copyright 2011
Roger Johnson

The right of Roger Johnson to be identified as the author of this work has been asserted by him in accordance with the Copyright, Designs and Patents Act 1998.

All rights reserved. No reproduction, copy or transmission of this publication may be made without express prior written permission. No paragraph of this publication may be reproduced, copied or transmitted except with express prior written permission or in accordance with the provisions of the Copyright Act 1956 (as amended). Any person who commits any unauthorised act in relation to this publication may be liable to criminal prosecution and civil claims for damage.

All characters appearing in this work are fictitious. Any resemblance to real persons, living or dead, is purely coincidental. The opinions expressed herein are those of the authors and not of MX Publishing.

Paperback ISBN 978-1-78092-050-4
ePub ISBN 978-1-78092-051-1
PDF ISBN 978-1-78092-052-8

Published in the UK by MX Publishing
335 Princess Park Manor, Royal Drive,
London, N11 3GX
www.mxpublishing.com
Cover design by www.staunch.com

In memory of
BASIL

"There are two means of refuge from the miseries of life: music and cats."

Albert Schweitzer

Mrs. Dudley: We live over in town, miles away.
Eleanor Lance: Yes.
Mrs. Dudley: So there won't be anyone around if you need help.
Eleanor Lance: I understand.
Mrs. Dudley: We couldn't hear you. In the night.
Eleanor Lance: Do you have any idea when Dr. Markway...
Mrs. Dudley: [*cuts her off*] No one could. No one lives any nearer than town. No one will come any nearer than that.
Eleanor Lance: I know.
Mrs. Dudley: In the night. In the dark.

The Haunting (1963)
Screenplay by Nelson Gidding, from *The Haunting of Hill House* by Shirley Jackson

CONTENTS

"Things that Go Bump in the Night" (Tales from the Endeavour)

The Scarecrow	7
The Watchman	20
The Interruptions	32
The Wall-Painting	48
The Searchlight	63
The Taking	76
The Melodrama	92
The Prize	106
The Breakdown	124
The Pool	131
The Clues	138
The Night Before Christmas	156
The Soldier	175
The Souvenir	189
Sweet Chiming Bells	198

"Things from Beyond"

Aliah Warden	216
The Dreaming City	225
Custos Sanctorum	237
Ishtaol	250
From the Desert	259
The Fool's Tale	262
The Man Who Inherited the World	269
In Memoriam	282
On Dead Gods	306

"More Things in Heaven and Earth..."

The Serpent's Tooth	310
Enigma	315
Desideratum	317
Love, Death and the Maiden	324
"Oddities Investigated" - Tales from a Hero's Casebook	338
A Butcher's Dozen: Tales in Verse	357

"Things that Go Bump in the Night"

Tales from the Endeavour

THE SCARECROW

"Going abroad, are you?" said George Cobbett, incuriously.

"Not this year," I said. "Mike Williams and I are off to the Cotswolds next month, for a couple of weeks. I came here tonight to tell him that I've booked us into a pub at a village near Banbury."

"Ah. Nice little town, Banbury. I rather envy you. What's the name of the village?"

"Saxton Lovell."

"Good God!"

It's never a good thing to surprise a man while he's drinking. Old George coughed and spluttered for a good half-minute. When he had regained his breath he said, "Then the pub must be — just a moment — the *Belchamp Arms*?"

"That's right. Obviously you know it."

"Oh, yes," said George, very deliberately. "I know it all right, though I've not been there in nearly fifty years. A little place, just off the road to Chipping Norton. Heh? And some three miles to the west is a hamlet called Normanton Lovell, which has one single and singular distinctive feature."

He paused, in that irritating way he has, and started filling his pipe.

"You're being cryptic," I said severely. "You've roused my curiosity now, and I want to know why. Is there a story behind this?"

The old man smiled, sheepishly. "I'm sorry, boy," he said. "Yes, there's a story, though I haven't told it in a long time. Ah, well... I'll tell it to you if you'll be a good fellow and get me another pint. I think you'll find it worthwhile."

I refilled both our glasses, and after we'd taken a good long draught I lit a cigarette and settled back to listen.

It happened while I was an undergraduate at Fisher College, Cambridge (said George). I was actually reading Classics, but much of my time was spent on the archaeology of ancient Britain — a theme that met with no approval at all from my tutor and was therefore the more cherished. He couldn't understand why anyone should wish to desert the crystalline delights of Rome for the dubious history of our uncivilised ancestors. My particular friend at Cambridge — *tamquam alter idem* — was one Lionel Ager, who was privately devoted to the pursuit of English custom and tradition. Already, by the time he came up to Cambridge, he was a member of the Folklore Society, and among his correspondents, he told me, were Alfred Williams and Frank Kidson, the great collectors of traditional song.

I was in my second year at Fisher College when I learned of the stone circles at Normanton Lovell. William Stukely seems not to have known of them, but in the college library's copy of his *Itinerarium Antiquum* I found a hand-written marginal note, referring to the Rollright Stones: "What of the Dancers of Normanton Lovell? More like Abury than this nearer neighbour."

The megalithic formations at Avebury — which Stukely called "Abury" — are unique, as I was well aware, both in their design and in their overwhelming size. All the other stone circles in Britain that I knew of — always excepting the uniquely complex structure of Stonehenge — were, like the Rollright Stones, simple rings of free-standing monoliths. None of them could approach the size or complexity of Avebury.

The riddle of the Dancers came to my mind again that evening, when my friend observed that the long vac was only three weeks away, and that neither of us had yet made arrangements.

"I know that your people are abroad, Cobbett, and my father's gone to Carlsbad, so we're our own masters at last. Now, I suggest that the two of us go off to Oxfordshire for a couple of weeks." (Oxfordshire? I was startled by the coincidence.) "I gather it's a rare place for folk songs, which will keep me occupied, and you should find enough of your precious Druid stones to amuse you."

Ager could never be convinced that the Druids were not responsible for Stonehenge and its fellows.

His suggestion was like an omen, and at the time I took it for a good omen. I immediately proposed that we should base ourselves at Normanton Lovell. A perusal of the one-inch map of the area failed to prove the existence of the village, but — to my delight — the stone circles were clearly marked, and so was the nearby village of Saxton Lovell, where the usual symbol indicated an inn. We decided then and there to take rooms at that inn for four weeks in June and July. Its name, as we subsequently learned, was the *Belchamp Arms*.

Upon our arrival we discovered that there actually was a village of Normanton Lovell — if half a dozen houses constitute a village — but I didn't regret our choice of accommodation. The *Belchamp Arms* was a grand example of the English country inn. The rooms were scrupulously clean, the service cheerful, the food good, and the beer excellent. The local farmers and labourers, too, appreciated the beer, so the landlord said, for they thronged the bar of an evening. It was a prospect that greatly pleased my friend.

We spent our first afternoon walking about the village, which was compact and seemed to us very pretty after the austereness of Cambridgeshire. In our youthful enthusiasm we were able to ignore the reality of life in those picturesque thatched cottages. The church was early Romanesque, with some fine pre-Reformation features that occupied my attention for a good couple of hours. By dinner-time were both ravenous, and happily did justice to the landlady's game pie, after which we settled ourselves in the lounge with half a bottle of port and our pipes, and Ager took the opportunity to ask whether there were any notable singers in the area.

Our host looked very doubtful. "I don't know," he said, "that we've anyone here that a scholar like yourself would care to hear. There's Tommy Wells, now, who plays the organ in church — he can sing fine, but I reckon all he knows is hymns, and between ourselves that's all right on a Sunday, but I reckon a man needs a change during the week."

That, said Ager, was just what he meant. Did any of the farm workers or such people come into the pub and sing?

"Why, bless you, yes! If you don't mind its not being polished like, just you come down to the bar a little later on. Old Harry Arnold'll be in about eight — he's got a fine, strong voice — and then there's Dennis Poacher and Percy Forrest and — "

Laughing, my friend assured him that it all sounded most satisfactory. The landlord, gratified, left us, and we fell to talking of those enigmatic stone circles that I planned to visit in the morning.

As we entered the bar, the landlord informed us that old Harry had just arrived, and that was him sitting over there, the big red-faced man, and yes, surely he'd be pleased to sing for us. Introductions were made, and Harry Arnold indicated in the subtlest way possible that he couldn't sing without something to wet his throat. As soon as we'd attended to that, I sat back, while my friend set about coaxing songs from the obligingly extrovert farmer. Before long Ager himself had been drawn into the singing, and he and Harry Arnold were swapping songs for all the world as if they were old friends. Even I was induced to join in the choruses, while the landlord grinned broadly behind his bar.

I remember very little about the songs that were sung that evening, though no doubt I've heard some of them many times since. The one that clings to my mind was a very intense, very powerful performance by Farmer Arnold of the ballad of John Barleycorn — the death and resurrection of the corn. He shut his eyes and threw his head back and sang as though every word and every note was forcing its way up from the very bones of him. He well deserved the pint of beer that the landlord gave him, and Ager's almost tearful congratulations. It was a remarkable experience, really remarkable.

The next song, though — that was something quite different. Harry Arnold took a deep draught from his mug and then, mopping his forehead with a large spotted handkerchief, he called out, "Dennis! Dennis Poacher!"

The man who looked up was stocky and weather-beaten. He had been at the forefront of the choruses.

"Give us 'Rolling of the Stones', will you?" said Harry. "It's a long time since I heard that, boy, and I'd dearly like to hear it again."

Now that, I thought, is a damned queer name for a song! My mind turned for an instant to the prehistoric remains that I'd come to see.

The stocky man began to sing, in a clear and surprisingly gentle voice: "Will you go to the rolling of the stones, the tossing of the ball... ?" A curiously enigmatic and charming fragment — a mere part, surely, of a longer song.

My thoughts were interrupted by the sympathetic voice of Harry Arnold: "Does me good to hear it again, sir, so that does, but there's no denying it's a strange sort of song. I can see you're wondering at it, and so did I when first I heard it. My mother used to sing that to me when I was a little child, and I always used to wonder at that bit about "the rolling of the stones". Of course, that's plain when you think about it: they mean fivestones — what my dad called knucklebones. But d'you know, the first stones that come to my mind over that was those great rings over to

Normanton way. Them, and that clump of 'em on our own farm — what we call Hell's Gate."

I couldn't help smiling. Hell's Gate. There was a name to conjure with! It suddenly occurred to me that, with a good amount of port and two — or was it three? — pints of beer inside me, I was really not quite sober. Otherwise I wouldn't be attaching any weight to the absurd name of a mere group of standing stones.

On the far side of the farmer, Lionel Ager's attention was confusedly divided between the singer (it was another singer now) and Harry Arnold.

"Hell's Gate?" I said, hesitantly.

"That's right," said Harry. "Over in Black's Meadow it is – though that's never been a meadow ever to my knowing. Always been ploughed over, that has." He looked from one to the other of us, and his broad red face broke into a grin, showing strong teeth. "You want to hear the story? Well, why not? It's quite a little ghost story, and it may interest you."

He drained his mug and set it down on the table.

"It's this way, you see – you know the name of this pub, the *Belchamp Arms*? Well, you won't find any Belchamps around here now, but for many long years they was the lords of the manor. As far as they was concerned, nobody else mattered. It was Yes, Squire, and touch your cap, or by God they'd know why!

"Now, this man was the very last Squire Belchamp, and he used to go over to them stones at night – without a by-your-leave to the farmer, of course – and he'd do things there that, well, I reckon they're what gave the name of Hell's Gate to the stones. O' course, all this was something like a hundred years ago now..."

Sir Richard Belchamp, it was clear, was something more than the traditional wicked squire. Certainly he was an unbending autocrat, and eccentric to the point of madness. Equally certainly he had a strong reputation as a whoremaster, and was rather less widely thought to be a necromancer. *Oderint dum metuant* – that was his motto: Let 'em hate, as long as they fear. Legends of his diverse misdeeds were not uncommon in the neighbourhood even now, particularly the tale that Harry Arnold told of the squire's last sin, which led directly to his unmourned death. He had been caught in a rather horrid act, at those same stones, by the father of a young woman who was unwillingly involved. The father was a farmer – in fact, the owner of the land where the megaliths stood. He was also a man of few words and telling action. Being rightfully incensed, he took a staff and quite simply beat the squire to death.

There must have been some juggling with the law. The killer received the surprisingly lenient sentence of five years' hard labour, which he accepted with calm resignation. He knew that justice had already been done; whatever the law might do couldn't alter that fact. His sons were strong and well able to care for the farm in his absence. Only one thing troubled him. It was slight at first, but through the years in gaol it grew, and it gnawed more and more at his mind. Sir Richard Belchamp had cursed his killer as he died, and the curse was an awful one: *Hell shall lie within your farm, and your filthy scarecrow shall be its gateman!*

Yes, there was a scarecrow in Black's meadow, a harmless thing, if old and ugly. Still, the farmer's sons had taken it down when they heard of the squire's words, and thrown it into a corner of the hayloft, and there it had lain, untouched but much thought of, through five long years.

The farmer was welcomed most heartily upon his release from gaol. Food and drink were provided in quantity, and all ate and drank – some a little too freely, perhaps, for it seems that no one noticed just when, in the early hours, the farmer left the house.

He did not return.

They found him some while after dawn, lying among the great stones, crouched in an attitude of intense fear. The fear did not show on his face, however, for there was nothing left to call a face. The whole body was most terribly burned. And yet — there was no other evidence of a fire, and the night had been rainy.

And the scarecrow? Somehow or other the scarecrow had found its way back into its old place in the middle of the field, where it now stood, as large as life, staring with its empty sockets at the appalling scene.

Harry Arnold smiled broadly and signalled to the landlord to refill his mug. "Nice little story, ain't it?" he said.

Nice little — Ye gods!

"Interesting," I ventured.

"Fascinating!" said my friend. His face was gleaming with the disinterested delight of the scholar, and beads of sweat stood out on his forehead. "Absolutely remarkable. So coherent —

"Those stones are still there?" he asked abruptly. "On your farm?"

Harry Arnold nodded. "On my farm. You see, that old farmer, he was my great-great-grandfather."

"Remarkable," said Ager again. "And what of the scarecrow?"

"Well, I don't suppose it's the same one — not likely, is it? — but there's still a scarecrow in that field. We reckon to let well enough alone, and every seed-time out he comes from the barn, and when he's not needed in the field we put him back there. Matter o' fact, we do often let him stay in the field rather longer than needful. We reckon he belongs there, and we don't want to upset him."

I didn't like the way the conversation was tending. It had taken a turn that was both morbid and fantastic, and at that moment I wasn't in the mood for either. Don't misunderstand, though: I had no presentiment of what would happen. In any case, I didn't believe in such warnings. I was very young.

My friend persisted with his questions. Had there been any other evidence of the gateway to Hell? But Harry was vague upon that point, and unwilling to commit himself. It was true that over the decades some people had disappeared, or died mysteriously, but that might happen anywhere. No, nothing certain could be said.

Ager fell silent, and I took the chance to steer the conversation towards the stone circles at Normanton Lovell. We were still engrossed in that subject when the landlord firmly called "Time!" and amid a clattering of heavy boots, a jingling of glasses, and a cheerful buzz of talk, the bar began to empty. The farmer held out his enormous hand and expressed the hope that we'd meet again the next day. And so Harry Arnold set off home, and we two went upstairs to our own rooms. My friend, I could see, was still preoccupied.

At breakfast, Ager's first words were: "Did you know that it's St John the Baptist's Day on the 24th of June?"

"That's seven days' time," I said. "Midsummer Day. What of it? You're surely not intending to rush back to Cambridge for Midsummer Fair?"

"No, of course not. But think! St John's Eve is rather like Hallowe'en — a pagan festival, when ghosts and witches walk abroad."

Being in no mood for my friend's obsession with occult tradition, I merely snorted, and returned to my bacon and eggs.

Then I realised what he was implying. "Oh, God! You don't mean that you're going to follow up Farmer Arnold's ghost story?"

"I mean that *we* are going to follow up Harry's story ."

"*We* most certainly are not! I came down here to look at megalithic remains, and that's what I'm going to do. You can go ghost-hunting if you like, but count me out."

I could see that he was disappointed, but I was determined not to give way.

He was equally determined. "I can't pass up a chance like this," he said. "Don't you see how important it is? The Folklore Society will be delighted to get this story, but it must be investigated properly. Even if you won't come with me — and even if Harry Arnold won't agree — on St John's Eve I'm going to Black's Meadow to see if anything happens."

"All that will happen is that you'll catch pneumonia," I said, rather tartly. I was on holiday, with a good friend, and in a most charming part of England — but my mind was not easy. *Post equitem sedet atra cura.*

We agreed that after breakfast the two of us should walk over to Black's Meadow. After all, I did want to look at the stones that the farmer so picturesquely called Hell's Gate. However, my interest was purely archaeological, and I had no wish to see the demon scarecrow.

But of course I did see it, and I can see it now, quite clearly. It was a horrid, ragged thing, with most of the straw stuffing gone from it. The clothes — I don't know how they held together. They were threadbare and rotten. The Scottish word came appropriately to my mind: *tattybogle.* I think that the coat had once been black, but it was a dull, nasty green now. For all I know, it might have belonged to the original scarecrow, back in Sir Richard's day. And the face — my God! The head had been carved from a turnip, and it was all shrivelled and wizened, but there was a distinct and rather frightening *expression.* The half-moon grin and the vacant eye-sockets combined to give a look of utter and menacing idiocy.

Even Lionel Ager was glad to turn his attention to the group of stones that stood on the western side of the field. Their formation was of singular interest to an archaeologist, in that the central stones formed the only genuine trilithon I knew of in Britain, outside Stonehenge. Ager was fascinated too, but I could see that to him the shape formed by one massive stone lying as a lintel on two great megalithic posts reinforced the idea of a gateway.

"Hell's Gate," he said, quietly. "Hell's Gate indeed. Cobbett, I simply can't miss this opportunity. Are you quite sure you won't come and keep watch with me?"

I thought of the scarecrow's face, and furiously dismissed the image from my mind. "I won't come," I said. "It's a very silly business, and besides, I see no fun in spending the night in a field when there's a comfortable bed back at the inn."

Ager merely grunted. Clearly his mind was made up, and St John's Eve would see him in Black's Meadow, watching for the gateway to Hell. The matter seemed to bar all other subjects from his mind. This was to be a major contribution to the study of folklore, and not until he'd seen it through would he return to more mundane matters.

He didn't object when I suggested that we should go and look at the stones of Normanton Lovell, a couple of miles away, but he spoke little as we walked along the narrow roads. It was plain that his thoughts were revolving around Black's Meadow and Hell's Gate.

Harry Arnold wasn't well pleased when he heard of Ager's plan, but he couldn't give any concrete or coherent reason why my friend shouldn't stay the haunted night in the haunted field. At length, seeing that his advice to leave well enough alone had no effect, he grudgingly agreed. "You'd go anyway," he said, "so you may as well go with my permission."

When St John's Eve arrived, Harry came into the *Belchamp Arms* looking rather embarrassed, and carrying a shotgun. "You've forced an agreement on me," he said, "and for your own sake I'll force one on you. You'll take this gun with you tonight. I don't know that it'll be of protection to you, but it may be, and I'll sleep sounder for knowing you have it."

With some reluctance, Ager took the weapon, and thanked the farmer for his concern. But Harry hadn't finished. "There's one thing more," he said. "I want you to promise that you'll stay on the east side of the field — away from the stones."

To my surprise, and rather to my relief, Ager agreed, smiling wryly as he saw the farmer's face clear.

"Good lad!" said Harry, and clapped him on the back.

Even so, he insisted on accompanying Ager from the inn at closing-time, so that he could be sure when he went to his bed that the terms were being adhered to. As you can imagine, I approved of this notion, and when the landlord called time I went with them to Black's Meadow. There was nothing more I could do, except offer to share the vigil, and I was not prepared to do that.

When Ager was settled fairly comfortably on a travelling-rug, with the shotgun and a flask of whisky beside him, we said our good-byes, and Harry Arnold and I went our ways.

I had difficulty in sleeping at first. Although I was very tired, my mind was so full that there seemed no room for sleep. Curiously, whenever I shut my eyes, one image predominated, making a clear picture, so disturbing that I had to open them again. It was as if I sat alone on the edge of Black's Meadow, gazing across at the strange cluster of menhirs and seeing the gateway that they formed. It was odd that the stones appeared so sharply to my inner eye, because, as I suddenly realised, I could see nothing else — nothing at all. The blackness that covered everything, everything but that unpleasantly distinct image of Hell's Gate, was so very black as to be the darkness of the tomb rather than of night. It was almost like a living thing, and it hid everything except those damnable stones.

No, not quite everything, as I saw the fourth or fifth time that my eyelids involuntarily closed. Far off, by the stones, and silhouetted against them, seeming tiny by comparison, was an awkwardly moving figure. It was more human than animal, as far as I could tell, and yet not quite human either. It was walking in a very unnatural manner, almost like a wooden doll that's made to caricature its young owner's gauche stride.

By the time I realised that the gaunt figure's awkward motion was bringing it rapidly through the stygian blackness towards me, I was struggling to stay awake. But our bodies at best respond perversely to our minds, and I found myself fitfully dozing, and observing, with something like terror, the progress of the black featureless creature across the black featureless field. As it drew nearer, I found that it brought with it waves of heat, as though furnace doors had been opened — an evil-smelling heat, but with no accompanying light. Whatever illuminated the stones remained itself hidden, and still I could discern no features on the gothic silhouette that approached me.

Yet something about it — something in that damnably sharp, gaunt outline — scratched at the doors of memory in my brain, and

I fought against recognition, while knowing that it could make no ultimate difference.

The heat became — not unbearable, for I bore it — but, like that appalling darkness, it seemed to take on a life of its own, a pulsating life, as though it was generated by some great unimaginable heart. The figure came ever closer, its stride implacable and unhindered. It moved so stiffly, as though it had no knee-joints. Its arms were spread wide, seeming fixed in a mockery of benediction. Its head — ah! — its head was small and round, wrinkled and very, very old. Rank shreds and tatters of clothing flapped from its thin frame, and now I could see coals of fire within the deep eye-sockets, as finally it stood before me, and the crushing waves of heat brought with them great gusts of a mirthless laughter.

The doors broke open, and I awoke, screaming — I'm not ashamed to say it — to find myself alone and secure in my room at the *Belchamp Arms*. Almost sobbing with relief, I lay back on my pillow and expelled my breath in a long sigh. God, what a dream! And what a story to tell Ager in the morning! I was almost amused at this glimpse into the depths of my unconscious imagination, but, feeling sleep approaching again, I turned on to my side and let it come.

I slept easily this time, falling almost immediately into a dreamless slumber, and didn't wake again until a heavy knocking at my door aroused me at about six o'clock.

Only half-awake, I climbed from my bed and opened the door to my untimely visitors. My yawn became a gasp of incredulity as I saw the urgent faces of the landlord and Harry Arnold, the latter biting his lip nervously, and with fear in his eyes.

The farmer had risen early as usual that Midsummer morning, and gone straight to Black's Meadow to see how Lionel Ager had fared. In the meadow he had found Ager's body, and he had stood looking at it for a long horrible moment, unable to move. It lay between the uprights of the trilithon — Hell's Gate indeed! — and it was hideously burned. The whole corpse was seared and blasted, and still smoking a little, and the face was no longer a face. The hands, still clutching the twisted frame of the shotgun, had actually broken around the weapon.

"I couldn't touch it," said Harry, later. "And I dared not, for fear it'd crumble into ash."

And yet, despite the condition of the body, Lionel Ager's clothes were quite unharmed, except that they were wet with the summer dew.

Harry Arnold turned and shook his great fist at the scarecrow. "Old devil!" he cried. And then he saw that the scarecrow had somehow been turned around during the night, and now stood facing the group of standing stones. On its turnip face, the crudely carved features no longer wore their customary vacant aspect, but had twisted themselves into an expression of malign triumph.

My cigarette had long since burned itself out in the ashtray, and I'd hardly touched my beer. Old George's hands were shaking a little as he fumbled with his tobacco-pouch and pipe. I knew that anything I could say would be inadequate, but I said it anyway: "That's quite astonishing. Quite astonishing."

George was silent for a moment, while he re-lit his pipe. When he had it drawing to his satisfaction, he looked up and stared gloomily at me.

"It was a pretty village," he said. "And those stones were really remarkable. But you can understand now why I've never been back there."

Afterword

I began to write ghost stories in the mid 1960s. If Ramsey Campbell can do it, I thought, then I can — but of course I couldn't. August Derleth rightly rejected the two stories I sent to him, though he did print some of my verse in *The Arkham Collector*.

A few years later, *The Times* ran a ghost story competition, nominally in tribute to M.R. James. I retrieved one of those rejected tales, completely rewrote it and entered it for the competition. It was unplaced, but I was consoled by the fact that the winners, published as *The Times Anthology of Ghost Stories*, were mostly flat and disappointing.

Then Jan Arter introduced me to *Ghosts and Scholars*, and again I dusted off my manuscript. To my delight, Rosemary Pardoe liked the story. She suggested a few changes, which I was happy to make, and "The Scarecrow" was finally published in *Ghosts and*

Scholars 6. Better yet, Karl Edward Wagner selected it for *The Year's Best Horror Stories XIII*.

Rosemary had already told me that Ramsey Campbell's superb "In the Bag", having failed to place in *The Times* Ghost Story Competition, had gone on to win both the British and the World Fantasy Awards for best short story. Now I discovered that Karl Wagner's entry, "Sing a Last Song of Valdese", had also been dismissed by the judges, and had later been chosen by Gerald Page for *The World's Best Horror Stories*. I was in good company.

Publication in my collection *A Ghostly Crew* gave me the opportunity to recast the narrative in the first person. In fact, I have revised all the previously published material, to a greater or lesser extent.

I borrowed "Fisher College" from that good detective story *The Cambridge Murders*. It seemed appropriate as the author, Glyn Daniel, was a notable archæologist, specialising in the prehistory of Britain.

The *Endeavour* (need I say?) is my favourite local pub, named after Captain Cook's ship.

THE WATCHMAN

Simon Wesley stubbed out his cigarette and asked, "Are you familiar with Woolton Minster?"
"Woolton in Suffolk?" I shook my head. "I know of it, of course, but..."
We turned to George Cobbett, who was scraping the bowl of his pipe. He looked up.
"Woolton? Yes, I've been there. A handsome church, mainly Norman. There's a very fine west window, and some remarkably grotesque gargoyles. One of 'em, right at the top of the west front —"
"That's the place," said Simon, "though you must have visited it before the war." (George nodded.) "In 1944, a German bomber on its way to Norwich got into difficulties and had to jettison its bomb. The thing landed right in the Close. Remarkably, no lives were lost, but the west front of the Minster was destroyed. The window — yes, it was a fine one — was shattered, and the gargoyles were pulverised. It was a sad business, but it brought me into the story."

You see (he continued), I was assistant to Sir Martin Runciman, who supervised the restoration work when it finally started. The building had been patched up, of course, but it wasn't until 1951 that they could afford to do the job properly. Money was short, and funds came in slowly, but at last we were able to begin.

Fortunately, there were plans and photographs to work from, and we aimed to make that west front look just as it did before — or very nearly. We used the same Barnack stone, and the window was fashioned as near as could be to the original, though somehow the glaziers didn't quite manage to reproduce the colours. I don't know: there's something about mediæval glass... It was a miracle really that the window had survived the Reformation, but Adolf managed to achieve what William Dowsing and his chums had failed to do.

Anyway, we did good work. You must go and have a look at the church, Roger. It really is very handsome.

The only real difficulty was over the gargoyles. You'll remember, George: there were three of them at the west. Oh, dear. I'll have to describe the place. That west front comes to a peak, about eighty feet high. The porch doesn't project, and there are no towers there; the building is roughly cruciform, and has a sturdy, fairly low central tower. The church is almost entirely Norman, with an apsidal east end, but the west window is — or was — a very nice example of a fourteenth century Tree of Jesse.

At each corner of the gable was a gargoyle — grotesque enough, to be sure, but not uncommonly so. You can see similar figures on many churches: rainwater pipes carved into demonic shapes, with the water coming out of their mouths. But the thing in the middle, right at the peak of the gable, was something else.

Strictly speaking, it wasn't a gargoyle at all, but a statue. It was extraordinary. The only thing I've ever seen like it — and remember: I only saw it in photographs — was the so-called Baphomet of St Bris-le-Vineux in Brittany. It had bulging eyes under thick brows, a heavy moustache, and huge hands that gripped the edge of the roof. And it had female breasts. A very strange and sinister creature indeed. It was crouched, as if ready to launch itself into flight. Yes, there were wings too, folded behind, so that you couldn't see them properly from the ground. There were the traditional goat's legs, and small horns, and the teeth were bared in a rather disconcertingly confident grin.

Well, there was much discussion among the Church Council, and with the Bishop's agreement it was decided to replace this particular demon with a statue of St Michael. That would be more fitting, they said, especially as the Minster is dedicated to St Michael and All Angels. They got John Elen in for this; it was his first major public commission, and he did a fine job. The saint, in armour, is standing, legs astride, looking up, and holding his sword hilt-upwards in front of him. It's hardly what you'd call *avant-garde*, but that's not what was required. It's a very impressive conventional — no; traditional — work of art, and somehow it gives quite a different aspect to the building.

Our work was finished towards the beginning of 1953. A new history of the Minster was published, written by the Vicar — a decent fellow, who was something of an antiquarian — and commemorative copies were presented to Runciman and me.

I've got my copy here: *The Collegiate Church of St Michael and All Angels at Woolton*, by the Revd Edmund Wheatley, M.A. There are photographs of the west end before and after the war, so you can get some idea of what sort of a job we did.

Wheatley and I got on very well together, and before the end of the restoration work, when Runciman had gone off to supervise another project in Shropshire, he suggested that rather than stay on at my hotel in the town I should move into the Vicarage, which stands on the site of the old Deanery, just south of College Gate. This was very agreeable to me, as you can imagine, and we'd often sit up of an evening, chatting about antiques, or music, or ghosts — or just reading.

Now, while the work was going on there was a watchman stationed in the Close — to protect my men's implements, mainly — and after Evensong Wheatley always used to come with me to his cubby-hole and have a few words with him. This was sheer good nature on his part, you know, because the church plate — some of it pre-Reformation — was kept pretty safe under lock and key in the vestry.

Bob Chater, the watchman, was a big man: an ex-Bombardier, sociable and cheerful. I wondered occasionally how such a person could cope with the solitude of the job, and was rather taken aback when I discovered that he spent the quiet hours in teaching himself classical Greek. That's by the way, though. Bob would take three or four turns around the Close — at no set time: we agreed that was best — but mostly he'd sit in the little room built into College Gate, with a lantern and his books and a flask of coffee.

I might add that the room had been the janitor's lodgings in the middle ages, and Wheatley told us that it had been used again early in the nineteenth century, when the resurrection men were at work. Still, Bob wasn't likely to meet anything quite that gruesome, we thought, and it became something of a standing joke when we said good-night for the Vicar to add, "Keep an eye open for the body-snatchers, Bob."

Body-snatchers, eh?... Yes, well —

It was early one March morning, a Tuesday, when I was woken by a hammering at the Vicarage door. I thought perhaps it was an urgent call on behalf of a sick parishioner, so I was surprised when Wheatley came into my room and said, "There's been an attempted burglary at the Minster. No, it's all right — nothing's been taken. But Bob Chater's here with a rather curious story, and I'd like you to hear it."

He waited while I got into my dressing-gown and slippers, and we went downstairs to his study, where he already had coffee brewing on the gas-ring. Bob declined a cup, but accepted a shot of whisky. Then he gave his report.

"It's a dark night, sir, as you can see — dry, but very cloudy — and about ten past three I decided to take a walk around the Minster, my third tonight. I started at the west end, opposite my sentry-box, and went round the south side, and everything was fine. Then the east end — nothing. And then I started along the north wall, and as I cleared the chapter house I saw a light in the vestry, as it might be an electric torch, where there oughtn't to be a light at all.

"I don't know sir, but somehow I never really expected burglars here, since everyone in the town knows that I'm on duty in the Close of nights. Still, I knew it couldn't be anyone who'd a right to be there. Any of the clerical gentlemen, or you, Mr Wesley, would have come and had a word with me first. Now, I don't usually carry a stick, as you know, so I had to be very cautious. I put my ear to the vestry door, not knowing what I might hear. I certainly didn't expect to hear what I did: it was a man's voice, sobbing! With fear, too, I'd stake my oath.

"A rum do, I thought, and ever so gently I tried the door-handle. The door was unlocked. I screwed up my nerves, and suddenly flung back the door and stood in the doorway, with my fists clenched, looking as menacing as I could — not knowing what I was up against, you see.

"Well, there was a man there, all right; just one, crouched over by the other door, the one that leads into the choir. As soon as he heard me, he looked up, and his face was grey. There was fear in his eyes, sir — real fear. And now there was another shock. He said, 'Thank God!' — just like that. 'Thank God! A human face!'

"Things were going too fast for me. I said, 'Of course I'm human, my lad — and just in time, by the look of things.' (For I could see that he'd already started to break open that big safe of yours, Padre.) 'What did you expect?' I said, '— a ghost?'

"And at that his eyes opened wide, and his jaw dropped as if he was going to scream. I walked over to him, and I saw that he was hanging on with both hands to that iron ring that's the handle on the choir door — hanging on as if for fear of his life — and he seemed to be twisting it in his hands, trying to open it.

" 'You stop that!' I said. 'Your night's work's done, my lad!'

"Then the movement stopped, and for a moment I thought he was kicking his heels against the floor, because I could hear that hollow sound — you know? But it was a harder, sharper sound that he could have made, because he was wearing rubber-soled boots; and anyway I could see now that his feet weren't moving. Yet I could still hear the noise for a moment. Then it faded away.

"Well, I was curious, sir, as you can imagine, so I collared this fellow. He was quite small and lithe, like you'd picture a cat-burglar to be, but he was so broken up that I could see he was no match for me.

" 'Now,' I said, 'you're coming along to the Police Station. Robbing a church is a very serious offence.'

"I'll swear, sir, that he was actually relieved. 'God, yes!' he said. 'I'll be safe there. Just take me away — I couldn't face *that* again!'

" 'Face what?' I said, and on the way over to the Police Station he told me. Very strange! I left him with the law (and they'd like you to go over, Padre, as soon as convenient, to see about preferring charges), and then I came back here straightaway.

"What he told me was this:

"He was from out of town, and he'd heard about the church plate. Well, it's no secret, is it? He'd found out where it was kept, and all on his own he planned to steal it. He knew that I was there — and that's no secret, either — so he hadn't tried to come in by College Gate or Dean's Gate, but had climbed over the high wall to the north-east, the one that gives on to the gardens in Wells Street. I said I thought he looked like a cat-burglar, didn't I?

"He seems to have had no trouble getting into the Close and across to the Minster — he knew just where the vestry was — or in picking the lock on the door. He found the safe all right, and noticed that the door into the choir was closed but not locked. That didn't bother him; not until he'd actually started to break open the safe.

"Then he heard the footsteps.

"Quiet at first, they were, but clear — ghostly, you might say — and they were coming towards him from the other side of the choir door. They grew harder, and stronger, and heavier: more — more *real*.

"Now, I should judge him to be quite a brave man, and perhaps violent too on occasion; but he wanted to know what the opposition was like. The footsteps still sounded some little distance away, so he switched off his torch and stuck it in his pocket, and then he opened the door a crack and looked through, into the church.

"What he saw made him slam the door shut and hang on to the handle for dear life, wishing that he could lock it. He was too frightened to call for help, and I really don't know whether it was in order to attract attention or simply from fear of the dark that he switched on his torch again. That, of course, was the light I saw, and when I burst into that room, he says, he was never so glad in his life to see another human face!"

I couldn't stand this. Bob Chater certainly knew how to build up suspense.

"What the devil *did* he see?" I said — shouted, almost.

But Bob's face was very serious.

"You must remember," he said, "that he only saw it for a moment, and in poor light, but he says he never wants to see anything like it again. As to describing it, he was — what's the word I want? — he was incoherent. It looked like a man, he says, but it was big, really big. Ten feet tall or more, he reckons. And it was grey; and, as I say, it looked like a man, but it didn't *move* like a man, not quite. And it was coming towards him, as if it knew just where he was, and what he was.

"So he clung to that door-handle, and he could hear the man — or whatever it was — coming closer, right up to the door. Then he could feel the handle moving in his hands, against all the strength he could put to it; and he was sobbing with fear... And then — well, then I came in."

My mind was full of questions, all unasked. I turned to Edmund Wheatley, trying to frame some words; but they didn't come, and they didn't need to, because I could see excitement and something like understanding in the priest's face. Without a word, he stood up and went over to one of his book-cases, at which he peered, shelf by shelf, until he had found what he wanted. It was a smallish red-bound volume, which I guessed to be about a hundred years old.

"This," he said, and his voice was very restrained, "is a curious little book which I bought some while ago at an auction. It's the work of Dr Davey, one of my predecessors, and was privately printed in 1847."

As he opened it, I could see that the title page read: *Quaint Historical Anecdotes and Legends of Suffolk, compiled and re-told by the Rev. John Davey, D.D.*

Wheatley and I kept in touch, you know, even after he retired from Woolton; and a few months before he died — that would be in '76 — he gave me that same copy of the book. Here it is, and this is the chapter that he read to us that morning. It's quite short, and if I may I'll read it to you now.

The Guardian of Woolton Minster

Woolton is a small and rather decayed town which stands a few miles from the coast to the north of Leiston. The chief glory of the place is the Minster Church of St Michael and All Angels, which will be well known to the antiquary and the ecclesiologist. For details of this fine building, however, the reader must consult a guide book. We mention it here because to it attaches a curious legend, which we have collated from several sources. The reader will appreciate that we have used our imagination somewhat in the telling of this tale, but be assured that the essentials have been followed faithfully.

In the days of the fourth King Edward, there dwelt in the town a merchant, one Thomas Drinkall, or Drinkale, who was neither pious nor amiable. He respected neither God nor man, for his creed was that Wealth is Power, and being both wealthy and powerful he believed it wholeheartedly.

This Thomas led for many years a life without crime but without charity, until on a day he found himself bereft of his wealth and consequently of his power, for his two ships, bearing between them the greater part of his fortune, were lost at sea in a storm of præternatural fury. He was forced, in order to meet his debts, to sell much of the property remaining to him in the town, and was thus reduced to a state that to him at least represented poverty. As the reader may surmise, however, Thomas Drinkall was not the man to accept such a fate. He foresaw months, perhaps years, of hard toil before his trade could again flourish; and truth to tell he was no lover of hard toil. He quickly resolved, therefore, to steal what he would not gain by honest labour, and to set himself up in some place far away: Norwich, perhaps, or better, the thronged streets of London.

Now, the house of Sir Giles Flambard, whom he did not love, was nigh impregnable, and only one other house in

Woolton held so much treasure for the taking: the House of God, to wit: the Minster Church of St Michael. For the moment fate seemed to conspire with the evil man, for he recalled that his father had been Sacristan at the Minster, having charge of a key to the church. At the old man's death, Thomas had through mere indolence retained this key rather than return it to the Dean and Chapter. Now he thought that perhaps his indolence was vindicated. He determined to "strike while the iron was hot", and to rob the church the very next night.

Meanwhile, he prepared himself by procuring a farm-waggon and a light load of hay, for he intended to leave Woolton as soon as might be in the character of a lowly freeman, which guise should, he thought, protect him from footpads upon the way. He muffled the wooden wheels of the cart and the hooves of his solitary nag, and provided himself with a number of large sacks to contain his spoils. Night fell, and the Angelus sounded, as if urging him to his task. The merchant waited for as long as he could restrain his impatience, until he was sure that the townsfolk were abed, and then he took his horse's reins and set off towards the Minster.

Fortune remained with him, for the night was neither too dark nor too light. Steadily, but without haste, he led the horse along Market Street, past Fish Street and Rosemary Lane, and at the *Golden Cross* turned right into Gracechurch Street towards the Minster Close. He did not directly approach the great gate, but as a precaution led the horse and waggon into Crown Alley, where they would not be seen by the Watch. Then, be it never so gently, he forced the lock of the wicket-gate and entered the close.

In those days there was an old man, a pensioner of the College, who kept watch in the Close by night, which is to say that he sat in a little room by the great gate and drank small ale. Thomas Drinkall went quietly to the door of this room and rapped gently upon the wooden boards until the old man peered out. Then, swiftly and silently, Thomas struck at the wizened neck, rendering the watchman unconscious, and caring nothing whether or no he had snuffed out the frail glimmer of life. He bundled the body back inside the room and softly closed the door upon it; then he turned to face the mighty west front of the Minster.

High above, at each corner, the gargoyles' faces stared in silent reproach, jutting as the old watchman's face had jutted upon its long skinny neck. Thomas looked up, at the vast window, and over that at the largest dæmon of all: the great grinning figure whose bulging eyes seemed to regard him with scorn and whose huge hands gripped the ridge of the building that it had guarded for more than three centuries. The merchant averted his gaze from this stone watchman and ran silently to the dark safety of the west door.

His father's key fitted snugly into the lock, and turned, ponderously, but with little effort, until the bolt sprang from its socket. Gently he drew out the key and replaced it in his belt, and then grasped the huge iron ring that served for a door-handle. Again a slow, heavy turn, a slight creak, and the latch was free. As quickly as he dared, he pushed at the door, and shortly there was a space wide enough to step through.

The merchant gathered up his sacks and slipped inside the porch, pushing the great door to behind him. It was quite dark, but he had no difficulty in finding and opening the smaller door into the nave; here there was light enough, for the moon was now clear of the clouds and shone through the arched windows of the south wall, while far ahead the candles burned upon the parish altar of All Saints. As his eyes became accustomed to the eerie half-light, Thomas could distinguish the great golden crucifix and the golden candlesticks grouped upon either side of it. Now, he felt, he was committed to his sacrilege, and soon he stood before the altar, stuffing the cross into a sack and putting candlesticks in after it. The sweat fell from his face with mere exertion, for the weight of these holy treasures was considerable. He must not, he thought, be over-greedy, else he would be unable to carry his booty away! With this cheerful reflection he passed beneath the pulpitum towards the Chantry Chapel of the Flambards.

Here he was faced with riches unsuspected, and his evil heart rejoiced. Eagerly he filled a second sack, and began to stuff treasures into a third, bending or breaking those that were too large. At length he opened a fourth sack, delighting in the merry clatter of gold against gold, and it was at this moment that another sound came to his ears: footsteps, hard and heavy, stalking inexorably along the nave from west to east.

His first thought was that the old janitor had recovered and had perhaps alerted the Watch. That would indeed be a blow! He quickly determined, however, that the steps were those of but one man, treading firmly and surely. One man might be dealt with, he thought; for had not he, Thomas Drinkall, trailed a pike in the wars? Swiftly he took the great cross from the altar and secreted himself by the arched entrance to the chapel, thinking to have the advantage of surprise.

Nearer and yet nearer came the stranger, seeming to know exactly where to look. The footsteps echoed solidly and deafeningly among the great pillars, accompanied by a slight creaking that suggested a man in armour. Yet, strangely, there was nothing metallic about the footsteps. Thomas thought that his brain would give way before the hard, reverberating sound. He lifted the cross as he heard the steps approach the chapel, with no diminution in their speed or their volume. Truly, the newcomer seemed to lack all caution. The merchant's arms were tiring quickly, for the big crucifix was very heavy, and the sweat streamed from his brow. He set his teeth, and as Nemesis stalked commandingly into the chapel he shut his eyes and swung the cross down with all his considerable strength.

The cross struck a hard surface and merely glanced off, throwing the merchant off balance. With remarkable agility, he jumped to his feet again and prepared to deal another blow.

He never did, for he saw now what manner of being it was that towered over him. He let the cross fall from his hand, and, overcome by the dæmonic horror of the thing, he slumped to the cold, hard floor. Then the other bent down over him and began to do certain things.

The next morning the Sacristan was appalled to find the old watchman lying dead in his little room, with the mark of a blow upon his neck. Hastily he summoned the Dean, who with some half-dozen of the Chapter followed the trembling Sacristan to the great west door of the Minster. It was unlocked. They stepped into the church and were at once confronted with the desecration of the parish altar, for the candles were snuffed and the precious ornaments missing. Now the Sacristan seemed to take leave of his senses: he let forth a cry of anguish and ran straightway to the high altar in the choir, sobbing with relief when he found it untouched. More sedately, the Dean and his fellows went to the Chapel of St Botolph, off the north aisle, but it too was undefiled. Then they crossed the nave towards the Flambard Chapel. At this time was distinctly heard a metallic *clank* from the west end of the church, as if some heavy iron object had been dropped by the great door, but so intent upon its purpose was the little band that no one stopped to wonder what it might be. At the entrance to the chapel they paused momentarily and then boldly entered.

Not for a little while did they remark the sacks upon the floor or the golden and bejewelled ornaments that lay scattered about, for something else demanded all their attention. The man who lay dead in a pool of his own blood might have been friend or foe, neighbour or stranger, for he was quite unrecognisable. The eyes had been torn from his head and the heart from his breast. There was another wound also, of which it were better not to speak.

As the priests and the Sacristan, shaken and wondering, passed out through the great west door, they saw the thing that had been dropped to the ground. On the lowest step, covered with gouts of drying blood, lay a mighty key. Warily they looked up, to see the grey stone figure of the guardian dæmon leering down at them. The grinning jaws of the statue and the huge hands that gripped the edge of the roof were dark with blood.

"There's another paragraph or so," said Simon, as he closed the book and set it down in front of him: "just a few lines in which old Davey draws a moral. Very sound, no doubt."

He accepted a cigarette from me and drew on it gratefully. "Well," he said, "you've heard my story. Have you any comments?"

George pulled at his grey moustache, pondering. Then, after a pause, he said, "You told us, I think, that the gargoyle — the statue — was completely destroyed by the bomb?"

Simon nodded, soberly. "That's quite true."

"You also said that there had been no loss of life."

"That was the official report."

"Ah. The report would refer, of course, only to human life. Normal human life."

As I was considering this, a thought occurred to me, and I said, "How strange — how very strange — that it should happen there, of all places!"

George looked up, quizzically, and Simon raised an eyebrow.

"Don't you remember the dedication of the church?" I said. "St Michael and All Angels! Ironic, don't you think?"

I heard a suppressed chuckle from George, and then: "I never get your limits, Johnson. There are unexplored possibilities about you."

I frowned at him, and said, "Don't quote Sherlock Holmes at me, George. What do you mean?"

The old man's face and voice were serious as he answered: "There are Angels of Darkness, you know, as well as Angels of Light."

Afterword

This is another very early story, re-written for *Ghosts and Scholars*; the original narrative is what appears here as the chapter from Dr Davey's book. The plot derives from a note in H.P. Lovecraft's "Commonplace Book", as published in *The Shuttered Room & Other Pieces*.

A re-reading of "The Residence at Whitminster" by M.R. James led me to G.H. Cook's *English Collegiate Churches of the Middle Ages*, whence the setting of "The Watchman". The church is essentially an amalgam of Southwell Minster and Tewkesbury Abbey.

The town was originally called Stockbridge, because I liked the name, and wasn't aware of how famous the little place in Hampshire is. I took the name of Woolton from *The Importance of Being Earnest* — though I have since found that there really is a Woolton, near Liverpool.

THE INTERRUPTIONS

"Your friends are taking their time," said George.

Be fair," I said. "They're coming over from Hertford. It's quite a distance."

But I didn't have to defend the Campions further, because at that moment Miles walked into the bar. When I'd introduced him to George Cobbett and bought him a drink, I asked him why he was alone.

"Sarah's got a meeting this evening," he said shortly. "You know how it is for teachers in the first week of term." He took a drink of his beer and continued: "Perhaps it's just as well. You asked us to come and tell you our ghost story, and I'm quite willing to do that, but Sarah — well, even now she doesn't like talking about it. Don't get me wrong: she doesn't have nightmares or anything like that, but she doesn't like talking about it."

A pity, that. I'm very fond of Sarah, and had been looking forward to her company. Still, for this evening the story was the thing, and I was curious to know what could have happened to subdue her high spirits.

It was the Easter holidays five years ago (said Miles), and we had been married for just over a year. What time and money weren't taken up with our work had been spent on the house. You've been there, Roger, and you know how much we've put in to it.

Well, Sarah came home from school on the last day of term and said firmly, "We need to get away for a while. Otherwise I think I'll have a breakdown."

She was quite right, you know. Both of us badly needed a break — only we couldn't really afford it. I lay awake half the night trying to think of a way around the problem, but without success.

Then the next day I had lunch with Mike Williams, who was over in Hertford on business, and he gave me the answer. The summer before, he said, he had gone cycling all around the borders of Essex, putting up at pubs and guest houses on the way. It was a strenuous sort of holiday, but cheap. He got the idea, I think, from one of Jim Garrett's songs, which points out that the county's surrounded on all four sides by water. Do you remember? The one that goes:

From Stour and Lea
To Thames and sea,
God bless old Essex Isle.

Mike is a more energetic soul than I am, and I wasn't taken with the notion of a cycle tour. The idea of staying at a pub out in the country appealed, though. I asked if there was any particular place Mike could recommend, and of course there was. He said that we could get right away from it all without travelling more than sixty miles, if we headed due east, out beyond Maldon onto the Dengie peninsula. The place he had in mind was a delightful pub on the far side of Tillingham, where we could get bed, breakfast and dinner, and where the only other likely guests would be there for the bird-watching. It was called the *Dog and Shepherd*, and the proprietors were Mr and Mrs Wakelin.

Mike said that he thought the building had once been a private house. It was known locally simply as "The Dog", which is mildly interesting but unimportant. There's a pub I know that's called "The Cuckoo" by all its regulars, though its name is actually the *Thatcher's Arms*. So don't go jumping to conclusions. What we saw was not the phantom dog of the marshes. It was nothing like that. Nothing like that at all.

Sarah liked the idea as much as I did, and that same evening we phoned Mrs Wakelin and booked ourselves in for five nights, starting the next day. Just to hear that kindly Essex voice gave me a lift, you know. Then we set about packing: old and comfortable clothes, a couple of books, and an electric torch. Mike had warned us that there were no street lights out beyond Tillingham.

That torch came in useful later, though not in a way we could have foreseen.

It was misty when we set out, but by the time we'd got to Sawbridgeworth the sun was shining in a clear sky. We couldn't have wished for a better beginning. We drove on to Chelmsford, and then through Woodham Mortimer, Latchingdon-cum-Snoreham, Steeple — all those places with the funny names — and eventually found ourselves in Tillingham.

It's a delightful village. There are no outstanding features, but it seems to be perfectly put together. Did you know that there's a chapel there belonging to the Peculiar People? It may be the last of its kind.

Well, we turned eastward when we got to the green — the Square, they call it — and drove past a couple of tiny shops and a solitary terraced house, deprived of its neighbours and propped up with brick buttresses. Within a few dozen yards we were in the open country again. Less than two miles more and we were at Kidds End. Only two miles from a sizeable village, and yet, do you know, I've never been anywhere where I was so conscious of the isolation. Sarah said that she could feel the past all around us. I knew what she meant, but for one exhilarating, almost frightening moment I felt that there was *nothing* around us. A very strange sensation.

The hamlet of Kidds End seems to consist of the inn and one other house, a tidy little white clapboard affair a hundred or so yards away. The inn by contrast is a sturdy red-brick building, clearly dating from the mid-eighteenth century. The square front is set back a little from the road, and there's a central door, with a modest porch, between the windows of the downstairs rooms — the public bar and the parlour. On the upper floor are five fairly narrow sash windows, equally spaced, then a pediment, and a low-pitched roof. It has a very welcoming, homely appearance, and we were very grateful to Mike for his recommendation.

It was only just gone ten-thirty when we pulled up outside, and there was no-one about. The door was unlocked, so we went in, to find ourselves in a hallway, with doors to right and left. Further along on the left was a staircase, and at the far end was another door, leading, I supposed, to the kitchen and scullery.

Sarah said, "What do we do now? Try the bar?"

And so we did. I led the way through the door marked "Public" — it was the one on the right — and sure enough there was a middle-aged woman, with a strong, intelligent face, standing behind the bar and polishing a pint glass. She could only be Mrs Wakelin. She looked up as she heard the door open, and gave me a most welcoming smile, which suddenly seemed to freeze on her face. Rather disconcerting, you know.

She blinked rapidly, seeming to collect her thoughts. Then she put down the glass and said, "You must be Mr and Mrs Campion."

"That's right."

She seemed suddenly nervous of something — a nervousness that hadn't been in her when we'd first come into the room.

Hesitantly, she said, "I can't — I can't give you the *best* room. You must understand that."

An odd thing to say, eh?

"I'm not sure," I said, "that we could afford your best room, but I'm sure that we'll be quite happy whichever room you give us."

She laughed at that. "Oh, my dears! You needn't worry that I'll put you in the attic or the cellar. It's just that the best room is locked up at the moment. It — er — has woodworm."

We couldn't think of anything to say to that. It seemed unnecessary, and I think Mrs Wakelin realised it. She went on briskly, "Well, I'll just call my husband to look after the bar, and then I'll show you upstairs."

Wakelin was a stout, cheerful man, agreeably easy-going. He blinked a little as he came into the bar, but that may have been because it was darker in there than outside. He certainly didn't give the impression that his wife had, of being somehow taken aback to see us. He said hello, and slipped behind the counter to carry on where she had left off, polishing glasses that were already sparkling.

We emerged at the top of the stairs, almost opposite the central one of three doors.

"This is a single room," said the landlady. "It's empty at the moment. The one to the right is the one that's locked. You'll be in this one." She walked over to the left-hand door and opened it. "Here you are."

It was a nice, plain, comfortable room, with the usual sort of furniture, old and well cared for. There was nothing exceptional. In the wall opposite the door were two windows. This was the front of the building, with a southward view that was uninterrupted for miles. It didn't take much imagination to guess that the "best" room also had two windows, leaving the single room with one.

Sarah smiled contentedly and said, "This is just what we needed."

"That's good," said Mrs Wakelin. "Now, I can do you dinner tonight in the parlour any time after seven, and breakfast up until nine o'clock in the morning. Will that suit you?"

"That's just fine. Now, if we may, we'd like a bath, and then we'll go out and leave you in peace."

The bathroom was on the other side of the landing, opposite the best bedroom. "Don't make a mistake, now," said Mrs Wakelin. "That's our door opposite yours, and you don't want to be coming in there during the night." She paused and added, "Of course, if you need us at all, you'll know where we are."

There was one more curious incident that morning. Sarah had left the bathroom door ajar while she was running the hot water — to let the steam out, you know — and she just glimpsed the landlady creeping very stealthily along the corridor to the room opposite, where she took a key from her apron pocket and actually locked the door. So it hadn't been locked before! Nothing very odd in that, really — but why didn't she want us to know?

By the time we were washed and changed it was nearly midday. At the bottom of the stairs it occurred to me that we ought just to pop our heads into the bar and say, We're off now — or something similar; only as we got to the door I could hear voices. To be accurate, there was one distinct voice, evidently Mrs Wakelin's, and a low mumble, presumably from her husband. The fragment of conversation that we heard went like this:

"They made the booking by phone, and I could hardly tell from that, could I?"

Mumble.

"Well, we'll do our best for them, but it's just as well that we've no-one else staying here at the moment."

With the mumbling reply to this, Sarah and I decided that we'd best go straight out. If there was something that we ought to know, then no doubt we'd be told about it in good time.

We had a delightful afternoon. We walked into Tillingham and had lunch at the *Cap and Feathers*; then we spent the hours just wandering, enjoying the sunshine and each other's company. It was the most pleasant aimless rambling that either of us had indulged in for a long time, and we were both tired and hungry by the time we got back to *The Dog*. Mrs Wakelin's cooking completely lived up to Mike's praises, and so did the beer in the bar afterwards. We're both fond of a good bitter, and it certainly was good.

That evening in the bar rounded off the day perfectly. Wakelin introduced us to a couple of his cronies from the nearby farms, and we had a few rounds of darts, then settled down to teach Sarah how to play dominoes. Our weariness left us during the evening, but when the landlady called time it flooded back very suddenly, and we were ready for the best night's sleep we'd had in weeks.

We were too optimistic. As we went into the bedroom, I heard a faint, persistent knocking or rapping sound that I couldn't place. I say it was persistent, but infuriatingly it wasn't regular: it would stop, and just when I thought I was rid of it, it would start up again. The strange thing was that Sarah couldn't hear it. She told me I'd had too much to drink, and at first I thought she might be right – but that damned noise continued, and anyway, I knew that I hadn't had more than four pints of beer all evening. It would surely take more than that to make me start imagining things. No, I was convinced that the sound was real. I even drew back the curtains and shone my flashlight on to the road, thinking that it might be some late drinker fooling about outside, but there was nothing to be seen.

It was very puzzling.

Especially puzzling because, as I say, Sarah couldn't hear it, and yet somehow it was making her uneasy. Not because she thought I might be hallucinating, though I suppose that would be upsetting for her: no, it was – and I can't put it any more clearly – as if she heard the noise without being aware of it. Can you understand what I mean? It was annoying to me, but it was actually depressing Sarah.

Each time we drew together, that dull insidious feeling got worse. After a while, and a very long while it seemed, I could hardly hear the noise at all, but the miserable feeling increased. We had a pretty rotten night, as you may imagine. Oh, fatigue won its victory in the end, and we slept at last, but restlessly.

When we woke up, the sky was already light, and both of us knew that we'd had bad dreams, though we couldn't remember any detail. And here's a curious thing: the bedclothes had come off us both during the night, but instead of falling to the floor, as you'd expect, they had worked their way between us. It was like a wall between Sarah and me.

Over breakfast I asked Mrs Wakelin about the rapping sound, but I couldn't get any sort of satisfactory answer. I had to make do with a reluctant suggestion that it might have been the beams settling or the pipes knocking. I knew it wasn't that, though; if it were, Sarah would have heard it as well.

There was something furtive about the whole thing, something that our hosts knew about, but hoped they wouldn't have to tell us. That was my impression, and I said as much to Sarah as we set out for the day in the car.

She made just one observation: "Did you notice that Mrs Wakelin didn't ask us whether we'd slept well?"

I hadn't noticed, but it was unusual, and it rather made me suspect that our landlady already knew how well – or how badly – we'd slept.

An excellent breakfast had set the tone for an excellent day. We just took it easy, driving through Southminster and Latchingdon, and all sorts of other nice places, until we came to North Fambridge, where we had lunch at the *Ferryboat Inn*. Then we turned eastward again and headed for Burnham on Crouch.

I don't need to tell you what an enchanting little town Burnham is. The waterfront, down by the quay, is lovely, with all the various craft in the river and that delightful jumble of old buildings. During that very pleasant afternoon, we made up our minds to stay and have dinner at a nice restaurant before going back to Kidds End, so I phoned Mrs Wakelin and asked her not to cook for us that evening. She was quite amenable to the idea, and said that she'd only charge us for the meals that we actually ate.

In the event, we were able to get a table at a good seafood restaurant and enjoyed an excellent meal. We had a bottle of wine with it and an Irish coffee afterwards; then, just tired enough and very contented, we drove back to *The Dog*.

By the time we went to bed, we weren't in the least worried about things going bump in the night — and yet, as soon as we got to the top of the stairs we could both feel that same amorphous depression settling upon us. As we entered the bedroom, the knocking started again. Within seconds my head felt as if it would burst, and poor Sarah looked as miserable as sin. For a moment I held her, but she pushed me away, very gently, saying that it actually made her feel worse. I was tired, headachy and angry, and I felt too horribly weary even to rouse our hosts and complain. My body felt, well, as if it was weighed down with water — I can't describe it any more accurately — and my poor wife was worse still.

That night was more wretched than the last, though I insisted that Sarah slept in the bed alone, while I curled up in the easy chair with a blanket over me. Again, we woke at dawn, Sarah shivering because the bedclothes had slid off her, and me feeling as if I'd been on my feet for forty-eight hours.

Those bedclothes! This time the blanket had formed itself into a ridge on one side of Sarah, and the eiderdown on the other.

Again, it was like a wall, protecting her. No, not protecting — it was imprisoning her.

But daylight had come at last, and the malign influence was gone. For an hour or so we were able to sleep soundly and peacefully until the landlady awoke us.

The mornings lately had been very misty up until about ten o'clock, but that day was all so bright and clear that it was almost painful. Breakfast was quite as good as we'd come to expect, but Mrs Wakelin was even less forthcoming. She seemed to be waiting for something, but there was no pleasure in the anticipation.

We drove off to the north after breakfast, intending to visit Bradwell and see the Saxon chapel. As we left Tillingham behind us, Sarah put her hand on my arm and said, "You want to get to the bottom of this, don't you?"

I knew that we would have to talk, and I pulled the car over at the first opportunity. We got out and propped ourselves against the bonnet, and I lit cigarettes for us both while I considered how best to phrase my thoughts.

"As I see it," I said at length, "we have two choices. Either we leave *The Dog* today, or we stay on; and if we stay, it's in the knowledge that there is, well, something in that house that wants to hurt us. If it were just me, I'd say be damned to it and I'd get the truth somehow from the Wakelins. They know — or they suspect — what we're up against, and yet they won't tell us."

"No, they won't," Sarah said, dully, "because they're afraid. Oh, they aren't bad people, Miles. You know that! But they are afraid — of — of *it*."

"And *it*, whatever it is, is out to get you."

She blinked, and protested at this. "Not me, surely! Why, I didn't even hear the knocking."

"That's right. I'm the one who heard it, and I think it may have been offered to me as a warning, which I have defied. But you, darling... You weren't given any warning. You were simply attacked. You don't have to tell me how you felt, because I could see it in your face and hear it in your voice. The thing was sapping you, making you too listless even to try to save yourself. And last night I felt that I was falling too. That's where the danger lies."

Sarah closed her eyes. Her face was very pale, and I knew that I'd hit the mark. She had felt herself sinking into the Slough of Despond, and it was a horrible thing to bear. If she had been less strong-willed, or if she'd been alone... What then, eh?

She forced a smile, and took both my hands in hers. "It will be settled before dawn tomorrow," she said. "Don't ask me how I know, but I am certain of it." She kissed me, suddenly and lightly. "Now, let's get back in the car and head for that chapel. There's something I want to do."

What she wanted to do, and I could only admire and love her for it, was to pray, quietly and privately. When we left the chapel, we walked hand in hand the few yards to the shore. We stood there for a few minutes, looking out over a leaden sea, before turning back to take the path, across the field and past the farm buildings, to the little patch of wasteland that serves as a car-park. A chill wind had blown up, and there were dark, threatening clouds overhead, but I felt better able to face threats now, because the rugged, unassuming little building we'd just left was one of the country's great survivors. How can anyone fail to be impressed and moved by a church that's stood, quietly and confidently, against all that man and nature could do to it, for thirteen hundred years?

We were within yards of the car when the storm broke, and mighty raindrops pelted down like liquid golf balls. We ran, and threw ourselves into the car. Sarah shook her head vigorously, spattering me with little drops of water, and said, "Right — what do we do now?"

"The first thing," I said, "is to get the car back onto the road before this track becomes a morass."

You've seen heavy rain hammering the surface of a pond? The road looked just like that. It was no time to be out in the open country. Clearly our best move was towards the nearest town, so we headed straight for Maldon.

That storm just went on and on, though by mid-afternoon it had settled down to a dull, steady rainfall. We decided to make our way back to Kidds End. Even if the night was to be no worse than the last two, I reckoned that both of us would be better for an hour or two's sleep that afternoon.

We got back to *The Dog* to find that things had been happening. There had been hailstones like shrapnel, and one great freak lump of ice had actually shattered the left-hand window of our room, right above the bed, and sent the pitcher of water crashing from the bedside table. The water from the jug and the rain that belted in through the broken window had soaked the bed right through to the mattress. On such a day, of course, there was no chance of drying it.

That's what confronted us when we arrived — that and Mrs Wakelin's eagerness to tell us that one of the pubs in Tillingham could surely put us up if we liked to move our things out. Terribly bad luck, of course, but her only available room was the small one with the single bed, and she was sure we wouldn't want that, now would we?

She was not a little surprised when we said that the single room would suit us quite nicely, thank you. We'd made up our minds to stay, and we were going to stay. The bed was a four-footer, and we've managed to sleep in much narrower quarters than that. So, over-ruling our landlady's protests of inadequacy, we moved our belongings, mostly untouched by the storm, into the room next door, and there we had the nap we'd promised ourselves.

The result was that we were awake and alert when night came. Sober as well — we'd made sure of that, so that we should be ready to face, well, whatever we had to face.

The rapping sound that night was much clearer and closer, and this time Sarah could hear it too, though faintly. To me it was like the sound of someone drumming on the wall of the next room.

Of course! That was it. It was obvious now that the mystery centred upon the locked room — the one that "had woodworm".

Curiously, the black depression that had fallen upon Sarah the last two nights was diminished now that she could actually hear the knocking. It was something tangible, something that she could hold on to and say, "This is real."

Perhaps we should have done something straight away, something positive. Collared the landlord, maybe, and asked bluntly what the hell was going on. But we didn't. We stood the row until after midnight, and then I said reluctantly that we should make our move. That hellish irregular rapping was shredding my nerves, and Sarah was sinking into the black state of the previous nights. We had to do something, even if it was just to pack our bags and leave.

"It's in that room," said Sarah. "Whatever it is, it's in that room, and it wants to hurt us."

That much at least was plain. Now that we were committed, I felt calmer and stronger. Picking up the torch and the key to our room, I said, "These are old locks, and there's a chance that our key may open that door. I'm going to see if I can find out what's behind all this. You stay here."

I opened our door cautiously and checked for signs of life from our hosts, but they had retired some while back. There was no light from downstairs, and none under the door of their own quarters. All that could be heard was that infernal tapping. At the door of Bluebeard's chamber I quietly fitted the key into the lock, but as I began to turn it I sensed that Sarah was beside me. She couldn't wait alone, and I couldn't blame her.

The key turned quite easily, and the latch sprang back with a sudden muffled click. Equally suddenly, I pushed the door open and shone my torch into the room.

There was no sign that it was anything but well used. Nicely furnished, very much like our own room — the double one, I mean. There was nothing out of the ordinary except for the damnable persistence of that knocking. I swung the torch over to the left, to the connecting wall, and with horrible distinctness I saw it: a human figure, a man, crouched at the foot of the wall, and with its arm raised, fist clenched, in the act of striking. That arm was appallingly thin. The muscles were wasted, and there seemed to be teeth-marks in the scrawny flesh.

The arm was lowered to support the creature as it turned its face towards us. I never want to see anything again like that face. It was little more than a skull, with straggles of grey hair and beard clinging to it. The skin, tanned like leather, was tight over the bone; the nose was just two black holes, and the lips were stretched back over yellow teeth in a dreadful travesty of a smile. It was the face of a dead man, but the eyes were alive in their sockets, and full of hatred and pain. I didn't immediately realise that their venomous glare was not directed at me, but at Sarah.

The thing steadied itself on its two arms and began to move towards us, crawling, as though its legs were crippled, and with that appalling glare fixed upon us. The movement seemed to break the spell, and I too was able to move. I slammed the door shut and turned the key, cursing my own slowness.

Sarah shivered violently and said, "God, I'm cold!" And then, "Miles, what was it? All I could see was a — a blur: a nasty yellowish blur, over by the wall."

I was saved from having to answer her then, because the door of the landlady's room opened, and she came out, followed hastily by her husband. She switched on the landing light, and for a moment the two of them just looked at us. Then she said, all of a rush, "Oh, my dears, I'm so sorry! I shouldn't have let you stay — I should have warned you, only I didn't know how bad it would be. Please forgive me — "

It was the quiet, easy-going Wakelin who took charge. He persuaded us gently into their apartment and sat us down on the sitting-room sofa with a glass of whisky each. With my arms tight around her, Sarah began to feel less infernally cold, but we were still bewildered. And I, at least, remembered that ghastly thing in the locked room.

At last the landlord spoke.

"I think I can guess what you've been through, at least up till tonight, though it's never happened before in our twenty-four years here, and I can't blame you for going to look. I can see by your face, young fellow, that you've seen it — him — and there's only one person known to have seen him before. Maybe you won't accept our apology, and maybe you'd be right, but I hope you'll hear the story, and then perhaps you'll think that we weren't altogether to blame."

Sarah said, "Of course we'll hear your story, and there's no need to apologise. We've known all along, I think, that anything wrong here was none of your doing. But — please, please, what was it? Miles, what did you see?"

So I had to tell them about the dead man whose eyes were alive with agony and hatred. They listened in sober silence — and it's odd, you know, but it really was silent: since I'd shut the door on that thing I couldn't hear the rapping any more. The poison was still there, but it couldn't be heard now.

Wakelin said, "I think perhaps my wife had better tell you the tale. She knows more about it than I do, for all that I was born and brought up in the area, and she's not been here above thirty years." He patted her hand encouragingly, and she gave us a nervous smile.

"Very well," she said. "It was like this. This house wasn't always an inn, you know. It was built around 1750 by a retired seaman, whose name was Bullock. He'd made his fortune, and he decided to settle down quietly and live the life of a gentleman. This Captain Bullock was a small, slim man, with a mane of grey hair and very taking ways. If you're wondering how I know all this, well, I got it from what they call a broadsheet that I bought years ago when the auction was held up at Gray's Farm. I bought something else, too, which I'll tell you about later.

"Now, the Captain hadn't been here a matter of months before he took himself a wife. She was a young woman he'd met in London, and you only had to look at her to realise why he fell for her. It was the old story, though: he loved her for her beauty, and she loved him for his money. It wasn't long before she decided that she didn't love him at all, only the money, and she became very bitter. She knew that his fortune would come to her when he died, but he was a strong, hale man, for all his grey hair, and in these marshlands he might well outlive her. So the greed and the bitterness festered inside her.

"Then, perhaps two years after they were married, something happened to change things, and not for the better. Captain Bullock was riding home from Maldon one winter evening when his horse bolted. The result was that he was thrown off the horse, and both his legs were broken. This was what the woman had been waiting for — some chance that would give her the upper hand. The Captain was confined to his bed, of course, and she put up a public show of pity and devotion, but within days it was known that she was entertaining lovers.

"She no longer slept with her husband, but moved herself into the next room, and there she was quite shameless with her fancy men while the Captain lay groaning with the pain from his broken legs — for she did little enough by way of tending to the wounds.

"Of course, it wasn't long before the poor man realised what was going on, though no doubt she was all honey the few times a day she went to take him his food. So, of a night, while the woman took her pleasure, he got himself out of bed, crawled over to the wall, and rapped upon it, loud, to disturb them.

"Well, you may be sure that it did disturb them, and I'll wager her fancy man that night left the house pretty quick, but she was not to be denied. She just moved herself and her lovers into the farther room, and still the brave old man would crawl from his bed and hammer on the wall. She must have been as mean as they come, you know, and she wasn't to be denied her pleasure. She took to tying her husband to his bed, but that was no use, for he was a sailor and could loosen any knot that she could tie. So still her games were disturbed, and at last she hit upon a final evil, desperate plan.

"She was too mean and too cowardly to kill him outright — that at least would have been clean and definite. What she did was simply to let him die. She locked the door of his room and left him to starve: no food, no water — nothing but pain and anger. She left off her affairs, of course, for several days, until she judged that he was too weak to leave his bed, but she must have been quite insatiable, for she didn't even wait for him to die before she started to bring her men-friends to the house again.

"And so, for perhaps another two weeks, she continued, as shameless as before, while in the next room her husband lay dying.

"I think that in those last days he must have gone quite mad. He had nothing but agony and hatred and the one thought of disturbing her wicked adulteries. At all events, when she finally roused the courage to unlock the door of his room, she found him as dead as she had hoped — but he wasn't in the bed. He had crawled — and what torment it must have been! — right over to the wall, and his hand was raised to strike a blow that he never made, for his brave old heart had finally failed him.

"She had him buried, saying that in his illness he had refused to take food and had wasted to death. If she stood by his grave-side with tears in her eyes, then they were tears of joy, for now she was free of him at last, and his fortune was hers. That very night, as you may suppose, she celebrated her release in the best way she knew.

"When she heard the knocking on the wall that night, she must have thought she was losing her own sanity. Then, perhaps, she suspected a gruesome joke; but when her lover had gone, and she looked into the old man's room, she found it quite empty.

"The same thing happened the next night, and the next, but the man who was with her the following night was a nerveless brute. While she cowered and trembled, he strode, naked as he was, to the Captain's room, and wrenched open the door. Then he slammed it shut and, with never a word to the woman, he gathered his clothes and fled from the house. He had seen what you saw tonight.

"A couple of days later, when nothing had been heard from the woman, a local farmhand broke open the door of the house and searched for her. He found her hanging from a beam in the wash-house."

Mrs Wakelin stopped and expelled a long breath. This was obviously the end of her story, and it was certainly a horrible tale enough. To think of the pain and the hate that had festered in the room over two centuries! But there was one important thing it didn't explain.

"Why us, Mrs Wakelin?" I said. "Why should we see and hear it, when you say no-one else has in over twenty years?"

She stood up and went over to the sideboard, where she opened a drawer and took something out. Before handing it to me, she said, "This is the other thing I bought at the auction. There's no positive identification, but I showed it to an art expert who stayed here once for the shooting, and he told me it dates from about 1750. You have to press the little stud to open it."

The thing was a golden locket, oval, and about two inches by one and a half, with a miniature portrait inside.

It was a picture of Sarah.

We looked at it for one horrible long moment, and then, suddenly and briefly, Sarah screamed, as she had not done before during the whole foul business. I put my arms around her and held her very tightly, and soon she stopped trembling.

After a moment I looked at the picture again, more closely this time. It was a pretty face, but the likeness to Sarah was only on the surface. The nose and chin were sharper, the eyes less widely spaced, and the mouth smaller. The expression was quite different. It was like a caricature of my wife, and that superficial resemblance was damnable. Can you understand if I say that it was Sarah *gone wrong*?

Well, that's really all there is. The Wakelins were full of apologies, but Sarah had been quite right, of course; the evil in the house was none of their doing. On their advice we slept separately for the rest of the night — as much as we could sleep. Sarah had the spare bed in our hosts' room, and I went alone into the single bedroom. Neither of us was disturbed by knockings or any other manifestations, though I at least had some pretty unpleasant dreams. You won't be surprised to learn that we left the following morning and went home.

There was a long pause while George and I looked at each other and at Miles.

"Well," I said at last, "much as I'd like to have seen Sarah this evening, I can quite understand that she'd rather not recall such an experience."

Miles nodded, and I thought I heard a murmur from George: "Alas, poor ghost." Then he said, "Was anything done? I mean, has any attempt been made to give peace to that troubled spirit?"

"About a week later," said Miles, "we had a letter from Mrs Wakelin. The Vicar of Tillingham had come to the house and held a little service of blessing in that room. Nothing as formal or dramatic as an exorcism, I gather, but it does seem that there have been no disturbances since then." He pulled a wry face and added, "But then, of course, Sarah and I have never been back there."

Afterword

The plot of this story derives from a real haunting in Devon.

I couldn't think of a name for the (non-existent) hamlet beyond Tillingham, so borrowed that of Hook End, near Brentwood. However, I've invented one for this revised text. "Kidds End" is a nod of thanks to A.F. (Chico) Kidd, whose ghost stories I have enjoyed for a good number of years. The story was originally called "The Dog" — an unnecessarily misleading title.

The inn, though I didn't consciously make it so, is rather like the *Tower Arms* at South Weald, near Brentwood.

Those who have nothing better to think about may like to know that what I long thought to be a "solitary terraced house" in Tillingham is actually the mill house. The mill itself is long since demolished.

I'm grateful to John M. Garrett for allowing me to quote from his song "Old Essex Isle".

THE WALL-PAINTING

"You must understand," said Harry Foster, " that this isn't my own story." He looked at us both with some concern. "I say, I hope you don't think I'm here under false pretences!"

He was a large, tweedy, red-faced man, giving something of the impression of a corpulent and amiable fox. I had been surprised to learn that he was — as he still is — an antiquarian book-seller, with premises in the West End and a house in Upper Norwood.

"That's all right," said George Cobbett. "It's the story itself that we're interested in."

He began to fill his pipe, waiting for our visitor to justify his journey into Essex.

"Good, good. Well, it came into my hands after a house clearance. I specialise, as you know, in sporting books, but I keep a fair amount of general material on the shelves, which usually comes from auctions and clearances. This particular item was among a job-lot from a house in Surrey. The owner had died, and the heirs — distant cousins — simply sold up the house and the entire contents. They couldn't tell me anything about the book, and I've been quite unable to find out how it came into the old man's possession. Maybe we'll never know.

"At all events, here it is."

He placed on the table a large notebook or diary, rather battered, with dark blue covers that were fading to grey. It had probably come from a cheap stationer's some seventy or eighty years ago.

"The name inside the cover," said Harry, "is the Reverend Stephen Gifford, Vicar of Welford St Paul in Essex. I used to know the place fairly well — a friend of mine had a cottage nearby — and that's what persuaded me to read the thing. It's — well... unusual, you know."

He put on a pair of horn-rimmed glasses and began to read to us in a slightly hoarse, fruity voice.

This parish of Welford St Paul is large in area and small in numbers. Visitors are often surprised to learn that the church is dedicated to St Lawrence, and I am obliged to tell them that the village, like so many in Essex, was named for the Lords of the Manor: in this instance, the Dean and Chapter of St Paul's

Cathedral. They owned and still own a good deal of land in this county, which for centuries constituted the greater part of the Diocese of London. Indeed, they might well be accounted the oldest landed "family" in England!

The parish church is very old. Much of the fabric is Norman work, but the chancel walls and the north wall of the sanctuary were built by the Anglo-Saxons and cannot be less than one thousand years old. It is a respectable age, even for this ancient county. The building is small and plain, with no really distinctive features, consisting of sanctuary, chancel and nave, with a squat western tower. There are no aisles, and the modest southern porch was erected by one of my predecessors early in the last century. Within, the walls are plastered and coated with a solution of lime, whose whiteness gives the small building a surprisingly light and spacious appearance.

Upon my first visit I noticed a number of cracks in the plaster, and experience suggested that I should call in a building surveyor. The result was as I had feared: the northern walls of both nave and chancel were in a very sad state. With the subsequent arrival of the builders began a period of disruptive activity such as this little church had not known for centuries.

It was on the afternoon of the fourth day that the patient and cautious work of the repairers uncovered a small patch of startlingly bright colour beneath the whiteness of the chancel wall. I took upon myself the responsibility of sealing off that wall and calling in a specialist. Fortunately I knew just the man. His name was Howard Faragher, and I had met him some months previously at the London Library, when I had dropped by to visit my friend the sub-librarian. I did not have his address, but Lomax was able to furnish it, and I telegraphed to him at once. He arrived at Welford St Paul two days later, a tall rangy man in his middle thirties, with untidy yellow hair and an amiably eager expression.

"Well," said he, after he had examined the little patch of green and red, "it is certainly a mediaeval painting, and from the colours and the way they're applied, I should say it's an early one — possibly late twelfth century."

"But it looks so fresh!" I protested. "I thought that in fresco —"

He interrupted me: "Not all wall-painting is fresco, you know, though all fresco is wall-painting. That technique consists of applying paint to wet plaster, and it's really only suitable in a warm, dry climate. It's hardly known in this country. No, this is what's called *secco*. The paints were mostly compounded of oxides and applied to a lime-wash surface that had been fixed with casein — simple skimmed milk. The colours can remain bright for centuries.

"Now, Gifford, I shall need several days to remove the rest of this covering — no doubt it was put on during the Reformation — and I dare not attempt to make up my mind about the picture until I've finished, so please leave any questions until then."

He worked for nearly a week, with meticulous care, patiently and cheerfully fending off my eager curiosity. Each evening he would hang a cloth over the painting and return with me to the vicarage. My attempts to draw him out met with a polite but firm refusal, and our conversation turned mostly to history and music.

After dinner on the fifth day he folded his napkin and said abruptly, "Well, I've finished. No, don't go rushing out to look at it just yet. I'd rather show you the thing by daylight, and besides, I want a word with you before you see it. I think you told me that you keep a rather good brandy in your cellar. Would you be averse to cracking a bottle? I think I deserve a drink!"

He would not say more until we were comfortably settled in my study, each with a glass of the rich, golden spirit. Then, after inhaling the piquant "nose" and taking an appreciative sip, he looked at me rather quizzically and said, "I think that we have found Saint Tosti."

Frankly, I did not know what to make of this. The name was quite unknown to me. "Tosti?" I said. "An Italian?"

Faragher chuckled. "You're thinking of the composer," he said. "No, no. The saint was as English as you or I — more so, I suppose, for he was pure Anglo-Saxon, with no Norman blood in his veins. He was never, I think, widely known, but he flourished in the early decades of the eleventh century."

I began to understand. "He lived too late, then, to be mentioned in Bede's history."

"Just so, and too early to have encountered the Norman invaders. But really, you know, you should be telling me about him." Again that sardonic smile.

"I? But — " I was lost for words.

"You really don't know, do you? The fact is that your church was once dedicated to St Tosti. Oh, there's no doubt about it. When we met at the London Library, I was actually researching the ecclesiastical history of the Tendring Hundred for a client, and that was one of the facts that came to my attention. But as to Tosti himself, information is not plentiful: a few scraps in the Library, a little more among the London Diocesan Archives – that's all. The name is certainly Anglo-Saxon. You may recall that King Harold had a brother called Tosti or Tostig, who treacherously allied himself with Harald Hardrada at the Battle of Stamford Bridge."

"But this is remarkable!" I exclaimed. "There's no mention of it in the Parish Records. I take it that Tosti was what you might call a local saint – not recognised by the Vatican."

It was certainly true that the Pontiff did not reserve to himself the right of canonisation until the thirteenth century. Before then there had been all sorts of irregularities, which the new decree swiftly crushed. The cult of St Tosti, like many others, must have found itself regarded quite suddenly as an unorthodox and unacceptable excrescence upon the body of the Church.

"That would explain why I had never heard of him. And yet many of these local saints were eventually granted official recognition and canonised. What was there about this man?"

Faragher shrugged his narrow shoulders. "I really don't know. He just seems to have been – well – dubious. Records are scarce, as I told you, and I didn't take any particular note of them, but I can recall nothing in the man's life that suggests sanctity. One account, written, I think, in the late twelfth century, did lay particular stress upon his celibacy, but where you would expect some suggestion that the saint was following the example of Our Lord, or was wedded to the Church, there was nothing. Just the bald statement. In fact, he doesn't seem to have had much to do with the Church at all."

"How very interesting. Then what was it that caused people to regard him as a saint?"

"There are the vaguest references to miracles. For the moment, Gifford, you will have to be satisfied with that. You see, all the records that I've come across date from long after Tosti's supposed death."

Faragher's thin face brightened suddenly. "Ah, yes! That is an interesting matter. A clerk who wrote in or about the years 1120 says that Tosti was actually in the midst of an address or sermon to his brothers – that's the word he uses – when he simply disappeared. The statement is quite unequivocal. He did not die; he disappeared. That is the only surviving account of the end of St

Tosti, and our clerk says that he had the story from an eye-witness. Curious, eh?"

"Very curious," I said. "And why do you think that the wall-painting depicts this rather doubtful saint?"

My companion stifled a yawn, and I suddenly realised how tired he looked.

"I think," he replied, "that I shall answer that question tomorrow, when you see the picture. Afterwards, perhaps, the two of us could make the journey in to Colchester and investigate the Archdeaconry records. Now, if you don't mind, we shall change the subject. I should like just one more glass of this very passable brandy, and then I'll be ready for a good night's sleep."

My first duty on the next day was to conduct a short Eucharist. This weekday service was rarely well attended, and I was gratified that Faragher elected to join the congregation. Indeed, his presence increased the attendance by fifty per cent. The simple and moving words of the ritual, hallowed by the Spirit of God and by the spirit of our fathers, absorbed my attention throughout, so that it was not until after I had pronounced the Benediction that my curiosity about the wall-painting returned. Howard Faragher was waiting for me outside the vestry when I had slipped off my surplice and cassock. His eagerness to show me the painting was quite as great as mine to see it. We crossed the sanctuary to where a sheet of dark cloth, some seven feet by four, covered this unexpected treasure. Faragher raised his hand and, with an almost theatrical gesture, whipped the cloth from the wall.

I am sure that I gasped. My first reaction was of astonishment at the sheer beauty of this hidden jewel of the church, but it was followed closely by another feeling — of unease, engendered by something too subtle to define. Was it the proud, ascetic expression of the man who stood, fully life-size, before us? Was it the extraordinary brightness of the eyes with which he regarded us? Was it the strangely uncertain figure, as it might be the shadow of a dog or a wolf, that lurked at his feet, half-hidden by the folds of his robe?

The whole painting measured just over six feet high by two and a half wide. There was a border, painted in clever imitation of a Romanesque arch, the pillars no more than two inches wide. Within it, against a grey background and upon a floor of green, stood the saint.

I could not doubt that he was regarded as a saint — why else would his likeness be enshrined in a Christian church? — but there was that about his calm and arrogant expression which suggested something other. The figure was tall and thin, with hairless and rather nut-cracker jaws and the most remarkable eyes. At first I had taken these piercing orbs to be blue, but a closer look showed that the colour was actually a curious and indeterminate grey.

I was pondering upon this when Faragher spoke: "You've noticed the eyes? No doubt the man's eyes were actually blue, as was common among the Anglo-Saxons..." He paused for a moment, then resumed: "By Tosti's time, of course, the various invading races — yes, including the Norsemen — had become melded into a truly English people, in whose veins also ran much good Celtic blood. Besides, this part of north-eastern Essex was variously claimed by the East Saxons and the East Angles, and there is no telling to which people the saint himself belonged."

A longer pause, while he seemed to gather his thoughts.

"Ha! Yes — blue eyes. Well, real blue is rare in mediaeval murals. It was made from an azurite, and not easy to come by. Mostly the artists used, as here, a cunning mixture of black and lime white, with the slightest touch of red ochre. You would expect the result to be a sort of dull brown, but there's no doubt that this is intended to be blue. No doubt at all..."

His voice trailed off, and I looked away, with some reluctance, from the compelling gaze of the painted figure.

The left hand was raised, as if in blessing, but instead of the first two fingers being extended, as I had seen before, only the forefinger was raised: it pointed directly upwards.

I mentioned this, and my companion, roused from his reverie, replied, "Yes, interesting, isn't it? It gives credence to the notion that there was something unsaintly about this saint. The forefinger, extended on its own, is usually a gesture of condemnation in these paintings, and as this one is pointing upwards — well, one wonders. I'm curious that it should be the left hand, too, and not the right.

"Have you observed, by the way, what he holds in his right hand? Uncommonly like a cat-o'-nine-tails, isn't it? That's what really convinced me that this must be St Tosti. You see, he is mentioned in more than one of the records as driving his enemies before him with a scourge. *His* enemies, notice, not the enemies of Christ."

"It was not a symbol of martyrdom, then?"

"Ah, that would naturally occur to you. You are thinking of the grid-iron associated with St Lawrence. No, it was certainly Tosti who wielded the whip. Still, our Lord himself flogged the money-lenders in the Temple, so perhaps we should read too much into that. But tell me what you make of this."

He indicated the shadowy figure to which I have referred. It seemed to stand or squat, perhaps half the height of the saint, just by his left foot, partly concealed by the folds of his red gown. No features could be distinguished, and, indeed, the closer I looked, the less sure I became that the figure was actually there. It might have been merely a darker stain upon the grey background of the painting. Yet such was the meticulous care with which the saint had been depicted that I was inclined to doubt this notion.

I asked Faragher, "Is there perhaps some animal, a dog or a wolf, which is associated with the legend of St Tosti?"

His reply was negative. "And yet," he added, after a moment's thought, "something, some fact or suggestion, is nagging at my mind." He gestured, wryly. "Perhaps we shall find out when we look at the Archdeaconry records. And that reminds me: the time is getting on. If we are to get any real work done in Colchester we had better go now."

With some reluctance, I left the presence of that enigmatic and dubious saint, and scurried towards the vestry to collect my greatcoat and hat. As I went, I observed that Howard Faragher was gazing intently at one portion of the wall-painting and murmuring, almost to himself, "What are you? I wish you would show yourself, so that I could be sure."

The journey in to Colchester is not a long one, and usually, upon a morning in early spring, it is particularly pleasant. My impatience, however, made it seem long and tedious, and I could see that my companion found it so as well. Still, we reached the town at last, and made our way to the offices of the Archdeaconry.

Our eagerness was not well rewarded: the information about St Tosti and the early history of Welford St Paul was quite as scanty as Faragher had supposed. After nearly three hours we had uncovered no more than a few very uncertain references to miraculous events, and one late version, dating from the mid-thirteenth century, of the story that Tosti had whipped his foes before him. Here, though, there was the qualifying statement that "the Brethren of Tosti cried aloud to magnify the name of Christ" — but this was probably a pious interpolation.

At two o'clock the Archdeacon's clerk remarked rather pointedly that of course the archives could be made available for our inspection another day, but at present his duties were pressing. Indeed, I myself had begun to feel that our quest was something of a wild goose chase.

But at that moment Howard Faragher gave a sudden exclamation of satisfaction: "Ha! Gifford, listen to this. It's from a pamphlet issued in 1612 by the Puritan Richard Fine of Colchester. The pamphlet was called *England, Rome and Babylon*, and it cost Richard Fine both his ears in those intolerant times. All copies were destroyed, except for this one page, and that is charred along one edge —"

"But what does it say?" I cried.

"It starts in the middle of a sentence, thus: '... to his Lorde while in Converse with his Brethren.' A reference to the disappearance, I think. Then it continues: 'This Tosti was knowne to consorte with an Angell, as some say, others a Sprite of different sorte, not being a Creature of *God* but of the *Divell*.' After that there's a new paragraph, fulminating in general terms against Popish superstition."

The clerk, uncomprehending, interrupted with a discreet cough, and Faragher hastily laid down the ancient paper.

"I do beg your pardon," he said. "We must not keep you any longer." He glanced at his watch and added, "We should go now, in any case, if we are to find anywhere open for luncheon."

Polite but triumphant, he accompanied me from the office. He spoke no more for a while, but his look as we bade farewell to the harassed clerk plainly said: "What do you think of that, my friend?"

There was but one thought in my mind: that the shadowy figure that lurked beside the painted saint had little about it of the angelic.

As we drove into Welford St Paul, Faragher said, "If you don't mind, I should like to stay here for a few days longer. This matter becomes more and more curious, and I'd rather like to put off unveiling the picture until we know what there is to know about it. I suppose that the builders...?"

"You need not worry," I replied. "The builders know only that a painting of some kind has been uncovered, and that it is being examined by an expert."

"Capital! Well, shall we go and have another look at it while the light lasts?"

The shade that clung to St Tosti was as disturbing and indefinable as ever. After peering at it for several minutes, Faragher said, "Please go if you want to, Gifford. I must see if I can date this thing at all accurately." He looked up at me with a smile. "Who knows? I may yet be able to tell you who the artist was."

I left him, but with slight and amorphous misgivings. Whatever the truth about St Tosti, I was sure that the painting itself was unholy. The proud face of the ascetic, the lazy and arrogant way in which he held his wicked-looking scourge, the sinister and almost shapeless figure of his unknown companion —

The companion! I could not be certain, but the suspicion would not leave my mind that the shadowy form had actually moved since we had last seen it.

The light was almost gone when Howard Faragher returned to the vicarage. He looked and sounded preoccupied, tapping his long fore-finger against his lips and muttering to himself.

In answer to my question, he said, "No farther, I'm afraid. My original estimate of the date may even be too late: it might just be eleventh century. Did you notice the folds of the saint's robe, how carefully they were moulded? That is a pretty sure sign of early work in this country. Later artists tended away from the continental ideal and concentrated on an essential purity of outline. I doubt that we shall ever find out who painted Tosti for us — he was simply too early."

Faragher said little more until after dinner, when he observed, "Tomorrow, I think, I shall pay a visit to the Diocesan archives in London — I don't think there's much point in going to Rochester or St Alban's. I'll see if the London records have anything more to offer. I shall bring my camera back with me, and a magnesium flare, and we'll try to get a clear photograph of our mysterious saint."

I retired early that night, leaving Faragher to his musings. I was very tired, and yet I did not sleep well, for I had a most unsettling dream. It was not a nightmare, in the sense that there was nothing gruesome about it, but it was instinct with a sense of isolation and intense loneliness.

I stood in the churchyard of Welford St Paul, and about me was only a dark, vague greyness. The church stood before me, its windows illuminated fitfully by the feeble glow of candles. From the building came the sound of singing or chanting, though that too was faint, almost ethereal, and I cannot recall whether the words or the music were known to me. I walked unsteadily to the porch and unlocked the door. As I entered the building, it was abruptly darkened, though the singing continued, as faint and attenuated a sound as before.

I did not realise the fact until I came to consider the dream in the morning, but the interior of the building was not that of my church. I had an impression of vast, almost infinite space, huge, dark and cold — made to seem more so, perhaps, by the singularly distant quality of the incorporeal voices. As I progressed, there came upon me the conviction that I was not wanted here, nor ever would be, though for what reason I could not tell. Something — something huge, perhaps the building itself — was, with a disturbing subtlety, hostile to me. That is all I remember, but it is enough.

At breakfast, Faragher, though still seeming abstracted, was now more open. He greeted me by asking, "Did you sleep well?" Not waiting for an answer, he continued, "I didn't — I had a rather frightening dream."

Putting aside my own vision, I said, "Tell me about it."

"I was walking alone," he said, "through some sort of forest or heathland. The sky was darkening, and I knew that I must reach my destination before the light was quite gone. No, I have no idea what that destination was, nor why I was in such haste. I walked faster, and as I did so I became aware that something was stalking me. I could not see it, nor tell precisely where it was, but I could hear it moving, with a rather horrible ease, not very far from me."

"It was something, then, and not someone?"

"I can't be certain. That's the devil of it! I could only sense the rustling and stepping of its long legs as it kept pace with me. I think that it was toying with me, as a cat does with a mouse. Yes, it had very long legs — but, Gifford, I couldn't tell *how many* long legs!"

Before he set out for Colchester and the London train, we went once more to look at the wall-painting. My friend said nothing, though he glanced at me rather uneasily, but again it seemed to me that Tosti's shadowy companion had moved.

I was crossing the churchyard after Evensong when he arrived back from London. He smiled ruefully and waved to me, then began to unload two large packages from the dog-cart: a square, bulky object that contained his camera and glass plates, and a long bag like those that golfers use. This held the tripod. I went over to help him carry them into the house.

"We shall have dinner first," I said, "and then you can tell me what you've learned."

"There is little to tell," he replied. "One thirteenth century document, written by a clerk of St Paul's, which refers cryptically to a *reliqua Sancti Tostigii*, and an episcopal order from the reign of Edward VI that a monstrance be destroyed at Welford church. That's all. There was nothing to identify the relic, and only the absence of other probabilities leads me to wonder if the monstrance had been made to hold it."

After dinner, we took the photographic equipment into the darkened church. With the magnesium flare, of course, there was no need for adequate light in the building, and half a dozen candles sufficed while we erected the tripod and set the camera upon it. Only then did we look closely at the painting.

Faragher's next words made my heart sink: "When we first examined this, wasn't Tosti's companion partially hidden by his robe?"

"It was," I replied, hesitantly. "But now there is a clear gap between the two. The shadow has definitely moved towards the edge of the picture."

Insanely, the thought occurred to me that it was trying to get out! But this quite impossible happening seemed only to have increased my friend's interest. With calm deliberation, he took three photographs of the painting — I averted my gaze each time, but the sudden flash of light seemed to sear my eyes — and then he began to pack up his equipment, saying, "I shall develop these in the morning, and we'll see whether any secrets are revealed."

I carried the tripod out of the church, while Faragher took the camera and the precious photographic plates. The moon had not yet risen, and a thick cloud obscured the stars. It seemed almost unnaturally dark in the churchyard. No lights could be seen in the vicarage, for my housekeeper had left long before. Fortunately the walk is short and straight, so that we had no difficulty in reaching the vicarage gate, but there, as chance would have it, I slipped upon the step and fell, giving my ankle a severe twist. I had dropped the heavy bag, but Faragher retrieved it unharmed. Then, carrying both loads, he supported me while I hobbled, and we shortly reached the door of the house.

I found my key and unlocked the door, so that he might go in and switch on the electric light before helping me. I felt, rather than saw, him enter and feel for the light-switch, which is just inside the door and to the right.

There was a dull click, but no light. Faragher's voice said, "I'm sorry about this. I think the bulb must have blown. Shall I try the light in the study?"

"If you please," I replied. "The door is just a few feet along, on the same side."

A moment later I heard the study door open, and again a muffled click in the darkness. Then Faragher returned to me.

"This is most annoying," he said. "I think we shall have to make do with candles tonight, and tomorrow we'll see about getting the electricity restored."

I sighed, no doubt with some petulance. "Very well. The candles are kept in the scullery, in a cupboard beneath the sink. That's through the kitchen — the second door on the left, remember — about twenty feet along."

"All right," he said, and I heard him feeling his way along the wall. The moments seemed interminable, and when I heard his voice again it was curiously muffled.

"Gifford! You did say it was the second door on the left, didn't you? Only I must have gone twenty feet already, and I haven't come across a door yet."

Something like fear touched me then. It was true that I had not lived long at the vicarage, but long enough, surely, to know where all the rooms were.

Then came the voice again, clearer this time, but fainter: "There seems to be a bend in the hallway here. I don't remember that."

Neither did I. I *knew* that the hall ran quite straight from the front to the back of the house, where it gave on to the back garden.

There was, I think, a note of hysteria in Faragher's voice as he continued: "I'll try down here — perhaps I'll find the door this way!"

A moment later the faint voice said, "There's no door here."

There was a dreadful long pause, and I heard my friend's voice for the last time, seeming to reach me from an infinite distance. The words were simple and, in the circumstances, terrifying: "Dear God!"

The sound seemed to ring, echoing, as though from an abyss. I heard it for long minutes after it had actually ceased.

Desperately, I stood upon the doorstep, not caring for the pain in my ankle, and fumbled hopelessly for the light-switch. I found it, pressed it — and the light came on, revealing the hallway as I had known it, running straight from the front to the back of the house.

"Faragher!" I cried, and again: "Faragher!"

Then the pain and the confusion overcame me. My ankle gave way, and I fell to the floor in a faint.

I awoke in the greyness of dawn, my body shivering with cold, and my head feeling as if it would burst. Desperately, hopelessly, I hobbled and crawled throughout the house, seeking for some trace of my friend, and finding none. The back door was locked, and had not been unlocked. The windows too were all closed against the chill night, and while I could not swear that he had not returned to the front door and stepped over my unconscious body, yet I knew that it was not so.

The answer was not outside the house, nor was it within. I lay for fully two hours upon the couch in my study, with both my head and my ankle throbbing, and at the end I could only think, as I had thought at the beginning, that the answer lay in that damnable wall-painting, with the false saint and his infernal companion. It was an answer, I thought, that they would keep to themselves for ever.

In that, I was mistaken.

With the aid of a strong stick, I staggered across to the church and let myself in, not knowing, but fearing, what I might find. In the chancel, the sheet of dark cloth still covered the painting, but before removing it I knelt at the altar and prayed for understanding of what I should do and for resolution to do it. Strengthened, but no less uneasy, I went to the north wall and firmly pulled down the cloth. The light was quite sufficient for me to see the painting clearly, and every detail of it is impressed upon my mind. For several minutes I gazed at it, a sickness growing within my spirit, and then I did what I knew I had to. Blessing the caution that had prevented my from letting the workmen see the picture, I raised my stick and hammered at the wall, blow upon blow, until every scrap of painted plaster was gone from it. Then I ground the lumps of plaster beneath my feet, so that soon there was nothing but dust upon the floor. It would not be hard to devise a story that would satisfy the builders. At last, sobbing and choking, I knelt before the altar again, and prayed for the soul of my friend.

The wall-painting upon that last day was just as we had first seen it, save for one small detail. The gaunt figure of Tosti still stood, clutching his whip and pointing derisively toward heaven. The shadowy form of his companion again lurked by his left foot, partly hidden by his robe. But now the features of the shadow could be distinguished: they were faint, but quite clear, and they were the features of Howard Faragher.

Harry Foster laid down the book and removed his glasses. "There's just one thing to add," he said. "Gifford says that when the photographs were developed he found that they showed only the figure of Tosti. There was no stain or shadow or any kind of a companion. He burned the prints and had the plates ground to powder."

Harry looked from one to the other of us with a sardonic smile, as if to say, "What do you make of that, my friends?"

Hesitantly, I said, "Have you made any enquiries about the story — in the parish records, for example? And what about this Tosti — ?"

Harry lit a cigar and drew upon it before answering. "I haven't been back to Welford St Paul," he said, "and I don't intend to do so. Perhaps because I'm afraid that the story is true, perhaps because I'm afraid that it is not. All I can tell you is this: a few weeks ago I acquired a copy of Crockford's clerical directory for the year 1910, and I found that one Stephen Gifford actually had been the vicar of Welford St Paul since February 1907." He shrugged his shoulders. "Let's leave it at that, shall we?"

I glanced at George Cobbett, whose eyes were fixed on the table in front of him. His brow was furrowed, and his lips pursed. I could see that he was thinking, as I was: "Shall we?"

Afterword

This tale was written for the Haunted Library special, *Saints and Relics*, where it was graced with a stunning illustration by Allen Koszowski. My knowledge of mediaeval English murals comes mostly from E. Clive Rouse's excellent little book *Discovering Wall Paintings* — a fact that David Rowlands recognised when he first read the story.

The village was originally called Wickham St Paul, but then I discovered that there really is a Wickham St Paul in north Essex and hastily invented a name.

Karl Wagner picked "The Wall-Painting" for *The Year's Best Horror Stories XII*, and Richard Dalby later included it in *The Mammoth Book of Ghost Stories*.

THE SEARCHLIGHT

John Chisholm looked at me for a moment and said, "You were born after the war, weren't you?"

"That's right," I said. "Nineteen forty-seven."

"Thought so. George, I think, was in the army, as was I. I can't say I enjoyed it, but for the first couple of years at least I had what they call a good war. I'd remember Shakespeare's words and think how ironic they were: "We are but warriors for the working day". Eventually I became a real warrior, but that's another story."

George Cobbett scowled impatiently and said, "Never mind that story. Let's stick to this one. It was something that happened to you in the early days, I understand?"

"Ah, yes." John waved away the stream of blue smoke that wafted from George's pipe, and cleared his throat. "It was in late 1940. I was newly promoted Captain and had just been appointed Adjutant to a military training establishment — never mind the details: they aren't relevant. My first task was to arrange the removal of the unit from just outside Watford to somewhere more isolated. The top brass had settled on a house in a village called Salting."

"I've never been there," I said, "but I've seen it on the map. It's out beyond Tollesbury."

"That's right. In absolute terms the place isn't very far from civilisation — twelve miles or so from Maldon, and a little further from Colchester — but in winter-time forty years ago it seemed like the edge of the world. Was it Edith Wharton who said that miles aren't the only distance? The village was tiny then — just a straggle of houses alongside a marshy creek — but we weren't to be actually in the village."

He broke off again to swat at the smoky air, and George took the opportunity to drain his mug and ask me to get another round in. When I'd seen to that, John resumed.

The house is called Salting Hall (he said). It's still standing, I believe, a couple of miles beyond the village, right out on the marshes. About three years before, some dispute had arisen over the ownership of the place. The last resident, a man named De Bourg, had died childless, and two branches of the family claimed his inheritance. The case just went on and on, with the litigants getting poorer and the lawyers getting richer. Meanwhile, the house stood empty, until the War Office stepped in. They requisitioned the estate — it could be done just like that in those days — and I was ordered to prepare it for my unit.

That was where difficulties arose. I was given just twenty-four hours' notice, and after innumerable phone calls — most of them to the wrong people — the sum of my knowledge was roughly this: that the house would be suitable for our requirements *if* it was still habitable. The legal dispute was so bitter that neither side would allow the other to install a caretaker. Nobody lived on the estate, which wasn't very large in any case, and as far as I could discover not a single person had set foot even in the grounds for nearly three years. Officially, that is. Who could tell what tramps, poachers or thieves might have done?

Well, I could only hope that the isolated situation had discouraged trespassers. A pretty feeble hope, eh? Meanwhile, I tried to arrange for some respectable body from the village to give the house a cursory inspection and perhaps a clean-up before I arrived. But that was out of the question, it seemed. The man I spoke to was most apologetic. He was the Parish Clerk and also, by good chance, the landlord of the village's only pub. That fact was about the best news I had all day. He cheerfully agreed to have some food and drink ready for my driver and me when we arrived in Salting.

I detailed my batman, Scott, to drive me, and the two of us pored over the Ordnance map until our heads throbbed. The signposts had all been taken down, remember, and we'd be travelling through the blackout, so it was essential that we should know the route thoroughly. The weather that day was pretty bad, and when we left Watford at about five o'clock the rain was pelting down. It was not a good journey.

Be grateful, boy, that you don't remember the blackout. It's bad enough today driving along narrow country roads on a cold, wet night, but then — ! Out beyond Maldon the roads were like a mud-bath. Our headlamps were reduced to the merest glimmer, and, as I say, there were no signposts. All the precautions seemed thoroughly sensible at the time, but that didn't stop one cursing them left, right and centre. If it hadn't been for Scott's good road-sense we might several times have found ourselves in a hedge or in a ditch. As it was, the journey from Watford took us something like four hours, and you can imagine that we were very glad when we finally reached Salting and pulled up outside the *Chequers*.

An hour later, a little relaxed and a good deal refreshed, we set out again. By now, the rain had stopped. The roads were still awash, but the sky was clear; the stars were bright and hard, and a gibbous moon was well above the horizon. In moonlight, then, we approached Salting Hall.

The narrow road curved round to the north, flanked on the left by a high brick wall. Then, suddenly, there were the gates. They were of iron, and very plain. The gateposts, about nine feet high, were topped with stone sphinxes, badly worn; the one on the left, beside the little bungalow that served as a lodge, had lost its head. The lodge was empty, of course, and boarded up. I opened the big padlock on the gates — there was no sign that it had been tampered with — and we entered the grounds of Salting Hall. Ahead of us, square and dignified, stood the house, white brick and stone clear in the moonlight. A handsome building of severe design, erected, I supposed, some time early in the eighteenth century. There were four pilasters rising to a central pediment, and two rows of tall sash windows, all shuttered on the inside. Those on the ground floor were boarded up, but the upper ones weren't, and as far as I could see all the glass was intact. It was a better start than I'd hoped for.

We had quite a lot of equipment with us: bedding, food and drink, a tool-kit, oil lamps and a cooker, petrol for the generator. We had hardly dared hope that the generator would be in working order, but now it seemed at least possible. These things had to be taken into the house, but our work would have to wait until daylight. We'd had a long journey, and we were both dog-tired.

The first thing we were aware of when we entered the house was the dust. It lay everywhere, like a thick grey carpet. I made a mental note that as soon as we'd uncovered the windows in the morning and got the generator going, our first task should be to get rid of the dust. As it was, every step we took caused little clouds to rise from the floor, swirling gently and taking an infinite time to settle again. After bringing our gear into the hall, we carried our personal effects up the big staircase and into the library. There were white dust-sheets on the chairs, of course, but apart from these and the ever-present dust itself, in the yellow gleam of our two oil lamps the room looked much as it must have done in old De Bourg's time. The walls were lined with bookshelves, except for the centre of the west wall where, above a handsome marble fireplace, hung a single life-size portrait — a man, in the dress of a Regency beau. I made up my mind to take a closer look at this gentleman before retiring to bed.

Scott found a dressing-room leading off — quite a large room — and I told him that he could bed down in there if he wished. For myself, I would stay in the library. While I checked the great wooden shutters on the windows, he went downstairs to fetch the rest of our kit. There'd be no roughing it here if Scott could help matters. He laid out my bedding on a couch between the two windows, then got my uniform ready for the morning, and finally produced a water-jug and a shaving mirror — one of those concave mirrors that magnify your face and let you see every little pore. These things he placed on top of a sideboard that stood over by the southern wall — the right-hand one as you looked away from the house. I knew that by the time I woke up Scott would have hot water ready for me to wash and shave.

The time was — what? — getting on for half past ten. Back in Watford the evening in the mess would be coming to a close; here, on the edge of nowhere, such things seemed a world away. Dowsing the lamps, we unfastened and opened a couple of the shutters, and stood for many minutes at the window, gazing eastward, across the overgrown estate and the marshes beyond. In the moonlight, the effect was tantalising, almost like a filigree pattern, with serpentine streaks of silver water and irregular patches of black earth. I had never, I think, felt so cut off, and I was about to make some remark when suddenly, over to the north-east, a thin column of light shot up into the sky, and another, and another, and they began to sweep majestically across the blackness. They were the searchlights of an anti-aircraft battery near Mersea Island. A moment later I heard the faint droning sound of their prey. Strictly against all training, the two of us stood watching, enthralled. We had no fear for ourselves.

We heard quite clearly the thudding sound of the ack-ack guns, momentarily drowning the noise of the aircraft, and saw, infinitely high up, the tiny explosions of light that were the deadly shells. The whole thing lasted less than a minute. The droning of the engines faded into silence, and then at last, one by one, the searchlights were extinguished. By now, other probes, near Chelmsford, perhaps, or Colchester, would be searching the sky. Isolated we might be, but the war was no less real here than it was in London. While Scott re-lit the lamps, I closed the wooden shutters over the windows.

"That'll do," I said. "It's time we both got to bed. Mrs Parmenter from the village should be here before eight in the morning, and there are all sorts of things to be seen to before she arrives."

"Like the generator," said Scott. "Very well, sir. If you don't mind, I'll take a book with me. I like to read a little before I sleep, and I don't somehow get the chance in the dormitory. Now, your washing things are all ready, and there's water in the jug — I can heat it up if you like. No? Well, there's a lavatory, should you need it, two doors along by the top of the stair, though I shan't be able to get the water running until the morning. Goodnight, sir."

He picked a book from the shelves — a work on natural history, I think — and, wishing me goodnight again, disappeared into his makeshift bedroom. The dust stirred sullenly as he opened and closed the door, and then settled again. If Mrs Parmenter does nothing else tomorrow, I thought, she must at least clear out this infernal dust.

Now that it was time to sleep, I felt quite unreasonably wakeful. I glanced with no real purpose along the bookshelves, not particularly attracted by any of the titles, and finally picked up a volume from a desk or table that stood in the shadows in a corner of the big room. It was leather-bound, evidently privately printed: a history of Salting Hall, written by one Christopher Holroyd, librarian to Valentine De Bourg esquire. The date was 1897. Having chosen my book, I thought again of the single, rather striking portrait that hung over the fireplace. I took a lamp and went to examine the picture more closely.

It certainly was rather impressive. The man, about thirty-five years of age, was not particularly tall, but he carried himself well and was good-looking in a dark, rather gipsyish fashion. There was something very attractive about his face, which held the same sort of confident half-smile that the so-called Laughing Cavalier has. He could be a jolly drinking companion, I thought, and perhaps a good man to have at one's side in a fight. Or perhaps not, for there was a lurking devil in his eyes, and their humour was not wholly cheerful. If he was a sheep of any colour, then that colour was probably black. For the rest, he was dressed in plain but expensive clothes — plain for his period, I mean. He wore a royal blue coat and stockings, with a white waistcoat and stock, and buff pantaloons. The expression on the handsome face belied any suggestion of sedateness given by the clothes.

On the frame below the picture was a small brass plate, on which were the words: "Adrian Lee, Esq., by F G Gainsford," and the date 1810. I was not sorry to have Adrian Lee's likeness in my bedroom, but it occurred to me that I was probably better off not sharing quarters with the man himself.

After I'd washed and brushed my teeth, I got into my sleeping-bag and opened Christopher Holroyd's book. I had set one of the lamps on a small table beside the couch where I was to sleep, together with a box of matches in case of emergency during the night.

The book had no index — I'd hardly expected one — but I was pleased to find that the chapters were headed with the dates that they covered. I turned to the chapter dealing with the years around 1810 and searched for references to the subject of the portrait.

Adrian Lee was the stepson of Mr Charles Everard De Bourg, who had married Lee's widowed mother in the year 1792, when the lad was sixteen years old. My estimate of his age, you see, was not far wrong. At the time his picture was painted, he would have been thirty-three or thirty-four. Mrs De Bourg survived only three years of marriage, dying shortly after she had produced a much-desired heir for her husband, but her darkly handsome son had endeared himself to his stepfather, and he continued to live at the Hall.

There was no mystery about Adrian's own father, who was an impoverished Suffolk gentleman with more romantic imagination than pecuniary sense. He claimed, though with what justification he never said, that his family had originally "come over from Egypt with the Romanies". It's true that Lee is a common Gipsy name, though, and Adrian's looks suggested that the tale might be true.

What else did I note before I finally fell asleep? When Charles De Bourg died in 1806, Adrian, who had got himself sent down from Cambridge a few years earlier, acted as guardian to his step-brother Howard. He seems to have performed his duties tolerably well, and perhaps they weren't entirely uncongenial. It's apparent that the man and the boy were genuinely fond of each other. In 1810, however, Adrian Lee bought himself a commission in Wellesley's army. The picture may have been painted for the occasion, though if that were so I'd have expected it to show him in uniform rather than civilian dress.

After that, references were scarce. They concluded with the stark report that in July 1812, shortly after the battle of Salamanca, Captain Adrian Lee of the 44th Regiment of Foot was ignominiously stripped of his rank and executed by firing squad. He died instantly.

So that was the end of it all.

At that appropriate point I laid down the book, extinguished the lamp, and tried to compose myself for sleep.

You know what it's like when you want to sleep, and you need to sleep, but for some reason you just can't sleep. In my case, I think it was just the strangeness of my surroundings; it always takes me two or three nights to get used to a new bed. Well, I lay there, dead tired but sleepless, for what may have been five minutes or an hour before I finally dropped off, and my mind seized on trivial little things and pondered them, as it does in such circumstances. What I noticed most, and with surprise, was a silvery grey disc of light on the dusty floor. It took a little while to realise that it must be moonlight, shining through a hole of some sort in the wooden shutters. I lifted my head — by now it took some concentration just to do that — and found that, as I'd surmised, there was quite a large knot-hole in the left-hand window shutter, the northern one. Just so, I thought; I'll see about getting that plugged tomorrow. And with that, I fell asleep.

It was the distant thudding of the anti-aircraft guns that woke me up, and once awake I could only lie listening to the guns and the far-off drone of the German bombers. So it was for a perhaps a minute, and then something quite extraordinary happened.

I realised afterwards that one of the searchlights must have swung out of control, just for a moment. Yes, it can only have been that, I think, because quite suddenly the picture of Adrian Lee was held in a disc of intensely bright light. It lasted for less than a second, but it was as if the man himself stood there, and the image remained in my eyes for some minutes.

No, the *two* images — for there were two, though I wasn't immediately conscious of the fact. You see, I'd been looking directly at the figure on the wall, and it was only afterwards that I was aware that there had been a second figure on the edge of my vision. I had seen it, though, just for a second, and it was stretched out upon the floor.

I can only surmise, of course — real explanation seems impossible — but I think that what happened was this: the most unlikely circumstances had combined briefly to produce the effect of an epidiascope. You remember those devices that used to be used in schools and colleges to project a picture on to a screen? We actually had one as part of the standard equipment at the training unit, though I'd never had to make use of it myself. Well, all the components, you see, were there in that room: the intensely powerful, concentrated beam of light, the picture itself, and the lens. Yes, that's right — my concave shaving mirror. And for the fraction of a second all were aligned correctly to project the image of Adrian Lee's portrait on to the horizontal screen that was the dust-covered floor of the library.

No, I don't know whether that notion would stand up scientifically, but it's the best that I can think of. In any case, I suspect that there was more to it than mere physics, in view of what followed.

I was left in darkness, so complete by contrast with the sudden brightness, that all I could see was the remembered image of that sardonic figure on the wall, and the other image, half-seen, of the same figure lying on the floor. In my bedazzled state, I may have dozed. It certainly seemed like it at the time, because the strange and disturbing notion came to me that the figure on the floor was moving, trying to stand up.

It can only have been minutes later, I think, that I suddenly found myself fully awake and wondering what could have disturbed me. It wasn't the guns this time, or the sound of aeroplanes. Gradually it came to me that there was movement actually within the room, though the sound was so quiet, so subtle, that I wasn't at all sure I'd really heard it. I had the unmistakable and unbearable impression that I was not alone in the library.

The intruder could not have been Scott, I was sure, for I should have heard the door of the ante-room opening — and even on that thick carpet of dust Scott could never have trodden so softly. With considerable misgivings, I reached my hand out for the matches on the little table and struck one.

What I noticed first of all was so thoroughly unlikely that I thought for a moment I must still be dreaming; but no, it was real enough. In itself it was simple, but it was sufficient to make me feel very uneasy indeed.

The room was no longer dusty.

The dust-sheets were still in place, but the dust itself was gone.

As I realised that even that was not quite true, the match burned down to my fingers, and with an oath I shook it out. Fumbling in my haste, I struck another and lit the lamp with it.

Incredulity and — yes — fear mingled as I gazed at the figure on the floor. It was grey, like a stone statue, but oddly stretched and slightly blurred. With increasing confidence and strength, it was pulling itself to its feet. I cast a hasty glance at the portrait on the wall, though I was already sure of the creature's identity. The features and the figure were the same — the clothes too, though as I say the apparition had no colour to it, and its shape was somehow distorted. I felt a funny sort of relief when I recognised the reason. It was so simple and obvious: the image had been projected on to the floor at an angle, you see. Naturally the figure was mis-shapen, but it was Adrian Lee — there could be no doubt of that — and strongly, awkwardly, he was coming towards me.

How do you read the expression in the blank eyes of a statue? No, I could only feel sure that this — this *thing* — had no good purpose, that it was enemy, not friend. On the grounds that attack is the best defence, I rolled from the couch, cursing my clumsiness in extricating myself from the sleeping-bag, and warily aimed a punch at the thing.

My fist sank into something soft, dry and powdery. It was like hitting a pile of dust.

Of course — that's what it was! That's where the dust had gone! I was so relieved that I started to laugh. Why, this creature could be no match for a solidly built soldier, I thought. But it kept coming, and I began to feel uneasy again. Another punch, and still it came, trying to press its dead self against me. I suddenly felt sick as I realised the purpose behind the expressionless face. Fool! Of course it couldn't hurt me, not with its hands or its feet — But the dust! If it pressed itself against my face I was done for. That was where the danger lay. At all costs I must prevent it from *choking* me to death.

I back away, trying now to keep out of its reach, not knowing where I was going. What happened at the last was inevitable: I found myself firmly wedged between a book-case and a large desk or bureau. I was trapped. There was no escape. I lashed out desperately. My hands and feet connected with that dry, soft body, sinking into it. Ugh! But try as I might, I couldn't part it. The will that held it together was too strong. It yielded but would not break. This was the end, I thought.

Then I heard Scott's voice, never more welcome. Half-blinded, I couldn't see him, and the sound was muffled, but I did hear it: "Excuse me, sir, but I thought — Good God!"

I imagined him standing, baffled and irresolute, and I opened my mouth to call out — but it was instantly filled with dust. I had to put both hands to my face, plucking the deadly stuff out, spitting and coughing, trying not to choke. I was weeping tears of frustration. The windows! If only Scott would open the windows — but I couldn't speak, couldn't tell him.

I was on the very edge of consciousness, and not sure that I really heard the snap of the bolts, the slight creak and the bang as the shutters were pulled back, the crack of the fastening and the slow, muscular strain of the sash being heaved up. The first clear sensation was the vital coldness as I was hit by a blast of wind from outside. Scott had done it. This really was the end — not for me, but for the living dust.

That wind was life itself to me, and a second death to Adrian Lee. Immediately, the dust began to disperse, blowing reluctantly and swirling about the room, as the spirit that animated it lost control. I think that at the last I heard a thick, inarticulate cry from the creature, but it may have been only the wind.

Scott had all sorts of questions, of course, but for the present I was too shaken to say anything. In silence, I gathered my bedding and my clothes and carried them into the dressing-room, where I would spend what remained of the night. We closed the windows and shuttered them, and took our lamps with us into the other room. The last thing I did before leaving the library was to take the portrait down from its place above the mantel and prop it against the wall, facing inwards. Adrian Lee, I think, had taken his last gamble, and lost.

I've not much more to tell. Shortly afterwards, such are the ways of the Army, I found myself posted to the Pacific, and from then on the war itself occupied most of my thoughts. It wasn't until the early fifties that I made up my mind to pursue the subject of Adrian Lee, and after a couple of abortive attempts to get information through the public library, I took the obvious step of writing to the new owner of Salting Hall. The law-suit by then had been settled, to someone's satisfaction at least, and a young cousin of old De Bourg was now in residence at the Hall. He wrote me a very civil letter, and enclosed as a gift this little book, published in 1847: *Recollections of a Long Life* by the Very Revd Thomas Woodhall, Dean and Rector of Catton. For six years, until 1813, Woodhall was Perpetual Curate at Salting, and he knew both Howard De Bourg and Adrian Lee pretty well.

He calls Lee a "free-thinker" — very much a term of disapproval — but whether he means that the man was an atheist or a deist or something else is not clear. I'm inclined to think myself that "something else" is nearest the mark. Fortunately, the old Dean seems to have had very good recall, and he quotes several conversations that he had with the young squire's stepbrother. Here are a couple of passages that I think may be relevant:

> It was in this year also that young Mr De Bourg expressed a wish to have his brother's portrait done. The painter chosen to undertake this commission, a Mr Gainsford, was at that time little known: indeed, this may have been his first important work. Some few years later, as the reader may be aware, he became associated with the group whose *animi* were the notorious Lord Byron and Mr Shelley. I believe that his Lordship's friend and physician, one John Polidori, sat for him not long before his, the Doctor's, early death.
>
> The picture of Adrian Lee was kept concealed by the artist until such time as he considered it complete. When that time came, Mr De Bourg gathered a small group of friends to see the likeness unveiled, myself among them. I am constrained to say that the portrait as I first saw it was a most striking work of art. The resemblance to its original was quite remarkable: so much so that I was obliged to cast my eyes several times from the one to the other. At length I realised that the subject of the picture was himself quite as fascinated as I. *Omnia vanitas*, says the Apostle, and yet it seemed to me that there was rather more of awe than of vanity in Mr Lee's steadfast gaze. Becoming aware that he was observed, he came to me and posed the following question: "Are you aware, Sir, that there is among primitive peoples a superstition which claims that a man's likeness inevitably captures within it something of its subject's soul?" Not waiting upon my reply he continued: "By G—, Sir! I would

almost take my oath that Mr Gainsford has imprisoned a part of me within this canvas. Remarkable, is it not? Ay, truly remarkable!"

The other passage actually comes a little earlier in the book, but I've left it till last for reasons which I needn't explain. It's a conversation between the parson and the free-thinker:

"Sir," said he, "in your Christian burial service there is a sentiment expressed that has long held a peculiar interest for me. Namely, *Earth to earth, ashes to ashes, dust to dust.*"
"In what, then, consists your interest?" I inquired.
"Why, Sir, may not this very earth, these ashes, this dust, be themselves inspired with life?"
"Surely they shall," I replied: "by the will of God and in God's good time. There follow, you must recall, the words: *In sure and certain hope of the Resurrection to Eternal Life.*"
"Sure indeed, and certain," said he; but my pleasure at such a sentiment was dashed by his *addendum*: "Yet why should not such transpire by the will of Man and in Man's good time? I tell you, Sir, I am certain in my mind that Man will come at last to rival your God. Man will cry, Let there be light, and there shall be light. I do not speak of your penny candles and your tallow lamps, but of a light to equal the sun itself. Man in time will make matter and even life. But these things are beyond your imagining, I see, and perhaps beyond my own. I do assure you, though, that at last Man's will shall be strong, even as my will is strong, and he will not be content to die. Mark me! for we commit ourselves to Death only through the weakness of our will. There shall be those whom Death cannot hold, even as he could not hold your Jesus. Mark me!"

John paused, frowning, and absently picked up his glass. When he had drunk off what was left in it, he smiled wryly and said, "It is relevant, I think — eh?"

George glanced sharply at him, but only nodded his head and said nothing.

In my own mind there was a question: "Why did the ghost — let's call it that — why did it attack you? You were a harmless stranger, so why such animosity?"

The answer came with an impatient snort from George: "Plain enough, I'd have thought. The dust was no more than a temporary housing for an ambitious and desperate spirit. Adrian Lee needed something more stable to live in."

"Good Lord! John — ?"

John Chisholm sighed. "I think that's right," he said, "though it's not a thought I care to dwell on. And first, of course, he had to get rid of me." He picked up our empty glasses, but before taking them across to the bar he added, "It was his last gamble, as I said. Thank God he lost."

Afterword

"The Searchlight" was an attempt to do with another substance what M R James had achieved with crumpled linen. The idea was suggested by a story called "Dust" by one Max Chartair — actually a pseudonym for John S Glasby, whose weird tales should be much more widely known and appreciated.

Margery Allingham set her last novel, *Cargo of Eagles*, in a fictional village called Saltey, a fact that I had forgotten when I wrote this story. I was surprised a few years ago to learn from her sister, Joyce Allingham, that Saltey combines elements of Tollesbury and Salcott-cum-Virley — pretty much where I'd sited Salting.

Adrian and Lee are both family names on my mother's side. It was her uncle, Frank Lee, who claimed that his family had "come from Egypt with the Romanies", which is too good a line not to use. I'm grateful to J J C Monk for suggesting the concave shaving mirror, and for letting me name my central character after him.

THE TAKING

Robert Lovewell looked at each of us in turn over his glass of John Jameson. He glanced thoughtfully for a moment at the whiskey itself, and then asked diffidently, "Did you ever see Carl Dreyer's film *Vampyr*?"

George Cobbett drew his heavy grey eyebrows down in a momentary scowl, but merely said, "No."

"I've seen it," I said. "It was at the Scala in Charlotte Street, on a double bill with the silent *Nosferatu*. The print was pretty bad, but for all that it was a wonderfully strange and powerful movie. Why do you ask?"

"Well, because I'd like you to consider a remark that Dreyer made about the film. 'Imagine,' he said, 'that we are sitting in an ordinary room. Suddenly we are told that there is a corpse behind the door. In an instant, the room we are sitting in is completely altered: everything in it has taken on another look: the light, the atmosphere have changed, and the objects are as we conceive them.'"

"*As we conceive them*," George repeated. "Well, that's an interesting way of putting it. But look here, young Lovewell. I thought you were an artist, not an expert on the European cinema."

Robert took a sip of his whiskey. "I'm a professional painter," he said, "as you well know. Whether I'm as much of an artist as Dreyer is another matter, but my line of work does have some bearing on the story, as otherwise I shouldn't have gone to stay at Abbotts." He glared briefly at the old man. "Don't side-track me again, George, or you shan't hear the story at all. Ha! Very well...

―――

Abbotts Farm (he continued) was a smallish concern that had been bought up by a neighbouring farmer in the early fifties. Most of the farmyard buildings were pulled down, and the new owner was wondering what to do with the old house when Jack Iszatt, the R.A., happened to spot it and made him an offer. As a result, Iszatt found himself the owner of a country retreat at a price that would seem ludicrously small today.

Iszatt is a good fellow, and not one to keep his fortune to himself. I suppose that by now nearly all his friends have been offered the use of the house for a couple of months or so. My turn came about six months ago, in early September, and I accepted it most gratefully. I was going through a bad period creatively — it was something like writer's block — and a change of situation seemed the best possible solution. North-west Essex in the late summer — it sounded perfect.

Abbotts stands outside a village or hamlet called Winstock. You'd need a pretty large-scale map to find it, but it's just off the road between Thaxted and Little Sampford. On the corner is the local pub, the *Whalebone*; then there are a couple of cottages and an evangelical chapel, and then no buildings at all for half a mile or so — just a high hedge on both sides of the road. At last the road takes a turn to the north, and just around the corner, on the left, is the house.

It's an attractive building without being particularly distinguished. You can see similar houses all over the eastern counties. The shape is that of a flattened letter H, with the crosspiece as the main part. I could bore you with a lot of technical terms, but I'd rather not; you'll have the essentials in your minds. The roof is tiled, though it may have been thatched at one time, and the walls are of lath and plaster over a strong timber frame. I was pleased to see that successive owners had resisted the urge to strip off the plaster and expose the beams. It's a practice that our ancestors would have thought about as logical as stripping away your own flesh to expose the bone.

I was able to draw the car up to the front door — which is over to the right in the central block, facing east — and while I carried my bags inside I found myself trying to estimate the age of the building. It appeared to have been constructed from the first with two storeys, which suggested a date no earlier than the fifteenth century. There might be another clue in the name. Had the place been built or owned at some time by a man named Abbott, or had it perhaps belonged originally to a monastery? It might be instructive, I thought, to have a look at the parish records.

Upon entering, I found myself in a fairly narrow hallway, with the main staircase at the far end. On the right, as I knew, were the kitchen and pantry, while to the left were the sitting-room, dining-room and study. Behind the house was a small plot of land, where Iszatt had converted one of the original farm buildings into a rather nice studio, small but light and airy.

The sitting-room somehow managed to be both spacious and cosy. No doubt it had been larger originally, taking in the hallway, with the front door opening directly into it. As it was, it stretched from the front to the back of the house. In each outer wall were two windows, which had probably been enlarged two or three hundred years ago. Between each pair of windows was a tall bookcase, one containing a nice selection on the pictorial arts and the other a surprising little library of rather tempting antiquarian books. Facing you as you entered the room was the big fireplace — early Victorian, I think — with the door to the dining-room on its left. Over the mantel, Iszatt had hung one of his father's paintings, a very fine watercolour of the abbey ruins at Bury St Edmund's — you know, the west front of the church, with the houses built into it — and elsewhere in the room were other pictures. I remember a rare couple of Lafcadio's early figure studies, and a good Welsh landscape by Boddington.

A rich green carpet covered the middle of the floor. Remember that carpet, by the way. It's important. And there's another feature of the room that's relevant: all the illumination came from wall lamps. Iszatt had told me that he disliked overhead lighting, so I wasn't surprised to see a cluster of lamps on either side of the fireplace and another on each side of the door opposite, the one into the hall.

I settled for a lazy evening on that first day, leaving work until the following morning. I didn't even bother to check out the studio right away. Instead, I got my things stowed away in one of the guest bedrooms and then went to see that the kitchen was properly stocked up. Having satisfied myself on that point, I thought it would be a nice idea to make myself known at the local pub, and as the time was now coming up to eight o'clock I took a walk down to the *Whalebone*. There I had a sandwich and a couple of drinks, a chat with the barmaid and a game of darts. Then I walked back to Abbotts.

I suppose it was getting on for eleven when I arrived back, but I wasn't feeling particularly tired, just comfortably lazy, so I helped myself to a glass of whiskey from the sideboard, put a record on the gramophone, and settled in an armchair with an early volume of *Punch*. Nothing deep, you see. I didn't want to bother with anything taxing. The music was Vaughan Williams' *Job* — the Adrian Boult recording — which suited both the place and my mood deliciously. In any case, it's a work that I'm particularly fond of, one that perfectly bears out Sidney Smith's dictum that music is the only cheap and unpunished rapture upon earth. I actually played the whole thing through twice, though I did refrain from refilling my glass, but at last it seemed that it really was time I turned in. I switched off the record-player, put the book back of the shelf, and went over to the door. Before turning out the lights, I just stood for a moment or two, looking at the room, drinking it in, as it were. Perhaps you've done the same thing. Then I opened the door, flicked the light-switches off, and turned to go out.

I must be rather precise about this, because it's quite important, as you'll see. Now, there were two switches by each door, so that you could turn off both sets of lights whichever way you left the room. Being unfamiliar with the switches, I had inadvertently turned off the nearer lights first, so that for an instant all the illumination was directed towards me, throwing shadows in my direction. The next moment the room was in darkness, and I was half-way out into the hall.

Only then did I realise that I had seen something on the floor, something rather curious. You know how you sometimes see a thing but don't immediately register the fact? Well, I went straight back into the room and pressed those switches again until the lights were on as before, on the far side of the room only. Then I crawled on my hands and knees the length and breadth of that nice green carpet, but there was nothing. Not a single blessed thing out of the way at all. At last, thinking that my imagination must be stronger than I'd given it credit for, I left the room again.

What had I seen? Well, you'll remember that just for a brief moment all the illumination, shadows and all, was directed towards me. On the carpet I had clearly seen the impressions of a dozen or more pairs of feet, large and small, all sharply defined, as if they'd been made in damp sand. Now, I said that the carpet was important, didn't I? You see, it was made of pure wool, and wool has one very interesting property that the man-made fibres don't have: it doesn't retain impressions. After the pressure is lifted, the pile springs right back into place. Odd, eh? Besides, you know, if they were just footprints left in the ordinary way there ought to have been many more than just the dozen or so that I'd seen. It occurred to me that perhaps I'd been visited by a party of invisible people; and with that rather bizarre thought I gave the whole thing up as a mystery and went to bed.

I fell asleep pretty quickly, and at once found myself dreaming. Now, this dream is really the greater part of my story, so again I'll have to be rather specific. The effect was not one I'd experienced before — and nor have I since, though I understand that it's not actually unknown. I was myself, Robert Lovewell, and perfectly aware of it, but I wasn't in my own body. It wasn't a wish-fulfilment fantasy, and I didn't suddenly find myself a Hercules or Adonis. I mean exactly what I say: the body belonged to someone else, and that someone was there as well.

Whoever my — er — host was, he was unaware of me. That much was plain; but he was in full control of our shared flesh. I could neither influence nor anticipate; I could only observe. With his eyes and ears and nerves, I could see, hear and feel — but that's all.

No, not quite all, because I could smell things too, and it was this that suggested that I might be in a real situation, rather than your usual surrealist dreamland. The odour that reached me was mostly a mixture of dust, sweat and dung. That last was rather faint, but it struggled bravely against the scent of flowers that someone had thoughtfully provided to cover it all. The sense of smell was the first to clarify, so to speak, forcing upon my mind that it had encountered something physical. Admitting this, I had to admit the evidence of the other senses. It came to me that I could distinctly feel the rather coarse stuff of the leggings that my man was wearing, with a much finer shirt, and what I took to be soft leather boots. The temperature, for what it's worth, was comfortably mild, like a good day in late spring.

For a little while my sight was fixed upon the floor immediately in front of me. It was made of wooden boards, partly covered with, I think, dried rushes — quite clean, it was — and just at the edge of my vision there was someone standing. I could make out a long robe or gown that just avoided brushing the floor. A woman, probably. For a second my gaze flicked towards this figure, and then back again immediately. And I distinctly felt a frown on my forehead.

You've probably seen films that are shot in the first person, so to speak. Mamoulian used the technique for the opening sequence of *Dr Jekyll and Mr Hyde*, where everything is seen through Jekyll's eyes. But it's a very strange sensation indeed to feel another person's frown.

While my eyes were set on the floor before me, my mind turned to what I could hear. It was Babel. From a little way off came the squawking, clucking and grunting sounds of a well-stocked farmyard, and above this, within the room, a dozen voices were talking, subdued but desperate, and in a tongue that meant nothing to me. From the vowel sounds and the occasional guttural, I thought it might be Dutch or possibly Scandinavian, but even as my sight was raised at last to the figure in front of me I could not be sure.

Slowly, even with reluctance, my host's gaze took in the long dark grey gown, moving upwards to rest for a moment on the hands. They were beautiful hands, slender and elegant, meekly folded, the right over the left, but tense with a disconcerting nervousness. The skin was of that exquisite glowing pink that sometimes goes with real pure blonde hair. When you've spent much of your life studying the human body from an æsthetic viewpoint, you come to realise that each part can have its own special beauty. I tell you. Those hands were remarkably beautiful. They made me very curious to see the face of the woman who owned them.

I became aware of other people in the room. With something of a shock, I realised that there were two large men standing firmly, one on either side of the young woman. Oh, I was convinced by now that she was young, and as beautiful *in toto* as her hands.

For some reason, my host seemed reluctant to look her in the face. He turned his gaze away abruptly to the left, to where a little knot of people stood nervously chattering by an open door, casting occasional glances in my direction. Now that I could see them, and how they were dressed, a part of the puzzle fell into place, and it seemed the most natural thing in the world that I should find myself among country folk in the late sixteenth century. And the room — yes, that looked familiar now, as it should, for I'd spent much of the previous evening in it. There was no separate hallway then, of course, and the sturdy front door led directly into the room. The furniture, what I could see of it, was quite different, being much more chunky and solid, but with that curious dignity that perfect rightness has. The walls were covered with linenfold panelling to a height of about five feet, with plain lime-washed plaster above. All this I had to notice when I could, being wholly at the mercy of my unwitting host, but there could be no doubt about it: I was in the main room of Abbotts farmhouse.

That would explain the apparently foreign language. My guess at a Nordic tongue hadn't been a bad one. As you know, Elizabethan English really did sound rather like that, and in such a remote place there would be the local accent to confuse things further. Even now it's very strong in some areas, despite creeping uniformity, but can you imagine how it was four hundred years ago? Realising this, I discovered that I could actually distinguish an occasional phrase from the confused babble that came to my ears.

At this point, my host turned his gaze away from that of an elderly, strong-faced woman who was standing near the door, a little apart from the group. He had at last resolved to look fully upon the young woman who was the centre of the drama.

Yes, she was young — no more than twenty-five — and she was beautiful, but with something more than a superficial classical beauty. Above the plain grey gown and white lace collar, she wore a close-fitting cap of grey velvet that framed her face. It hid most of her hair, but a stray lock on her left cheek was of the perfect light gold that I had expected. The mouth was neither large nor small, but well-shaped, and the eyes, though not exceptionally large, were of a very clear and candid grey. It was a finely proportioned face, but what made it beautiful was the very evident spirit within. I never saw the girl smile, but her smile, I think, would have been ravishing.

Her grey eyes returned my stare, and noticeably hardened, though she said nothing. Her mouth was calm and apparently without expression. That she was contemptuous of this man I could not doubt, even though fear might be mingled with the scorn. But what were his own feelings? I thought I could sense in him a strong nervous tension, and something that was only too plain to read as lust.

The two men standing beside her were massive brutes, roughly dressed, who might perhaps have been labourers on this very farm. In their bovine faces I could see only a rather frightening blankness. They stood so close to her, as if guarding her, that they put me in mind of policemen effecting an arrest. And plainly the situation was something very like that.

As this fact forced itself upon me, I found that I could distinguish more and more of what the people around me were saying, though there was one word, muttered or whispered, that somehow eluded me. Then this puzzle too was solved, by a voice behind me, masculine and assured, which cut through the chatter and silenced it. Some official paper was read or quoted, and with this at last the whole tragedy became clear. The word that seemed to form most of the conversation in the room, the word that I'd not been able to make out, was "*witch*".

The tension in my body was painful, seeming about to erupt, as if the man had been waiting for this. He looked sharply at the girl, but her grey eyes were like slivers of ice in the warmth of her pink skin, and he turned his gaze away to where the older woman stood, rather aloof from the crowd. He looked long at that still-handsome face, and the tension gradually came under control.

This woman, now — I called her elderly, but the word isn't quite right. People did grow old before their time in those days, of course, but for all her fifty or so years she was not old, but rather in vigorous middle age. She looked as if she could live to be a hundred, by the strength of her will. Her eyes gazed very steadily into mine — his — and I fancy that there was something like suppressed amusement there. Only once did she glance towards the younger woman, and even then not a flicker of expression crossed her handsome features. I think the man took strength from her. At last he looked back at the girl, meeting her own cold stare with growing confidence.

The voice behind me finished speaking, and the silence that followed was like something tangible. The girl's elegant hands were clasped now, so tightly that the knuckles appeared a vivid white. It was the only sign of fear that she showed, and her voice was quite calm as she spoke. The accent was still strange to me, but that voice was pure and clear. She said, "Before God and His angels, I do swear my innocence."

She was allowed no more. With a terrifying suddenness the man's hand — *my* hand, God help me! — had drawn from its sheath a long-bladed knife, and he had leapt at her, bellowing like an animal. The abrupt release of rage appalled me. In my own mind I was cursing with frustration that I couldn't stop him. I could only watch, through his own damned eyes, as the knife swept across her face — as she started back, but was firmly held by the two uncomprehending oafs beside her — as she threw up her right hand to save her eyes — and as the sharp blade sheared cleanly through flesh and bone, severing the slender forefinger.

Strong hands grasped my arms, pulling me back, that fearful rage still burning throughout my body — and I awoke. Awoke, with the girl's scream of bewildered pain sounding about me, and her horrified eyes clear— in my sight, starting with appalled accusation directly at me.

I felt foul. My vision was blurred, my head had a dull ache, and I was thinking quite lunatic thoughts. Fortunately sleep came over me again, and the next I knew was that I was fully awake in broad daylight. I began to think again, but coherently this time.

What should I make of it all? The few dreams I'd had before that I could recall in any detail had been thoroughly inconsequential — "as beautiful as the meeting of an umbrella and a sewing-machine upon an operating-table", which after all is the essence of surrealism. But there was nothing surreal about this. It was solid and logical. I couldn't doubt that I had been party to some real event.

Well, I decided to spend a while in the studio, where I could occupy my hands and make up my mind on what course to take. Having reached that small decision, I washed, dressed and went downstairs.

In the sitting-room I found something that set my mind racing again. It was small enough in itself, but — the significance of it! In the middle of that rich green carpet it lay, just where the girl had stood in my dream, and where I couldn't possibly have missed it the night before.

You've guessed, of course. It was a severed finger. There was nothing of beauty left in it. It was quite clean, but withered and almost fleshless, though the nail was intact, and I could clearly see how the blade had cut through the bone. It looked — as it was, I suppose — some hundreds of years old.

I examined it carefully, even minutely, and then wrapped it in cotton-wool and locked it in a little box in the cabinet beside my bed. Then I took paper and chalks over to the studio, where I spent most of the day. It was already plain that I'd have to make some research into the history of the house, but what was I to do with the — the object found? That was the question that kept nagging at me, and by the evening I was no nearer an answer, though I had got down on paper quite a good likeness of the two women in my dream, so the day hadn't been wholly wasted.

I dined on something from a tin, and then went off to the *Whalebone*, as before, where I struck up a conversation with the landlord. He was an affable fellow enough, but unfortunately a foreigner — which is to say that he'd come from Cambridge and hadn't lived in Winstock above twenty years. Neither he nor the two old boys from the local farms, who spent the evening hunched over a game of crib, could tell me anything of the village during the period that I was interested in. One of them suggested that I ask the vicar, but the landlord scorned the idea, pointing out that Winstock church no longer had its own incumbent. The vicar of Great Sampford would drive over every third Sunday to conduct a single service, and as he'd only been resident for a few months it was unlikely that he could help me.

At last the landlord made the suggestion that should have occurred to me: that I should come into Chelmsford and consult the archives at the County Record Office.

Do I need to tell you that I dreamed again that night? But the dream was not the same. The hint, if that's the right word, had been taken, and I need not take part in the drama again. What I saw that night — what I remember, at least, was the young woman herself, alone and standing by my bedside in the moonlight.

Her face was calm. and there was none of the pain in her eyes that I had seen there before. I was grateful for that, for though I'd had no deliberate part in the events of her taking I hadn't been able to forget the bewildered accusation in those grey eyes. She stood quite still, until I had stopped gawping like an imbecile, and then she simply held out her hands to me, so that I could see clearly how sadly mutilated the right one was. The forefinger had been cleanly severed, and there were sharp cuts, dark with blood, across the lower joints of the middle and ring fingers .

Anger rose in me, perhaps at the marring of such beauty, and I came abruptly to a decision. The thing was obvious, after all. "Yes," I said. Just that. And although she made no reply I knew that I'd done right. She closed her eyes for a moment and expelled a gentle sigh. When she looked at me again, I could see relief in every feature. Then she was gone, and the morning was upon me. Perhaps it wasn't a dream this time. I'd like to believe that, but who can tell?

It took the best part of an hour for the people at the Record Office to find what I wanted, but they know their job, and in the end I had the whole sad tale. The information wasn't, as I'd expected, in the Winstock parish records, but in a copy of a report from the archives at Lambeth Palace. It was an account of the arrest, trial and execution for witchcraft of one Mistress Jennet or Janet Fisher, of Winstock in the County of Essex, in the year of Grace 1585, before Lord Brian D'Arcy.

Janet Fisher was the young widow of a farmer, whose house and land were "late the property of the Prior of Tilty in the same

County". He inherited the place from his father, who had bought it at the Dissolution, but he, the son, survived only a few years, being killed in a riding accident at the age of twenty-seven. Having no other immediate family, he had willed the property to his wife. And this bequest, it seems, was the basis for the whole drama. It would have been unusual anyway for a woman to have sole charge of a farm, and this particular woman was young and marriageable. In short, both the estate and its owner were desirable.

Desirable, eh? Well, she's described in the report as "fair and slender, full-eyed, her feet and hands of singular beauty". It's understandable that more than one young man should have had his eye on her. And one young man's mother as well. She was another widow, one Dame Alice Rosemary, whose only surviving son, Thomas, was the master of a larger neighbouring estate. Having so much, they wanted more, and although young Mistress Fisher — she was just twenty-four, and a widow for eighteen months — showed no desire to marry again, it seems that Alice Rosemary had determined that she should. The happy bridegroom, of course, would be Thomas.

Neither mother nor son comes out well from the affair, unless you count maternal ambition as a virtue. Alice Rosemary seems to have worshipped her late husband, and when he died she transferred that worship to their son, a taciturn lout of twenty-five, strong and quick-tempered. From his own later account it appears that he considered himself happy only when in his mother's company, and he would do anything to ensure her approval. She must have been a remarkable woman, you know. In a less patriarchal age she might have made good use of her verve and intelligence. As it was —

Thomas Rosemary seems to have been pretty much indifferent to Janet Fisher until, as he said much later, his mother advised him to court the young widow. Even so, it's clear that for the son, as for the mother, the main object was to gain possession of Abbotts Farm. To this end he did his clumsy best to woo the girl, and she, an intelligent creature, would have none of him. Every day Thomas would recount his lack of progress, and every day Alice would chide him for the fool that he was. So matters went for some months, and then Alice Rosemary chanced to consult a lawyer, and learned something that put matters in a new light.

Janet Fisher was an orphan with no surviving family. If she were to die unmarried, then the estate would revert to her late husband's family. So far, all was straightforward. The shock was to learn that the late Walter Fisher's nearest living male relative was Thomas Rosemary himself. This gave things a new urgency, for although the young widow might refuse to marry Thomas there was no telling when she might meet a more attractive suitor. Alice found herself with two choices: she could reinforce the efforts of her miserable son to make love to the girl, or she could see to it that Janet Fisher simply did not live to marry again. Rejecting straightforward murder, she made up her mind to a simple and devastating plan. She would see that the respectable Mistress Fisher died as a witch.

Thomas Rosemary, some fifteen years later, confessed to his own part in this nasty business. He claimed that the idea was entirely his mother's, and I see no reason to doubt him. He was violent enough by nature, and ready to avenge what he saw as the slighting he'd received from this stubborn chit, but he lacked his mother's intelligence. And in those days, you know, the plan could hardly fail: an accusation of witchcraft was almost proof of guilt in itself. Oh, there were a few enlightened souls about, like George Gifford of Maldon, but even he didn't deny the reality of sorcery, and for the most part opinion went along with writers like William Perkins. Well, you can look him up, if you like. He wrote *A Discourse of the Damned Art of Witchcraft*, and it's a very disturbing glimpse into the mind of a fanatic.

Dame Alice set to her filthy task — with some relish, if we can believe her son; certainly with effect. Rumours were spread. Simple folk began to believe that they had seen what they'd only been told. Those who were sick or wounded became convinced that they were actually bewitched. Even Mistress Fisher's own servants came to be wary of her, while she, poor child, remained falsely secure in her real innocence.

Then came the taking. On the morning of the fifteenth of May, the widow Rosemary and her son triumphantly conducted three officers of the County Sheriff, followed by a nervous group of villagers, to Abbotts Farm, where Janet Fisher was formally accused by that public-spirited citizen Master Thomas Rosemary, whose own bailiff, he said, had but lately been stricken lame through the sorcerous arts of the said woman.

All this was recounted in some detail at the trial, so we know pretty well exactly what happened. At first the young woman was struck with horrified disbelief, but quickly controlled herself, and appeared to all to be quite calm. This fact was noted against her, but I suspect that she'd been overtaken by that comforting sense of unreality that's sometimes instilled in us by the utterly outrageous.

She spoke only once on that occasion, and I can quote the words exactly. After the Sheriff's man had read the formal deed of arrest, she said, "Before God and His angels I do swear my innocence."

You can imagine what a queer feeling it gave me to read that simple statement in the cramped print of the old pamphlet!

All this was minutely recorded, because something quite unexpected followed. The brazen words of the witch aroused such an excess of wrath in the good Master Thomas that before he could be restrained he had drawn his long-bladed knife and attempted to slash at her face. She threw up her right hand, saving her eyes, but receiving a savage wound none the less. In short, one of her fingers was wholly severed, and the hand badly cut. At this she cried aloud and swooned. The constables had to carry her from the house.

The trial was held at Chelmsford on the twenty-seventh of June, and Janet Fisher found herself only one of three women arraigned before Lord Brian D'Arcy. The others were simple, ignorant souls, and their cases were speedily despatched. It isn't surprising that more attention was paid to the young, intelligent and attractive mistress of Abbotts Farm. I wonder now if she was at all aware of D'Arcy's reputation. If so, she must have known that she was already lost. He'd been the presiding judge in at least two previous witch-trials and had proved himself to be quite without mercy.

I read the whole report very thoroughly, though it told me nothing that I hadn't already surmised. The several villagers who gave evidence were plainly overawed by the situation, and in one or two cases words were actually put into their mouths by the prosecution in a way that quite sickened me. Nearly all mentioned the part played by Master Rosemary in building up suspicion against the accused, and yet none of them was questioned upon this point. Every insinuation appeared to be accepted as fact. Dame Alice didn't testify, and her son's evidence was kept to a minimum. No mention at all was made of the fact that he was the sole heir to the estate of Abbotts.

The verdict was inevitable — guilty. The sentence was death by hanging. It was carried out the next day in the open space in front of the Sessions House, where Tindal Square is now. The old courthouse was replaced, as you know, in 1789 by John Johnson's Shire Hall, and the whole place is so changed that when I walked around there after leaving the Record Office I could gain no impressions at all.

That was the end of Janet Fisher: branded as a witch and hanged without compassion. But it wasn't the end of the story, because about fifteen years later Alice Rosemary died of a fall. Her son Thomas must have had a spark of independent humanity in him after all, because the day after her funeral he went to the Sheriff's office and confessed to the whole sordid plot. He said that he was troubled by the thought of eternal ignominy attaching to the memory of an innocent woman. Maybe he really did love her a little, or had at least managed to persuade himself that he did. His confession was duly noted, and a copy of it survives in the County Archives, but no action was taken. Can you beat it? Nothing was done, and Thomas Rosemary went back to Winstock and his family. He died, according to the parish register, in March of 1611, much mourned by his wife and three sons.

Well, that's the story of the reality behind my vision. But of course I already knew that it was so, and the details of the story had combined to explain my own part in it. I knew what I was to do with the severed finger, and now I knew why.

Oh, I must tell you what the pamphlet said on that point, because it clarified matters wonderfully. There was just a brief casual statement in the report of Janet Fisher's arrest. Thomas Rosemary, in his savage attack on her, had cut off one of the fingers of her right hand — and as I knew, because I had seen, it was the forefinger. Now, in the confusion following all this, when the poor child had collapsed, nobody had given any thought to the severed finger, and when one of the constables had looked for it later it was not to be found. The assumption was that some servant, still faithful, or some ghoul among the bystanders had pocketed it as a gruesome memento. It was a reasonable notion, but quite wrong, as you can see. Quite wrong.

I am certain, positive, that it had been waiting for me. Somewhere — or nowhere — it had been waiting for me.

George was busy filling his pipe. Without looking up, he asked — although we both knew the answer — "What did you do with it?"

Robert spread out his strong hands. "Just what I promised I'd do. I sealed the box I'd put it in, and that night I took it along to Winstock churchyard. I found a quiet corner where it wouldn't be disturbed, and I buried it." He looked sharply at us, as if daring us to dispute the rightness of the action. "I took along a copy of *The Book of Common Prayer* that I'd bought at Clarke's in Chelmsford, and I read over the burial service. She wouldn't have had a Christian burial, you see."

I toyed with my glass a moment, and as George didn't seen inclined to speak I asked the obvious question: "Why? I mean, it was a nice gesture, and a good one — perhaps I'd have done the same. But why this insistence on it? You speak as if you were paying off a debt."

"I'm sorry, but I thought you knew. 'Paying off a debt' is about right. Ah, well... I've not been able to trace the family all the way back, but it's a pretty distinctive name, and there's no doubt at all in my own mind."

"You see, my mother's maiden name was Rosemary."

Afterword

This story started out more than thirty years ago as a bad (*very* bad) imitation of H P Lovecraft. Only the dream motif and the severed finger survive.

My home town of Chelmsford saw the first major English witch-trial in 1565, and several others during the next hundred years or so. Peter Haining's book *The Witchcraft Papers: Contemporary Records of the Witchcraft Hysteria in Essex 1560 - 1700* is a wonderful collection of first-hand accounts, from which I've drawn gratefully. George Gifford, William Perkins and Lord Brian D'Arcy were real people, and appear to have been much as I've indicated.

Sax Rohmer occasionally dreamed that he was in another person's body, as his friend Cay Van Ash relates in his engaging biography, *Master of Villainy*.

"Rosemary" doesn't seem to exist as a surname, but it ought to — perhaps as an English equivalent of the Scottish "Primrose". I wanted a name that was very unusual but not outlandish, and found it in Margery Allingham's short story, "The Old Man in the

Window". The reference to the painter Lafcadio is by way of an acknowledgement to Margery Allingham, as readers of *Death of a Ghost* will recognise.

"The Taking" appeared in my first book (or rather, booklet) *Deep Things out of Darkness*. I revised the story a little for Richard Dalby's anthology *Tales of Witchcraft*, and have revised it further for this book.

THE MELODRAMA

"At last," said Stephanie Cowles, "I've been able to track down our family ghost story."

"You've hinted at this before," I said. "Something to do with your aunt?"

"My great-aunt,' said Stephanie. "You knew her, I think, Mr Cobbett."

George Cobbett rubbed a finger across his grey moustache. "Yes," he said at length. "She was a friend of my mother's, and a good few years older than I. Didn't she die in a nursing-home about twenty years ago?"

"That's right - when I was a child. I remember her as a little old lady dressed all in black, rather like Queen Victoria. Lucy Underwood her name was, and she was my mother's aunt.

"The story's all contained in some letters that she wrote to her younger sister - my grandmother, you know - in 1910. I'm fairly sure of the year, though it's not mentioned in the letters, and it all happened in September. At that time the family were living in Maldon, where Great-Grandfather was a solicitor, and Lucy had gone to visit her fiancé's family at a village called Wormingford, the other side of Colchester. They were married the following spring, and just five years later he was killed at Gallipoli. She never remarried.

"My grandmother found the letters again only the other week, among a pile of papers that she was discarding before she moved down to Sussex to live. She's over ninety, poor dear, and she's firmly convinced that the climate's healthier on the south coast; I can't see it myself. Anyway, she passed the letters on to me. I found the writing a bit hard to decipher in places, so I've made a typed copy.

"And now, if someone will get me another drink, please, I'll read it to you:

Letter I

Wormingford
September 17th

Alice, my dear,
	Firstly I must tell you that the Mallows send you their love — Francis in particular, of course, but also his parents and his younger sisters (what dears they are!). The house is just as I remembered it: square, white and austere without, but so welcoming within that I might already be a member of the family.
	The journey from Maldon seemed almost interminable, and yet it was by no means unpleasant in this fine weather, with the clear blueness of the sky as a perfect backdrop for the many shades of green, and the late summer flowers showing their colours brightly and bravely. There is so much of interest to be seen from the railway! Still, it was good to arrive at Bures Station and to be met by Dr Mallow with the gig.
	Now, you may be sure that I shall write to you every day, for I fully intend to enjoy myself throughout this little holiday.

Your loving Lucy.

P.S. Your own note has arrived just in time for me to add this brief reply. Dear, silly Agatha! What ever could have possessed the girl to leave so precipitately? And with a man she hardly knows! Still, you say that Cook reports him to be a handsome, swaggering fellow, so perhaps I should confess to a pang of romantic jealousy — but I am sure that it will not last the night, for I shall be with Francis again at breakfast-time. I do hope that the foolish child is happy with her man.

Letter II

September 18th

My dear Alice,
	You will never guess where we have been today, Francis and I! (Yes, and Dr and Mrs Mallow too, though they stayed mostly inside the church while we explored the village.) Why, we have

been to Polstead, just over the border in Suffolk. Do you recall how we saw the travelling players perform the old drama of "The Red Barn" when we were impressionable children? How frightened and yet how delighted we were by it all! How we pitied poor Maria Marten, and how we hated the wicked Squire – and yet I remember your telling me in a moment of confidence that you felt perhaps that you might have been able, were you in Maria's place, to turn his evil thoughts in a higher direction. (Or perhaps you were more than a little in love with the villain! For I am brazen enough now to confess that I was.)

And then, my dear, when we learned that the story was true! Oh, how we begged Mama and Papa to take us to Polstead so that we might see Squire Corder's house, and Maria's cottage, and her grave – and the fatal Red Barn itself! Ah, but our dear parents thought that the whole matter was too gruesome and sordid for our young minds. The artificial world of the stage was one thing, but the reality —! Perhaps they were right, but when Dr Mallow asked if we should care to go with him and his wife over to Polstead, you may be sure that we agreed at once. "It is just a few miles away," said he, "but the village is a very pretty one, and I think that you will find it interesting. The church has much to commend it. I understand that it possesses the only stone spire in Suffolk."

Francis declared that, as the weather was so delightful and the company so charming (my blushes!), he would welcome an afternoon in the open air, particularly (he added) if I should like to visit the very spot where the Red Barn murder, that most notorious and romantic criminal affair, took place. Then I blushed indeed, and agreed willingly.

Oh, Alice, you *would* like Polstead! Dr Mallow was quite right: it is a lovely village. The church is very handsome (though of more interest, I suspect, to the good Doctor than to me), and there are such quaint old houses... After we had dutifully admired the church, Francis and I asked leave, readily given, to explore the churchyard and the village. We started by looking for poor Maria's grave, and I can only add that I *think* we found it. This may seem strange, but in eighty years so many people have come to Polstead (morbid sensation-hunters, no doubt) and have chipped pieces from the gravestone for a ghastly *memento mori* that little is left of it. Just think – the great Gospel Oak still stands after a thousand years, but this modest stone memorial is likely soon to vanish altogether!

Still, Squire Corder's farmhouse stands as it did in 1827, very near the church (such irony!), a most picturesque black and white half-timbered building, in the shape of a letter E, but without the middle stroke, which Francis tells me is a sure sign that it dates from before the days of the Tudors. Its calm and beautiful exterior gives no hint of the dark passions that raged within so few decades ago — but then, the old place has seen so many people come and go, of such different tempers, virtues and vices, that it must have achieved tranquillity or itself gone insane. (What a strange thought!)

Maria's cottage survives also, and while meaner than the farmhouse it is no less charming. The garden grows gay, showing off perfectly the neatly whitewashed walls and densely thatched roof. It makes quite the prettiest picture. To be accurate, of course, it was never Maria's cottage but her father's — and Francis, who knows so much more about it all than I, told me that old Mr Marten (whatever you and I might have gathered from the play) was not a tenant farmer but a mole-catcher! I do not know quite why that should surprise me so; no doubt it is a very necessary occupation.

I suppose that you will want to know about the Red Barn itself. Alas, there is little to tell. Francis had brought with him a map that showed the village as it was in 1825, so we knew where we ought to have found the barn, but when we reached the spot there was nothing to see but a ploughed field. We spent some little time in discussing whether the map might be at fault, and in attempting to identify nearby buildings as the scene of the murder, but it became plain that the Red Barn simply exists no longer. At last we called upon the present occupant of Maria's cottage, a sweet old woman who was able to tell us that she remembered as a young woman seeing the barn ablaze one night, a conflagration that utterly destroyed it. So, my dear, the very site of poor Maria's death has now disappeared. I do not know whether to be sorry or glad, for certainly so majestic a destruction has saved the barn from the ignominious slow erasure that afflicts Maria's grave.

Poor Maria, I said, and yet the old woman seemed to have little sympathy with the victim, which appeared strange to me until I asked her to explain. "Why, my dear," said she, "if you'd feel sorry for anyone, then feel sorry for poor William Corder. The whole affair was so altered, so distorted, that all today think that he was purely wicked and she purely innocent — but it wasn't so, I tell you! I wasn't so..." She spoke for several minutes, and most interesting it was, though far too much for me to recall and recount here. In essence, we learned that the old worthy had herself been a child of nine years old at the time of the murder, and remembered it quite clearly, garnering further details from her mother afterwards. I must tell you, then, Alice, that whatever you and I may have thought, it is fact that Maria Marten, though undoubtedly the belle of the village, was by no means the pure maiden that she has been painted (she had already borne a child out of wedlock before meeting William Corder), and that William himself was not the heartless, suave, middle-aged rake. He was a cultured, if wild, young man, and fully three years his lover's junior! It would be so convenient if one could picture everything in plain black and white, but alas! The world is deeper and darker than we imagine. The intrusion of sordid reality into the drama should, perhaps, have rendered it less fascinating, but somehow I found that the fact was more poignant than the fantasy.

  The afternoon did not, after all, take quite the turn that we had expected, but I cannot deny that it was a most stimulating and interesting visit to Polstead.

  Now, Alice, what of your own news? Do write soon (as I know you will).

Your loving Lucy.

P.S. The dear old soul at the cottage told us something further about the infamous Red Barn — which I am ashamed to admit that I have quite forgotten!

Letter III

September 19th

My dear Alice,

  Thank you so much for your sweet letter. So there is still no news of that foolish girl Agatha! No doubt she is an impressionable and romantic child, but I never thought that she would leave her position so suddenly and without notice. Has Papa written to her parents? (Oh, no! I have just remembered — she was a workhouse child, wasn't she? Poor thing. Well, I am sure that you will tell me *at once* when there is news of her.)

Now to my own news. You will remember that we spent such a pleasant afternoon yesterday in Polstead? Well, the most extraordinary and delightful thing has happened! At breakfast this morning, Dr Mallow folded the local newspaper to a particular page (they take the *Colchester Gazette* here, you know) and handed it to Francis, saying, "If we are to give Lucy a real treat while she is with us, my boy, then I suggest that we pay attention to this notice." The dear boy glanced smilingly at me as he took the paper, and as he read the notice his eyes widened and his smile broadened. "I say!" he exclaimed. "This is topping! Listen, Lucy: 'Mr Cain Foxborough, the celebrated actor, has brought his talented and versatile company to Colchester this week. Readers will hardly need to be reminded that Mr Foxborough is one of the last of the once numerous race of "barnstormers", who do not confine their performances to the luxurious playhouses of the metropolis but bring culture and diversion to the provinces. Mr Cain Foxborough's company specialises in innocent old-fashioned "blood-and-thunder" such as our parents and grand-parents enjoyed...'"

Francis chuckled and cast a mischievous glance towards his father. *That* gentleman was smiling broadly. "There is more," my dear boy continued. "During his week at the Corn Exchange in Colchester Mr Foxborough will present his two most celebrated rôles: Sweeney Todd, the Demon Barber of Fleet Street, and — " I understood his pleasure. "And William Corder in *The Murder of Maria Marten*!" I exclaimed (for it could only be that). "How wonderful! Oh, *may* we go? Please?"

Dr Mallow said that at that moment he could deny me nothing, which was sweet of him, and Francis grinned and blushed like a schoolboy. And so, my dear, it is all settled. Tomorrow afternoon all six of us are to go to Colchester to see Cain Foxborough himself enact for us the very drama that we were investigating yesterday. I suspect that we may return rather late from the town, so I may not be able to write to you then, but be sure that I shall give you a full account on the following day!

Your loving Lucy.

Letter IV

September 20th

Alice, my dear,

It is actually long past midnight, so I really ought to have put "September 21st" at the head of this letter. I am sitting in my bedroom, writing by the light of a candle. By now I should be fast in the arms of Morpheus, but — oh, my dear! — I *cannot* sleep! This evening past has been a time of drama and horror, and I simply must tell you all about it while it is fresh in my mind. To be sure, the dread of it will remain with me all my life, but now I must chronicle all that has happened before the details fade. It was so strange, so very strange...

We had borrowed a neighbour's dog-cart, which Francis drove, his mother and I being the passengers, while Dr Mallow drove his own gig, with his two young daughters behind him. We arrived late in the afternoon at the *Red Lion* in Colchester, where we stabled the horses and had ourselves a capital severe tea before walking the few yards to the Corn Exchange.

For a moment we stood facing across the street while the girls and I gazed at the big posters flanking the doors of the Corn Exchange. They promised so much! But we were sure that the promise would be fulfilled. My reverie was broken by a discreet cough from Dr Mallow and by a sudden tightening of Francis' grip upon my arm. "Look!" he whispered, pointing upwards and across the street. "How very curious!" The dying sun had bathed the roof of the Corn Exchange in a dull red glow, like a ruby held before the embers of a fire: it was a sombre and most impressive sight — a fit prelude, I thought, to the delicious drama that we were to witness. I wondered how the Maria and the William that we should shortly see would compare with what we had so recently learned of the sad reality.

We were entranced from the moment that the curtain arose upon a scene of village revelry, which introduced the rustic clown Tim Bobbin and Maria's pretty sister Ann. Their simple good nature provided a most telling contrast to the suave and sinister charm of the newly returned squire, William Corder. What a fine actor Mr Foxborough is! One could not call him handsome exactly, but his heavy-lidded eyes and expressive features are instantly appealing, while his personality is so powerful that I was conscious of restraint upon his part lest William should appear to be the only character upon the stage.

But then Maria appeared, and if Sister Ann was pretty then Maria was beautiful. There is no other word for her. She glowed in her sweet innocence, and William (like every man in the audience, I dare say!) fell in love with her. He was all honey, but there was venom beneath the sweetness, and I knew in that moment that I hated him. (How foolish this looks written down! But you may take it, if you will, as a tribute to Mr Foxborough's skill, for it was William Corder that I hated and not Cain Foxborough. For me, then, Cain Foxborough did not exist.)

I need not recount all the details of the story, for you will remember them well enough. Suffice it that all was consummately done: the seduction of Maria, the sorrow of her uncomprehending parents, the honest bantering love of Ann and Tim, the revelation of Corder's true villainy by the brother of the gipsy girl whom he had deceived... and the culmination of that villainy — the murder of Maria Marten in the Red Barn.

Ah, but that murder was harrowing! The pitiful pleas of the wronged girl, the fiendish intensity of the wicked man... It was then, I think, that I began to feel truly uneasy, though looking back I realise that the unease had begun to make itself felt earlier yet. Perhaps it was when the gipsy lad, Pharaoh Lee, first appeared. For the life of me I could not recall before ever seeing on stage the ghost of his wronged sister, Zorah; and indeed I was not quite certain that I saw her now. Yet I *think* that while Pharaoh Lee stood at the front of the stage, in the full glow of the limelight, swearing vengeance upon Squire Corder (and callously consigning poor Maria to the flames) there lurked behind him in the shadows a slim, dark-haired young woman, whose face I could not discern, but who exuded an almost tangible fervour.

The actor who portrayed Pharaoh Lee was a most attractive young man, far more obviously so than Mr Foxborough. Handsome — almost rakish. I was very taken with him.

Then came the inexorable process of discovery and retribution. The old woman in the cottage at Polstead had been most insistent upon the truth of the story here: that Maria's mother (really her step-mother, I think) actually had been visited in her dreams by Maria's ghost, urging her to search the Red Barn. I know that it all sounds too much like *Hamlet*, but why, after all, should such visions be granted only to the high and the mighty? So we saw the poor creature settling down to an uneasy sleep in the cottage (so empty now, without her daughter's radiant presence); we saw the spirit of the murdered girl seeming to hover in the shadows behind her, and we heard a faint cry: "Vengeance!"

At least, I saw and heard. And here unease set in again, and I began to suspect that something (I knew not what) was seriously amiss. For the figure in the gloom was unmistakably that of a dark-haired young woman in a black robe, whereas Maria had been a true English rose, pink-cheeked and golden-haired, and when we had seen her at the infamous barn she had been charmingly dressed in men's breeches, boots and a white shirt. I tried to call Francis' attention to the enigmatic figure, wondering if perhaps the play had been adapted to refer to some further deed in Squire Corder's past, but the dear fellow was so enthralled that he simply brushed away my hand without noticing. I wondered if I might be suffering from some mild hallucination, for at that moment another figure appeared on the stage, and this time most surely it was Maria. Her cheeks were now a ghastly white, and the yellow hair and white shirt were shockingly stained with red, but it was certainly she. When I looked for the other girl again, she was not to be seen.

The drama progressed. We discovered that the gipsy (as we had known all along, those of us who had seen the play before) had joined the Bow Street Runners and was now officially as well as privately committed to the execution of justice upon Squire Corder. We saw his meeting with the elders of his tribe, who urged him on to revenge. And, Alice, I am *sure* that at the edge of the group, half-seen, was the figure of a woman who was not one of the tribe! What was I to make of it? I was quite as fascinated by the events on the stage as the rest of the full audience, but now it was for rather different reasons.

Relentlessly the play moved to its gruesome climax. Pharaoh Lee effected the arrest of William Corder, who turned frighteningly from a swaggering bully to a horror-struck coward — and ever at his side I seemed to see the apparition of the dark girl, and to hear (was it only in my own mind?) her whispered cry of "Vengeance!" We saw the hapless villain in his prison cell (a pitiful wretch now he seemed!) and his last visitor, the gipsy, who called upon him to repent. As the gipsy entered, so did the ghost of the murdered Maria. Now, thought I, Squire Corder will surely confess, and beg God and man for forgiveness; but no! Not seeming to see the spirit of the woman he had so cruelly wronged, he regained something of his former imperious manner and defied his captor. Then Maria must speak, I thought, and at the sound of her sweet voice he must collapse and admit his villainy! But when I looked again, the figure standing so close to the side of the handsome young avenger was not that of Maria Marten, but of the dark young woman whom I had seen (as it seemed to me) before. So Pharaoh Lee departed the dreadful cell, to the sound of defiance from the murderer, and as the latter mused upon his black deeds, so there did indeed enter the blood-bespattered but glorious angel whom he had deceived and slaughtered. She appeared not to notice the third figure in that cramped and gloomy place of confinement, but went directly to the author of her woes, addressing him in some such words as: "O, William! William! Will you not repent? For see! Thy Maria forgives thee." Francis told me afterwards that it was a truly affecting moment, and that the dawning penitence of the wicked man represented a triumph of art for Mr Cain Foxborough; but my own attention was fixed upon the other participant in this act, the slim young woman who seemed always to be half-hidden in the shadows and whose face I still could not plainly see. Yet two strange notions occurred to me: the first, that somewhere perhaps (and not upon the stage) I had seen this figure before, be it never so briefly; the second, that she was not merely slim but of an almost terrifying thinness. The close-cut black dress, such as a housemaid might wear, served only to emphasise that, and when, as on occasion, she stood in profile to me, her face appeared to be of a somehow unwholesome shape. Throughout, she took no active part in this, the penultimate scene of the play, but I thought that occasionally there floated up an indistinct whisper that did not come from either Maria or William.

The dreadful conclusion arrived all too quickly. The curtain arose upon a starkly realistic representation of the gallows whereon William Corder was to expiate his crime. The awful figure of the public hangman stood ready to pull the lever that would set the execution of justice in motion, and near him were the governor of the prison and the parson, in his bands. William Corder (now a truly pathetic sight) was led in by a turnkey, and ever at his side was the ineffably gracious spirit of his victim. A little below stood old Farmer Marten and his wife, Tim Bobbin and his dear Ann, and the gipsy, Pharaoh Lee — but only I, it seemed, could also descry, more plainly now, the shape of the dark young woman, standing upon the scaffold beside the hangman.

All proceeded as it should — William making his confession and imploring the Martens for pardon, a solemn little homily from the parson, murmurings from the crowd — but then suddenly something was wrong. The hangman pulled the lever that should have opened the fatal trapdoor, and nothing happened. He pulled harder, and then went and stamped gingerly upon the trap. There was a hasty whispered exchange with the prisoner (who for this moment was no longer William Corder but Mr Cain Foxborough), which led to a summons to Pharaoh Lee, the Bow Street Runner, to step up and test the trap while the hangman again attempted to pull the lever.

I can scarcely bear to write of what followed, swift though it was. The handsome young gipsy, his face a stern mask of duty, mounted the scaffold and gave one hearty stamp upon the recalcitrant trapdoor. At that moment, the thin dark figure ran from the hangman's side to his (though no one else that I have spoken to admits to seeing this) and flung her bony arms around him in a cruel embrace. The trap swung suddenly open, and there was an appalling cry from the young man, followed by the sound of splintering wood and a sort of dead thump as the two of them fell through the raised stage.

There is little more that I can report directly. Mr Foxborough, much shaken but still the master, signalled for the curtain to be lowered. The audience sat in a shocked hush which rapidly developed into fierce murmurings and excited debate, and then Mr Foxborough appeared at the side of the stage. He called for silence, and after a pause announced that there had been a grave accident, resulting in severe injury to one of the most promising young members of his company (yes, only one was mentioned). He hoped that we had enjoyed the play up until this sad occurrence, and that we would not let it displace his company and himself from the high esteem which they were fortunate enough to occupy, &c., &c. And now, if we pleased...

It was a most subdued audience that left the hall. At some point after Mr Foxborough's exit Francis left us, but he returned some ten minutes later, as we were giving our names and addresses to a hastily summoned police constable in the vestibule. He told us then that he had been taken briefly unwell, but as he was helping me in to the dog-cart he whispered an instruction to meet him in the kitchen after his parents and sisters had retired. The look on his face was both troubled and excited, and I knew that he had learned something of the supposed accident.

The story he told me was this. An old acquaintance of his was employed as a carpenter and handyman at the Corn Exchange, and it was to him that Francis had gone for information. The tale was strange enough, though whether it falls into place with the strange things that I had witnessed (but Francis had not, I am sure), I simply do not know. Briefly, the young man who had portrayed the gipsy was a newcomer to the company, with them only a matter of weeks, but being both talented and personable he had been given this important rôle by the percipient Mr Foxborough. The company had for the previous two weeks been performing, with deserved success, in Chelmsford, and after closing there the young man had left his colleagues, saying that he was going to call upon a friend but would be with them again at the first rehearsal in Colchester. He had duly arrived, accompanied as always by his big wooden trunk and by a large and apparently new leather suitcase. The trunk, with other possessions and properties, was thenceforth kept in a large storage area some twenty feet directly below the level of the stage at the Corn Exchange. ("And it took two men to carry it down there. Thirsty work!" said Francis' friend.)

It was on to this very trunk that the young man fell. This accounted for the sound that I heard, of splintering wood. Of course, he was killed instantly. A very sad story, to be sure, you will say, but what of the mysterious woman? Why, simply that when the carpenter arrived, the first upon the dreadful scene, he found not *one* body but *two*. The second, hideously mutilated, had been inside the trunk all along. It was that of a dark-haired young woman, dressed in black. The carpenter was appalled to see that as the young man had landed, crushing the corpse horribly, its decaying arms had been flung up and over him, as if in a mockery of embrace.

Good-night, my dear. I hope that you, at least, are sleeping soundly tonight! We shall talk about all this when I return on Tuesday.

Your loving Lucy.

"No doubt," I said hesitantly, "we've all drawn the obvious conclusion?"

"No doubt," said George, with a grunt. He was, as so often these days, trying to get his pipe to draw satisfactorily.

"Oh, that's plain enough!" Stephanie sounded impatient. "I'm wondering just what it could have been, though, that the old woman at Polstead told my great-aunt. You know — the thing she couldn't remember."

I considered. "Perhaps that old Marten's wife was actually Maria's step-mother and not her mother? No, that's not likely, since Lucy mention the fact in her last letter. Could it be that William Corder wasn't in fact the squire of the village?"

George interrupted tetchily. "You're forgetting, boy, that it was something to do with the barn itself." He turned to Stephanie and adjusted his features into an avuncular smile. "Now, my dear," he said, "do you know just why it was called the Red Barn?"

"I always assumed it was because of the murder. Blood — you know... "

"Not at all. It was known by that name long before."

"Was it built of red brick, then?" I asked

He scowled momentarily. "No," he said, "but you're closer. It's an odd tale, and it throws a rather interesting light on something that Great-Aunt Lucy says in that last letter of hers. It was believed in East Anglia in the early nineteenth century that the rays of the dying sun had the power to single out a place where evil had occurred — or would occur. The people thought that if the sunset cast a red glow over a building, that was a sign that no good would ever happen there. And it seems to be a fact that the barn on Corder's land, even though it was a thatched wooden structure, could often be seen at the end of the day bathed in a glow as dark and red as blood... "

Afterword

I wanted to write a story about the music hall, but I'll settle for having written one about that other favourite theatrical form, the melodrama. The perceptive reader will notice that I have re-used the theme of M R James's "The Story of a Disappearance and an Appearance".

Again I've drawn on one of Peter Haining's books: *Buried Passions*, a very readable account of the Red Barn murder and its aftermath. My actor-manager is a sketch of the great Tod Slaughter, whom I never saw on stage, but whose surviving films give at least some idea of how melodrama should be played: larger than life, but with complete sincerity. John M Garrett suggested the inspired name "Cain Foxborough".

This story is affectionately dedicated to my good friend Bernard Davies, who as a young actor worked with Tod Slaughter, and who shared some of his memories with me.

I took a risk in having the play performed in the Corn Exchange at Colchester, and was very relieved to discover that a century ago it actually did house touring theatrical productions. The subterranean arrangements of the building, however, are imaginary.

THE PRIZE

"It's Penny's story really," said Roy Plummer. "Or rather, it's about her. My aunt, you know; but though she was twenty or so years older than I, she was always a good friend, and I don't think I ever called her anything but Penny."

George Cobbett grunted, and I asked, "Penny who?"

"Oh — Penelope Carter. There's nothing very much to say about her, except that she was intelligent and very likeable. She'd been widowed about three years before all this happened, and had moved out of the house in Leytonstone to a pleasant flat in Bow. It was very handy for the London Hospital, where she worked as a laboratory technician."

Roy paused while he offered round a packet of panatellas. (I accepted one, but George chose to stick with his pipe.) Then he said abruptly, "Do you remember the book *Sorcerous*?"

The title stirred vague memories. "Something about a treasure-hunt?" I said.

"Just so. That was the starting-point of the whole damned business."

At least (he continued) you can hardly have forgotten Kit Williams' *Masquerade* and the quite extraordinary excitement inspired by the quest for the golden hare. In some cases it amounted almost to a religious fervour. Well, Williams' book and its success naturally provoked several imitations — pot-boilers mostly, entirely lacking the spirit of the original, which was far more than a simple treasure-hunt. But then came *Sorcerous* by Charles Device.

It certainly followed *Masquerade* into print, but it wasn't produced in imitation of the earlier book. In fact it had been written two or three years before, and only the publishers' caution had prevented it from appearing before then.

In a way, it was a complement to *Masquerade*, which is a book of pictures. The pictures actually lie at the heart of the riddle, and the text was written to match them, not the other way about. In *Sorcerous* the text is everything. It's a novel, and all the clues are in the words. Read it sometime — never mind the puzzle. Device has a very powerful and bizarre imagination, and his depiction of magic in Celtic Britain is masterly. But at the time, of course, the book's intrinsic quality was hardly considered. What mattered was the riddle.

And the prize.

The prize was thoroughly in keeping with the theme of the novel: a beautiful reproduction of the Gundestrup cauldron, in silver, like the original. It's a large bowl, dating from the Iron Age, and exquisitely decorated with portraits of Celtic deities and rather macabre religious scenes. The cauldron itself wasn't actually buried in the ground — unlike the golden hare. The idea was that the solver of the riddle would find a sort of sheet of silver, with an inscription to the effect that the quest was over. This was to be presented to the publishers, who would then hand over the cauldron.

Well, it was Penny who found the silver sheet.

Now, that was rather curious, because Penny was really no great hand at puzzles — I never knew her complete the *Telegraph* crossword — but she'd set her heart on this hunt. She read the book goodness knows how many times, and filled several notebooks with theories. The difficulty was that none of the hunters (the word will have to do) even knew what form the clues took — whether they were mathematical, literary, wordplay or what — so those notebooks contained any number of different ideas, all of which had to be tested, and eventually, all but one, discarded.

So we thought.

Myself, I'd read the book once and enjoyed it. I'd even toyed with a couple of possible leads, and got nowhere. But Penny was obsessed. It was rather awe-inspiring. She'd once seen the original Gundestrup cauldron in the Danish National Museum, and now she'd decided that if she couldn't have the real thing she was going to try as hard as she could for the copy.

Like everyone else, no doubt, she assumed at first that the author's name, Device, was itself a clue, and was a little put out when she discovered that the name was real. Oh, there's no need to try and recall every wrong path she took. Certainly she seemed to devote all her free time to the quest. Her attendance at the Amadeus Society, of which we were both members, ceased, and she was quite ecstatic when influenza obliged her to take four days off from the hospital.

The decisive clue, she thought, was a double reference to fangs. It was a sufficiently unusual word for her to take notice.

Eventually she thought of vampires; and after considering Augustus Hare's Croglin Grange — somewhere in Cumberland, isn't it? — and a few other places, she decided that there might be a connection with Count Dracula. Even that gave her headaches, as several places in England play important parts in Stoker's novel, but with fatalistic determination she tried all those that she could identify, ending at Whitby, the farthest from London. And at Whitby, on the cliff-top near the Abbey, she found the silver sheet.

With a sort of nervous joy, she took it along to the publishers' office in Russell Square, and waited on needles and pins while it was authenticated. She said afterwards that she nearly fainted when they told her that she really had solved the riddle, and that the cauldron was hers.

The next day she was taken to meet the author: a pleasant fellow, she told me, in his early thirties and with a mind like a razor. And then the bombshell exploded.

Penny hadn't solved the riddle after all.

By remarkable good fortune, she had actually misinterpreted a couple of minor clues, while ignoring nearly all the major ones, and she'd ended up precisely where she would have been if she'd correctly followed Device's straightforward, elegant, but cunningly concealed thread.

Nevertheless, she hadn't cheated in anyway, and since the author's announcement in the book clearly stated that the cauldron would be won by the finder of the silver sheet — rather than by the solver of the puzzle — the trophy was legitimately hers.

The riddle, however, remained unsolved — but not for long. Among the correspondence that arrived at Device's house that same morning, while Penny was actually there, was a letter from a Doctor Venetia Caracalla, giving a perfect, complete and beautifully reasoned solution. Dr Caracalla merely awaited confirmation before she started to dig.

I shan't ask you to imagine how Penny felt — or how Device felt, for that matter. Things were as they were. Venetia Caracalla had, quite fairly, solved the riddle; but Penny Carter had, quite fairly, won the prize. No one could change that. The only question that remained was, would this state of things satisfy Dr Caracalla?

The question was soon answered.

Publicity for the *Sorcerous* treasure-hunt had dwindled from the enthusiastic to the indifferent. By this time Kit Williams' golden hare had been found, and there was little interest left for anything else of the same sort. Oh, the national dailies duly reported the matter, but most of them gave it no more than a paragraph. There was nothing on the television news that I can recall. But there was an interview on Radio 4 — the *Today Programme*, or something of the sort — to which the three principals were invited: Charles Device, Penny and Dr Caracalla. Naturally Penny told me about it in advance, and naturally I listened. Not just out of loyalty to my aunt, but because I was curious to hear what the riddle-setter and the riddle-solver had to say.

It was a live interview, not recorded. Otherwise, I think, most of it wouldn't have been broadcast at all. It was, even for me, embarrassing. Uncivilised. And of course it all came down to the unknown factor, Venetia Caracalla.

All Penny was asked to do was to describe the cauldron; then Device said a little about how he'd prepared the trail of clues (no one seemed interested in the literary merits of the book); and finally Dr Caracalla explained how she had unravelled the thread. Her voice was clear, rather deep, and exceptionally well modulated. I remember thinking that she must have a remarkable mind, to seize upon the important features, to reject the irrelevant, and now to explain so concisely and elegantly that even a dolt like me could appreciate the logic and beauty of it all. Happy as I was for Penny, I thought it was unfair that this brilliant woman hadn't been a day or two earlier with her solution.

But she didn't stop with the explanation. Her next words startled me, and they must have made Penny and Device want to creep into a corner and hide.

She said, "I have solved the puzzle and I have won the prize."

There was no anger in the voice. She spoke in a tone of utter and devastating conviction. Penny said something inarticulate, and Device cut in with, "But we've already explained, Dr Caracalla; and the statement in the book is quite clear — "

With a breath-taking haughtiness, she dismissed this as irrelevant. "The letter of the law does not interest me," she said. "Only the spirit matters. Morally, even you cannot feel justified in allowing this woman to take the trophy."

Her tone became condescending as she addressed Penny: "You must see, my dear, that I am right. Come, I have no wish to harm you. The cauldron rightly belongs to me, but I am prepared to compensate you for it. You will accept one hundred pounds — "

I heard Penny's gasp of disbelief — for the thing was worth fully two and a half thousand — and then the announcer's voice broke in: "There, I'm afraid, we must leave *Sorcerous* and the sorcerers..."

I switched off the radio, and waited for the inevitable phone call from Penny.

It came nearly two hours later, and though she'd taken the chance to cool off by walking around the streets near Broadcasting House — and, I suspect, to have a couple of gins — her voice was still shaking with anger as she spoke. "That damned woman! Do you know what she had the nerve to say, Roy?"

I told her that I'd heard Dr Caracalla's insulting offer.

"Not just that," said Penny. "I know that bit went out, and then they stopped transmission, but that bloody woman carried on, utterly blind to all decent manners. 'It's all I shall offer,' she said, 'and you may consider it a great favour. The cauldron is mine, and I shall have it. You may sell it to me or you may give it to me, but I shall have it.'

"Roy, I'm afraid I lost my temper then. Unforgivable, I know, but it's true."

Penny was one of those people who sometimes lose their temper with inanimate objects — I've heard her use some very salty language to her vacuum-cleaner when it was malfunctioning — but very rarely with other people.

"Don't let it worry you," I said. "The cauldron is yours, fair and square, and not even Charles Device can take it from you now. Where is it, by the way?"

"Eh? Oh, it's at my bank, in safe keeping. Nothing to fret about there.

"Roy, love, I know it's silly, but at the moment I feel quite drained. I think I'll take a couple of aspirin and have a nap this afternoon. Then, if you promise not to be chauvinist about it, I'd like to treat you to dinner. I think I deserve a little celebration. Would Simpson's suit you? Good. I'll leave it to you to make the booking, then, and we'll meet there at eight."

She arrived at the restaurant a little before eight, no less flustered than she'd sounded that afternoon.

"It's that woman!" she said. "I can't get her off my mind. She's so damned superior. I know she's got a brilliant mind, but that doesn't give her the right just to disregard the rest of us. Ugh! I think I'm a little frightened of her."

I urged her to forget the whole business, but over the meal she returned to it again: "Roy, you know that I'm not super-sensitive, or whatever the word is, and I'm not especially nervous."

"Well?"

"Oh — it's... Oh, dammit! It's just that I think I may have been followed here this evening."

"What — by this mad doctor?"

"No! That's what makes it seem so silly. Not by a person at all, but by some sort of animal. A dog or something. Only I can't be sure. I kept catching glimpses of it out of the corner of my eye, and once I saw it when I looked quickly behind me, but if ever I tried to look straight at it, it wasn't there."

"Odd," I said. What else could I say?

By the time coffee was served, her nerves had quietened considerably. She gave my cheek an affectionate peck as we left the restaurant, and she told me not to let myself be worried by a silly woman's fancies. It wasn't an entirely convincing performance, though, and I knew better than most that Penny was far from being a silly woman.

For most of the next week I was out of town on business, and though I made a couple of dutiful phone calls to Penny she seemed rather preoccupied and uncommunicative. I was pleased, then, to get a call from her on the morning after my return, a Saturday. I was less pleased to hear the tension in her voice. She sounded very guarded as she told me that she'd taken the cauldron out of safe keeping at the bank, and now had it at her flat.

"Why did you do that?" I asked.

"Why not? What's the point of having it locked away where I can't see it? And where you can't see it! Come over to the flat, Roy. I'm sure you're dying to see the thing."

"Well, if it's — "

"Please come."

Just that. So, of course, I went.

She looked awful. Not that she's let herself go to piece; she was as neatly dressed as always, but her face was unnaturally pale, and her eyes unnaturally bright, with dark shadows under them.

"Good Lord!" I said. "You must have had a bad night."

"That's not the half of it." She sounded listless, uninvolved. "I don't think I've been free of nightmares throughout the week."

"And this sense of being followed — ?"

"Oh yes, I'm still being followed, and still by some sort of animal. But not continuously — and it's the very devil!" She seemed to be close to tears, which wasn't like her at all. "Every so often I feel safe — free — and it's such a relief! I think that life is back to normal again... And then it starts. Shall I tell you what happened to me yesterday?"

"Mm."

"I had to go over to St Pancras, to the Tropical Diseases Hospital, and decided to go by tube rather than by bus. It's a fairly short walk from King's Cross Station, but I must have been preoccupied, because I went past the station and had to get out at Euston Square. Take a bus from here, I thought, but — would you believe it? — there didn't seem to be any going in my direction. All right, I'd walk. I don't know those back streets very well, but I only had to get to St Pancras Road and I'd be all right.

"God, but Somers Town in a depressing place! Even though, for the time being, I was free of the feeling of being shadowed, I was still nervous.

"Then I came to a street on the right, which ought to have led me directly to the main road and to the hospital.

"It was mean and unprepossessing, but no more than the rest of the area, and it led fairly steeply upwards, with a gentle curve to the left. I wondered what I should see from the top of the ridge. Oh, it seemed never-ending! There were shabby buildings on either side, seeming to press towards each other as I climbed slowly upwards: mysterious offices, all apparently closed; seedy shops, locked and barred... At one stage I turned to look down the hill, but the curve in the road was sharper than I'd thought, and all I could see was that double row of faded, dun-coloured buildings, seeming to stretch on forever.

"Then I saw the antique shop. Can you imagine a more unlikely place for such a business, among those shabby newsagents and second-hand clothes shops? But there it was: smart, discreet and clean, with the name 'Wolf' in plain letters above the window, and a cheerful yellow light inside.

"It was like a beacon, a haven. I felt very weary as I crossed the rough, dirty street, wondering why everything here was so quiet. I thought afterwards that I ought surely to have heard sounds from all around — traffic on the main roads, trains from the great stations, just people's voice — but it was as if there was a wall of fog between me and the outside.

"What I could see in the shop window wasn't particularly encouraging: a couple of quite nice walking-sticks, a small carved pipe of the sort that your father used to collect — but mostly the usual reproduction brassware. Still, at least the place seemed to be alive. I opened the door and went in.

"The shop was filled with metal bowls, dishes, cauldrons — all of them chased or incised with the most horrible and obscene designs imaginable. They seemed to stretch back, beyond the small counter, into the darkness, piled on to shelves and tables, hanging from the ceiling. Someone evidently heard my gasp of astonishment, and came padding out through a narrow door behind the counter.

"No, not someone — some*thing*. It was an immense dog, like a huge grey alsatian. It stood on its hind legs and placed its front paws on the counter, and it was the very type of the thing that had been following me. Just before I woke up, sweating, it spoke, in a voice I recognised at once.

"It said, 'You see. I shall have it.'"

I breathed an immense sigh of relief. "Thank God!" I said. "It was only a nightmare, then?"

"Was it?" said Penny, wearily. "I told you that the dreams weren't all. This morning I phoned the London Hospital, and was told that I had actually set out at the right time for St Pancras. When I called the Tropical Diseases Hospital, they said that I'd arrived there right enough, but a full two hours later than I should have done. Now, I don't remember getting to the hospital, and I don't remember getting home — and for pity's sake, Roy, what happened during those two hours?"

I was wary of mentioning the subject, but I knew that I had to. "Do you think that this is something to do with the Caracalla woman?"

"Magic, you mean? Or it might be hypnotism — I'm sure she's capable of that. I don't know. Probably."

"And — er — have you thought about letting her have the cauldron? I mean, if this is torturing you so — "

She flared up suddenly, like a candle before it burns out. "I'll be damned if I do! All right, I felt bad when they told me that I hadn't solved the riddle and she had, and if she'd been poor — if she'd only been *nice* to me — I think I'd have sold the thing and given her a share. But that blasted superiority of hers — ! I made some investigations — oh, I've not been idle! Do you know where she lives? Flask Walk in Hampstead. She retired at the age of forty-three from a very good post at the University of Bristol, and now she lives on an independent income. She doesn't need the cauldron, and certainly not at the laughable price she's offering! No, I — "

At that moment the telephone rang.

After Penny had announced her number, I could quite clearly hear the cultured voice of the woman at the other end of the line: "I shall ask you once again, Mrs Carter. Will you sell me the cauldron for one hundred pounds?"

Penny somehow managed to keep her anger under restraint. "Dr Caracalla," she said sourly, "I have just been telling my nephew precisely why I will not sell it to you. To you I say, I shall be damned if I do!"

There was a sound of amusement from the caller. "Very well, Mrs Carter. I have made you a most generous offer, but the cauldron is rightly mine, and I shall have it. You have refused to sell it to me. If you are wise, you will give it to me."

"What the devil — ?"

"Dear me! Such language. I repeat: if you are wise, you will give it me." Amusement drained from the voice, and it became hard. "Mrs Carter, as you and I know full well, you have already failed to solve one riddle. I shall you another. Its solution may help you to your senses. One of four, Mrs Carter, and twenty-one of six."

"Go to hell."

"One of four, Mars Carter, and twenty-one of six. Learn and be wise. You have three days."

"Three *days*? But — "

The line went dead, and Penny slammed the receiver down. She was almost rigid with fury.

"Did you hear that?"

"Every word," I said. "And I don't like it at all. The woman may be brilliant. She may be mad. But whatever she is, she's dangerous. What about this new riddle?"

"Damn the riddle! And damn her! She knows I'm no good. She knows I'm no match for her... Oh, God! Roy, what am I going to do?"

"Right now," I said, "you're going to come and have lunch with me. There's a very good Turkish restaurant I know in Hornsey. We'll eat, and we'll talk this business over. Now, you're sure you won't change your mind about letting her have the cauldron?"

"Quite sure, thank you." She was already in the hall and putting on her overcoat. "Lunch is an excellent idea. Come on."

As we left the building — it had once been two Victorian houses, but was now divided into six flats — we had to step around a sizeable hole in the pavement where some sort of work was going on, to do with the telephone cables, I think. Then we were at my car, and soon we were out of Coborn Street, away from the East End, and heading towards Hornsey.

The meal, thank heaven, was good; and the staff at the restaurant didn't mind us lingering over our coffee — which was just as well, because there was a lot to talk about.

When I'd asked Penny whether Dr Caracalla mightn't be responsible for her strange (and, after all, possibly quite subjective) experiences, it was hypnotism that I'd had in mind. Yet Penny had immediately mentioned magic. I wondered why, and asked whether she knew what post the woman had held at the university.

"Oh, anthropology," said Penny. "Reader in Anthropology, and with some sort of responsibility for comparative religion as well. By all accounts — well, the ones I've got hold of, at any rate — she was a very queer fish indeed. A positively brilliant scholar, but a highly eccentric lecturer, and with a disturbing tendency towards the occult. At one time she was on close terms with Gerald Gardner, and she was a sort of posthumous disciple of Aleister Crowley. She seems to have taken most of what Crowley said as gospel. That's hardly the right word, but you know what I mean. I suppose she's just old enough to have met him, but she's have been no more than thirteen or so when he died. It's hardly likely. Anyway, she'd got herself a very odd name at the university, and from what I gather it's as well she retired when she did."

I liked it less and less. I knew no harm of Gardner, but Crowley was something else. Whether or not his "magick" was genuine, he certainly had remarkable mental powers. If Venetia Caracalla was gifted in the same way, and able to influence people's minds, then Penny could be in real danger.

"What about this riddle?" I asked again. "'One of four and twenty-one of six'?"

"Oh, I don't know." Penny sounded bored. "Perhaps it's some magical formula. You belong to the London Library, don't you? Maybe you can check it out there."

Maybe. It didn't sound right, though. Dr Caracalla had allowed three days — and what she meant by that I didn't care to think. She knew very well that today was a Saturday, and that the weekend isn't the best time to go researching in esoteric volumes on the occult. I suspected that the answer was nearer at hand. If Penny was too lethargic to investigate, at least I might be able to do something.

I dropped Penny outside her flat and drove on home, thinking furiously. I might not believe in magic, but it seemed pretty clear that the Caracalla woman did; and whether she had merely exercised some sort of mental force over Penny, or had actually placed a curse upon her, the conclusion was inescapable: the woman was dangerous. But if it was a curse, now — what form did it take? I was at a loss. All I could do was to review the events of the past week, and to ponder on that infernal riddle.

It seemed reasonable to suppose that Penny's nightmares and her sense of being followed amounted only to a sort of mental or psychical warning. Caracalla had not had any direct contact with Penny since the radio interview — not until the phone call that morning — so if there was a curse, then it was implicit in that riddle: "one of four and twenty-one of six".

Three days, she'd said, and that was a threat if ever I'd heard one.

"One of four and twenty-one of six." It all came back to the problem of *Sorcerous*: first you had to identify the clues and then decide how to solve them.

An idea suddenly occurred to me, and I reached for the telephone. Penny was slow in answering, and her voice betrayed that same distressing lethargy that I'd hoped to shake out of her over lunch. Whatever had caused that, though, I mustn't let it affect me. There were two questions to be asked.

"Listen, dear. It quite slipped my mind earlier, but perhaps you'll tell me now: while we were out, did you feel at all that we were being followed?"

"Mm? Oh, I don't know. Perhaps... Roy, why did you call now? I feel so blessed tired, all I want to do is sleep."

"In a minute, Penny. Can you be more specific? What do you mean by 'perhaps'?"

"Well, after all, a dog isn't exactly an unusual thing to see in the streets of London, is it? And as for — no! It's just silly."

I'd never known her in such a mood.

"What's silly, Penny?"

"Oh, the noise in the car. I mean, you don't expect any car but a brand new one to be entirely free of odd sounds, so of course the snuffling noise I heard must have come from the engine. Your VW does have its engine at the back, doesn't it? I mean, the sound can't actually have come from the seat behind us — "

I had to take a moment or two to digest this. It was true that my car was a rear-engine model, but all the same I hadn't heard anything like a "snuffling noise". That's the sort of sound you'd expect from a —

"Penny," I said, "have you got your copy of the book by you? *Sorcerous*, I mean. Only I've had a thought about that riddle."

"Oh, that. Yes, I've got the book here. Why?"

"Turn to Chapter Four, and tell me what the first word is. Then look at Chapter Six and read out the twenty-first word."

After an infuriating pause and a yawn, came the answer: the words were "that" and "witch".

"That which?" Or could it be a pun — "that witch"?

Perhaps, but what the devil did it mean.

"All right, love. Just one more try, and then I'll let you sleep. Look up the first word on the fourth page, and the twenty-first word on the sixth page."

That was no better. It produced "table better".

I said goodbye, and left Penny to her drowsiness.

There might be wordplay involved, but somehow I didn't think so. "That witch" certainly sounded appropriate, but it was only a pun, after all, and it could hardly be construed as a curse or a warning. As for "table better" ...

No, I was sure I was on the wrong track. Perhaps it was a mathematical puzzle. "One of four" seemed straightforward enough, but what was I to make of "twenty-one of six"?

Or could it be connected with astronomy? Or astrology? The possibilities and ideas kept revolving in my brain until I felt almost as exhausted as Penny had sounded. Maybe Dr Caracalla's connection with Aleister Crowley might provide a lead. I just didn't know, and I found myself wishing all sorts of perdition on the woman's head.

Late Saturday afternoon. It was a hell of a time to be engaged in this sort of puzzle! Penny's suggestion of the London Library would have been sensible at any other time... And Dr Caracalla had specifically allowed three days!

I sat up very late that night, but made no progress, and it won't surprise you that I overslept the next day, so that it was nearly noon when I phoned Penny and invited myself over to her flat.

She looked no better than she had the day before, but at least something had shaken her out of her lethargy. Something that had started the previous evening, when she'd realised that she was out of milk, and had gone out to a shop in the Mile End Road to buy a bottle. The familiar feeling of being followed, even accompanied, was still with her, but she'd managed to persuade herself that it was purely subjective, so you can imagine her shock when the shop-keeper started to say, "I'm sorry, lady, but you can't bring that — " and then looked around in bewilderment, as if for something he'd seen a moment ago that wasn't there any longer.

An when she got back to the block of flats, it was to be greeted by an irate neighbour, who tartly reminded her that tenants were specifically forbidden to keep pets of any kind, let alone a great grey —

Penny fled upstairs to the first floor, where she flung herself into her own flat, locked and bolted the door, and collapsed in tears, unable to sleep or to stay fully awake, and hearing every little sound as something hostile.

Whatever had been in my mind when I'd arrived at the flat was now quite forgotten. Penny was in no state to be left alone, and at least my presence must give her some sort of reassurance. While she slept, fitfully, on the sitting-room couch, I busied myself in re-reading *Sorcerous*, searching for clues to the riddle. It all seemed to come back to that book, you see.

I took the cauldron out of its glass case and studied it thoroughly, but its sinister beauty now seemed more sinister than beautiful. There was something decidedly unpleasant about the stylised human heads moulded on the outside of the bowl, and as for the cult scenes depicted on the inside — no, I couldn't take to the thing at all.

Penny continued to sleep, and it became clear that the best thing I could do was to stay with her overnight. In the morning I should have to decide whether to go in to work, of course, but that decision could wait until then.

She woke up at about eight in the evening, making incoherent little protesting sounds, but even then she didn't seem to be fully conscious. It was as if she was under sedation. She soon fell asleep again, while I carried on trying to make sense of the riddle. "One of four and twenty-one of six... "

Eventually, of course, I dozed off as well, in the big armchair where I was sitting.

I decided for the moment just to let things ride. Half a dozen times I was awoken by inarticulate sounds from the couch, but I went over and held Penny's hand until she fell asleep again. Besides, the light was still on, and that seemed to comfort her.

Until the last, my own sleep was very shallow, so I was surprised to find myself being shaken into wakefulness shortly before seven o'clock — shaken by Penny, and a smiling Penny at that, though the smile was rather thin.

All she would say as first was "Thanks," and "Let's have a cup of coffee."

Over coffee and biscuits she opened up a bit. "I must have had a pretty rotten night," she said, "and so must you, you poor dear. Still, I'm more than grateful to you for staying. It's all right now, though. I can feel it. Whether the curse or whatever worked itself out in my dreams, or whether — well, I don't know, but for the first time in over a week I feel free. It's a wonderful sensation."

I didn't ask her about the dreams. I hoped in any case that she'd no memory of them. They must have been pretty foul, you know. But if she felt relieved of a burden, so did I, though where she simply accepted it, I couldn't help wondering ...

I looked down at my rumpled clothes and felt my stubbly chin. Penny leaned over and stroked my cheek, and her delighted smile gave way to a look of concern. "What have I got you into?" she said. "You'll have to rush home and change, and then go on to work. Oh, well. If you're a bit late, you can say that you were up all night looking after your sick aunt. What's the time? Oh! Seven-fifteen. Let's see what the local news has to say."

She switched on the radio, and tuned it in to one of the local stations just in time to catch the news summary. Nothing of immediate importance there, except for traffic conditions on the A11, but we were suddenly riveted by the news flash that followed the traffic bulletin. At last, it seemed, the whole beastly business really was over:

"Police report that the body of a middle-aged woman was found about half an hour ago in Rosslyn Hill, Hampstead, apparently the victim of a hit-and-run motor accident. The body has been identified as that of a Dr Venetia Caracalla of Flask Walk, Hampstead... "

Well! So much for my half-formed notions of going to Hampstead to confront the woman, to tell her what Penny was suffering. Just as well. I could imagine what sort of reception I'd have got: "I know precisely what your aunt is going through, Mr Plummer, and it's no more than she deserves. 'As ye sow, so shall ye reap.' But if Mrs Carter has her pride, Mr Plummer, you may tell her that I also have mine. I have allowed her three days in which to give me the cauldron. She may consider herself very fortunate. That is all I have to say."

Yes, I could imagine it all, even down to the unctuous Biblical quotation. But the affair was over now, thank God. All over.

As it happened, I wasn't late for work — which was fortunate, because I found myself exceptionally busy that day. It wasn't until nearly half-past seven that I was able to phone Penny, but all was well enough with her. She'd managed to struggle through a day at the hospital, but had given way to overwhelming tiredness when she got home. Now, after a couple of hours' sleep, she felt fine.

So it really did seem that it was all over. And yet — There was something scratching at the back of my mind, warning me not to be complacent. Something to do with the fact that we still hadn't managed to solve the riddle. I began to feel uneasy again. Of course, it all came down to hypnotism or something of that sort — but just suppose there really *was* a curse... Was there any reason why its working out should be cancelled by the death of its instigator? None that I knew of.

Meanwhile, unfortunately, there was too much work to be done for the office to allow me to penetrate the mystery of "one of four and twenty-one of six".

I was still uneasy the next morning, and by ten-thirty I could stand it no longer. Ten-thirty — and that phone call from the Caracalla woman had come through at ten-fifty on Saturday, just three days ago.

"You have three days," she'd said.

I can't remember what excuse I made as I rushed out of the office and down to the car-park. Of course I wouldn't be able to make it in to Bow in twenty minutes, but at least I could *try*...

I got to Coborn Street just on eleven, and the police were ahead of me, gathered around that hole in the pavement, where the telephone people were working on the cables. If any of the workmen had been by the hole at the time, the tragedy might never have happened, but they had left it temporarily, and for a moment the street had been empty.

There was one witness: that same neighbour who had laid down the law to Penny about pets in the flat. She had happened to glance out into the street, as she sometimes did (evidently she was that type), and had seen Penny, standing on the pavement, with her back to the hole. She was staring, horrified, at something in front of her, below the level of her own eyes – something that the neighbour couldn't see. Then she suddenly threw up her arms, as if to protect her face, and staggered backwards, knocking over the flimsy barrier and falling straight into the deep hole.

She was impaled instantly on a thin pole or pipe that was sticking up about two feet above the ground.

Naturally, I was called at the inquest. After all, it must have seemed pretty odd that I should turn up so quickly after my aunt's death when I should still have been at work in Snaresbrook. All I could say was that Penny had appeared to have a kind of persecution complex over the previous ten days or so, and that it seemed to be connected in some way with the cauldron. I made no mention of Venetia Caracalla, but even my reference to the cauldron caused the coroner to tighten his lips and frown.

The verdict, as you might expect, was "misadventure". Mind you, if I hadn't been able to prove that I'd been at my office until half-past ten that morning, I fancy there'd have been more directed at me than the few distinctly funny looks I got as I left the court.

But there was more, of course, and it was connected with the cauldron.

Before, I might have been able to dismiss Penny's troubles as subjective, but now —

The autopsy had revealed that when Penny's body was brought into the operating-room there was no heart within. Some ghoul, it was thought, had removed it through the wound caused by the pole that killed her. When or why, though, no one could say, and of course nothing was proved.

That was horrible enough, but you must also consider what the police found when they broke in to Penny's flat. A disgusting practical joke, they said, and there was even some talk that it had been perpetrated by Penny herself. After all, she worked at a big hospital, and she had been acting very strangely of late. The blood group matched hers, but type O is one of the commonest, so that proves nothing.

It was a human heart, fresh, lying inside that sinister silver bowl, itself still locked in the glass case.

Roy's hands were still shaking a little as he re-lit his cigar. "Get another round in, someone," he said, with an attempt at calmness. "I think we could all do with a drink."

While I saw to this, George was musing, pulling at his moustache. "Caracalla," he said at last. "Was it her real name?"

Roy gave a sour smile. "Not in the sense you mean." He said. "I found out that she'd changed her name by deed poll when she was twenty-three. The name she was born with was Woolf. Suggestive, eh?"

"And Caracalla," said George, "was perhaps the most vicious and debauched of the Emperors of Rome. I find that suggestive too,"

"What about the riddle?" I asked. "Did you ever solve it?"

"I did," said Roy. "And it's what convinces me that there was more to the case than just paranoia. The riddle does refer to a book, but not the one I was thinking of. 'One of four' is the first of the four Gospels, and 'twenty-one of six', of course, is the twenty-first verse of the sixth chapter."

The pause that followed was broken by a sudden comprehending exclamation from George: "Oh, my *hat*! A joke!" More soberly, he added, "A wicked joke."

Roy nodded, and said bitterly, "I told you, didn't I, that I could imagine that woman quoting from the Bible for her own purposes?"

"The Gospel according to Matthew, chapter six, verse twenty-one. It reads: 'For where your treasure is, there will your heart be also.'"

Afterword

H R Wakefield, Brian Lumley, Ron Weighell and Christopher Fowler are among those who have written variants on "Casting the Runes", so I knew I'd be in good company. I wondered what might happen if the black magician's curse *wasn't* thwarted at the last minute.

The idea for this one came while I was reading Ron Weighell's story "An Empty House". Part way through I thought: I know how this is going to end — please let me be wrong! And I *was* wrong, which meant that I enjoyed Ron Weighell's story to the full *and* had an idea that I could use myself.

The mechanism of the story was suggested by Bamber Gascoigne's account of the phenomenon that Kit Williams had unintentionally produced with *Masquerade*. The golden hare actually was won, fair and square, by someone who hadn't solved all the elegant clues in the book, while the two people who had solved them were just waiting for confirmation before digging. Fortunately they weren't vindictive, unlike Venetia Caracalla.

THE BREAKDOWN

"It was only three nights ago," said Alison Myers, with a rather charmingly shy earnestness. "Richard happened to see Mr Cobbett yesterday and mentioned it to him."

"That's right," said George Cobbett. "I thought you might be interested in hearing the story, and as young Richard wasn't able to come along this evening, I asked Miss Myers here to tell it to us." He pulled a face. "She might be more coherent than he was. In any case, I think you'll find it's rather up your street."

The girl was clearly making an effort to appear composed, but her slender feet were fidgeting nervously under the table. "I'll do my best," she said. "And, please, call me Alison."

"Thank you," I said. "Now, we're all friends, so there's no need to be formal with the old man here. Address him as George. That'll put him in his place. Please tell the story from the beginning and in your own way. Oh — and if you'll forgive a jealous question, who is Richard? Your fiancé?"

She smiled gratefully and nodded. "That's right. He lives in Romford, and that evening he'd picked me up from my home in Epping and taken me to a party somewhere in the country, not far from his own home — about ten miles, I suppose. It's fairly near Ongar and fairly near Brentwood. The village is called Navestock, and it seems to be all spread out and very rural. You probably know it a lot better than I do, because it's only a few months since my family moved down from Sheffield.

"The party was a good one, very good fun, and we met a lot of nice people. There was music, and food and drink, and dancing — all that you'd expect; but the party itself isn't important. What's important is that it found us as we came away right in the depths of the countryside at about half-past two in the morning. Oh, I know it's very close to London — it can't be more than about fifteen miles to the City — but somehow it seemed far more cut off than anywhere I could remember being before. You see, I've been used to cities, or to great open stretches of moorland and mountains. This area around Navestock isn't like that at all: it's all hedges and trees. The roads twist and wind until you don't know where you are. It's like being in a maze. You can't see more than a couple of hundred yards, and whatever is around the next corner, you know that it'll be just the same — hedges and trees. You feel that you're miles and miles from the nearest town, and that you could go wandering along those narrow roads forever and always take the wrong turning, so that you'd never get back to home and safety.

"Maybe I'm making rather much of this, but I want you to see the place as I saw it. I'm familiar with the open country, but this was all so closed-in that it seemed just a touch spooky. I didn't mind it on the drive in to the party because it was all so fresh after a day working in Town, but in the small hours I found it — well — oppressive. I could fancy that a little voice was telling me that I was trapped, that we'd be there for ever, just driving on and on.

"That's not what happened, of course. We'd only been gone about ten minutes from the party when the engine of the car began to knock. I felt a sort of tight feeling in my stomach, and I'm sure that I actually said to Richard (though he denies it), 'Oh, Lord! We *are* going to be here for ever.'

"He just said, 'She's done this before, love. Don't worry. She'll get us back to Romford at least, and you can spend the night at my parents' place.'

"He's a good driver, but honestly he doesn't know much more about cars than I do. That car certainly didn't sound to me as if it would get us even as far as the next turning. I wasn't frightened, but after the high spirits of the party I suddenly felt very low.

"Sure enough, just around the next bend in the road — it was to the right, I remember — the noise in the engine became a rapid drumming, and even Richard realised that things were not good. He stopped the car and hastily turned off the ignition. In the sudden silence, I discovered that I'd been quite unconsciously holding my breath. Even the feeling that we were caught in a labyrinth couldn't shut out a sensation of immense relief.

"It didn't last long. Richard gave the engine ten minutes or so to cool down, and then he tried the ignition again. Nothing. Absolutely nothing. And at last he began to lose his patience. I won't tell you exactly what he said, but part of it was apology to me, and part of it was that he would have to call out the A.A.

"It's silly, I know, but I quite clearly remember thinking, 'Surely they don't have telephones out here?'

"Richard said, 'Now, let's make sure just where we are. If I haven't made a wrong turning — ' (If? My heart sank. I hadn't realised that he'd never driven along these roads in the dark before.) ' — we should be about at Horseman Side. I think there's a pub along here where there might be a public call box.'

"What could I say? I was a total stranger to the area, and all I could do was to trust him. I was terribly afraid that he would tell me to stay in the car while he went off to find a phone. He didn't, though, and I blessed him for it. I don't think I could have borne to be alone in that weird place just then. We locked the car and started to walk along the road in the direction we'd been heading in.

"Thank heaven it was a fine night. The sky was quite clear; the stars were bright and hard, and there was an icily light half-moon low down. It was a little cold, as you'd expect in late September, but not bitterly so, and our raincoats were enough to keep us comfortably warm. The road was dry and firm, and there was no traffic at all. You'd think that we might at least have heard the odd late car at a distance, or seen the reflection of headlamps on a nearby road, but there was nothing.

"Nothing, until —

"That road just went on and on, and we could never see more than about twenty yards ahead. They say that a long road has no turning, but it's certainly not so around Navestock. We can't actually have walked much more than a mile and a half, but oh! It seemed so much further. More than once I thought of taking my party shoes off and walking barefoot, but the road was so hard and cold that I couldn't bring myself to do it. At last I said that I really must stop for a few minutes and rest my feet. And it was then that we heard a car at last. Richard squeezed my hand tightly and said, 'Pray that it's coming this way.'

"I still don't know whether that car was coming our way or not. Certainly we didn't *see* any sign of it, though we heard it quite clearly. I suppose it must have been some lunatic driving without lights on a road parallel to ours, and yet I could swear that as it seemed to pass us I could actually feel the breeze it set up as it rushed along.

"Richard didn't seem to notice anything odd. As the sound stopped, rather abruptly, it seemed to me, he just said, 'No help there. We'd best carry on walking, Ali.'

"No help from that car, maybe, but as we reached the next shallow bend in the road it seemed that fortune was with us after all. Ahead of us, no more than thirty feet away, was the one sort of person we could most have wished to meet. No details were apparent, but the shape was unmistakably and blessedly that of a policeman. He was standing quite still and seemed to be facing in our direction. There was no need to run up to him, even if I'd felt like running. All we had to do was to walk those few yards and explain our problem. He could help us if anyone could.

"He wasn't facing us, though, as we could see when we got nearer, for the moon was pretty well behind us now. He was standing quite still, as I said, and his back was turned towards us. I think that at that moment I began to feel truly uneasy. You see, my shoes were clicking quite sharply on the hard surface of the road, and it seemed to me that this man must have heard and turned to see who on earth could be walking in that lonely place at such an ungodly hour. But the policeman didn't move. Not until Richard came right up close to him and said, 'Excuse me, Constable.'

"Then he turned around, and the moonlight fell full on his face.

"I think I screamed, though Richard says not. I know I felt deathly frightened, and turned away to avoid the sight of that face. Then Richard's arms were around me, and we were both, for a moment, shivering uncontrollably.

"When we looked up again, the policeman had gone.

"There was nothing in his expression to upset one, because he had no expression, but his face was the saddest, most horrible thing I've ever seen. It had no eyes. There were just two holes, black, and circled with crusted blood. That man was dead. He *must* have been. And yet —

"That's really all there is to the story. We ran. I lost the heel of one of my shoes somewhere, but I kept on running, and soon we heard the welcome sound of a car approaching, and saw the gleam of its headlamps. Thank God, it *was* on our road. We flagged it down, and explained our predicament — though you won't be surprised to know that we said nothing about the dead policeman. The driver was a doctor on his way home after a late call, and he gave us a lift to his own house, not very far away, where we could phone the AA. A patrolman came within the hour and fixed the car sufficiently to get us home. And — well — there you are.'

"And here you are," I said. "Thank you for telling us about it, Alison. It must have been quite a testing experience for you."

She shook her head, soberly. "No, I'm very grateful to you for listening. You're the only people I've felt could hear me out without making stupid remarks.

"But now it's your turn. Mr Cobbett — George — " (she gave him a shy smile) "— suggested that you might have some idea of what's behind it all."

Perhaps I had, at that. "I think —" I began.

But George interrupted me: "I'm sure you do, boy, but if you don't mind, I'll take over. I spent some time yesterday evening checking the facts." He turned to Alison. "First of all, young lady, tell me whether you noticed anything particular about the policeman's uniform."

"His uniform? But he had his back to us, as I told you, and it was really too dark to make out any details... Oh! Just a moment. Yes, there was something — about his helmet. You know that the County Police wear those helmets with a crest — Roman-style, rather like the City of London Police? Well, this man's helmet wasn't like that: it was what I'd call the traditional kind of helmet — like the Metropolitan Police wear. You don't suppose he could have been a member of the Met, do you? I mean, we weren't all that far from their patch."

George shook his head. "I don't think so," he said. "You see, up until 1969, when they merged with the Southend Constabulary, the Essex Police did wear the more usual kind of helmet."

He paused to fish his pipe out of his pocket, and I took the opportunity while he filled and lit it to get another round of drinks in.

"There are," he said eventually, "many theories about what ghosts actually are — that's assuming you believe they that they exist, of course. I have my own idea, naturally, and it seems to me that you and your young man have been privileged (not the right word, perhaps, but I can't think of a better one) — privileged to see something very sad, and in its way rather noble.

"Now, what was the date when all this occurred? The 26th — am I right? Very well, then. I'll tell you what Roger and I believe lies behind your experience.

"In the early hours of September the 26th, 1927, two unpleasant characters named Browne and Kennedy went by train from the East End of London to Billericay, where they intended to steal a car. They had their eyes on a particular car, a Riley, that was garaged in the High Street. Fortunately for the owner, they were frightened off by a dog — but that's where good fortune ends. They were still determined to take a vehicle, and they walked through the dark town until they found one that was suitable.

"As it chanced, the one they chose belonged to a doctor. Hmph. Well, that's just coincidence, I'm sure. At any rate, they forced the door of his garage and pushed the car out on to the road. Then they started driving back to London.

"As far as they could, they kept clear of the main roads, avoiding places like Brentwood, where they knew that policemen were stationed during the night. Well, they drove along those back lanes that run between Ongar and Romford, and they must have thought themselves pretty safe – that is, until a police constable saw them approaching and waved his torch, signalling them to stop.

"They didn't stop.

"The policeman – his name was George Gutteridge – did what any conscientious copper would do: he blew his whistle. He must have been gratified when the driver pulled the car over to the side of the road and waited for him to come up to them. As Gutteridge took out his notebook, Browne, the driver, shot him dead.

"Perhaps we're getting inured these days to crimes of violence, but sixty years ago the killing of a police officer on duty was considered a particularly horrible offence – rightly, I think. And this crime had an especially gruesome flavour to it. As the policeman lay dead or dying on the road, Browne got out of the car and shot him at close range through both eyes.

"The usual theory, which I see no reason to dispute, is that he believed in the old superstition that the eyes of a murdered man retain the picture of the last thing he saw before he died. Then again, Browne was known to have a violent hatred of the law... Whatever the cause, the result was the same, and for myself I think that it accounts for what you saw. It's my belief that PC Gutteridge — or a part of him — is still occasionally doing his duty on that lonely country road."

"How awful!" said Alison. She was clearly and understandably fascinated. "But where did you learn all this? And where can I find out about it?"

"Ah, well... If you want to know how the two men were tracked down, arrested and convicted – it was largely through the new science of bullet identification — then there are several books you can turn to. Try *The Encyclopædia of Murder*: your local library should be able to help you."

"That poor man!" she said. "To mean no harm, and yet to terrify people just by your appearance — "

We considered the thought for a moment, and then Alison asked hesitantly, "Should I – do you think that perhaps I ought to have spoken to him? Would it have helped at all?"

George shook his head wearily and rubbed a finger across his bushy eyebrows. "I think not," he said. "You see, if I'm right — and we know so little of these things, after all — then the policeman himself wasn't there, not in any real sense. What you saw, because you chanced to be there at the right time — and perhaps because you're sensitive to these things — was only a fragment of personality, a residuum. You might call it a visible manifestation of shock.

"I'm sorry, but I can't put it more clearly than that. At all events, I'm pretty certain that P.C. Gutteridge himself has gone to wherever he was bound for, and has left nothing more than a reflection in a glass."

A last question occurred to me: "Alison, did you happen to notice the name of the road where your car broke down?"

"No," she said. "I'm sorry, but I didn't see any signposts at all. Oh! Wait – there was something... Yes, of course! When Richard phoned the A.A. that nice doctor had to tell him where their man should come to attend to the car. It was — " Her hand flew up to her mouth as she realised the final macabre touch. "I remember now. It was *Murthering Lane*."

Afterword

The murder of PC George Gutteridge certainly ought to have given rise to a haunting — however you define the word. Once the idea had occurred to me I found it irresistible, though it wasn't until some time later that I learned that some people actually have claimed to have seen Gutteridge's ghost.

The murder took place outside the village of Stapleford Abbots, not far from Navestock. I've taken a minor liberty in siting the apparition near the gruesomely named Murthering Lane.

Since the story was first published, the Essex Police have established a fascinating museum at their headquarters in Chelmsford, which features a display about the murder of PC Gutteridge.

THE POOL

"My night in the Forest," said Mike. "Pour me another whisky, and I'll tell you about it."

"That's better," I said. I topped up his glass and handed the bottle on to George Cobbett, who was firmly settled in my favourite armchair.

Mike Williams had been very reticent about this particular episode. All that I or anyone else knew was that he'd gone walking after "having drink taken", and had woken up to find himself somewhere in the depths of Epping Forest. It was pretty clear, though, even to me, that there was more to it; something had frightened him, and since Mike is an unimaginative and phlegmatic fellow I was curious to hear about.

"You can regard this," he went on, "as a sort of repayment for putting me up for a few days. God knows I needed this break. And fond as I am of the north-east it's good to be home for a while." He paused to light one of the small cigars that he's recently taken to in an effort to give up cigarettes. "I couldn't somehow bring myself to talk about it back in the pub, but now that we're back home — "

"Get on with it," said George, ungraciously.

"You don't change, do you?" said Mike. "Very well, then. It was the night of Miles and Sarah's wedding, back in the late seventies. You'll remember it, Roger; it was while you were still living at Harlow. I'd better be precise, though, for the old man's benefit. The wedding itself was at High Beach, pretty well in the middle of the Forest, and handy for the main road. The reception was at a village hall just outside Waltham Abbey, and after we'd all had time to digest there was a barn-dance.

"You may remember which band it was that played. All I recall is that they were good, and they managed to get just about everybody up dancing — even me, and I'm not much of a dancer. Well, I reckon that I pretty much exhausted my reserves before the evening was half over, and I just sat and chatted with friends for the rest of the time. Chatted and drank, until after the bride and groom had left, and the band played a set of polkas to finish off."

"Most of us went home then," I said. "I got a lift back to Harlow with Jack Simmonds. You went on somewhere else, though, didn't you?"

Mike sighed. "Yes, I did, and I wish that I hadn't. Tony and Vicky Ramsden invited a few of us back to their house for coffee.

It was only a mile or so away, in Waltham Abbey, and we decided to leave our cars at the hall and walk. The night was fine and warm, and we were all in good spirits... Well, you know what Vicky's hospitality is like, as if we hadn't eaten enough that afternoon, and Tony's idea of coffee usually includes alcohol, so the merriment went on well into the small hours, until I finally decided that it was time I made my way home.

"I remember looking at my watch and being mildly astonished to find that it was some time after three in the morning.

"Vicky offered me a doss-down, but for some reason that escapes me now I was determined to go. I still had sense enough to realise that driving was right out of the question, so I decided to walk. After all, it isn't that far to Loughton. The night was still warm, and there was a high three-quarter moon. If I stuck to the main roads, I'd have no trouble at all.

"But I didn't stick to the main roads. My mind was in that dangerous state that I've only experienced a couple of times in my life — pumped up to bursting, with images and ideas leaping about like grasshoppers, all too fast to catch, or even to see clearly. I remember walking out of the town along Honey Lane until the street lamps gave out, and up the hill past the Jewish cemetery. Then I came to a side road — I forget its name — and thought that it would make a handy short-cut. Vaguely, I noticed the trees crowding in, but the moon was still fairly high, and I could see everything pretty well."

Mike paused, to stub out his cigar and to concentrate his thoughts. After an irritating moment he said, very deliberately, "The next thing I remember is meeting an old friend.

"Dick Morton had been at school with me until his family moved down to the west country. After that we'd lost touch with each other, until I went to take my post-grad course at Exeter, when I bumped into him again. I was standing on the steps of the Union building, thinking of nothing in particular, when a voice beside me said, 'I know that face!'

"Dick had married and gone into business in a small way near the city, and he was calling in at the Union that day to see one of the porters about a car that had been advertised in a local paper. Well, the long and the short of it is that we took up out friendship exactly as if there hadn't been a five-year gap. He was a grand fellow. We kept in contact after I'd finished my course, and occasionally I'd go and stay with him and his wife.

"It was a great shock back in seventy-three when I learned that Dick had killed himself.

"And here we were — what? four, five years later — meeting up again in Epping Forest.

"Oh, it was a dream, of course. But I'd dreamed about him before. You see, Dick and Janet weren't good correspondents. She simply hadn't thought to contact me after his death, and I actually found out about it from a notice that his parents had put in our local paper. By that time everything was over — funeral, memorial service, everything. I sent formal condolences to the parents and made a brief phone call to Janet. Then I got thoroughly sloshed at the pub and went home and cried. That night I dreamed about Dick. I dreamed that we were sitting over a pint in the *Rose Tree*, as we'd done so often, and he was explaining to me that it was all a mistake.

"Perhaps — because I'd missed out on the funeral and all the rest of it — perhaps, subconsciously, I had a hope that it really was all a mistake, that Dick wasn't dead, that we'd meet again and pick up our friendship just as before. And yet, you know, all the time I was aware that this was a dream, something to be savoured, because it wouldn't last. Two or three times I met him again, in my dreams, and each time it was the same: a renewing of the old jokes and the old comradeship, while knowing that soon I'd wake up, and Dick would be gone, as he really was gone.

"Tonight was different.

"It was natural, I suppose, that I should encounter him in the Forest, where even my unconscious mind knew that I really was. I could accept that. What jarred was his attitude. Oh, it was friendly, but the cynicism and humour were gone. Instead there was a mystical earnestness that seemed quite out of place. And for the first time he admitted that he was dead.

"No, that's the wrong word, I think. Admission implies reluctance, and there was nothing reluctant in the dreadful conviction with which he talked about his death.

"And mine.

"'It's so easy to bugger things up,' he said. 'Take my word for it, son, and don't use a knife. Death shouldn't mean pain, and knives are painful.' He paused and frowned. 'I suppose gas isn't too bad,' he said at last, 'but it smells so bloody bad. Water — that's the thing. Come on, son. I know just the place. Think of it: no more problems, no more pain — just peace and oblivion.'

"He took my hand in his own thin claw and began to lead me through the trees, dextrously skirting the undergrowth, keeping up a monologue of death. Faster he went, and faster, until I had to beg him to stop.

"'Not much further, son,' he said, and he turned his face to look at me.

"It was then, I think, that I became really afraid. I knew then that whoever — whatever — this creature was, it wasn't my old friend. He was still talking, with a sort of terrible cheerfulness: 'This way, son. It's just along here — ' I tried hard not to listen, to concentrate on anything except that voice — the voice that was so damnably like Dick Morton's. Concentrate on the trees that seemed somehow to make way for us as we slid onwards. Concentrate on the tight grip of that bony hand. Concentrate on the thin face, with its dead eyes.

"The face — yes. It wasn't as thin as it ought to be, but somehow swollen, almost bloated. And the colour —

"I shouted something incoherent, but powerful enough to stop him, so that he let go of my hand and faced me again. There was no expression at all in the eyes, and the features were no more than a mask.

"'What's the matter?' said the voice, but now it didn't even sound much like my friend's.

"'Stop it!' I shouted. 'Dick's gone — he's dead, and you're not him!'

"I swung my right hand wildly at the solemn mask, felt it enter something horribly soft and giving, until it came out the other side and landed with a stinging blow on the trunk of a tree.

"That woke me up, I can tell you.

"I was on my feet, surrounded by thick-growing trees. The sky, what I could see of it, was a dull dark grey. There was no sign of moon or stars, and my hands were both throbbing. It was painful to put the right hand into a pocket and fumble for my lighter. No less painful to light the thing and hold the valve open, but in the light of the little flame I could see that my right hand was black and bloody, the skin broken and the flesh bruised where it had struck the tree.

"Death's messenger had gone with my awakening, thank God, and I expelled a long sigh of relief.

"But if he hadn't been real, then why did my left hand feel so painful? I'd hit nothing with it as far as I knew, touched nothing with it. But pressing deep into the flesh and against the bone there were thin livid marks.

"No, I mustn't think about that. I was sober now, and awake, and I must set about finding a way out of the Forest. For God's sake, I didn't even know where I was!

"Above all, I must resist the temptation to go forward, along the almost invisible path that seemed to open ahead of me. I was still afraid, you see.

"I turned and walked resolutely in the opposite direction, only to stumble almost at once over a root. Steadying myself, I took several deep breaths and looked around me. Behind lay the path that I feared, leading to — well, to nothing wholesome. But as I stood up I felt a sharp pain dart across my head, and a slowly diminishing throb. For a moment I was dizzy, and when I came to, I wasn't sure any longer. Was the path ahead of me or behind? Or did it lead between the trees to the left or right?

"I just couldn't tell, and I felt so weary that I almost didn't care.

"It was hardly a conscious decision to go where the shadows seemed less dark. Unsteadily, I made my way towards the left, hoping to come upon one or other of the roads that lead through the Forest. After a short while I really thought that I'd made it.

"What I actually saw when I emerged from the trees was a deep, wide runnel: a trough with water at the bottom, black and sluggish. There was little scrub on the banks, and no brambles; I was able quite easily to walk to the edge and look down. And in the diffuse grey light I saw death.

"I can't put it more accurately. In that sluggish pool was something that was death. I felt dizzy again, and unspeakably weary. There seemed to be nothing to life that was worth all the pain and the effort. Peace, I thought. Peace and oblivion were here, just below me, and all I had to do was to let myself go. There was no exhilaration, not even relief, but just a longing for rest.

"Peace and oblivion. Something deep in my mind caught hold of that phrase and held me back — I couldn't for the moment think why, but the effort of concentration, I'm convinced, helped to save me. Peace and oblivion. That was what *he* had said — the creature that wasn't Dick Morton. I must fight against it, I told myself. Must fight it. Must.

"But, God, it was such an effort, and my head was throbbing again, and it would be so easy just to let go.

"Straining nerve and muscle, I pulled back from the edge, with painful slowness, unable to take my eyes off those enticing waters. They were deep, deep — with the deepness of eternity.

"Something pulled at my ankles as I backed away, but there were no brambles, and I couldn't bring myself to reach down with my hand. Even when I could no longer see over the lip of the trough, I felt the pull. Physical or whatever it was, I still felt it as I backed away from the pool. I couldn't resist it much longer.

"What rescued me was another tree-root. Unable to look where I was going, I fell sharply backwards over it, driving all the breath out of my body, so that I whooped loudly and painfully, trying to inflate my lungs. The sheer ordinariness of the sensation helped clear my mind, and once I felt recovered I turned and ran.

"God knows how long I ran, but at least I couldn't feel the pull now. I just blundered through the trees, under a steadily lightening sky, until at last, bruised and exhausted, I stumbled on to the main road. The sky was clear now; soon the sun would rise. And I had come out of the Forest not as I'd expected from the west, but from the east.

"Shivering uncontrollably, I sat down by the edge of the road and wept."

Mike's hands were unsteady as he lit a fresh cigar. "That's it," he said. "That's the story. Perhaps you can see why I've not felt able to tell it before."

George nodded soberly. From his withdrawn expression, I guessed that Mike's tale had awakened unwelcome memories in him. In my own mind too something was stirring. At last I muttered an apology and went through to the dining-room, where I spent a few minutes looking for a certain copy of a short-lived county magazine, *This Essex*. Finding it at last, I returned to my friends and opened the magazine at an article, written years before by George Monger — whom I had once, God forgive me, accused of romancing.

"I think you'll find this instructive," I said, and I read aloud: "*Another interesting Epping haunting is at a place known as Suicide Pool.*"

Afterword

The twelve issues of *This Essex* contain a good deal of interest, not least George Monger's article on Essex ghosts. After I asked George whether he'd invented the story he kindly showed me the letter he had received telling him about Suicide Pool. My description follows that given by George's correspondent. The pool is dry now, but it still has an unpleasantly compelling feel about it.

Mike Williams's experience of snapping awake half-way through a long walk home after celebrating with friends was inspired by a similar unintentional exploit of my friend Mick Graves.

This story is dedicated *in memoriam* Robin Ager, who was the real Dick Morton.

I wrote "The Pool" for the Ghost Story Society's first competition. It achieved a respectable place in the top ten, and was subsequently published by Chico Kidd in the first (and so far only) issue of *Picatrix*. The story is consciously influenced by A.N.L. Munby's "The White Sack".

THE CLUES

"Martlets," said Frank Retford in a reminiscent tone. "Heaven knows what's become of it. Long passed out of the family, no doubt."

George Cobbett looked up from his beer and scowled momentarily, but said nothing.

"Martlets?" I prompted.

Frank looked sharply at me for a moment; then his face relaxed. "Ha! Yes. Martlets. Well, it was a long time ago, and I was much younger then — "

"Of course," said George, unhelpfully. "How long ago, though? You're among friends, old man. Pray be precise as to details."

If Frank recognised the quotation he gave no sign of it. "I don't see any reason not to tell you," he said. "It was before the war — the early summer of 1938. Satisfied? Look: get me another G and T, will you, and you shall hear the whole story."

George, who had drawn his pension that day, saw to the drinks, and after an appreciative sip Frank settled down to his narrative.

Martlets (he said) was a house, at a hamlet called Holland Green, a couple of miles out of Newport. That's Newport in Essex, of course; not the place in Monmouthshire. Martlets stood in quite extensive grounds that had been landscaped in the 1790s by Humphrey Repton. The house, which faced west, dated from some fifty years earlier, though Repton had made his mark there as well. It was a solid, square, handsome building of mellow red brick, two and a half storeys high, and five bays by five. The west front was capped by a pediment bearing the arms of the original owner — whose name I never learned. Below this was the portico, with a pediment supported on Ionic columns.

In short, you see, it was a very civilised, very agreeable house. At the time I thought how lucky my friend was to be living there. Now I'm less sure.

His name was Edward Langley. We'd been up at King's together, and although he was reading classics, while mathematics was my subject, we'd found enough in common to ensure that we got on very well. Our backgrounds too had been quite different.

My father was a mechanical engineer, but Langley Senior had been a house master at Felsted School. Beyond that I knew little of my friend's family, so you can imagine that it was something of a surprise for me to receive a letter from him after a hiatus of a couple of years, inviting me to spend a few days with him at Martlets.

The address meant nothing to me, though it suggested something substantial, and I was very curious to know how Langley had come by such a place. I wired back at once to say that I'd be happy to pay him a visit at the beginning of the summer vacation; and so, for a couple of weeks, the matter rested.

Well, I've given you some idea of how the house looked, but it would be very difficult to convey the impression that it gave me as I approached along the drive. You could see it from the main road, looking in the clear sunlight like a Georgian dolls' house — like something not quite real. Then, as you turned in to the long drive, the low wooded hills seemed to rise and hide it. At times you'd catch glimpses or warm brick behind the trees, and at last, just as you thought you'd never reach the house, there it was.

I was enchanted; and more than ever I wondered how such a jewel had fallen into Langley's hands.

I drew the car up before the front door and was almost immediately greeted, in his usual silent fashion, by Langley's manservant, an old acquaintance. I refrained from asking him any questions; he carried discretion to extraordinary lengths, and would only have nodded and smiled indulgently. Fortunately, at that moment Langley himself appeared, and Shepherd picked up my bags and carried them off to whichever part of the house had been assigned to me.

"Luck?" said my friend, as we sat over a glass of port. "I should say so! I'd only heard vaguely of this place during my childhood — the rich relations that everyone dreams of. And then, when the old man died, to find that I was his sole heir — ! Yes, I'd certainly call it luck."

"And who was the old man?" I asked.

"Ha! He was my father's cousin. You needn't offer condolences, because I never knew him — and you can't be more surprised than I was to find myself the master of such a house. As I said, I'd really very little knowledge of it. I never had any contact with the old fellow, and even when my parents died I didn't give a thought to letting him know. He must have found out, though, because when he died about three months ago he left the house to me, as his nearest living male relative."

"Remarkable!" What else could I say? "There were no children?"

"None. He was a widower and an only child. Would you like to see him?"

For a moment I had an unnerving notion that Langley was about to introduce me to a mummified corpse, but he merely produced a leather-framed photograph. My expression as I looked at it amused him.

"Yes," he said. "Not really an old man at all. The picture can't have been taken earlier than 1932, and, as you can see, Paul Vivian was little more than fifty at the time. My father always used to talk of 'the old man', and I rather think that he confused Paul with his father, David Vivian. Now there was an interesting character, if you like."

He showed me another, much older, photograph. The son's face had appeared scholarly, but bland. The father's, however, bore a very intense expression on its gaunt features. It was the face of a man who knew many things, not all of them good. I didn't like the look of it very much, and I said so.

Langley grinned. "Don't think too badly of the old chap," he said. "If he hadn't restricted himself to the one child, I shouldn't be here now, and you wouldn't be enjoying my hospitality. Besides, you know, he seems to have developed quite a pious streak in his old age."

"Oh, I don't know anything actually bad about him, though his son's diary does report that in 1920 he paid an extended visit to Cefalu in Sicily. His host, plainly, was Aleister Crowley himself."

"Well, that's pretty strong stuff," I said, "but after all, Crowley has entertained visitors of all sorts. What of this piety you mention?"

"Oddly enough, it's in a rider to his will, and again I got the information from Paul's diary, in which he quotes a particular verse from the Old Testament. It runs, in part, 'I the Lord, which call thee by name, am the God of Israel.'"

After lunch, Langley proposed a stroll around the nearer part of the grounds, and on such a golden day it seemed a far better prospect than remaining indoors. The disposition of the trees in the park, single and in copses, was exquisite, a fine testimony to

Repton's foresight. They must have taken over a hundred years to reach this state of perfection.

On a low rise, to the south of the house, stood a small folly: a circular Doric temple, apparently built of white marble, and standing no more than eight feet high. I asked Langley about it.

"A funny little thing, isn't it?" he said. "It isn't very old, though — late nineteenth century, I believe. The work of David Vivian's predecessor. And it isn't marble, either, as you'll see if you look more closely."

He was right. What I'd taken for solid stone was actually stucco. The floor, some three feet in diameter, was paved with ordinary house-bricks. Almost inevitably, the architrave at the cardinal points was inscribed with the names of the four winds. It was a pretty little ornament.

As we descended the slope, my eye was caught by something white, partly hidden behind a clump of trees. I pointed to it.

"That's a monumental column," said my friend, "and of all things it commemorates the fall of the Bastille. Some early owner of Martlets must have had romantic republican sympathies."

"Like Wordsworth," I said. "'Bliss was it in that dawn to be alive, but to be young was very heaven.' Bloody revolutions always seem to start among the intellectual middle class. May we look at it?"

"If you like. It's not a very good example, I'm afraid. They tell me that it can't compare with the one at Audley End. Still, there isn't much ornament in these grounds, and I certainly don't intend to get rid of it."

A few minutes' walk took us to the column. Surprisingly, it stood on low ground, almost as if its builder had been ashamed of it — and perhaps rightly so, for it was not a thing of beauty. I wondered what Humphrey Repton could have thought of it. It was a plain Tuscan pillar, set upon a large box-like plinth, and rising to a height of about fifty feet. At the top was something that might have been intended for an urn, but it was so weathered and broken that I couldn't be sure. The whole structure had worn rather badly, and at close quarters it quite lost the appearance of integrity that distance had lent it. Even the inscriptions on the base were barely legible. On the eastern side, facing the house, was what I took to be the date of its erection: 'mdccixc'. On the far side appeared some letters that might have formed part of a longer inscription, though whether they too indicated a date, I couldn't tell. I could just make out 'D..T.xxxii..xxiv'.

"Don't you think," I said, "that the stone on this side seems to be much more worn than elsewhere — almost excessively so?"

"Yes, I'd noticed that. It's quite artistic, isn't it? Well, that's another riddle, to set beside old David Vivian's conversion."

And for the moment we left it at that.

I shan't weary you with a description of the interior of the house, except to say that its beauty gave the impression of being faded. It seemed, like the park, to have been rather neglected in recent years. Langley must have divined my thoughts.

"That's the problem," he said, wryly. "Money. Isn't it always so? I have the house and grounds, and I mean to keep them intact. Just how I'm to do it, though, I don't know. There was precious little money came with them. And don't go thinking that Cousin Paul gambled or drank it all away, because as far as I can discover, he and his wife lived a life of shabby-genteel seclusion."

"What about his father?" I asked.

"Ah! There you put your finger on it. Yes, old David certainly had money when he died, but quite what he did with it, no one seems to know."

Something tugged at my memory for an instant, but it was gone before I could identify it. While we were having dinner, however, it came to me again.

"That Biblical quotation in old David's will," I said. "How did it go again?"

Langley repeated it, and added: "But it seems that the will didn't give the text in full. It only specified the chapter and verse."

"Better yet! Well, my Biblical knowledge is a trifle rusty, but I rather think that both you and Paul Vivian have fallen into a trap. David Vivian hadn't suddenly turned evangelist; on the contrary, he was trying to convey a very material message.

"If you've got Paul's diary to hand, look up the exact reference, and we'll see."

Langley went into the library, and presently emerged with what was evidently one of a number of mock-leather-bound volumes.

"Here we are," he said. "September 1924." He looked through the pages for a moment; then: "Ah, yes. Isaiah, chapter 45, verse 3. Just a minute and I'll look it up."

He'd had the sense to bring a pocket Bible from the library, and only seconds passed before he gave a low whistle and said, "By Jove, you may be right after all! Listen to this: 'And I will give thee the treasures of darkness, and hidden riches of secret places, that thou mayest know that I, the Lord, which call thee by name, am the God of Israel.'"

"Just so. I think we can ignore the last part. It seems pretty clear that David was telling his son that the money was hidden, and that Paul would have to find it."

"Curiouser and curiouser. I wonder if it was some sort of joke."

"I don't know, and I'm not sure that I like the old fellow any more for it."

"Where on earth do you suppose it could be hidden?"

But I could make no answer to that, and it wasn't until the following day that one became apparent.

We were part-way through a good, solid breakfast, when Langley suddenly and loudly clapped his hands together and exclaimed, "By Jove! The picture! I wonder — "

"Which picture?" I asked, thinking of the various portraits and landscapes that hung on the walls of Martlets.

"Oh, it's a rather odd and garish thing — a symbolic portrait of Britannia, if you please! Cousin Paul evidently didn't think much of it, for it was tucked away in an attic when I came to the house. I respected his judgement and left it there. But as I remember, there is an inscription on it that mentions riches and treasure."

The attic proved to be the usual country-house lumber-room, full of assorted bric-à-brac that I'd have loved to spend a day sorting through. Against one wall was a stack of paintings and prints. Langley sorted through them, and pulled out one of the largest. He set it in the light, by the window, and waited rather nervously for my opinion.

The painting was certainly an oddity, though I couldn't agree with his use of the word "garish". At first sight, the representation of Britannia was conventional enough. The lady appeared much as she's depicted on the back of a penny-piece. A real penny, I mean; not the nasty little things we have these days. She sat facing the spectator's right, her left hand holding a trident, and her right resting on a burnished shield — which reminded me, incongruously, of the wheel of a bath-chair.

Not all was conventional, though. Despite the stern Grecian helmet, the flowing Grecian robes managed to reveal a good amount of a very well-shaped figure. The pale, sad-eyed face wasn't shown in profile, but was turned to look directly at us. For no apparent reason, I thought of Shakespeare's Cordelia. Stranger yet, lying on the ground beside the shield was a copy of *Whitaker's Almanack*; but the date on its cover was concealed by a tuft of grass. Behind the rod of the trident, partly hidden by it, a lighthouse reared up from the sea, while high on a cliff to the left was an imprecise daub of white — perhaps a building of some kind, and one that looked just a little bit familiar. Strangest of all, there were letters, written in a distorted fashion upon the grass before the shield, and reflected in it.

That's what I saw in my first, cursory look. Before investigating these individual features more closely, however, I made a comprehensive study of the painting. The whole was no less curious than its parts.

"Langley," I said, "I'm no expert, but it looks to me as if someone highly talented has imitated the style of Harry Clarke."

"What — the illustrator?"

"Yes. He did work in other mediums — I'm sure I remember hearing of some impressive stained glass — but he's best known for his black and white illustrations to Poe. I've never heard of his working in oils, and I'm pretty sure that he didn't paint this, but the shape of the figure and the lines of the drapery look right, and the face is very much like the Marchesa in his picture for — what was it? — 'The Assignation'."

"How very curious! You don't think this is by Clarke, then?"

"I doubt it. For one thing, look at the colouring of the face. No, I think it's rather too late to be his work. I'd say that it dates from shortly after the Great War."

My friend was silent while he digested the possibilities. At last he said, "Could it be just another device? I mean, to attract someone's attention to the thing and to its strange details? For instance, the inscription in the lower right-hand corner — there! It's just about where you'd expect to find a signature."

The writing, enclosed in a cartouche, was very small and very fine, in imitation of late eighteenth century script. It read: "Length of Days is in her right hand; and in her left hand Riches and Treasure. PRO. iii:xvi."

"Surely," said Langley, "it's just a patriotic metaphor: Britannia as the symbol of a benevolent Empire, offering health and wealth to her subjects. A very conventional idea."

"You're thinking too conventionally yourself," I said. "What do you make of that thing on the cliff-top there, eh? Doesn't it look just a little like your miniature Temple of the Winds?"

"By Jove, it does! What do you suppose it means?"

"I'm not sure," I said. "Just let me think for a moment."

It actually took me several minutes to reach a decision, but Langley remained silent throughout. At last I looked into his questioning face and said, "Please understand that I've no complete answers, and I'm at a loss as to where any treasure might actually be concealed. However, the temple, if my reasoning isn't faulty, is only there as a pointer — an indication that the picture does contain the information you need. I said that you were thinking too conventionally; it might have been more accurate to say that you weren't being bold enough. Look at the object near the right hand."

There was a brief silence, and then: "You're right, by Jove! That almanack is a fair candidate for 'length of days', isn't it?"

"Quite so — but that's the easy part. What about 'riches and treasure'?"

"Hm. Ha! Yes, of course!" He actually grabbed my sleeve in his excitement. "Look near the other hand, Retford — look at that lighthouse, and see whether it doesn't remind you of something!"

Rather sceptically, I did as I was told; then, suddenly, I realised.

"Good Lord, that's it! What's the time, Langley? Will there still be light enough this evening to go and have a look at that mysterious inscription, or do we have to wait until the morning?"

What we had quite reasonably taken to represent a lighthouse was actually an accurate depiction, as it must have looked when it was new, of the Bastille column in the grounds of Martlets. It didn't take much imagination to connect this fact with the inscription on the western side of the great square plinth — the inscription that seemed to have been so artistically worn away.

To my friend's impatient regret, it really was too dark by then to make our researches. I tried to take his mind off the matter by getting him to show me properly around the library, but my efforts weren't wholly successful. It was painfully clear that the collection had been sadly depleted. In all probability, Cousin Paul had been obliged to sell off the rarer and more interesting volumes in order to keep the house and grounds in good repair. Certainly there was little there to detain a scholar, and nothing at all that might have related to old David Vivian's bizarre character.

Well, if our surmises were correct, and if we hadn't been somehow beaten to it, Langley should at least have the chance to keep his beloved Martlets in proper style.

By the morning the weather had changed, and there was a grey drizzle from low-hanging leaden clouds. We weren't to be put off, though. Manfully, we made our way through the sodden park to the column, where I insisted that we first examine the carved date on the nearest side of the plinth. That seemed to be perfectly in order, however, and after a few minutes we turned our attention to the opposite face.

Here matters were less certain. I was struck again by the apparent excess of the weathering it had undergone, and at last became convinced of what I had merely suspected before. The stone had been artificially eroded, to make the inscription seem much older than it was. Langley declared that he could see the marks of a chisel, but I think he was letting his imagination get the better of him. At any rate, I was sure that some of the deeper hollows had been skilfully worn down, to make it seem that letters had existed where in fact there had been none.

"Our only certainty," I said, when we were back in the house, "lies in what we can actually see there: that partial inscription. Let's see if we can reconstruct it."

"Right. Here — I've written it out: 'D..T.xxxii..xxiv' What do you make of it?" Langley seemed happy to leave this side of things to me.

"Well, first of all, let's assume that David Vivian was responsible for the inscription, since we've already concluded that it's much more recent than the column itself. Now, David seems to have been fond of quoting Holy Scripture for his own purposes, so it's reasonable to infer that he's directing us towards a verse from the Bible."

"By Jove, you make it sound as if the old fellow were here with us!"

It wasn't a thought that appealed to me. I continued: "On previous experience, I'd say that we should look for a book in the Old Testament, and if that's so, then surely 'D..T' can only be 'DEUT'."

"Deuteronomy! Then it must be chapter 32, verse 24."

"All right. Let's look it up."

What we found was no at all encouraging. "They shall be burnt with hunger and devoured with burning heat, and with bitter destruction. I will also send the teeth of beasts upon them, with the poison of serpents of the dust."

"It's a joke!" said Langley, angrily. "Damn the man!"

I calmed him down as well as I could, and pointed to his copy of the inscription. "No, we've missed something here. Look: there's too wide a gap between 'xxxii' and 'xxiv'. There ought to be another figure in there. The question is, whether it belongs to the first or the second number."

"Then it could be almost anything – we could search for ages!"

"Hardly. In fact, there are only two possibilities. It's either 'xxxiii.xxiv', or it's 'xxxii.xxxiv'."

Eagerly, he looked up chapter 33, to find that the twenty-fourth verse refers to the blessing of Asher. So our first possibility was wrong. Logically, the second had to be right.

It was. This is what we read: "Is not this laid up in store with me, and sealed up among my treasures?"

"Laid up in store with me... " I didn't like the sound of that.

Langley too was rather startled. "Good heavens! Do you think the old fellow had it buried with him?'

"It looks very much like it, in which case our search comes to an end."

"I'm damned if it does! He couldn't leave clues like that and not expect his heirs to follow them."

Perhaps he was right. Perhaps that was what David Vivian intended. I still wasn't easy about it, though. I remembered that first verse we had consulted: "They shall be burnt with hunger and devoured with burning heat... " I wondered if it had been meant as a warning.

"The first thing to do," Langley was saying, "is to find out just *where* he was buried."

A thought occurred to me. "Before we do that," I said, "I want to have another look at that painting. There's something we've forgotten — those letters reflected in the shield."

"Good idea. They may give us a lead."

The letters really were most peculiar. Whoever the artist had been, Clarke or another, he'd painted them with enormous skill.

They were made to appear as if cut out from cloth and laid upside-down on the ground to form a circle. They appeared distorted, because we saw them from a low angle and close to. "Anamorphic" is the word, I think. But because they were laid out in reverse, the letters were reflected in the shield the right way round, appearing as a regular circle around its inner edge. They were in groups of six; and, clockwise from the top, they read thus: "pusoba ligivo geecce munobn inonte mulamn isoere".

"Hell!" said Langley, and his expression summed up my own thought. This was evidently a code or cipher, and it looked to be well beyond my own capacity to unravel.

"Shall we see what we can make of it?" I suggested, rather half-heartedly.

But before my friend could answer Shepherd arrived, carrying a telegram. To my surprise, he silently handed it to me. Its content pushed thoughts of treasure-hunting to the back of my mind.

"My mother's badly hurt," I said. "She stepped off the pavement in front of a car. Look, Langley, I'm terribly sorry, but I really must go."

He was instantly solicitous. "Of course you must. Do keep me informed of events, and — er — give her my very best regards."

"Thanks. I'll do that. And if you get the chance, see whether you can make something of that code."

Thank heaven, my mother's condition wasn't nearly as bad as the telegram had led me to expect. She'd broken her left arm, and was suffering from several nasty bruises, but she was a tough lady, and when I saw her at the hospital in Norwich I was left in no doubt that she intended to make a full and rapid recovery. Still, I felt obliged to stay nearby for a week before turning my mind again to Martlets and its secrets.

Just before the end of the week came another telegram. This time it was Langley who needed my attention, though Shepherd, who had sent the message, refused to go into details, except to say that his master was ill. I began to wonder how I would come out of all this myself.

My mother, who knew Langley slightly and liked him, was recovered enough to urge me to leave her and attend to my friend. "Wish him well for me," she said. I nodded, kissed her, and left.

Shepherd had evidently been keeping watch for me at Martlets. His habitual composure, I could see, had been shaken, almost enough to make him garrulous. If I hadn't been concerned for my friend, I might have taken a slightly malicious pleasure in seeing him so put out.

"Do you know what's the matter?" I asked.

"Indeed I do, sir," he said. "But I must leave it to Mr Langley to tell you. This way, sir, if you please."

We had barely reached the door of the smoking-room before a hoarse voice called out: "Shepherd! Is that you, man?"

"Yes, sir; and Mr Retford has arrived."

There was what I can only call a groan of relief, and the voice, rather stronger now, said, "Thank God! Come in, both of you — come in!"

Langley was a distressing sight. He lay stretched out upon the *chaise longue*, swathed in a blanket and shivering, slightly but continuously.

"God!" he said. "I'm glad to see you, old man — by Jove, I am!"

I couldn't doubt it, and I said so. "Is this to do with — well, with old Cousin David?" I asked.

"Yes, it is. And you needn't worry about mentioning our treasure-hunt in front of Shepherd. He knows all about it now. And I'm not sure, but I think he may have saved my life."

I looked at Langley's servant with a new respect, but he had relapsed into his usual imperturbability, and his face was blank.

"Go on," I said.

"Oh, well. I'd better tell it from the beginning. Don't rush me, though. I really have had a nasty experience. There don't seem to be any bones broken, but I'm rather cut about and bruised, and I feel quite infernally hot and feverish. Maybe I caught some infection when I was down — down there. I don't know. This perfect summer weather doesn't help, but Shepherd keeps me supplied with cool drinks. Besides, I'm not sure it's an entirely physical thing. Oh, I'll get over it in time; only for God's sake just hear me out, and please stay on for a while, if you can. It's company I need more than anything else."

"I don't think there'll be any difficulty about that," I said. "My mother's well on the way to recovery — "

"Oh, Lord! Your poor mother! Are you sure she'll be all right?"

"Yes, yes. Don't worry." In spite of his injunction, I felt strongly inclined to push him into telling his story. Fortunately, there was no need.

"Good. Well, you'll remember that when you left you suggested that I should try to find out where old David Vivian was buried. I tried, old man, but with no success. There was no record of his burial in the parish registers, and of course there isn't a chapel here at the house. Then, when it seemed that I'd come up against a brick wall, I thought of looking again at Cousin Paul's diary.

"At first I thought I'd just reached another dead end, because all that Paul says of his father's interment is: 'Arrangements proved satisfactory. Legal quibbles are resolved, and he is buried where he wished to be.'

"'Where he wished to be...' Yes, but where was that?

"Perhaps there was a clue in that phrase 'legal quibbles'. If the old fellow had chosen to be interred in a churchyard or cemetery, then surely there shouldn't be any problems with the law! There might be some with the church, but... No, I just couldn't believe that he'd choose a Christian burial. All the evidence we have, though it's scant enough, to be sure, suggests that he wasn't a Christian.

"So where did that leave us?

"I discounted the notion that he'd chosen to rest at Cefalu, or wherever the Great Beast had moved on to from there. Paul recorded just the one visit to Sicily, and there's no hint that his father had any lasting correspondence with Crowley. In fact, the more I thought about it, the more likely it seemed that David Vivian would have been buried here at Martlets.

"Of course, if we'd been able to decipher the letters on that wretched painting, we might have had some sort of confirmation, but I'm afraid that any message there is lost on me.

"I don't suppose you've been able to make anything of it, Retford? No, I thought not.

"Well, if my surmise was correct, that still left me with a pretty large area to search. The grave could have been in the house, or in the park somewhere. I just didn't know. On the fourth day I went to bed feeling thoroughly exhausted, and too frustrated to sleep. My mind turned the matter over and over again, until finally I drifted off. And when I awoke, I had the answer.

"As I saw it, everything pointed towards the Bastille column. There was the depiction of it in the painting, masquerading as a lighthouse. You yourself put me on to the fact that column was indicated by that phrase in the inscription: ' — in her left hand

Riches and Treasure'. I actually laughed when I remembered how I'd thought that the text was just a bit of jingoism — 'Britannia rules the waves' and all that. Now I knew better, and I was a step further ahead than poor Cousin Paul. The painting had led us to the column, and what did we find at the base of the column? *Is not this laid up in store with me?*

"I didn't need to look any further. This was the place.

"Now, I was as eager as any man would be, but I didn't want to rush into things. First I had to consider whether David had been lain below ground or above. Could he perhaps have been placed in that urn thing at the top of the pillar? It wasn't unlikely, because from there he would still, in a way, be master of Martlets, and it would make a difficult quest even more difficult.

"No. I had to discard that idea. Paul's diary definitely says that his father was *buried*, and he'd hardly say that if the body had been raised so high above the ground. The only probability, it seemed to me, was that he'd been placed in or under the plinth of the column.

"It's a large thing, that plinth: eight or nine feet high, and about fifteen feet wide on each face, while the diameter of the column is only about eight feet. There was room enough, I reckoned, and I resolved to make a start that very day. Perhaps I should have taken Shepherd into my confidence then — I wish now that I had, but all I told him was that I had some work to do in the park, and might be two or three hours about it.

"There's no need to bore you with my frustrated efforts to find an opening in the plinth. It's enough that I did find it, though it took me nearly three hours. As you might have expected, the door (why not call it that?) was in the western face, over on the right. It was cunningly disguised by apparent cracks in the stone, part of that very artistic ageing that we'd noticed. All I had to do was to prise out a panel, about three feet square, and there was the entrance to the tomb. That panel was damned heavy, I may say! Fortunately the base of it was at ground level, or I'd have had the hell of a job to stop it crashing down on me.

"By the time I'd opened the door, so to speak, I'd spent quite a bit longer than the couple of hours that Shepherd was to allow me. I knew he'd give me a while longer, though, before he'd come looking for me, and he had only the vaguest notion of whereabouts I'd be.

"I decided to go ahead, and enter the tomb straight away.

"The hole was quite small, and I could see only blackness inside, so for the moment I left my various tools — hammer, chisel, crowbar — and switched my flashlight on. It revealed something like a passageway inside the plinth, with a brick floor. It was no more than three feet from front to back, and about ten feet from the wall on the right to the one on the left. The light was strong enough to show me that there was a square hole in the floor over by this left-hand wall. I shone the light upwards, and was pleased to see that I was allowed a few inches' headroom. At least I'd be able to walk.

"I crawled inside, stood upright, and made my way over to the hole. Then a thought occurred to me, and I turned off the flashlight. Almost instantly I switched it on again. The darkness must have been falling even while I'd made my way in there, and I could see only a glimmer of grey where I knew the entrance to be. Where I stood, ten feet away in that narrow passage, it was as black as sin. Not a cheerful thought.

"I'd rather hoped for a set of steps, but the hole went straight down — for about twelve feet, as far as I could tell. For a moment I thought that I'd have to go back to the house and fetch a rope, but then I noticed that there were projections from the wall at regular intervals, evidently meant for hand- and foot-holds. Frankly, I didn't relish the notion of going down into that pit without proper lighting, but after all, I told myself, it was only twelve feet. I tucked the torch into my belt, so that the light shone upwards, and started down.

"It wasn't a long descent, but it was one that I shouldn't care to make again. There were odd noises — at least, I thought that there were — from beneath me, and I cursed the fact that I couldn't see down there.

"Phew! Shepherd, get me a drink, please — something stronger than lime juice this time. Just do it, man! I'll be all right with Mr Retford here. Besides, it's doing me good to tell the storey again. Catharsis — isn't that what they call it?"

Shepherd did bring lime juice, but he'd put a good measure of gin in it; and when Langley had drunk about half of it, he resumed his narrative:

"I reached the bottom of the shaft with no great difficulty, but I was quick to take my flashlight out and shine it around me. It revealed a room or chamber about fifteen feet square, whose ceiling just brushed the top of my head. Wall, floor and ceiling were all of plain grey stone slabs. In the middle of the floor was a much larger slab, on which lay a coffin of good oak. There was no plate on it, nor any sort of identification, but I could hardly doubt that I'd found the resting-place of David Vivian.

"I'd been too excited to notice it before, but I now realised that the air wasn't either excessively stale or excessively foul. The one unpleasant odour that came to me was certainly the smell of animal-droppings. Rats, most likely. That would account for the odd noises I'd heard. I hoped my arrival had frightened them away.

"Well, there was the coffin, but what of the treasure? I could hardly believe that I'd been beaten to it. No — that must be what I'd come for, over there. In each of the four corners was a pile of objects — bags and boxes. I smiled with profound relief as I thought of what this would mean to me. To me, and to Martlets.

"I approached one of the heaps, and was reaching out my hand for the leather bag on to when I noticed a small movement at the foot of the pile. Hastily, I dropped my hand. Damned rats! I thought. Very well, then. I started towards another pile, but that too began to shift slightly.

"I whirled around to look at the others. Each of them was moving. I said aloud to myself that I would *not* be put off by vermin!

"And then, from the corner of my eye, I caught a glimpse of a larger motion. I could hardly bring myself to turn and look. There was a foulness in the air that was more than rat-droppings, and suddenly I felt unbearably stifled and hot. In an agony of slowness, I swung the torch around. As I looked, horrified, the pile of bags and boxes shivered slightly, stood up, and stretched out its arms, as if to embrace me.

"That was when I dropped the torch. It broke instantly.

"And in the utter darkness, with noises about me that were not of my own making, I think I went mad.

"Mad for a time, at least.

"Before God, I can say that I've encountered as much naked terror as a man can without permanently losing his mind. Until Shepherd found me, panting and sweating, on the grass beside the column — well, I don't know what I did. I must have floundered about in complete darkness, knocking into things — and, though I hate to think of it, being knocked into.

"Perhaps I fell when I climbed up the shaft at last. I don't know; I simply have no memory of it. At all events, when

Shepherd found me, long after nightfall, I was severely cut and bruised, and as nervous as — as a kitten. I'll venture to say, though, that I was in my right mind. You'll agree to that, Shepherd? Thank you."

"What about the flashlight?" I asked.

He gave a short, barking laugh. "If you want to go down there and look for it, you're welcome! But really, old man, I shouldn't advise it."

"Shepherd clearly believed the story," said Frank. "And perhaps he knew his master better than I did. I wasn't sure then, and I'm not sure now.

"I will tell you this, though: that against Langley's advice, I did venture down into David Vivian's tomb, and, sure enough, I found the flashlight crushed and broken upon the floor. For the rest, everything was as he'd described it. That is, it was as it had appeared to him at first. The coffin lay squarely upon its slab in the centre of the floor, and the four piles of bags and boxes stood in the corners of the chamber. Only the broken flashlight showed that someone had recently been there — that, and a number of splashes of recently dried blood. I saw no movement from the heaps in the corners, but then I was careful not to approach them too closely. And I confess that I wasn't at all sorry to get out of there."

"What became of Edward Langley?" I asked.

"He recovered in time, though he continued to be plagued by attacks of something like fever for the rest of his life. He was lost at Dunkirk, poor devil. I think the worst thing for him was the belief that his cousin David had deliberately hidden the wealth that would have kept Martlets in good order, and made it impossible for anyone to use that wealth.

'Whether Langley's experience in the tomb was real or not, there's no doubt in my mind that David Vivian was a selfish old bastard."

"Hear, hear!" said George. "Now, one last question, and then it's Roger's turn to get the drinks in. Did you manage to decode the message on the painting?"

"Yes, I did. Oddly enough, it wasn't a cryptogram in any usual sense. The fact that the letters were reflected in the shield should have given me a clue. All I had to do was to find the right letter to start with, and then read backwards. After that, it was pretty plain sailing. The message is in very good Latin — from the Vulgate Bible, in fact. Another of David Vivian's mock-pious Old Testament texts: from Jeremiah, this time — chapter 44, verse 27. You start at about five o'clock on the shield, and simply read in reverse.

"In the Latin, it runs: *Ecce ego vigilabo super eos in malum et non in bonum.*"

George nodded in grim understanding, but I was slower to catch its import. Later I looked it up in the Authorised Version, where it's given as: "Behold, I will watch over them for evil and not for good."

Afterword

Bob Price's invitation to contribute to his magazine *Spectral Tales* impelled me to fulfil a long-standing ambition: of writing a variant on M R James's "The Treasure of Abbot Thomas". It was a bonus that I could throw in a folly and a passage in Latin (fortunately Essex County Library was able to supply a copy of the Vulgate Bible).

The description of Martlets is actually that of a private house in Norfolk, which I was privileged to visit in the mid 1980s, with a party from the Sherlock Holmes Society of London.

THE NIGHT BEFORE CHRISTMAS

"God, how I hate Christmas!"

Hilary Falkner crushed out her cigarette and scowled.

This early in the evening the bar was almost empty. I looked from her contemptuous face to the harmless and discreet Christmas tree that the landlord had placed near the fireplace. As she continued, the thought occurred to me that Hilary Falkner wouldn't be my choice for a companion on the last train home. Why on earth had George Cobbett asked her to come here? Not out of pity, surely.

But the old man's face was quite expressionless as he watched her and listened to her complainings.

"All this fraudulent decoration — I mean, the garishness of it! And always you have to spend Christmas Day with the bloody family. And, dear God — the children! 'I want this, I want that...' 'What's Father Christmas going to bring me this time — ?'"

"Ah," said George, "now we're coming to it. Father Christmas, eh? Isn't he behind it all — that fat, jolly, generous old spirit?"

Hilary's face relaxed suddenly, and she gave us a brief vulpine smile. In that instant I saw that, for all her sixty years and despite her mask of misanthropy, she was actually a very good-looking woman. She rubbed her chin with a rather masculine gesture; then she sighed, and looked at George with calm eyes.

"You're right, of course," she said, "though I'm blessed if I know how you knew. You're an artful old brute, George. Oh, well — since we're all comfortable, I don't see any reason not to tell you. After all, the season's appropriate."

She shivered slightly.

I'll tell you (she said) about the worst Christmas I ever spent. And — damn you, George! — yes, it does have to do with Father Christmas. Not one that you'd wish to meet, believe me. "A right jolly old elf?" Brrr!

When I was a child, my closest friend was a girl called Diana Calthrop. Diana and I were pretty much brought up together, because our families lived side by side, and our two birthdays fell within a fortnight of each other. She was a perfectly ordinary child, stolidly lower-middle-class, not unintelligent and not unattractive.

What I'm trying to impress on you is that there was nothing at all unusual about her.

Almost nothing.

You see, she suffered from a recurring nightmare — and "suffered" isn't too strong a word.

This dream — vision, or what you will — afflicted her perhaps three or four times a year, and for a day or so afterwards she would be in a truly pitiful state. It started, I think, some time before her third birthday. At least, it was then that she was, for the first time, able to be reasonably coherent about it. Her parents thought she was ill, and sent for the doctor. Those were the days when you could actually send for the doctor. He came, and he examined her — she shocked and silent all the while — and he could find nothing wrong. Nothing he could put his finger on. He prescribed some sort of sedative, and sure enough, within a couple of days Diana was as right as could be.

Then it happened again, and since the cure had worked so well the first time, the doctor was summoned again, with the same result. The next time, she told me, her parents began to suspect that she was shamming, especially as she seemed to recover quite satisfactorily without medical attention. But there was a next time, and a next, and it became clear ever to the unimaginative Calthrops that something really was wrong. But as the doctor said, it was nothing you could put your finger on.

Still, although the attacks (the right word, I think) occurred with erratic frequency, Diana always recovered within a few days. The worst after-effect was a sort of nervous melancholy.

Even then, you know, I wasn't sure that was a good thing. It seemed that every detail of the dream was forgotten within seconds of her waking, so that she had nothing tangible to tell her parents or the doctor — or to tell me, which in the circumstances she was rather more likely to do. All she could say was that she'd had "that dream" again, and we knew what that meant. For me it meant that there'd be an empty desk beside mine at school, and that I mustn't call at the house next door and ask if Diana could come out to play.

In time, as children do, I grew used to the situation, and so, I suppose, did she — to a degree, at least. But it wasn't a healthy situation. She was left with nothing to discuss, and nothing to exorcise.

Not healthy, and not pleasant, but the human child is a resilient creature. Somehow Diana adjusted to these attacks. She came to expect them, and she knew just what effect they'd have on her and on her parents. Occasionally, she could even laugh about them, but it was a disconcerting and nervous kind of laughter.

She was still afraid, you see.

The climax — the first climax — came at the Christmas just after our fourteenth birthdays. Diana was growing up more quickly than I was. In the physical sense, at any rate. You could have taken her for a young woman of eighteen, whereas I was very much into the pigtails and puppy-fat stage. She was good-looking too, with a sweet little heart-shaped face, framed by really glossy auburn hair. And her eyes were huge and clear. It was only the eyes, I think, that told you how young she really was.

Well, a small group of us had been invited to spend Christmas at the house of a friend — not a very close friend — whose people were rather better-off than ours were. There were the usual sort of tears from our mothers and warnings from our fathers, but I've a strong suspicion that they were all pretty glad to be shot of us. My own views on the family Christmas aren't by any means original.

The house was at Woodham Priors, not very far from Maldon. At the age of fourteen, and with the prospect of a lavish Christmas ahead, I didn't take much notice of the building. It seemed very old, and was both glamorous and luxurious to us provincial girls. The bedrooms seemed enormous, and you can perhaps imagine the novelty of having a basin with running water actually in one's room. If there was anything primitive about the arrangements, we either overlooked it or put it down to rustic charm.

The hall, where we ate, and in fact spent much of our time, really was vast. The one wooden table would have been far too big for Diana's house or mine, but it left plenty of room here. I remember being just a little disappointed that there were no swords or shields or suits of armour; instead the walls bore only a dozen or so landscape paintings. Rather dull, I thought, but they couldn't detract from the magnificence of the room.

We arrived on the morning of the twenty-third. Some came by car, but Diana and I and a couple of others were collected from Witham station by our host's chauffeur. There were no fun and games on that first day: as we were told, suchlike frivolity belonged properly to Christmas Day itself. Still, there was a treat promised for Christmas Eve, and that was only a day away. In the meantime we were put, in the most charming way, to earning our fun by helping to prepare the house. We hung decorations,

gathered holly and mistletoe, brought home the Yule log, decked the great tree...
I'd never enjoyed myself so much at Christmas.
The treat came after dinner on the following day, or rather, towards the end of the meal. We'd just started on our cocoa when there came a heavy knocking at the big front door. Our hostess said nothing as she motioned the housekeeper to open it, but we could see that she was barely suppressing a grin of pure delight. The door was flung wide, and we heard a resonant voice say:

> "Open the door and let us in!
> We hope your favours we shall win.
> Whether we rise or whether we fall
> We'll do our best to please you all."

One of the girls clapped her hands together and said, "Why, it's the Mummers! I didn't know you had them here."
We watched, fascinated, as a bulky figure strode in to the hall, still chanting:

> "A room, a room, a gallant room,
> And give us room to rhyme!
> We'll show you bold activity
> Upon this Christmas time."

From where we sat, Diana and I could see only one side of this extraordinary creature. He seemed to be completely enveloped in a vast dark green robe, with a hood that shaded his face from us.
"Who is he?" Diana whispered; but I could only shrug and watch, as behind their leader there marched in a quite bizarre little troupe. First a tall man, very stern, dressed in an old-fashioned military uniform and carrying a sword, blade upright in his outstretched fist. He was followed directly by a slightly shorter man, whose uniform was black instead of red, and who also carried a sword. Then came a little fellow, wearing a countryman's smock and a battered hat. Behind him was a thin man in frock-coat and top hat, carrying a Gladstone bag. Finally came another small man, in some sort of tunic and cap of red, holding, of all things, a soup-ladle in his hand. They were very grave, and they looked straight ahead of them as they entered, but we could see their faces clearly. The only face hidden from us was their leader's.

He walked slowly and deliberately to the centre of the hall, still chanting. There he halted, facing our host and hostess, pushed back his hood, and bowed to them. The others grouped themselves on either side of him, three to the left and two to the right. The two men with the swords faced each other. As the big man straightened himself, I could see the back of a bald pink head, rising from a fleecy mass of white hair.

Then he turned around, so that we could see his face at last.

It was quite the jolliest thing I'd seen on that jolly day. The fat cheeks glowed red from the cold, the grey eyes danced like stars, the mouth held a half-smile, and the beard and moustache fully matched the woolly whiteness of the hair. They weren't false, either: there was a distinct yellow tinge to the hairs around the mouth, which told you that this old fellow was a cigar-smoker.

He began to speak again:

"In comes I, Old Father Christmas,
Welcome or welcome not.
I hope Old Father — "

There was a sudden, shocking scream from beside me. The deep, confident voice faltered and stopped, and all faces turned to Diana.

But Diana was no longer in her chair. As we looked, she slid like a rag doll to the floor. She was completely unconscious as our host carried her upstairs to the bedroom that the two of us shared. He made no fuss when I slipped away from the table to follow him, but allowed me to help in laying Diana comfortably on her bed. Below us, from an infinite distance, I could hear voices raised in declamation. The Mummers hadn't allowed this interruption to put them off for long.

"The poor kid's had a shock of some kind," my host said, "but I'm blessed if I can think what." He turned to me. "Did you notice anything that might have caused her to faint like that?"

He was a sensible man, and compassionate. I liked him for that, but I couldn't help him. I told him all I'd seen, and suggested feebly that my friend's distress must have been brought on by the sight of Old Father Christmas. He had already reached that conclusion, of course, but the idea still seemed pretty wild.

After a moment, he shrugged his shoulders and said, "Well, we'll find out in time, I suppose. Meanwhile there's the more urgent question of what to do with your friend. In other circumstances I'd be inclined to let her be and recover her consciousness naturally, but — well, you can see her face. You don't think, any more than I do, that this young woman is enjoying a peaceful sleep."

It was true. The expression on Diana's pretty face wasn't at all a comfortable one.

The long and the short of it was that she had to be brought round, and this our host achieved in the gentlest way, by bathing her face with *eau de Cologne*. I was prepared, if necessary, to hold *sal volatile* under her nose, but it didn't come to that. Diana's eyelids fluttered briefly, and then her eyes suddenly opened wide. She took no more than a second to realise the situation. Her first words were, "Whatever must you think of me?"

My quick embrace was enough, I think, to show how I felt. At that moment I must have looked a good deal less calm than Diana did. Our host kept his composure, but there was a distinctly quizzical look on his face.

He peered intently at Diana, and then said, "Don't worry about the rest of us. You did cause a bit of a disturbance, I'm afraid, but it can hardly be called a sensation. Do you mind talking about it? Only I'm rather curious to know what's behind it all. Something upset you pretty severely, and your friend and I (by the way, I'm afraid I don't know your name. Hilary? And you're Diana. Well, I'm glad to meet you both, though it's rather an odd meeting. I'm Richard. Now, what was I saying? Oh, yes —) Hilary and I had reached the rather unlikely conclusion that your fit was brought on by the sight of Old Father Christmas."

Diana swallowed hard and nodded. For the moment she said nothing.

"Just so," he went on. "Well, you'll agree that it does seem improbable. Quite apart from the very unfrightening nature of the character, I'd have said that Uncle William was about the most amiable person I'd ever met — and, what's more, he looks it. So what's the story, eh? Do you know something nasty about the old boy?"

Diana managed a very creditable smile. "No," she said firmly. "I've never seen the old gentleman before, and I know nothing about him. Probably he does look as nice as you say, but I'm afraid he put me in mind of something rather awful, so it wasn't your uncle I saw, but — look here, do you really want to hear about it?"

Richard told her that we certainly did. I just nodded. I had a sudden notion of the truth, and I couldn't trust myself to speak.

Diana was very much more composed now, and looked like her old self. It was plain that she'd quite won over our host. She sat gracefully on the bed, with her legs curled under her, looking like a golden kitten. I perched myself on the other bed, while Richard sat in the one easy-chair. Having politely asked permission, he lit a small cigar, using the metal waste-paper bin as an ashtray.

"Hilary knows as much of this as anyone," said Diana. "As much as I did myself until this evening. I know that sounds cryptic, but it will be explained, honestly. You see, ever since I can remember, I've suffered from nightmares — or rather, from one single nightmare that's come again and again, several times during the year. Always it would leave me weak, nervous and frightened. And perhaps the worst part of it was that afterwards I couldn't remember a thing about the dream — except that it had terrified the wits out of me. I couldn't get rid of it, you see, because I didn't know what it was I wanted to get rid of. Do you see what I mean?"

He saw exactly, but, wisely, he said nothing.

"Well, now I know.

"In all that awful dreaming I've been haunted — menaced — threatened — by a man. A huge, bloated, grotesquely fat man, with a vast bald head and a big beard. The beard is thick and white, or very light grey. He looks at me with his little evil eyes, and there's a sort of dreadfully confident humour in them — and he smiles. Always he smiles. He never says anything, but I know what he's telling me: 'You're mine, all mine — and oh, what fun I'm going to have with you!'

"He picks me up as if I were a doll, and he leers fatly at me, while his fingers are squeezing and stroking — " She broke off, shuddering, but she didn't cry, though I'm sure I would have done so.

"Nasty," said Richard, at length. "Very nasty. And though I'd hesitate to call Uncle William at all grotesque, it's plain now why the sight of him should have brought the dream back to you. You'll admit, I think, that the old boy looks just like the Ghost of Christmas Present. The dream, now — you say it's been with you since your childhood?"

"Yes, I told you. Ever since I can remember."

"Odd that it should persist so. Can you remember anything else about the man? Has he changed at all over the years?"

"No. No, I don't think so — though I have, of course."

"Ah, he's followed you as you've grown up, eh? Well, I suppose that's to be expected. I'm no psychologist, but it does sound reasonable. Now, just one more question: do you connect the man in the dream with anyone you've seen or met?"

"No, not at all. Not even in a picture; otherwise I'd surely have remembered before. And really, you know — " (she smiled charmingly at him) " — your Uncle William doesn't look very much like the man in the dream. It's all — what's the word I want? — superficial. Besides — "

"Well?"

"Well, it's just that I'm not at all sure that the man in the dream is alive."

There's not much more to tell about that Christmas. The three of us, I think, remained pretty thoughtful for a while, but it became clear that, in remembering and recounting her strange dream, Diana had at last managed to exorcise her bogey-man. Father Christmas and the Mummers had gone their way, and the house was ours. Diana was soon her old self again, only more so, if you see what I mean. Bright, sweet and very happy. I was more than glad to fall in with her mood. We said very little to the others, and in any case they had more seasonal matters on their minds. Only Richard, who seemed to be a naturally reflective person, remained less than hysterically cheerful.

The holiday came to an end, as holidays must. I noticed that our host was particularly careful and particularly grown-up in his goodbyes to Diana and me. On one subject, at least, he seemed to regard us as equals, which I found very gratifying. It was something rather unusual, you know, to be on Christian name terms with the father of a school-friend. Diana's mood was still blessedly, quietly happy, but as he shook my hand Richard said discreetly, "Keep an eye on that young woman. If she doesn't tell her people about the dream, then it's not up to you to do so. They sound like nice, ordinary folk, and I somehow think that they're better off not knowing. You're a bright girl, though. Just keep your eyes and ears open, and if anything happens that you don't like — anything connected with the dream, I mean — drop me a line."

But nothing did happen, and for four years our only contact with him was a brief note in the Christmas cards that we exchanged. During all that time there was no repetition of the dream. Diana's parents suppressed their relief at first, but when six months had gone by and there were no disturbances, their quiet pleasure was almost painfully evident. I continued to watch and listen, though Diana herself seemed quite unaware of it. It was almost as if the nightmare had never been. At length she was even able to talk lightly of "that funny dream" that she used to have.

Then came another Christmas, the one just after we turned eighteen. By now, of course, we'd both left school. Diana, who was as lovely as she'd given promise of being, had got herself a good post as a private secretary; I was training to be a teacher. Our financial circumstances at that age weren't especially desirable, so we were both very pleased to receive a polite and friendly invitation to spend Christmas over at Woodham Priors. The only doubts were about what our parents would say, but there proved to be no difficulty there. My mother, at any rate, had been hiding some slight disappointment that we'd not been invited back to stay with the girl she thought of as our "rich friend", so she was quite as happy about it all as Diana and I were.

On the twenty-fourth of December we were met at the door of the house by Richard and his wife and daughter. The daughter — we hadn't seen her for something over a year — was like a stranger to us, though of course we made all the right social noises. Her mother was polite, pleasant, and a touch absent-minded, but Richard himself didn't seem to have changed at all: he was as sympathetic and perceptive as ever.

Eventually the two women went off to see to something or other in the kitchen, and Richard said, "I'm really glad that you could both come."

Diana's smile just avoided being impudent as she asked, "And was there a particular reason for asking us?"

His own answering smile was very engaging. "You mean, apart from the fact that we rather like you? Yes, there was a reason. Two reasons. First, I had an idle curiosity to find out what sort of young women you've become. You've both turned out pretty well, you'll be pleased to hear."

I caught a glance of amused naughtiness from Diana, and we curtsied in unison — but instead of laughing, Richard turned the joke back on us by gravely kissing our hands. Then we all laughed.

Then his face became suddenly thoughtful, and he said, "I had a second reason, you'll remember, for inviting you. The fact is that there's someone I'd like you to meet."

There was a brief pause, and I said, "Oh?" enquiringly.

"Yes. Someone you've both seen but haven't actually been introduced to. It's — well — it's my wife's uncle, Uncle William."

I felt suddenly nervous, wondering if this was a wise move. The picture came into my mind of my friend's face, tortured and haunted, as it had been the one time we'd seen Uncle William, but it was quickly dispelled by Diana's delighted exclamation: "Oh, how marvellous! He helped me get rid of my nightmare, and I'd so love to meet him and thank him."

I realised that Richard had been as delicately nervous as myself. His face perceptibly relaxed, and he said, "That's splendid. Now, I must tell you that the old fellow knows about your dream — which is more, by the bye, than my wife and daughter do. I thought it only fair to give him the story behind your rather dramatic behaviour when you were last here. You'll appreciate that he was just a little taken aback. He's not used to having young women faint at the sight of him."

Uncle William was waiting for us in the smoking-room, though he wasn't actually smoking. There was a half-finished cigar in the ashtray, and his comfortable, bulky figure was fast asleep in the big leather armchair beside it. I fancy Richard was ready to wake him, but it wasn't necessary. As soon as the door clicked to behind us, the old man jerked, or rather, bubbled into consciousness.

"Bless me!" he said. And then, when he'd fished a pair of horn-rimmed glasses out of his breast-pocket and perched them rather dubiously on his small round nose: "Well, this is nice! The young feller warned me he was bringing the two gels here to see me, but I thought you'd still be little things, you know. I wasn't expecting such well set-up young wenches. Bless me!"

It was obvious why he'd been chosen to take the part of Father Christmas. His face and bald head glowed pinkly above the fleecy whiteness of his beard. His eyes, surrounded by a network of cheerful wrinkles, sparkled merrily. His belly shook in happy sympathy as he chuckled. Altogether, he was a man you couldn't help loving.

He made a move to stand up, but was politely and firmly pushed back by Richard. While the three of us got ourselves seated, Uncle William busied himself in re-lighting his cigar.

"Now," he said, "one of you's the nymph who had the bad dreams. Am I right?"

"You're right," said Diana. "I'm the — the nymph."

He peered anxiously at her. "Young Richard says you told him that the bogey-man in your nightmares looked a bit like me."

"A bit." She smiled, charmingly. "But not very much. It's just that the man in the dream was — forgive me — fat and old, with a big white beard and a bald head. But he was huge — horribly, disgustingly obese — whereas you — "

He tapped his broad chest with a thick forefinger. "Me?" he said. "I'm fat. I know it, and I'm happy with it. But heaven help anyone who calls me obese! So, he didn't look a lot like me, apart from certain obvious superficialities, eh? Well, that's a relief. I'd hate to think I'd caused distress to a nice-looking lass like you."

"You did, though," I said, boldly. "But it turned out for the best, because seeing you brought the dream to the front of Diana's mind, so that she could see it and recognise it for what it was. It must have been a dreadful shock at the time, but since then she hasn't been troubled by it at all."

"Shock therapy, eh? Well, I'm glad it all came out well." For some reason he sounded just a little dubious.

Diana smiled happily. "It certainly did, and I'm very grateful to you." She darted a quick, mischievous glance at me, and then suddenly got up of her chair, went over to the old man, and kissed him on the top of his bald head. By the time the look of delighted surprise on his plump face had subsided into mere cheerful satisfaction, she was sitting demurely in her chair again. Richard was grinning broadly. I suspect I was, too.

Presently, I ventured a question: "Uncle William — may we call you that? — why was it that we didn't see you on Christmas Day that time?"

He waved a big hand, dismissively. "Ah, well, d'you see, it's because I wasn't here."

"Not here? But - "

"No. It's quite simple. I was down here from my home in Worcestershire, staying with my married daughter in Maldon, and I'd only called in at Woodham Priors for the jollifications on Christmas Eve. When my son-in-law suggested reviving the old Mummers' play for the occasion, since there was to be a party of young gels here, I was pleased to join in. I've often been called on to play Father Christmas, but it was nice to have something more meaty than just saying 'Ho ho ho!' and 'Have you been a good little boy?'

"Anyway. As I say, I'd only popped over from Maldon for those few hours. After that, it was back to my daughter's house, so that I could fight my way into the red gown and fill up the stockings for my grandchildren. We were kept pretty busy for the next couple of days, and then on the twenty-seventh I had to get off home. That's all there is to it. The past three years, the family's come over to Worcestershire to spend Christmas with me. This is the first time I've been here since you gave our little Mummers' play such an unexpected reception."

Richard said, "A while back, I gave the old man a full account of that little episode, including your description, Diana, of the nasty figure in your dream. It was then that he invited himself down here for the Christmas holiday."

Uncle William scowled, but not very convincingly, and said, "You know damn' well that I've got an open invitation to stay here. Or maybe it's just my niece who likes to have me along? Ha! Very well then."

He turned his eyes back to Diana and me, and again that note of uncertainty crept into his voice. "I had a reason for coming, d'you see, and between us Richard and I decided that it would be a good notion if you two young wenches were invited as well. The women of the house liked the idea, as I thought they would, so here we all are. I wanted to meet you both, of course, but there was more to it than that.

"Your description, my lass, of the incubus that haunted you since childhood put me in mind of something. The fact is that an ancestor of mine fits that description pretty damn' closely. All right, I know — there must be quite a fair number of grossly fat old men about, even when you've discounted the ones who are clean-shaven or who have a full head of hair. However, they aren't all wicked old men, are they? And my great-uncle was that, in spades. To put the cap on it all, he actually lived in this house. In fact, he had it built."

"The house," Richard explained, "belongs to my wife. As the only child, she inherited it from her parents. It'll go to our daughter when she dies. I'm only here on sufferance." He gave a short, contented laugh.

"But it looks so old!" I said. "Of course, we haven't had time to look at it properly today, but when we were here before I quite thought it must be Elizabethan."

"Sorry to disappoint you. It was actually put up in 1822. Of course, it was deliberately designed to look much older — "

"This wicked great-uncle," said Diana. "What was his name, and what did he do that was so wicked?"

"His name was Marcus Ridler," said Uncle William. "That's straightforward enough. He was born in 1756. Yes, it shakes you a bit to think of that, eh? But his brother, my grandfather, who inherited when old Marcus died, was nearly forty years younger. To be strictly accurate, of course, they were half-brothers. Marcus died in 1839. Or rather, he disappeared then. The circumstances seem to be very vague, and frankly very muddy. There's no doubt that he'd got himself a really bad name in the area, and folk weren't too eager to pry into the manner of his disappearance. Various reasons, no doubt. I rather fancy that they knew who was responsible, and were inclined to praise and not condemn. The best way of praising, in the circumstances, was just to keep their mouths shut. Don't go asking me who might have done away with the old villain, though, because I haven't any notion. It might have been any of several people. He'd made a powerful lot of enemies."

"How, though?" I asked. "What did he do?"

"Ha! Well, now we come to it. You'll notice that I've been skirting around the subject rather. The fact is that it's rather indelicate. I'm not especially worried about his being a relation of mine, because, after all, it was a long time ago, and he may have got his bad blood from his mother, so that it wouldn't have come down in our side of the family. I hope that's so. At any rate, we've all led quite blameless lives since his time.

"The man was a satyr. I don't mean that he had horns and cloven feet, though they'd have been appropriate. Marcus Ridler was a lecher and a sadist. In fact, he read and approved of the Marquis de Sade's theses, and it seems clear enough from the accounts that survive that he did his best to put the madman's theories into practice. Everything about him, as far as I can tell, was perverted. He turned love into lust, authority into tyranny. His learning took him along paths of sheer vileness. And he rejoiced in inflicting pain. I'll spare you what I found written in one of my grandfather's letters about the things that Marcus did to his mistress's pet spaniel. That's bad enough, but it wasn't only animals.

"Well, if Marcus was the bogey-man who tormented you, my dear, then I can only assume that at some time you must have heard of him, or seen a picture. Now, there's just one way I can think of to make sure whether it was Marcus Ridler who haunted you all those years. Richard, my boy, I'm too old, too fat and too lazy to go dashing about the place, so perhaps you'll be good enough to go up to my room and bring down my black dispatch-case. Thank you."

Neither Diana nor I could bring ourselves to speak while our host was gone from the room, but I had a strong notion of what was in that dispatch-case. Richard must have said something to his wife and daughter — though how he managed it without telling them anything explicit about Diana's nightmares was beyond me. At any rate, throughout the time we were closeted with Uncle William, we saw no sign of them.

Richard was back none too soon, carrying the dispatch-case. He handed it without a word to Uncle William, who unlocked it, but didn't for the moment raise the lids.

"You'll have guessed," he said, with more seriousness in his voice than I'd yet heard, "that I've found a picture of Marcus Ridler. I knew there was one — in fact, I'd seen it when I was a child, before I'd been told anything about him. I was too young and too trusting then to see beyond the humorous look on his fat old face, and my parents, bless 'em, would tell me only that he was the great-uncle who had built the big house. It was much later that I found out about his foul life and his doubtful end.

"I'd done my best over the years to put him out of my mind, but then Richard told me what you'd told him, and that brought it all back. I was particularly struck, d☐you see, by the coincidence: I mean, that it was in Marcus's own house that you'd remembered all the detail of your incubus. And since it was the sight of me that had sparked off your remembrance, well, I thought I owed it to us all to try and get to the heart of the matter.

"Now, my dear, would you rather you didn't see the picture?"

Diana's reply was emphatic: "I want to see it. I want to know! You must understand that."

He said, "Just so," and he opened the case and took out a small item wrapped in cotton wool, which he peeled off to uncover a miniature in a gilt frame. He gazed at it for several seconds, shielding it from our eyes, before handing it to Diana.

For a long horrible moment she looked silently at the picture. Her face was white, and I could see a tic working at the left side of her mouth, but she said nothing. She'll scream, I thought; if she doesn't, I will.

But she didn't scream, and she didn't faint. At last she closed her eyes and swallowed hard. Then she nodded.

"Yes," she said. "That's the man."

Uncle William expelled a long breath, and harrumphed. "Extraordinary!" he said. "I hardly dared think it was, you know. One builds these fantastic explanations, not really believing — " He lapsed into silence while he lit a fresh cigar.

Diana's colour returned quickly to her cheeks, but her hand was shaking as she passed the picture to me.

"There," she said. "That's my bogey-man."

The portrait looked like a cruel caricature of old Uncle William. The sitter was dressed in clothes of the early nineteenth century, and his bloated face leered at the viewer with a dreadful mock-benevolence.

"A nasty thing," I said, with restraint, as I handed it to Richard.

Uncle William looked at us both gloomily for a while, as if debating what to say. At last he decided. "I'm sorry, my dear. Truly I am. I seem to be fated to distress you."

"Cruel to be kind," said Diana, rather shakily. "No, you're an old dear, and you've acted very sensibly. I won't deny that it's just a bit upsetting, but I'm glad to have seen the thing. God knows how that horrible face got itself into my dreams, but at least I know now that it was a real face, and a real person. Besides, you know, I've been quite free of the nightmare for four years now."

The old man echoed her smile, but Richard remained grave. "I can't help wondering," he said, "just how Marcus Ridler did find his way into your unconscious mind. You're quite sure that you'd never heard of him, or seen his picture?"

"Quite sure. I was terribly young, remember, when I first had the dream, and if I'd seen anything as horrid as that then surely my parents must have seen it to. They'd have said something."

"Um. Perhaps — but they knew as little as you did what it was that made your nights such a torture." He shrugged his shoulders. "Well, we'll just have to give it up as a mystery. It's all over now, and we've got a merry Christmas to look forward to. I'll call the womenfolk in, and we'll break open a bottle. A good idea, I think. Let's drink to a happy reunion."

Merry? Yes, I suppose we were — though the word suggests a touch of, well, rowdiness, which certainly wasn't present then. There were few belly-laughs, but lots of smiles, and contented chuckles from old Uncle William. We were happy, which is better than being merry.

It was the last time that I was truly happy at Christmas.

We went to bed — at least, the female members of the party did — not long after midnight, because we'd all agreed to attend the morning service at the parish church. Diana and I had separate rooms this time, but we sat up in my bedroom for quite a while, chatting, before Diana said, "Goodnight, dear, and have sweet dreams. I know I shall. The bad nights are gone now, and there are only the good times to look forward to." She kissed me, and left for her own room.

Shortly afterwards, I heard the two men talking in low voices, and moving with exaggerated quietness along the corridor. Then I fell asleep.

I was awoken soon after six by a figure whose pale, drawn face I scarcely recognised as Richard's.

"Did you hear anything in the night?" he asked abruptly.

"No. I don't — I don't think so. I sleep pretty soundly. What's wrong? Richard, what is it?"

He came into the room and sat for a moment on the bed, taking one of my hands between his own.

"It's Diana," he said, and I could see that he was forcing himself to be calm. "She's gone from her room. Dear God, I wish I hadn't asked you to come here!" He peered anxiously at me. "She doesn't walk in her sleep, does she? If it were only that... But I'm afraid, you see — I'm so afraid!"

"What? What are you afraid of?"

"I'm afraid that she's been taken."

I shooed him out of the room while I hurried into my clothes. Then I went straight to Diana's room, where the four of them were. Our hostess was sitting in the easy-chair, just looking dumbly at the floor, while her daughter knelt beside her, holding her hands. Richard and Uncle William stood over the bed; they were talking, and their voices sounded low and desperate. As soon as they saw me, they stopped. Silently, the old man took my hand and gestured towards the bed.

The bed-linen seemed to have been roughly thrown or pulled off. Diana's frock and stockings were strewn across the floor, and to me that was the most sinister touch, because I knew her to be the neatest person with her clothes.

"My wife was woken by some disturbance," said Richard. "It took some while before she thought that it might be coming from Diana's room or yours. When she looked into the corridor, she saw that the door of this room was partly open. She looked in, and found things as you see them. I came as soon as she called me. By that time the other two were awake. I left the women with Uncle William and went to make a thorough search of the house. I looked into your room first of all, but you were clearly alone and asleep. There was no sign of Diana elsewhere, though, so I took the liberty of waking you on my way back."

All sorts of mad and horrible pictures were before my mind's eye. My sweet Diana!

"We must look again," I said. "This time I'll come with you."

I glanced at the two women, with their white faces and their inward-looking eyes; at Uncle William, who now suddenly looked very old. His plump features seemed to have fallen in; it was a terrible thing to see. These were good people, but right now they were quite useless. Only Richard and I could do what had to be done.

Until dawn came, we could search the house. That was all we could do, and we did it thoroughly. There was no sign of anything amiss — nothing that couldn't be put down to last night's merry-making. And there was nothing to be seen of Diana. The implications were terrifying.

When we got back upstairs, we found that Richard's wife had gone back to bed; her daughter had had the good sense to give her a sedative. Uncle William sat alone, an uncomprehending ruin of a man. We left him and went down to the hall, where the lights and decorations seemed to me like a cruel joke.

At first light we left the house and scoured the grounds. It wasn't long before Richard found traces of disturbance. It had rained at some time during the night, and in the mud of the stable-yard were foot-prints that shouldn't have been there — large, deep prints. What they suggested so frightened me that I clung tightly to Richard's hand as we followed the trail. It was broken and erratic, and at one point there was horrible evidence of something being dragged along the ground, but it led inexorably to the stable block.

What we found there gave rise to a great deal of wild speculation in the area. Fortunately, perhaps, it never made the national press. As it was, dear old Uncle William was taken with a severe heart-attack from which he never fully recovered. He lingered for some months, but he was no more than an echo of his true self. The effect on me was less drastic, but more lasting.

Inside one of the stalls, the immense stone slabs that formed the floor had been flung aside and broken, while the thick-packed earth beneath was disturbed to a depth of about ten feet. The police, when they came, found the digging surprisingly easy.

It wasn't long before they came to the body of my poor friend. That, I suppose, was inevitable. What shocked them, but left Richard and me with a sort of sick feeling of suspicions confirmed, was the other body.

It was, to be exact, the skeleton of an elderly man. The flesh was almost entirely gone, but there were fragments of clothing left, metal and bone. The skull had been crushed by something hard and heavy, and the bones of the arms and legs had been broken, probably before death.

That was bad enough, but it was the injuries done to my poor friend's body that truly appalled me. They matched his in every respect. And his hands, dry, broken and bony, clasped hers possessively.

Hilary's hands were shaking so much that she couldn't hold her match steady to apply the flame to her cigarette. With bad grace, she accepted a light from me, and inhaled deeply. Her features relaxed as she expelled the smoke, and she looked at us with that unexpected sudden smile that quite altered the character of her face.

"Since that time," she said, "I've been the one to suffer nightmares."

George peered at her with unusual sympathy. "I expect," he said gently, "that the expression on your friend's dead face would be difficult to forget."

She closed her eyes and drew at her cigarette again.

"You're right, of course," she said. "But it isn't that which haunts my nights. I see Diana, lying peacefully in her bed on Christmas Eve, waiting for Father Christmas — 'that fat, jolly, generous old spirit'. And he comes to her, you see. He comes! And he's grotesquely, obscenely fat, and he leers down at her with lust in his wicked little eyes. He stretches out his strong hands — "

Hilary shuddered. "Merry Christmas, everybody!" she said, and her smile was pure acid.

Afterword

Richard Dalby invited me to contribute a story to his 1989 anthology *Chillers for Christmas,* and this was the result. If anyone's noticed that the plot bears a similarity to E F Benson's "The Face", they've been too polite to say so.

The village is actually called Wickham Bishops, but I had devised the name "Woodham Priors" and was keen to use it.

When I was slimmer and more energetic, I used to play Saint George in a Mummers' play. These days Father Christmas seems more appropriate.

THE SOLDIER

"A Christmas ghost story?" I prompted.

Julia Kirkby's eyes widened. "Did I say that?" she murmured. "Perhaps I was exaggerating a little."

"Oh, I do hope not," said George Cobbett, in a dangerously polite tone that warned of dyspeptic ill-temper. Its import wasn't lost on Julia.

"Well, at least it took place towards Christmas, and if there was an end to the story, then it came on the day itself." She flashed us a brief, slightly nervous smile. "Mystery there to start with — and more to come. As to ghosts... I think you'd better make up your own minds about that."

"Straightforward advice," said George. "Here's some for you. There's a good fire going, your glass is full, and you're among friends — so begin at the beginning and stop when you think you've reached the end."

"Very well," said Julia, "though I should tell you that it isn't actually *my* story. If it were, perhaps I'd be able to understand it more clearly." She took a sip from her gin and tonic, and continued: "As far as I was concerned, it began with some research I was doing for an article on the City of London and its peculiar institutions — the Livery Companies, Gog and Magog, the Trial of the Pyx — that sort of thing.

"Well, I came across a letter in an issue of *The Athenaeum* from some time in the 1890s. The writer simply asked for information about the Worshipful Company of Militia — 'said to be the oldest volunteer corps in the British Army, and drawn entirely from men of the City.' The name meant nothing to me. You may not think that's surprising, but my father was a military historian, and I actually do know something about the subject. I looked through the following half-dozen issues of the magazine, but there was nothing further. Perhaps someone had got in touch directly with the enquirer. There was no way of telling. It did seem a little odd, though, that he'd been unable to satisfy his curiosity by simply asking at the War Office. I wondered idly whether the whole thing was a mistake. Maybe the body in question was actually the Honourable Artillery Company.

"Still, I had work of my own to do.

"The article eventually appeared a few months later in a magazine called *Your England*, which is distributed only in North

America, aimed at expatriates and potential tourists. By the time it was published I'd written a lot of other pieces and had quite forgotten about the Worshipful Company of Militia. I'd certainly forgotten making a brief reference to it in my article, so the Worshipful Company wasn't the first thing I thought of when a package arrived from Canada.

"Inside the package, which had been forwarded by the publishers of *Your England*, was a small batch of typed sheets and a covering letter. My correspondent — his name was Davies, which is of no importance whatsoever — had by interested by my reference to this mysterious body, because it was something he'd known of, by name, for several years. And he to had run up against a blank wall in trying to find out more. He actually had written to the War Office and the National Army Museum, but the replies had been courteous and completely unhelpful. He could add nothing concrete to the little I already knew, except what I should read in the enclosed pages. Yours sincerely, etc., etc.

"The typed sheets were a transcript from a notebook, kept in about 1880 by a boy who was some sort of cousin to Mr Davies's grandmother — the relationship wasn't entirely clear. Although more obviously important and valuable items had been discarded over the years, this notebook had somehow survived. There wasn't much to tell about its owner. His name was Richard Henry Wenlock, and he was nearly sixteen years old when he wrote this brief journal. Physically he was stocky and well proportioned, but mentally — well, I don't know. Not actually backward in any usual sense, but distinctly strange.

"He was the youngest child by several years, which wasn't uncommon, I suppose, in those days of large families. At least one sister had died in early childhood, and there was a brother killed at Balaclava. Perhaps it was the brother's career that had set the boy to the notion of becoming a soldier himself — or perhaps it was just the experience of being brought up in a garrison town. I can imagine the clash there'd be between that military ambition on the one hand and the over-protectiveness of an ageing mother for her last and youngest darling."

Julia paused and looked pointedly at the glass in front of her. George hastily emptied his own glass of bitter and handed it to me. Plainly this was my round. When I returned from the bar, I found that Julia had taken from her briefcase a neat loose-leaf folder. She thumbed quickly through the pages before turning back to the beginning.

"This is young Wenlock's story," she said. "I can grasp the significance of some of it, but... Well, let's see what you two make of it."

And she began to read.

I really did not think that I should be happy when I came here. They told me that it was not just London, but the City of London. Of course I knew that London is a city. It is the greatest city in the world. But that was not what they meant. The City of London is a very small place, they said, like a village, and the Queen does not live here, nor does Parliament meet here. It does not seem to me very much like a village, but I have learned that the City is very special.

It was strange at first, not being able to go out into the countryside, and not seeing soldiers everywhere, as I used to in Colchester. I loved to visit the Garrison in Colchester. It was even exciting to go to the chapel there, because it was a soldiers' church and had regimental flags and battle trophies. I made up my mind quite early on that I wanted to be a soldier, but somehow things did not seem to go right. My Father had served in the army, and he used to tell me wonderful stories of wars and campaigns, but Mother never liked to hear them, and she never wanted me to be a soldier. When Father died she tried to stop me going again to the barracks, but it was not hard to go there without her knowing. But then Mother died to, of what the Doctor said was her weak heart, and I was sent here to the City of London, to live with my Aunt. I have been here now for nearly three months. Soon it will be the twenty-fifth of December, God's birthday, and then I shall take my first steps towards becoming a real soldier.

It did not take me long to find out that where we live in Spicers Lane is not very far from the castle which is called the Tower of London. I think it is rather strange that the Tower of London in really in Stepney and not in London at all, but there are many strange and special things still to learn about this City. There are soldiers at the castle, and just occasionally I am allowed to see them. Some of them are old men and wear funny old-fashioned clothes. I have read also that soldiers come to the great Bank of

England, which is quite near, but they only come in the evening to stand guard, and I have not seen them yet.

I am going to be a very special kind of soldier, and that is only right, for I am a special person. I know that, for Mr Pater told me so. I must write down all that has happened so far, so that it is clear in my mind. It is most important for a soldier to have a clear mind. Father told me that. Some things, though, are secret things and must not be written down, and if the wrong people were to find out about them I should not be allowed to become a soldier.

So I must not tell where the Church is, except that it is only a short distance from Spicers Lane and it is in a little square churchyard which you get to by going underneath a building and along an alleyway.

There is a metal gate with a bull's head on it, and Mr Pater told me that it is usually locked, but I have never found it locked.

Many of the churches in the City have strange names. I have found this out while walking about the streets, with my Aunt or on my own. There are Saint Katherine Cree and Saint Dionis Backchurch and Saint Andrew-by-the-Wardrobe. So I was not surprised when I saw the board just inside the iron gate with the name upon it, Saint Denis Mitre. But I was surprised and excited to learn that it was a soldiers' church, the first I had seen since I left Colchester. I knew, because under the name on the board was written, The Church of the Worshipful Company of Militia. Militia means soldiers, so this church was a soldiers' church.

It was a Sunday afternoon, and the City was very quiet, like death. It was as if there had never been anybody alive there. Even the public houses were shut, and there were no shops open at all. If I had chosen to walk towards the Tower of London, then there would have been many shops open and busy street markets, because so many people who live just outside the City of London are Jewish and do not keep Sunday as a day of rest. But in the City all was still. I like to be here on a Sunday, because then I can feel that I have the whole special place to myself, and even the Lord Mayor is not more important than I am. It is even more peaceful than on Saturday afternoons, when so many of the people who work here go home for luncheon and do not come back until Monday morning. The stillness on Saturday afternoons is one of the reasons why the City of London is so very special.

My Aunt had been taken ill with a headache while we were at church, but it is not that church that I shall tell of. It was only our parish church, which is called Saint Michael Cornhill and which is old and gloomy and rather dull. After luncheon, Aunt said that she would lie down for a while, and as Cook and Ann, who is our maid, said that they were very busy, I asked if I might walk about the streets for a while. I said that I had not lived in London long, and it was important that I should know where famous places were, like the Guildhall and Saint Paul's Cathedral. That is what I said, but really I wanted to get out of the house and away from Aunt and Cook and Ann, because I could not make them see how very important and special it was to me that I should become a soldier. When I mentioned it to them they would laugh, but in a secret kind of way that they hoped I would not understand, but I did.

The sky that Sunday was grey and watery, and the sun looked like a dull sixpence, casting uncertain, fleeting shadows. It was the sort of day that suits well the greyness of this City, which was now mine. I am of a clever and enquiring mind, and I already knew where the Cathedral was, and the Guildhall in its secret square, back from the empty road. However, I resolved to follow the streets wherever my nose led me, now this way and now that, so that I might know my new home fully. In this way I discovered many special and important buildings and places, such as the Royal Exchange and the Mansion House, which is where the Lord Mayor lives, and the Founders' Hall and Leadenhall market, and it seemed to me that I ought to return to Spicers Lane and my Aunt's house. But my nose led me to turn to the left off one of the main roads and into a narrow lane where tall grey buildings seemed to reach up to the grey sky, almost shutting out the light.

As I walked along this lane I noticed, for I am very observant, that there was a number of older and generally smaller buildings among the big grey ones. One of these, which looked very old indeed, had a narrow passage or alley underneath it, leading away from the lane. I should have passed this by, thinking it a private way, if it had not been for the sign. It was just inside the passage, screwed to the wall with bolts that had rusted over very many years, and there was an arrow painted upon it, which pointed away from the street. Underneath the arrow were the words, To The Ch — . But that is all it said, because the rest had faded entirely.

The passage was rather dark beyond, and it still looked to me like a private and secret place, but if I had not been meant to go in, then there would not have been a sign with an arrow. So I went along the dark and narrow alley and found at the end of it a gate made of strips of black iron, shaped into strange shapes, and with a metal bull's head in the centre of it. Beyond the gate I could see a small square, whose grass looked colourless and unhealthy. There were tombs of blackened stone and patches of bare earth, but the grass was neatly shorn. Someone tended this little churchyard. Looking to the far side of it, I saw the church itself.

At first, and for a moment, I was disappointed, because I had several churches that afternoon, and even the dullest of them were more handsome than this one, which seemed rightly to hide away from the streets where people go. But then I saw the notice-board which told me that this was a very special church. It stood just within the gate, and it was cracked and faded, but I could clearly read the words, The Church of Saint Denis Mitre, and underneath, The Church of the Worshipful Company of Militia. So then I knew that it was right that I should go on, because this was a soldiers' church.

I pushed open the iron gate and walked across the grass to the big wooden door of the church, where I lifted the heavy latch and pushed, but the door was locked. I was about to go away, disappointed, when I noticed the knocker on the door. It was made of iron, black like the gate, and shaped like a bull's head. Almost without thinking, I raised the knocker and rapped smartly upon the door. The sound was very loud, like a martial drum. I expected to rouse angry people in the buildings that surrounded the little churchyard, but nobody appeared at any of the blank windows, and I remembered that it was Sunday. Probably these houses and offices were all deserted. Almost before the sound of that loud rap had died away, the big door was opened, and in front of me stood a tall man who wore a dark robe and had a curious kind of cap upon his head. As he saw me, he smiled. This was my first meeting with the Priest.

He said, My dear son, I have been waiting eagerly for you. I thank God that He has led you to us this day.

This was strange, because I had not known myself that I should even find this hidden church, so how could the Priest know that I would come?

But he was speaking again, and he said, Come in. It is good to have another soldier to swell our ranks.

I started to explain that I was not really a soldier, but that I hoped to become one, and he said, In God's good time you shall. We must give thanks to God and to the Mother of God that you have arrived. This is a special church indeed, and you are a special Son among the Sons of God.

He said that he was the Priest of this Church of Saint Denis Mitre, and that he was called Pater. Because of the cap that he wore, I was so bold as to ask if he was a Roman Priest, and at that he only smiled in a singular way and did not reply. But I thought that he was a Roman, because of the smell of incense that was all around the church. It was not very strong, but it was like the incense they use in the big churches in Flanders, where my mother had taken me when I was quite a small boy. I found this rather exciting, but I was not sure that my Aunt would like the thought of my visiting a Roman church.

It was a soldiers' church, though, and I had been welcomed as a soldier. That was very special and important.

I asked if the church was very old. Was it as old as Saint Michael Cornhill, which was our parish church? And Mr Pater said that it was very much older, older than all the churches that stood in the City of London, even Saint Paul's Cathedral. And it had always been a church of soldiers.

He said that he would show me something of the upper part of the church, and tell me a little about the soldiers who worshipped there. Alas, he said, there are very few of them now, but once they were numerous. They were the strongest and bravest of all the soldiers of the Empire, and they worshipped God from all its wide dominions. Those who are left still remember in their bones the great deeds that were done, and even now those few are proud to be of the Worshipful Company of Militia.

I said that I had never heard of this Company of Militia, and Mr Pater told me that it was very old, like the church. It is the oldest company in England, he said, and for a long time now it has met only here in the City of London. Ah, my son, he said, this City of ours is a very special place. It is more strange and special than you can imagine, and you are a privileged young man to be admitted to its secrets.

He took me to the altar and made me swear that I would say nothing to my Aunt or to anyone else of what he told me and what he showed me, and his eyes were dark and terrible as he spoke. When I asked why, he said that a soldier must be a fit person to have secrets entrusted to him, and that if I could not keep the secrets of the church then I was unfitted to be a soldier. Besides, he was an officer of very high rank, and I must learn to obey his orders. So then, of course, I swore as he commanded, by God and His great sacrifice, by which the world was saved.

Then his lifted up the embroidered cloth and showed me the altar itself. It was made of a single great block of stone, and on it were carved the signs of the stars and the words, LORD OF AGES, only the words were in Latin, and I could not read them. This, he said, is the altar of our Lord, even as the other is. Now come, and see what a proud tradition we soldiers have.

The stone walls, and even the strong low pillars with their rounded arches, seemed to be covered with plates and tablets of stone, recording the lives and deaths of soldiers who had worshipped at this church. All the names were of men. There were no women's memorials here at all. Many of these monuments were framed with stone wreaths, and above them was written the word, DEO. Mr Pater explained to me that this too was Latin, and meant simply, TO GOD. The names on some of the stones were quite ordinary, but many of them were strange names. They are among the secret things, and I must not write them down. Mr Pater was able to tell me a little about these soldiers, how they fought bravely for their country and for their God, and how they died uncomplaining when they were called. It was remarkable that he could tell me something about every man whose name was there, no matter how long ago he had lived. This one, he said, was a valiant Lion, and this a faithful Persian. I may not mention the name, but it did not seem Persian to me.

Before I left that afternoon, Mr Pater asked me to kneel with him in front of the altar and say a prayer of thanks to God for sending me to the Church of Saint Denis Mitre. The battle continues, he said, and we must have soldiers. Life and Death, Light and Darkness await the outcome.

When may I come again? I asked.

When you will, he said.

And will you be here?

When you come I shall be here, he said.

That was my first visit to the Church of Saint Denis Mitre, and my first meeting with Mr Pater.

When I got back to my Aunt's house in Spicers Lane, I found that I had hardly been missed. I was able to tell of the streets I had walked along and the buildings I had seen, but I said nothing about the church and the Worshipful Company of Militia.

In the evening, while Aunt read to me from the Bible, I thought of the stories that Mr Pater had told me. Stories of great battles, of brave soldiers and mighty deeds, of victories won and enemies defeated. The stories that Aunt was telling me were not exciting, but those that Mr Pater had told me thrilled my martial blood even as I remembered them. I called to mind the great wars in which the Soldiers of God had fought, the mighty clash at Maranga and the battle of Chalons, when the plains were rich with the red blood of brave men. I thought upon these secret and terrible things, and I said no word to anyone.

It was not always easy for me to leave the house alone and to go about the City. On the next Sunday I was kept indoors because my Aunt fancied that I did not look well, and that the winter chill would be unhealthy for me. Twice at the weekends Aunt told me to stay with her because special company was coming to tea. The people who came were not special at all, though perhaps Aunt truly thought they were. They were an old woman, who was about Aunt's age, and her son and daughter. I had hoped that the son might be a soldier who could tell me exciting stories of wars and battles, but he was only a lawyer and very smartly dressed and dull. Aunt told me to be very agreeable to the young woman, and I did as well as I could, though I could not think why. She was pretty enough, but not interesting. I wanted more than anything to visit the hidden church again and to learn more about the soldiers.

Once, on a weekday afternoon, which I think was a Wednesday, I was sent on an errand to Aunt's bank, and I thought that I might return by way of the church. The day was covered in a greasy yellow fog, so that I could not see many paces in front of me, and I had to take care not to jostle people or step into the road. There were boys here and there with torches in their hands, to guide gentlemen along their way, and after I had called at the bank I followed one of these boys because it seemed to me that he would lead me in the right direction. As he passed the corner of a counting-house I saw in the light from his torch the sign with the name of the lane that leads to the secret narrow passage and the church, but when I walked along the lane all was so dark and uncertain that I could not find the old building with the entrance to the passage. When I got back to Spicers Lane I tried hard to hide my disappointment, but my Aunt noticed that something was wrong. Happily, she thought that I must have taken a chill, and she made Ann light the fire in my room and give me a hot drink and see that I went to bed early. I did not mind this in the end, because in my sleep I dreamed of being a soldier and fighting in the most glorious battles.

I was at last able to visit the church again, and it was on a Sunday afternoon, just as before. Three weeks had passed since my first visit, but Mr Pater was there as he had said, and he greeted me like an officer welcoming a faithful soldier. I felt very proud and very humble at the same time. With the Priest was an old man who must have been over fifty years of age. I may not tell his name, but Mr Pater said that he was a brave and loyal member of the Worshipful Company of Militia. He had risen high in the ranks and was soon to be promoted again, to the rank of Courier.

I said that I had not heard of an officer being called a Courier, even though I knew of Captains and Generals, but he explained that it is a rank that is very special to the Worshipful Company of Militia.

I asked the old man when and where he was to receive his new rank, and at that he pointed to the rounded west end of the church and said, I am to by buried at the great Festival on the twenty-fifth of December, when we celebrate the birth of God and His coming into the world.

I did not like to hear that, because he was a fine old man, and I did not want to think of him dying, but the two of them just laughed kindly and told me that no harm would come of it. He will pass through Death to a new Life, said Mr Pater, and on that joyful day he will be reborn. God will take care of him. You have much to learn, my son, but if you are willing to be taught you too shall share in our feast, and be recruited with the rank of Raven. God has shed the Eternal Blood for you. Can you refuse Him your service?

So then I knew that this good man had accepted me as a fit person to be a real soldier. It was the most important thing that had happened to me, and I resolved that I should be brave and strong and worthy of my brother, who died in battle far away. How proud he would be! You will be a true Servitor of the Lord, said the old man, and my heart rejoiced.

Mr Pater left me in the care of this good old soldier, and he told me many things about the great and honourable company that I am soon to join. Some of them are secret things and may only be spoken of among those who know. They made my head swim with the wonder and the glory of it all. At last Mr Pater came back and told me that it was time for me to go. They will miss you at home if you stay longer, he said, but you shall come once more before the great day.

That was my second visit to the soldiers' church, and it was near the end of November.

The third time I went to the church was on a Saturday afternoon, just two weeks ago. Of course, there were more people about in the streets, and the public houses and some of the shops were open, but all the City seemed very quiet when I thought of how it had been only that morning. The sky was all over clouds of a greyish blue, and towards the west was a great uncertain patch, so dark that it was almost black. The air itself felt heavy with excitement, as if it had been charged with electricity. But I did not need excitement from the air, for this was my third visit to the secret church, and my last before the great Festival, when God is born, and the year turns.

The Priest and the old soldier were there again to greet me and to conduct me into the church. We knelt before the altar to offer our eternal service to the God of Battles, and the flames that burned in the little pottery bowls shook a little, even as my heart shook, with the majesty and the glory.

Mr Pater said, Now, my son, you have seen what may be seen of this church above the ground. Today you shall see beneath, where lie the heart and bowels.

They led me behind the altar, to where an archway was covered by a hanging curtain. In the archway was a wooden door, which the Priest unlocked. Then, with two candles to light us, we proceeded down a narrow and winding stone stair to the church beneath the church.

It is the same shape as the church above, and no smaller. The walls are of a plain white, and on the floor is a design in stone to remind us always of God and His sacrifice. Behind the door that we had entered through stands a statue of a most beautiful Lady, whose face is proud and commanding. She is the Holy Virgin, Who is to be revered. The smell of incense and wine was strong.

Mr Pater said, Here is the real church, of which that above is but a shadow. See the benches and tables, where the Communion Feast is taken! See the High Altar, where the Holy Mysteries are celebrated! My son, this shall be your glory when you join us.

He told me and showed me much more: of the roaring of beasts and the croaking of birds, of the liquid sweetness of the honey wherein the Lions bathe, of the spiced sacramental wine. This much I may write down, but the rest is secret. I knew and gloried that I was to be admitted to the ranks of an ancient and blessed company.

When the time came for me to leave, Mr Pater said to me, You are God's gift to our cause, for we are few in number now and grow old. Our faithful friend here is the youngest of our company. I myself am older than you think, old beyond your imagining. Your youth and vigour are sorely needed in the great fight.

How shall I arrange to leave the house and come here on the day of the Festival? I asked.

Never worry, he said. I shall arrange that. Pay no heed to those who celebrate other gods upon the twenty-fifth of December, but set your heart and mind upon the one true God. They have kept us under foot for so long! But we are soldiers, you and I, and we will prevail. If by chance you cannot come to us upon the great day, then we shall come to you. Be assured!

And so I left the Church of Saint Denis Mitre and the Worshipful Company of Militia, but soon I shall return, for soon it will be the twenty-fifth, the day of the Festival of God's birth, and I shall hear in my ears the terrible pain in the bellowing of the dying bull.

"Yes," said George. "It's certainly a strange story. Powerful strange. What became of the boy?"

Julia took a thoughtful sip from her gin and tonic. "There," she said, "we have to rely on third-hand evidence. Some while ago my Canadian correspondent found a letter, written to his grandmother by a cousin, who tells what she had heard from someone else in the family — oh, dear! This is getting very complicated. What it comes down to is a very brief report on the death of a younger cousin, who isn't named but is certainly the Wenlock boy.

"You'll remember how amused he was at his aunt's notion that he'd taken a chill? Well, apparently he really had, though he'd ignored it. He was such a withdrawn, secretive lad that he managed to keep the worst of it from the rest of the household until a few days before Christmas, when it became clear that he was seriously ill. His mother had a weak heart, and it looks as if the complaint was hereditary. At all events, he was confined to his bed, and the doctor was called. Pneumonia, that was the diagnosis, and the boy wasn't to be left alone. The pneumonia aggravated the heart condition, and he died shortly after ten o'clock on Christmas morning. Not a very merry Christmas in that household, I fancy. He ate little and spoke little, though he seemed, they thought, to be waiting for something to happen. When he died, he was smiling.

"There. Now you know just as much as I do. What do you make of it?"

I started to say, "One or two things seem pretty plain — " But I was interrupted by George's voice. He spoke in an almost dreamy tone, quite as if no one else had said anything.

"Some years ago," he said, "your old friend Michael Harrison wrote a book setting out the theory that much of Roman London can still be traced in the names of the present City — street names and so forth. He went into considerable sound detail. One point I particularly remember is the notion that a few of the churches, too, have names that indicate Roman origins. Dionis Backchurch and Magnus Martyr, for instance, at the very least suggest *Dionysus Bacchus* and the *Magna Mater*."

"Now that," said Julia, "is something that hadn't occurred to me. And you think — ?"

He waved a hand, deprecatingly. "Well, the City certainly is a curious place — very secret and special, as young Wenlock put it. And I suppose that a hidden cult would tend towards corruption, mental or spiritual. My knowledge of the later Empire is limited, and I wouldn't dare offer it as proof, but — well — to me, at any rate, the name Denis Mitre strongly suggests *Deus Mithras*."

"I think you've got it," I said. "*Mithras, also a soldier...* The highest grade was *Pater*, if I remember rightly. And wasn't Cybele — the *Magna Mater* — also known as the Mother of God?"

The old man nodded in approving silence. Then he turned his sharp eyes to Julia. "Young lady," he said, "you haven't told us everything, have you? I appreciate that you weren't able to find out any more about the ancient militia company, but what of the church, heh?"

She laughed. "You're right, of course. I've been doing some research there, and I can tell you that St Denis Mitre was one of the churches that escaped the Great Fire. The parish was small and neither rich nor populous, so in about 1710 there were proposals to demolish the church. Instead, it was extensively renovated. Some of it was attributed to Hawksmoor, but the few surviving pictures of the building don't show anything that looks like his work.

"The church did exist, though it was eventually pulled down. It had stood empty for something over twenty years, having been closed on the authority of the Archbishop of Canterbury on account of 'certain un-Christian practices'."

She hesitated for a moment, looking at each of us in turn. "Now," she said, "here's the twist. That journal was written in about 1880. The Church of St Denis Mitre was destroyed in December of the year 1855. Make of it what you will."

"George," I said, "you've got your Christmas ghost story after all. How about another drink?"

Afterword

This was written for Richard's next seasonal anthology, *Mystery for Christmas*.

Rosemary Sutcliff's novel *The Eagle of the Ninth* reminded me that the birth of Mithras was celebrated on the 25th of December. That in turn put me in mind of an "alternative universe" story by Brian Aldiss in which Christianity and Mithraism are confused. Then there are the classic stories by Vernon Lee ("Marsyas in Flanders") and John Brunner ("The Man Whose Eyes Beheld the Glory"), in which the mistaking of the pagan for the Christian results in supernatural havoc... But the model for "The Soldier" was "The White People" by Arthur Machen, one of the most subtly disturbing stories ever written. Most of Machen's best work in the field is set in his native rural Wales, but he also knew how to find mystery and terror in London. I hope I've managed to achieve something of that in "The Soldier".

The book that George mentions is *The London that Was Rome* by Michael Harrison (London: George Allen & Unwin, 1971). Michael would probably have found my fantasy philologically unsound, but I'm still quite pleased with it.

It was interesting to discover just how easily I could describe a Mithraic temple in terms of a Christian church. The nearest I've come to cheating is in using Kipling's phrase "God of Battles", which does seem very appropriate for the soldiers' god.

Karl Edward Wagner picked "The Soldier" for *The Year's Best Horror Stories XIX*.

THE SOUVENIR

"What do you make of this?" said Tony Rawdon, and he placed on the table a small, squarish box, made of some kind of hard wood. It looked pretty old; either that or it had been very hard used. The unknown maker had evidently taken great care over it, but the sinuous carved decorations were nearly worn away. It was curious rather than beautiful.

I glanced at George Cobbett, who was peering interestedly at the box. "North African?" I hazarded.

Tony shook his head. "Close," he said. "I'm told it's actually Arabian, though no one's prepared to be more precise than that. Not that I got it in Arabia. Ha! No, I picked it up in Harwich some years ago.

"At that time I was living in Leicestershire, working for a company that dealt in maritime supplies — yes, I know that Leicestershire's about as far as you can get from the sea, but that's the way these things are. At any rate, in the September I was directed to visit a client in Harwich and instruct his staff in using some new equipment. I was book in at the *George* for four days, but since I had some leave owing to me I thought I'd stretch it out a bit — make a holiday of it.

"Well, before I left, my sister asked me to look out for a little something for her. She has quite a selection of artefacts from what we used to call the Near East. No, not a collection: an accumulation. There's a fair amount of really interesting and attractive stuff, but it's almost stifled by a much larger amount of, well, junk. Still, it's all precious to Jenny, and I'm happy to look out for more material for her.

"The work that I'd been sent to do was rather more arduous than I'd expected, so I was pleased on the first couple of evenings just to relax in the hotel, with a book and a drink or two. On the Thursday after work my client had invited me to his house for dinner. It would have been bad manners and very bad diplomacy to refuse. I fully expected the evening to be dull, and so it was, but at least I could feel that I'd done my duty, and when the last training session was over my time would be my own.

"The funny thing is that on the Friday morning all I'd been trying to drive into the heads of my client and his staff suddenly seemed to penetrate at last. After that it was just a matter of clarifying a few details, and as a result we were able to call a satisfied halt shortly after four o'clock. Things had gone so well that I didn't feel in the least tired. I refused offers of tea and biscuits and made my way eagerly into the town.

"Now, the only time I'd been there before was when I took the ferry from Parkeston Quay to the Hook of Holland, and I quickly discovered that Harwich isn't at all like Parkeston. Even the old quay, where small ships still call to pick up and set down, is quite different from the efficient, aggressive modernness of the Continental terminal. Well, I shan't bore you by trying to describe the place — you certainly know it better than I do, anyway. I'll just say that the quiet streets and the narrow alleys, the atmosphere of ancient glory and of nineteenth century portentousness, the impression that the sleepiness of the waterfront just hid some momentous secret activity — I found it all both reassuring and stimulating.

"For a while I just wandered, not attempting to take in anything in particular, but vaguely noting the old light-houses, the inns, the splendidly Victorian Town Hall, and gazing in a rather desultory way in the windows of the few antique shops. Most of them, not surprisingly, seemed to be devoted to maritime equipment and memorabilia — which wouldn't at all interest my sister. As for myself, I'd had quite enough of modern marine equipment that week to want to look at its dubious predecessors. I was happy just to carry on walking, which I did until my stomach decided to point out that I'd taken only a very light lunch and had eaten nothing since.

"I wasn't entirely sure where I was, but that was nothing to fret over; Harwich isn't a large town, and there must be several pubs where I could get a meal and a drink. Sure enough, just ahead and to the left, at the corner of one of the cuts, was a place advertising itself as the *Hero of the Nile*, which seemed very appropriate in a historic naval base. Now, what was the time? The sky was still fairly light, and the pubs mightn't be open yet. I checked my watch. No, all was well: it was after half past six. I'd been walking for much longer than I'd realised. The lights were on in the pub, and now I came to notice it there was even a placard in the window announcing that meals were available.

"I peered along the alley and saw, a little further up, a lighted shop window that looked rather interesting. Nearly seven o'clock. Hm. If the shop was open now, it might still be open when I left the pub. In any case, I could return in the morning. I pushed open the door of the *Hero of the Nile* and went in.

"An hour later, feeling a good deal better for food and drink, I left the pub. The shop window was still lit, and I noticed now that the name above it was Redvers Mariner, which seemed almost too good to be true. When I got to it, however, I was mildly disappointed to find that the place wasn't actually open. The proprietor apparently left one bulb burning overnight — a canny move. Now, what could I see in the window? Well, there was an attractive *art nouveau* desk-lamp; a set of pewter mugs and dishes that looked to me like seventeenth century work; some clockwork motor-cars — the metal ones we cherished as children, that are considered dangerous these days... In short, Mr Mariner's shop seemed to have just about everything. Ah! And there, right over in the corner, was a small wooden box, old and battered, with what looked to my inexpert eye like arabesque carving on it. Just the thing for Jenny, I thought. Now, the shop probably opens at nine in the morning, but just to be safe I'll try to be here by half past eight. Good! And the shop is in — ? I looked around for a sign that would tell me the name of this particular alley, but could see none. Never mind; I had only to find the *Hero of the Nile*, and I should find Mariner's shop.

"Having made that decision, I made another: a couple more pints of beer would go down well. Not here, though. I really should find my way back to the *George*. And so I did, by heading initially for the quay and taking my bearings from there.

"I wasn't as early as I'd intended getting to Mariner's shop the following morning, because I overslept, but it didn't matter, because the place wasn't open yet, despite the fact that it was now nearly nine-thirty. Perversely, I'd set my mind on buying that wooden box, even though I'd no idea how much was being asked for it, nor indeed what it actually was! It was enough that I'd found just the sort of thing that my sister would appreciate.

"The shopkeeper eventually unlocked his door at ten o'clock. I'd expected perhaps to spot him coming along the street, bustling because he was late, all haste and apologies, but in fact he opened the shop from inside. It seemed that he lived on the premises.

"Not wishing to seem hasty myself, I nodded acknowledgement to his greeting and entered the shop as nonchalantly as I could. If I'd expected the usual questions, I was to be disappointed. Mr Mariner didn't want to know, it seemed, whether I was looking for anything in particular. He simply sat, polite but inscrutable, behind a very nice rosewood desk, keeping a fatherly eye on things. At last, though, seeing that I was carefully keeping my hands in my coat pockets, he said in a quiet, cultured voice, 'You're welcome to touch anything you like, you know. There's very little here that's breakable.'

"'Thank you,' I said, but I still made my way slowly towards the box, as if it wasn't the one thing that I was interested in buying. Occasionally I'd catch a glimpse of the shopkeeper out of the corner of my eye, but his gentle, courteous expression never changed. Eventually, after much putting-off, I picked up the box.

"At last the shopkeeper showed some signs of interest. 'Ah,' he said. 'I wondered if you'd spot that. Unusual, isn't it?'

"I took the box out of the window and looked at it more closely. 'Can you tell me anything about it?' I asked.

"He pushed his glasses up on his forehead and ruminated for a moment.

"'Not much, I'm afraid,' he said. 'I got it from the family of a man named Bob Walton, who died about five years ago. Oh, he was a character, all right! Dear me, yes! Old Captain Walton, one of the last of the old-time barge skippers. He reckoned to have brought it back from Arabia before the war.'

"'That was a bit out of his way, wasn't it?' I said. 'I mean, the barges are tough little craft, but — '

"He laughed. 'Ah, now you're thinking of the coastal vessels. Well, they might cross the North Sea now and again, but they wouldn't take on a long voyage like that. No, Bob Walton was master of a boomsail barge. Dear me! The old *Alice May*. I've heard of some of the boomies even crossing the Atlantic, but I don't think Bob ever tried that. He did take *Alice May* several times to the Mediterranean, though — that I do know, but more I can't say. He never told his people what the box was for, you see, so they couldn't tell me.'

"He paused briefly, then added, 'They didn't like it, I can tell you that. Mind you, they didn't very much like him either, so perhaps it's no wonder that they wanted to get rid of his things. Would you believe it? They were actually going to throw that box away! Well, I wasn't having that. I know it's not very pretty, but it is a curio, when all's said and done, and curios are my business.'

"I asked the price, expecting from his apparent artlessness that it would be higher than this strange little object deserved. Still,

I was prepared to haggle, because by now I was quite sure that I wouldn't find anything more suitable for my sister. To my surprise, he wanted only a couple of pounds for it.

"'It cost me next to nothing,' he said, 'and as I can't give you any guarantees of provenance it would be dishonest to overprice it. After all, I don't even know how old it is.'

"I was pleased enough with my bargain to want to buy more, and in the end I left the shop with both the box and the *art nouveau* lamp, to which I'd taken a fancy. It must have been quite a profitable morning for Mr Mariner. He showed me the trick of opening the box, and then we shook hands and parted.

"After lunch I took the train to Colchester, not returning until mid-evening. At various times I took the box out of my briefcase and examined it. I was sure that Jenny would be delighted with it, and I knew that she wouldn't be bothered about what Mr Mariner called its provenance. I was curious, though. I looked carefully at the shapes carved on the sides, and wondered if they might perhaps be Arabic writing, but they were so worn and battered that I couldn't come to any conclusion. I opened the box again, and remember being surprised that the trick worked so smoothly, considering how much the thing seemed to have been through. I sniffed at the inside of it, with some idea of detecting what it had once held, but all I could smell was the wood.

"The train home was pulling in to Harwich Station when the conviction came upon me that there was another compartment in the box.

"I sat for a while on a bench outside the station, trying by the light of a street-lamp to test this notion. I poked at the box, prodded at likely looking bumps and dents on the sides, and eventually took my pocket-knife to it. The thing was so solidly made that there didn't seem much danger of my damaging it.

"It was frustrating work, especially in the poor light, but I was determined, and at last there was a stifled click that told me that my instincts had been right. The base of the box had twisted around, and a sort of drawer was revealed. Now, was there anything in it? I held it up to the street-light and looked closely in to the narrow space inside. All I could see was a very small quantity of a fine brownish powder.

"There came from nowhere a gust of wind, and the powder was suddenly blowing into my eyes. It was as if a hand had snatched it up and actually *thrown* it into my face. For a moment I was blinded. The stuff stung like the devil, and tears were streaming down my face. I dropped the box, closed my eyes and rubbed them — did all the things they tell you not to do in such circumstances.

"My first thought was pepper, which can do permanent damage, and I cursed myself heartily, but the pain began to fade remarkably quickly, and I was able to hope that there was no real harm done to my eyes. Cautiously, I tried opening them, relieved to find that the pain had now quite gone. It was a little while before I could actually see again, because of the tears, but at least I was able to put my breast-pocket handkerchief to use by wiping my eyes and generally cleaning my face. I stooped to pick up the box, which had closed itself again when I dropped it. Then I looked up.

"There were no lights.

"I don't mean that I was in total darkness. The sun had set some while ago, but there was a bright sliver of moon, and the stars were clear in the velvet blackness of the sky. What I mean is that there were no *other* lights. Harwich isn't the place to go for night life, but the time couldn't have been much beyond nine o'clock, and there should have been illumination from pubs and houses — and from the station.

"I *was* still at the station, wasn't I?

"I looked around wildly. I was outside a building of some kind, to be sure, but whether or not it was the station... And I seemed to be completely alone. For all I could tell, this was a town of the dead.

"It wasn't a comfortable thought.

"Maybe there had been a power cut — but even that wouldn't explain all this strangeness, this alien quality that surrounded me. I called out, cautiously, 'Hello!' — and immediately wished I hadn't. My voice rang madly, echoing from unseen walls, coming back to me like bitter laughter.

"But then I heard a sound of movement, away to my left, in the direction of what should be the town centre. Thank God, I thought. I'm not alone. The noise, quiet as it was, momentarily ceased, and it was borne in on me that in such circumstances company might not after all be desirable. The sound came again, nearer this time, and I looked, with a taut eagerness, through the colourless dark, straining my tortured eyes to see what was causing it.

"Something coming along the street, I thought, but there was no sign of anything.

"Then I caught just a glimpse of movement, not on the road, but beside it, above a high wall. As I watched, unable to stir, I saw two blank eyes and an unpleasantly confident grin raise themselves above the wall, on a pair of very long arms. The creature, whatever it was, was silhouetted against the starlit sky, and the arms seemed to be horribly thin and hairy. I shouldn't have been able to see the eyes at all. It's pretty certain that they couldn't see me; they were quite dead, with a sort of shiny, opaque film over them. The grin never wavered, but the narrow head was gently turning this way and that, and now I could hear an animal-like snuffling sound.

"At that, my nerve broke, and I fled, leaving my briefcase on the ground, but still tightly clutching the box. God knows where I went — I was running blind in that near-darkness, running from something that was itself blind but had a dreadfully purposeful feeling to it.

"Was I still in Harwich? I don't know, and I was in no position to stop and look. There was still no artificial light to be seen, and the place seemed as empty of life as a cemetery. I ducked into a side-street, emerging moments later on to a broader road. Unrecognisable structures towered above me. I twisted and turned desperately, as behind me I still heard the easy long-legged stride and the snuffling of my pursuer.

"God knows how long I ran. My head was aching, my throat was painful, and there was a sharp stitch in my side. At one point I spotted an open door a little way along the street. Safety, I thought — respite! But just as I reached it, the door was slammed shut. If there was life in this place, then it was hostile. On I ran, occasionally turning my head, fearing to see something close on my heels.

"At last, just as I thought that I should collapse from exhaustion and fear, I glanced behind me once more, and at that moment ran smack into a wall. My head struck the wall ferociously hard. There was a sudden, brief impression of blazing light and an equally sudden explosion of pain. As I lost consciousness I could feel something tearing at my clothes.

"I came to in what seemed to be agonisingly bright light. My head hurt like hell, but slowly I opened my eyes — to find that I was lying on the pavement in what was unmistakably a normal, well-lit English town. A solicitous elderly couple were bending over me, and when they saw that I was conscious they told me that they'd called an ambulance. I wasn't sure at first that I needed an ambulance, but the pain in my body and my head was enough to convince me.

"No one, it seemed, had seen anything of my flight or my collapse. The assumption was that I had been mugged, and I had sense enough not to contradict it. Some interest was shown in the box, which was still firmly clutched in my hand.

"I spent some days at the hospital. My injuries were mostly superficial, though I was left with a permanent deafness in my left ear.

"That could all be explained quite straightforwardly, but the authorities were puzzled by the rents and slashes in my clothes, some of which had penetrated to the flesh.

"It won't surprise you that I left Harwich very soon after, and that I've never been back there."

Tony stopped, to finish his glass of whisky. "My briefcase was never found," he added. "But that may mean nothing."

George picked up the box. "I'm still curious about this," he said.

Tony laughed, briefly and without humour. "I'm not," he said. "I've managed to curb my curiosity sufficiently to make no further attempts to open the secret drawer — even though I'm pretty sure that whatever was in it is spent now. You'll have gathered, by the way, that I didn't in the end give it to my sister. Quite simply, I think it's too dangerous. I'd burn it, only I worry that doing so might release anything hostile that remains. Eventually I'll find a sure means of disposing of it, but in the meantime it stays with me."

I went to get another round in. When I returned to our table, I could see by the expression in George's sharp little eyes that he thought there was more to come. As usual, he was right.

"I did indulge my curiosity to this extent," said Tony. "I took the box to an old friend of mine, Paul Bensusan, who's a formidable linguist, and I asked him to look at the decoration on the sides. As I'd half suspected, it's actually Arabic writing, and still readable, despite its condition. It's a text from *The Koran* — from the Book of Ya Sin, to be precise — and it can be translated as 'This is Hell, which was promised to you.'"

Afterword

This was my entry for the Ghost Story Society's second competition. It just failed to make the top three, and was subsequently published in the society's journal, *All Hallows 6*.

The George and *The Hero of the Nile* are both fictional. The former has something in common with a real and very distinguished Harwich hotel, *The Three Cups*, which closed in 1995, a victim of the recession that made north-east Essex one of the most economically depressed areas in southern England.

"The Souvenir" is another variation on the basic theme of "Oh, Whistle, and I'll Come to You, My Lad".

SWEET CHIMING BELLS

"You were singing something!" Philippa Warren looked at me accusingly.

"Was I? Sorry" No doubt most people find themselves humming or singing to themselves, often without being aware of it. I set down the tray of drinks.

"Something about bells," she said. George Cobbett raised his head and peered quizzically at me from under bushy brows.

"Bells? Oh, right." I thought for a second. "Yes. *Sweet bells, sweet chiming Christmas bells*... It's one of the Yorkshire carols."

Philippa shivered, a reaction I hadn't expected. George and I looked curiously at her. After a moment she smiled, suddenly and briefly. "Sorry," she said. "It's just that there's a rather ironic aptness to it. Bells come into the story — oh, yes. And it all happened in Yorkshire...

"It isn't my story, I should add. In fact, I'm not going to tell you the full details — names and so forth. They aren't important. It's enough that a distant relative of mine, not long before the war, had moved with her husband to a small town in the West Riding of Yorkshire, where he'd been appointed assistant curate at the parish church." Philippa sighed. "They must have been very young, you know. At least, they were only recently married, and very much in love. This was his first appointment, and she had great hopes for him. He wasn't a Yorkshireman by birth, but his father's family had come from Scarborough, and that went some way to overcoming the local wariness of foreigners. The rest he had to achieve on his own, and it seems that he was doing very well, being intelligent and a genuinely good fellow. He'd thrown himself whole-heartedly into the life of the town, supporting the workers at the local coal-pit, proving himself very useful on the rugger field, and becoming an invaluable addition to the team of bell-ringers.

"His young wife was very proud of him, and only sorry that her own diffidence and shyness didn't allow her to make the sort of impression in the parish that he deserved. She felt, rightly or not, that the people regarded her with a sort of tolerant contempt. They'd been in the town for some nine months, and were looking forward to their first Christmas there — with rather mixed emotions. When it was nearly over, she wrote down the story as she saw it. I'll read it to you."

Philippa took from her bag a red-covered exercise book, of the sort that we used at school. She took a drink from her glass of white wine, and then, opening the book to the first page, she began to read.

Christmas is, above all, the time of peace to all mankind, the time when all should see themselves as brothers and sisters. I hoped that my Edward's popularity would ease the way for me to be accepted, at this season of the year, into the enclosed little community that was now our home. My intentions, I am sure, were for the best, but I lacked the social ability to reach out and touch these people. I was not one of them, though I hoped desperately that in time I might be. My intentions, I say again, were good, but I cannot now put from my mind the old saw about the Road to Hell.

How shall I describe the town? It has that curious quality that we sometimes find, of combining the industrial and the rural, seemingly without strain. In size, it would scarcely qualify as a town were it situated in the south and east of the country — say, in Essex, which is my own home — yet it is, so to speak, complete. All the usual offices are there, including a small, sedate, Town Hall. The parish church, where Edward and his vicar had the cure of souls, is a fine building, well kept and well appreciated by its parishioners. There are also at least two flourishing non-conformist chapels, belonging to the Methodists and to the Strict Baptists. The people are fiercely loyal to each other and to the town itself. I longed to show them that I too was capable of loyalty, and — for my husband's sake — deserving of it.

As we often find in places where the Methodists are well established, there is a grand tradition of singing. We had already attended a number of recitals by the Choral Society, and it was gratifying to see that men from our own church choir and members of the Methodist congregation raised their voices together, making one great and glorious "joyful noise to God". Edward and I were eagerly looking forward to the services at Christmas.

And then, of course, there were the church bells. Edward had become an enthusiastic ringer while at the university, and his superiors at theological college had by no means discouraged him, though it was understood that his parish duties should always take precedence. The ringing, I remember him saying, was an expression of praise to God. For some, it was their only way of expressing praise; he must respect that, but he as a clergyman had greater means and higher duties. It is no slur upon his integrity to add that he delighted in the bells and assisted in ringing the changes (as I think they call it) whenever his conscience would allow.

The holy time approached. The town was not a rich one, but the shopkeepers had made brave and festive work of decorating their premises, while the boughs of evergreen in the church were tasteful and comforting in their reminder of my far-away childhood. I made a determined effort to appear less nervous than I felt when meeting the people of the town. It was so frustrating! They had a sort of friendly tolerance for Mr Barnicott, the vicar, who was an elderly, benign, but rather unworldly gentleman. Me they seemed still to treat with suspicion. Edward, however, inspired a clear enthusiasm. If only, I thought, I could break through my own reserve, then perhaps I could break through theirs. And so, as I have said, I put myself out to be cheerful and accessible, and it seemed to be having some effect. I refused to mope alone in our little house, but went out into the cold and brightly lit streets, into the shops, greeting the townsfolk by name, forcing myself to appear tranquil, and tranquilly wishing to all the compliments of the season.

It was worth the effort, for the initial suspicious looks mellowed, not perhaps to actual friendliness, but at least to something like the amused patience with which the vicar was treated.

It was particularly pleasing that I should at last attract something more wholesome than silent contempt from Mr Hartley, the captain of the bell-ringers. He was a man in his fifties, with that quiet air of authority that the true leader has. A lifetime's work in the colliery had made and nearly broken him: he could have been taken for a man of seventy, bone-thin, but with a wiry strength in him that even Edward could not match. As leader of the ringers, he held a position of honour, admired by all those in the town who could appreciate the strength and the delicacy of touch that the bells required. Edward liked and respected him, and I am sure that he in his turn liked and respected Edward. There are, after all, few clergymen who truly appreciate the mystery of the bell-tower. At last it seemed that he was prepared to like me, and for my husband's sake I was glad of it.

A few days before Christmas, I was permitted to climb the narrow, winding stairs and watch the ringers at their work. No doubt I am stupid, or perhaps just unmusical, but I could not even then take in the intricacies of their art. I could only look, listen and admire, while my Edward and the others of the team, all under the quiet discipline of their captain, created the mathematical pattern of sound. After the course had been rung, Mr Hartley looked at me, apparently as stern as ever, then turned to Edward and said, "Maybe the lass would care to see the bells themselves?"

I knew then that a small, but significant breach had been made in the barrier. My dear husband looked at me, and there was such a wealth of proud love in that look I felt that Christmas itself could bring no greater joy. And so we mounted the sturdy old ladder and entered the bell-chamber.

There are eight bells in the peal, huge creatures of bronze, their weight seeming to strain endlessly at the wooden beams from which they hung. I marvelled that mere human beings could manipulate such mighty things, taming and directing their strength in the praise of God. Ringing was over now, and the great bells were at rest, each hanging below its beam. Mr Hartley reached out a hand and gently stroked one of the bronze giants. "Aye," he said, "near forty years I've rung in this tower, and these bells have been dear friends to me."

"Mind you," he continued, fixing his intense eyes upon us, "they demand respect as well as love. Oh, yes — you may smile, young fellow, but you're inexperienced yet, good as you are. I tell you both, you must treat the bells with respect, or they could turn against you. Still and all, they've been good friends to me."

Very practical advice, no doubt, but it sounded to me like a warning not to meddle in things beyond our capabilities. Very well, I thought; you need have no fear of me. I like and admire your bells, but I do not understand them, and you may be sure that I shall not interfere with them. In an attempt to brighten the sudden gloom of the atmosphere, I asked Edward which of the bells did he ring?

He smiled, and placed his hand upon one of them. "Here she is," he said. "This is the other lady in my life. Her name is Honour."

I was surprised. "Do the bells have names, then?" I asked.

"Indeed they do, and these are all called after Christian virtues. Let me see if I can remember them all." He thought for a moment, and then recited the list that I can still clearly recall: "Faith, Hope and Charity; Patience, Obedience and Honour; Joy and Mercy. Those are the names in order, from the smallest bell right up to the great tenor. It's a fine ring, Mr Hartley — a wonderful ring."

The captain nodded approvingly, his thin face momentarily losing its dour expression. "That it is," he said, "and old Mercy, well, she's about the finest tenor I've ever rung." Abruptly, he took out his watch, glanced at it, and announced that it was time to go.

We descended once more to the ringers' chamber, and thence to the floor of the high tower, where he opened the big door and bustled us out into the churchyard. For a moment he seemed to hesitate, and then, unexpectedly, he shook me by the hand, saying, "You take good care of him, lass. He's one of the good ones. Well, I may not see you before the day, so I'll wish you a merry Christmas."

Before I could recover my composure sufficiently to return the compliment, he had turned his back upon me and was saying earnestly to my husband, "I hope you've managed to get vicar's word to join us on Christmas Eve?"

"I think so," said Edward. "But you know how vague he can be. He's still quite likely to demand my services elsewhere." He smiled, ruefully it seemed, and added, "After all, I am paid to be a priest, not a ringer."

"Well, we'll see," said Mr Hartley. And with that he left us.

It was not until Christmas Eve itself that a visit from Mr Hartley reminded me to ask what special event should call for my husband's presence in the bell-tower that day. Edward looked rather sheepish, and said, "Oh, it is just an old Christmas custom." But Mr Hartley's bony hand was on his shoulder, and the fervent eyes were darting sharply, now at Edward, now at me.

"Old custom?" said Mr Hartley, slowly. "Aye, sir, it's a very old custom. We may believe that it's as old as Jesus Christ himself!"

Ignoring Edward's startled look, he continued, "Ringing the Old Lad's passing bell — that's what it is, ma'm."

"The Old — ?" I looked helplessly at my husband.

"The Devil," he explained. "It is believed that with the birth of our Lord, the Devil died. Or perhaps it was with the Harrowing of Hell — though in that case they should toll the bell on Easter

Saturday... " His voice tailed off, and there was an expression almost of guilty confusion on his face.

I did not understand. This seemed the merest nonsense to me. How could anyone look intelligently at mankind and maintain that the Devil was dead?

He made an effort to justify the matter: "It is, after all, harmless, my dear. The tradition is that, upon Christmas Eve, the great tenor bell should be tolled the same number of strokes as there have been years since Christ was born. Further, the final note should come with the last stroke of twelve, to welcome in the great day."

Mr Hartley's expression as his listened to my husband did not flicker by so much as a muscle. He had the look of almost feverish determination that we associate with the early Apostles. He spoke quietly and without fuss: "Welcoming the day — well, that's a nice thought, but it's not the reason." He turned to me, looking intently into my eyes, as if searching for signs of comprehension in them. "You see, each stroke is another safe year. It must be the right number of strokes, exactly, and it must end at midnight, or the Old Lad won't be held under any more. It doesn't matter whether you understand, ma'm, not really, but please understand that it is important to us."

I looked at my husband, whose face showed clear signs of embarrassment — and well it might. He cleared his throat and said, "It is just a custom, my dear, and quite harmless. Why, the same sort of thing used to take place in many towns and villages before the Commonwealth, when the Puritan reformers abolished so many charming customs. Even now, you know, there's a similar tradition in Dewsbury." There was a sort of desperate cheerfulness in his voice as he turned to the older man. "Isn't that right, Mr Hartley?"

"Dewsbury? Aye, right. But in *Dewsbury* — " (he pronounced the name with some scorn) "— the ringing was revived only a century ago. There's not the same force, you see, because in this town we've never ceased. The Puritans would have got short shrift here if they'd tried to interfere."

I shook my head in bewilderment. I thought of the great world outside, where the Four Horsemen ran riot, and I wondered again how any sane person could claim that the Devil was dead.

Before I could voice my thoughts, Edward spoke, brightly — as if an idea had just occurred to him: "It can only be for good, you know. Remember that all the bells are named after the Christian virtues, and that the Devil's knell is sounded upon the tenor — Mercy. It must be good, surely, to offer Mercy."

But Mercy to whom? I wondered.

"And to make assurance double sure," he continued, "I have just remembered. On one side of the bell's rim is inscribed the word Mercy, but on the other, done it seems rather earlier, is your own middle name — Ruth. And Ruth, as you know, means Mercy. I shall think of you, my dear, while Mr Hartley is ringing 'The Old Lad's Passing Bell'."

I gave up. The captain was looking meaningly at his watch, and had his hand on my husband's arm. "Very well," I said. "Go and toll for the Old Lad. I shall be in bed and asleep, I am sure, long before you even start, while you are still ringing the changes. Goodnight, Mr Hartley, and a merry Christmas to you."

The old man's expression relaxed, and he nodded courteously. My husband's face was stamped with relief as the two of them left the house. I closed the door quietly behind them and made my way to the kitchen, where, after feeding our cat Tabitha, I intended to tire myself out completing arrangements for the holy day.

But I could not pull my mind away from what seemed to me to be the most futile and superstitious nonsense. A line from an old song came to me unbidden: "Some say the Devil's dead, and buried in Coldharbour — "

"Not true!" I said aloud. It was not, and sadly could not be true.

Almost unconsciously, I heard the bells sounding the method — Stedman, or Grandsire, or whatever it was — in its mathematic precision, and I found myself musing upon the names of the bells. It was right, of course, that they should be called after good things; no one could object to Faith, Hope, Charity and the others. It pleased me to think that my dear husband should have been allocated the bell called Honour, because honour was the keystone of his life and career. But what of the great bell, the tenor, which bore the name of Mercy? God's mercy should indeed flow out over the town, like the sound of the bells, but should mere man presume to offer mercy to the Devil?

No, it was too hard a problem for me to unravel. I was even unsure about Edward's notion that some benefactor had made assurance double sure by inscribing the bell with both names, Mercy and Ruth. It is true that my second Christian name is Ruth, but though I am naturally aware of its significance the name has never been one that I cared for. Still, each to his own, as the townsfolk would say.

But the Devil? Perhaps he had been staved away from this quiet, comfortable little town, but he still held sway in the world. The Devil dead? I had only to think of the suffering, the fighting, the disease and the poverty that seemed to over-run our little planet, and from which the holy time of Christmas offered such blessed relief, to know that the Devil was far from dead.

Aloud I said, "You fools! You claim to keep evil at bay by ringing the church bells, but the Devil is alive — he is not dead, and in your hearts you know it!"

It is difficult to be accurate about what happened then. The very atmosphere seemed to change, to become electrically charged, as in a lightning storm, and I was suddenly aware that the single bell was striking — had been striking continuously — but now, for a moment, had faltered.

So, I thought, they are ringing the Old Lad's Passing Bell. Such foolishness! How could intelligent adults do such things? And one of them a minister of God! It made no sense.

Then I realised: the sound of the great bell, heard but unnoticed, had faltered. It was that very fact that had made me aware of the monotonous tolling. Suddenly I felt light-hearted — and, I should say, light-headed. The thought came to me, smug and unbidden, that my own unheard protests had interrupted these men in their silly ritual.

I stood at the kitchen window and looked into the night, at the cold bright stars shining in the infinite darkness, and I felt small and ashamed. After all, as my husband had said, it was a harmless custom, though to mind dependent upon a blinkered view of the world. And this was Christmas, the time above all when we can afford to indulge our loved ones. Let him enjoy himself.

In that mellow frame of mind, I made to prepare for bed, but was taken aback by sudden, insistent and frantic knocking upon our front door. Some call, no doubt, for my husband's good offices. Well, Edward would just have to forgo the rest of his time in the bell-tower; being the good-hearted fellow that he was, he would not resent it.

I vaguely recognised the man at the door as one of Mr Hartley's team of ringers: a strong, quiet fellow who earned his keep at a nearby dairy farm. His face, bereft of its usual ruddy and complacent expression, was now white and drawn, the scared eyes not daring to meet mine. The air once again seemed alive with electricity.

"Are you looking for my husband?" I asked, somehow knowing that it was not so. The only reply was a gulp for breath, and I continued, fearing the truth, "Isn't he with the ringers, in the church tower?"

My caller began to shake his head, then corrected himself and nodded, the frightened look never leaving him. Fear was upon us both, and I could not raise more words. He found voice at last, seeming to whimper as he spoke: "You must come, ma'm — to the tower. It's your husband, ma'm. I can't explain — you'll see for yourself!"

What could have happened? I did not know and dared not think. All that came to my numb mind as we hurried across the graveyard to the church was the realisation that above us the tenor bell, Mercy, was still tolling inexorably for "the Old Lad".

We reached the tower. The young man, in a fever of haste, wrenched open the great door. We hurried up the narrow, winding staircase to the ringing chamber.

Injury, havoc — whatever evils I might have imagined for my poor darling were both unrealised and surpassed. Mr Hartley, with great gentleness, raised the cloth that had been laid over Edward's body, and I saw that in death he looked at peace with himself and with God.

I did not faint, though it would have been a blessed relief to do so. Instead, it seems, I went temporarily mad. I remember nothing of the rest of that night; no, nor of Christmas Day, nor of the two following. On the fourth day, I woke as from a normal sleep, to find a nurse seated placidly beside my bed. Ah, I thought, I have been ill. But where is my husband? And then memory rushed back of the devastation of Christmas Eve.

The nurse looked me over, spoke a comforting platitude, and went to call for the doctor. That gentleman arrived quickly, and with him Mr Barnicott, the vicar, who for the moment merely took my hand in his and said nothing. I found his silent presence peculiarly comforting. The doctor's examination, more mental than physical, seemed to satisfy him, though the look of grave concern never left his face. Having assured himself that I was in capable hands, he made out a prescription for some tranquillising drug, which he handed to the nurse. Then he left.

For the first time, Mr Barnicott spoke: "How much do you know?" Not waiting for an answer, he turned to the nurse and said, "Have you told her anything?"

She shook her head, and at last I found my own voice. "I can speak for myself, and I must know all," I said.

The old gentleman nodded. "Yes," he said. "It is better that you should. But understand that I was not myself a witness. I was in my own study, polishing my sermon for the Christmas morning service. Mr Hartley, I have no doubt, can give you a first-hand account. For myself, as I say, I was working at the Vicarage, with my ears half-tuned to the tolling of the great bell, wondering idly how the ringers could keep a tally on nearly two thousand strokes. Then the steady progress of the ringing stumbled. It was momentarily interrupted, but only momentarily. Almost immediately, it was taken up again.

"As you will have realised, it was your husband who was sounding the tenor bell. Mr Hartley told me that he had taken a liking to young Edward and, knowing him to be a fine ringer, had decided upon this honour for him."

My feelings may not easily be imagined; certainly they cannot easily be described. I was at the same time proud for my dear husband of the esteem in which the ringers held him, sad that he could not enjoy the honour done him, and resentful that the same honour had taken him from me. I could not then fully appreciate my loss — indeed, I did not then know the full depth of it.

The vicar: "Suddenly, so the others say, Edward stumbled, pulling clumsily at the rope, falling to the floor in an apparent faint. Mr Hartley's first thought, he admits, was for the bell. He took the rope and continued sounding the old year's passing bell. I doubt that anyone who had not been listening closely would have noticed that briefest of interruptions."

And yet I noticed, I thought, and I had been unaware till then of the bells.

Mr Barnicott had not stopped. "One of the others knelt beside Edward and tried to rally him, but it would have done no god whoever had attended to him, for the poor lad was already dead. Were you aware, my dear, that he had a weak heart."

I shook my head, dumbly. I was aware of no such thing.

"Even so," said the vicar, "the doctor's examination plainly showed that he had suffered a sudden and lethal heart attack.

"You were called, I know, to the ringing chamber, though I do think that perhaps the news might have been broken to you more gently. It must have been a dreadful shock to you."

A shock indeed, but not really a surprise. I had not realised that before.

He did not apparently expect me to speak, though he paused for just a moment. His lips were pursed, and his fine brow furrowed. He sighed, and continued: "You did not faint. Instead, and I cannot blame you, you — broke down." (He was choosing his words, treading very carefully, not looking at me while he spoke.) "When I arrived, a little before Doctor Lake, two of the ringers were holding you firmly seated upon the bench. You were struggling to reach the bell-rope, perhaps seeing it as the instrument of your poor husband's death, and crying out — well — " (For the first time he seemed truly embarrassed. He paused, as if to draw courage to him, then turned to look me earnestly in the face.) "You were crying out," he continued, "upon the Devil for mercy."

There was no feeling of shame in me; it was as if he spoke of some other person. Instead, I felt a languorous, anaesthetic coldness in my breast. The vicar was a good man, a kind man, but he did not know everything. It was plain that the ringers had not told him the true meaning of that annual tolling of the great bell — not, I thought uncharitably, that he would have understood if they had told him. I do not think that my poor Edward had fully understood, and certainly I had not. How different things might have been if I had!

"There is little else to tell," said Mr Barnicott. "You shortly became submissive and allowed the doctor and me to lead you home. I arranged for you to have a nurse by you all the time, and we have both looked in upon you twice a day. The nurse was instructed to call us as soon as you recovered — and now you have recovered. Christmas is past, three days past, and a sad time it was.

"My dear, I have not told you how sorry I am at poor Edward's death, but I think you know that already. Besides, I believe — as I am sure you do — that he is in the safest keeping. We must give thought now to your future. You must rest and regain your strength, of course, and for as long as need be you are welcome to stay with Mrs Barnicott and me at the Vicarage. You will not, I suppose, wish to stay alone in this house.

"Well, I have told you all I know, all I can remember. Is there anything you wish to ask me — or anything you think you should tell me?"

No, there was nothing I should tell him. He was a good man, remote from the world. Let him remain so. There was something I should ask, however.

"It was Mr Hartley who showed me my husband's — showed me my husband. And yet you say that it was he who retrieved the rope. How could that be?"

He seemed curiously relieved, as if he had expected a different question. "That is simply answered: having got the ringing back on course, he had delegated one of the others to continue."

I had been unaware until then of the tension in my body; now I felt able at last to relax. The little town was safe again, and so was I while I remained there.

There was a pause, and I realised that the vicar was considering whether or not to tell me something further. He was a simple, gentle old man, and quite transparent. Eventually he spoke, as I knew he must: "One singular thing. Hartley seemed oddly perturbed by something quite trivial. 'We have lost count,' he said — over and again. 'We have lost count.' As if it mattered!"

The coldness within me became an icy clamp, squeezing my heart. They had lost count! Mr Barnicott did not understand the significance of that simple fact, but at last — and too late, perhaps — I did. What had Mr Hartley said? "It must be the right number of strokes, exactly." Just so. There was no safety here for me, nor for any other. It would have been good to accept the vicar's invitation, but I knew that danger lay that way. With what grace I could muster, I declined the offer. The decision had been made for me, and for the moment I must stay in the house that was now so empty without my husband's vital presence. There was no strength in me to weep, though there would be a time for tears. If I had no comfort now, at least there was company, in the affectionate little form of Tabitha, our cat.

The vicar left, promising that he or his wife would call upon me each day, and that they would remember me in their prayers. I was glad of that, for if ever a soul stood in need of mercy, it was I. Compassion, mercy, ruth... I thought of the great soul-less tenor bell whose pulling had destroyed my poor Edward's heart. Mercy was a scarce commodity, it seemed.

I dismissed the nurse, preferring for the moment to be alone, and in my solitude I wept. How long the fit was upon me I do not know, but at the last I felt emptied of all strength and emotion, with only a great weariness in me. I fed Tabitha, who had been well cared for during my illness, and went to my lonely bed, where sleep came directly to me.

I was half woken at some early hour by Tabitha's mewling and the movement of the bedclothes as she tried to pull them off me. Too tired for movement, aware vaguely of the coldness outside the bed, I called sleepily to her to stop, which she did, and I drifted again into sleep, to a world of dreams that I could never afterwards recall.

Only upon waking fully in grey daylight did I remember that before going to bed I had put the cat outside and closed the door behind her.

There was a sickness upon me, not of the body or the mind, but of the soul. They had lost count. Mr Hartley's words came back to me; it would be a sad jest to say that they haunted me. The ringers had lost count! The town was no longer protected, and I above all was in danger, for I above all had been arrogant and foolish. I should leave, as soon as I could, for only then might both be safe.

I had neither family nor close friends upon whom I could impose. Besides, the proprieties demanded that I stay at least until my husband's funeral was over. These things take time, and I must resign myself to that. In God alone could I confide, and it seemed that He had abandoned me to the Old Lad.

The days that followed were like a living dream. I try to recall detail, but all evades me; nothing is substantial. My nights were not my own, and I grew drawn and hollow-eyed for lack of rest. Again and again there came that tug at the bedclothes, and the pleading animal sound, until at last – whether consciously or not I do not know – I murmured an invitation. After that, something warm and momentarily comforting shared the nights with me, going some way towards assuaging my grievous loss.

The old couple at the Vicarage may have noticed some change or deterioration in me, but except on one specific occasion I cannot now remember if they said or did anything to indicate it. That was upon the day when I found just outside the kitchen door the sad little heap of fur and bones that had been my beloved

Tabitha. Someone, it seemed, would brook no rivals, and that would be hard to forgive.

The captain of the ringers tended to avoid me, and perhaps that is to be expected, for he at least had the knowledge and the native shrewdness to realise what I had done and what I had become.

The day of the funeral came. Many compliments were paid to Edward's sweetness of character, his honesty and strength, his courage and intelligence. Many pitying looks were directed at me, but no help was offered. The day went as it had come, bringing nothing and leaving nothing. My husband was dead, and nothing remained of him. There would be no children now. It was as if he had never been.

At last, with what money I could raise, I was able to move away from the town and from the area. The chance came none too soon, for the new curate had already been appointed and was due to take over the house that I could no longer call mine.

I went first to Cheshire, where I took a post as secretary to a lady, but after some weeks we parted — "by mutual agreement", as she said. After that I tried my hand once more at teaching, near Northampton; there was something in the faces of the children, however — a calculated knowingness that no child should be capable of — that I was glad shortly to leave. So I have made my way by stages, as perhaps I had known that I would, back to my own home county. It has been a curious experience in my progress to observe the demeanour of those I meet, and to gauge whether they realise that I do not travel alone.

Each morning I find myself almost surprised to wake, for sleep and I seem to be strangers these days. My nights bring little repose, but there are other things, and I usually find that there is an impress in the pillow beside my head.

Those strange events in Yorkshire — how pin-sharp some aspects are in my memory, while others are all uncertain. Nearly a full year has passed, and soon Christmas will be on us again. Will Mr Hartley sound the Old Lad's Passing Bell, I wonder? I hope he does, that the town may still have protection. He need have no fear that the barriers are useless now, for whatever came through last year left the town with me and has been my companion ever since.

It is a tale of irony above all, and the greatest irony is the name of that bell, the great tenor. Mercy it is called — but mercy for whom, I ask? Mercy for whom?

Soon it will be Christmas, and my baby will be born.

Philippa closed the book, quietly but decisively, and put it down on the table in front of her. "The poor creature was found dead a day or so before that next Christmas," she said. "The verdict was death by natural causes. The family found her book and tried to dispose of it, thinking that it reflected on their sanity. They evidently weren't efficient about it because my brother found it some months ago and passed it to me. There was no baby, by the way, and she wasn't pregnant."

Philippa drank what was left of her wine, and looked pointedly at me.

"Uh-uh," I said. "This is George's round."

The old man glared at me as if I'd betrayed him, but eventually he took out his wallet and handed me a note, saying, "I'll pay for 'em, but you can fetch 'em — and don't worry! We'll say nothing more about Philippa's story till you get back."

He was as good as his word, though I could see when I returned with the drinks that there was a question demanding to be asked. Typically of George, though, he put it off until we were settled and he had his pipe going satisfactorily. At last he took a swig from his glass of bitter and said bluntly, "Look here, young woman! Just how true is this story? You'll forgive my asking, but you've refused to give us names or even a date. So I repeat: is it true?"

Philippa waved a slim hand. "The book at least is genuine," she said, "and you're welcome to examine it. As to the story, I have no doubt that the poor woman believed it. But no, I won't tell you her name."

"Hm!" He was clearly dubious. "Well, I suppose I could look this Barnicott up in *Crockford*. That should give us a lead to the identity of the town — "

"You can if you want," I said, "but as it happens I know that town. It's on the outskirts of Bradford, and of course it's grown a bit since the thirties. It hasn't changed that much, though. I was there a few years ago with a friend who's a bell-ringer; he showed me the church bells.

"The tradition is officially known as 'tolling for the old year', much as Mr Barnicott knew it. Or rather, it *was* called that. The Puritans didn't manage to silence the bells, but Adolf Hitler did.

The custom wasn't continued after the war, though I understand that there's talk of reviving it now. No mention of the Devil, however; that bit seems to have been what you might call secret knowledge."

I picked up my glass and drank, finding when I put it down that Philippa and George were both gazing expectantly at me. I looked as innocent as I could, but said nothing, though the question in their minds was obvious. Perhaps I was being rather hard on Philippa, but it's a rare situation when I know something that George doesn't.

At length the old man lowered his bushy eyebrows, harrumphed, and turned to Philippa. "Will you ask him, my dear?" he said, in a tone that suggested that his patience was wearing thin.

"Very well," she said. "Roger, you told us that your friend had shown you the church bells. Was there anything strange about the tenor bell? Could anyone tell you why it should have two names — Mercy and Ruth?"

"It's not usual, is it?" I said. "George has probably guessed the answer, though. Despite what your unfortunate relative was told, the bell has only one name: it's called Mercy. But also inscribed on the rim is an appropriate reference to the Bible — "

George nodded grimly, and I saw understanding in Philippa's eyes. "Yes," I said, "to the Book of Ruth. Rather worn, but still legible, it reads, if memory serves me rightly, 'Ruth i xvi'. You'd recognise it as the loyal words of Ruth to Naomi."

"Very appropriate," said Philippa.

"Appropriate and ironic," I said. "Almost the last entry the young woman made in that book, you'll recall, was a comment on the irony of the name Mercy. The real irony is in the biblical text, because it contains the words of Ruth... Go on, George. You can quote more accurately than I can."

He closed his eyes and appeared to be searching his memory, but the words can fluently and precisely: "'Intreat me not to leave thee, or to return from following after thee: *for whither thou goest, I will go; and where thou lodgest, I will lodge.*'"

Afterword

Each December, if it's possible, my wife and I like to get up to Sheffield for the carol-singing in the pubs near the city. When I remembered that in Dewsbury they still ring the Devil's knell at

Christmas, I thought that the title of one of the Yorkshire carols would make a suitable title for the story — though on reflection "Voices of the Belfry Height" might have been even more appropriate.

The unnamed little town was inspired by Cottingley, on the edge of Bradford, which became famous in the 1920s when two young girls claimed to have photographed fairies there. Cottingley is a tiny but complete and very attractive town, which the traveller could easily miss.

"Sweet Chiming Bells" was written for Richard Dalby's *Shivers for Christmas*. It's the last "tale from *The Endeavour*" to date, but I fancy that there will be more, eventually.

"Things from Beyond"

ALIAH WARDEN

Witchcraft is an ever-present theme in the history of the county of Essex. It is like a sinister drum-beat below the even tenor of life, often unheard but always felt. I was aware, of course, of the great witchcraft trials held in the sixteenth and seventeenth centuries and of the infamous career of Matthew Hopkins, the *soi-disant* "Witchfinder-General," but I little suspected that behind these painted devils there lurked something deeper, darker, and infinitely more terrible.

Late in the year of 1902 I was invited to call upon a Mr Giles Chater, a Chelmsford solicitor, on a matter which has no relevance to my story. What is relevant is the fact that I accepted the invitation, for it was at Mr Chater's office that I met for the first time Aliah Warden. My business was soon concluded, and Mr Chater had just poured for me a glass of excellent Madeira wine — of which I was very fond — when his clerk entered the office and diffidently announced that there was a gentleman to see him, a Mr Warden. "Aliah Warden?" cried my host. "Then show him in, by all means. He may care to join us in a glass of wine."

The elderly man who followed the clerk into the office was a very singular personage. To begin with, he was not, in fact, as old as he first appeared, though his hair was quite white above a wide face that was lined with wrinkles. He and Mr Chater greeted each other cordially, and when I was introduced to him I took careful, but, I trust, unobtrusive, note of his curious appearance. His legs were thin, very thin, and gave the impression of being longer than they actually were, in sharp contrast to his squat, round torso. They were markedly bowed, however, and he carried his trunk bent forward at a sharp angle from his hips. This strange bodily configuration of curves and angles amounted quite to a deformity, and was largely responsible for the impression of age that hung about him. His hands and feet were large, flat and square — the hands in particular having one remarkable singularity: there were small but distinct flanges of loose skin between the bases of the fingers. The large, round head was placed directly upon the stocky torso, without any sign of a neck, and seemed to be almost split in two by the wide, flat-lipped mouth. The-eyes bulged uncomfortably beneath the lashless lids, and the low forehead, the small ears and the back of the very large stiff collar were almost completely covered by the shock of white hair. This hair was in itself rather peculiar, for it was worn long, in the style of thirty or forty years ago; I perceived that it was of a rather coarse, thick texture and of a quite lifeless shade of white. Physically, at least, Mr Warden was hardly a prepossessing figure.

Mr Chater's voice interrupted my thoughts: "I am sure you will excuse us for a few minutes," he said. "Mr Warden is shortly to retire from his practice over in Wrabsey, and we have arranged that most of his business will be transferred to me. There are just a few papers to be signed now, and then the thing is done. Don't go, however, for I understand that you have certain interests in common, and I should like you to know each other better."

Mr Warden pursed his wide lips and then smiled. "My practice is very small these days," he remarked. "The Law and the inhabitants of Wrabsey have little to do with each other."

The interests that were shared by this strange little man and me centred upon the study of that misty region of learning where psychology, anthropology and comparative religion overlap. Before the cheerful fire in our good host's office, we drank Madeira wine and talked a good deal about witchcraft, devil worship and magic, while Mr Chater smiled and puffed stolidly at his pipe. I recall Aliah Warden remarking at one stage, "Matthew Hopkins was a fraud, sir — a charlatan. In, that is to say, his capacity as a witch-finder. Ah, he was a cunning devil! What better mask could a fox assume than that of a hunter?"

I had barely time to consider this provocative question before the clock struck five, and I realised that I must be off to the railway station, and thence back to London, where I was to dine with some friends that evening. Before I left the solicitor's office, however, Mr Warden extended to me an invitation to call upon him at some future time at his house in Wrabsey, and made a remark — flattering, I fear — to the effect that he was always pleased to converse upon his favourite subject with one who was both intelligent and knowledgeable. I gladly accepted the invitation, for the strange old man had proved to be both charming and eloquent, and I suspected that his curious exterior masked a whimsical, if grim, sense of humour, which appealed to me. It was arranged that I should spend a weekend with him towards the end of January. "I have treasures in my house," he said as we shook hands. "Things that will surprise you." I did not doubt it.

When the appointed day arrived I packed my suitcase and set off for Liverpool Street Station. My feelings, as I boarded the train for Maldon, were distinctly cheerful, for my work of late had been prosaic to the extent of being boring, and I welcomed the thought of leaving the thronged and dirty streets of London for a few days. In Wrabsey, the air would be clean, and miles of marshland would separate me from the metropolis. I looked forward, too, to the erudite conversation of Aliah Warden.

Long before my train reached Maldon, however, I began to feel that I had seen enough of the Essex Marshes. I had forgotten how *very* bleak and how *very* flat is this region which is not quite land and not quite sea. The glistening, mud-flats seemed somehow sinister in their isolation, and the few lonely farms and decrepit clapboard houses only seemed to emphasize the loneliness. It was hard to realize that I was little more than thirty miles from the greatest city in the world.

Maldon is an enchanting little town, a small but busy port. There was a cheerfulness about the place that day that raised my spirits, and I felt that, after all, I had made no mistake in leaving London. Until, that is, I hailed a cab and instructed the driver to take me to Wrabsey. His answer was not encouraging.

I'll take you, sir," he said, "but I can't think why you would want to go there. 'Tis the most desolate hole."

I explained that I was visiting a friend there. At that, his manner brightened a little.

"Would that be Mr Warden, sir? Ah, he's a nice gentleman — if a bit odd. But I won't hear a word against him. He always asks for me when he wants a cab from Maldon." The cabbie was silent for a moment, brooding, while the horses pawed irritably at the cobbles. "Still and all," he said, "I don't take back what I said about Wrabsey. The place is run down something rotten, and so are the people. Huh. Rotten! Yes, I reckon that's the right word. Still — " (he gave a half-smile) "if you're visiting there I mustn't put you off. Get in, sir, and I'll drive you there."

As we travelled along the north bank of the estuary, skirting the jagged reed-filled inlets, it seemed that the landscape became more desolate. The mere flatness of the land made it difficult to judge distances, and I was surprised when suddenly the driver pointed ahead with his whip at a low, jagged prominence and said, 'There's Murrell Hill, sir. We'll be in the village shortly." I soon realized that the hill was covered in buildings — indeed, it was here that Aliah Warden had his house — and that it was this that gave it that curious rugged appearance.

The village, or rather town, had hardly spread at all on the landward side, but rather seemed to huddle about the little creek, where the weatherboarded buildings leaned precariously upon each other. We approached from the west, however, entering directly into the cobbled road that ran over the low hill. The houses were very large, suggesting considerable wealth, but it soon became evident that this wealth must have been spent long ago, for most of the buildings were in sadly poor repair. Only two or three houses survived in good condition—these and a solitary public building, a hall of some kind, whose Doric portico bore the single word "Dagon," in discreet Roman letters.

The cab pulled up before one of the better houses, and the driver climbed down and opened the door for me. 'This is the place, sir," he said. "Mr Warden's house." As I paid him the agreed fare, I could not help observing that even here three windows of the eight in the not unhandsome frontage lacked curtains. With some misgivings, I lifted the heavy brass door-knocker.

My welcome, however, was as cordial as I could have wished. Aliah Warden greeted me effusively, almost hopping along the hallway in his eagerness. This curious movement unlocked a door in my mind, and I realized with a start what I had unconsciously recognized at our first meeting — that Aliah Warden, physically, bore a remarkable resemblance to a frog. I was strongly reminded of Tenniel's depiction of the frog-gardener in *Through the Looking Glass*, and I was unable to restrain a smile, which, by good fortune my host misinterpreted. "Ah," he said, "you are looking forward to seeing my treasures? All in good time, my dear fellow. First, I think, a glass of wine, and then something to eat."

It appeared that Mr Warden was his own cook and housekeeper, and he suggested that while he prepared a meal for me I might care to inspect his collection of books and various objects d'art which he had accumulated during his delvings into what he called "the world's most fascinating pastime."

Here were treasures indeed. One large room was almost entirely taken up by his library, and I soon realised that the man must be possessed of learning far beyond anything I had suspected. I saw Scot's *Discoverie of Witchcraft*, Stearne's *Confirmation and Discovery of Witchcraft*, Mather's *Magnalia Christi Americana*, and others — numerous others — with which I was familiar, but many of the books were quite unknown to me, while others I had long believed to be fabulous, having no existence outside the imaginations of certain perverse cultists. There were handwritten volumes, bearing such titles as *Cultes des Goules*, *Unaussprechlichen Kulten* and *De Vermis Mysteriis*. Ah! And here was a title that I recognised, though I had never thought that book actually existed. The volume was bound in scarred and stained leather, and printed in tiny blackletter characters, and on its spine was the one word *Necronomicon*. The title page gave the information that this "treatise" was the work of one Abdul El-Hazred, translated into English by John Dee, Doctor, in the Year of Grace 1605. My host, it seemed, was a very surprising man indeed, and one very learned in dark and mysterious matters.

One particular name printed in fine gold characters on black leather, caught my attention. I remembered from my history lessons at school that Sir Geoffrey de Lacy had fought beside the Conqueror at Hastings, and that in the year 1067 he had been granted the manor and the earldom of Ashton in Derbyshire, which manor became the city of Ashton de Lacy. I knew nothing of any interest on the old warrior's part in matters of demonology, and yet here was his name above the Latin title: *De Potentiae Deorum Antiquorum*. Curious, I took the book from its shelf and glanced at the title page. This edition, it appeared, was revised and translated from the Latin in the year 1763 by one Thomas Dashwood Morley, who called himself *Frater Mednamae* — a Monk of Medmen-ham. I began to peruse its contents.

I was gazing with some awe at one of the diabolical engravings which illustrated the book, when I became suddenly aware of Aliah Warden, standing behind me and peering over my shoulder. "Interesting, sir, is it not?" he said. There was a peculiar tone to his voice. "That is a rather fanciful representation of one of the Dwellers in the Depths, a creature that de Lacy claimed to have met and conversed with. The Deep Ones, you know, are the legendary servants of Dagon, the fish-god of the Philistines."

He paused, but before I could compose myself and put the question that was in my mind about the pillared Hall of Dagon that stood upon this very hill, he had turned over a few pages, and was speaking again. "This set of characters, sir, is a paean to the transcendental Kingdom of Voor. It is written in the letters of the Aklo, which are said to be a revelation from certain dark forces to their chosen apostles. Not many *uninitiated* have seen those letters. You are a privileged man, sir. Privileged." With that, he closed the book and motioned me into the next room where my meal awaited me. As I had half-suspected, it consisted principally of fish.

The picture of the Deep One had impressed me considerably, for the creature it depicted appeared some half-way between a man and a frog, having distinctly batrachian characteristics, but standing almost erect, like a man. Despite the fact that it was clad in a long, diaphanous robe, and was adorned with various primitive, if rich, accoutrements, the thing, in its overall appearance, reminded me more than anything of Aliah Warden.

"The marshlands," said my host, as I reclined comfortably in an armchair, with a post-prandial cigarette, "have long been the haunt of witches. They are so isolated, you see, and their people are accustomed to uncover the secrets both of the land and of the sea. They are, one might say, amphibious." He stopped short for a moment, and I half fancied that I saw a faint blush beneath the gray pallor of his wrinkled face.

"What of Wrabsey, itself?" I asked. "The place seems so desolate, so decrepit."

"Hah! You may well ask! Half the houses are deserted — you have only to go down to the waterfront to see what I mean. The timbers are rotten, the walls are cracked, the windows are broken. And yet, people live here, though you would not see many of them, for they will have nothing to do with foreigners. Oh, yes, Wrabsey is *in* England, but do not delude yourself that it is *of* England. The allegiance here is to something much older and far more powerful. Let me tell you of Dagon, for he is the true master here."

Again, the old man paused, and seemed somehow to be ill at ease. Then, bracing himself, he continued: "His minions, who dwell in the Depths, are mentioned in many texts, some of which may be found on these shelves. It becomes plainer the more one reads that it is the supreme test of these creatures, the duty for which they are born and bred, to do nothing less than precipitate the final Armageddon. And that, sir, is fact. Fact!" His voice was low and husky, and his expression arresting. I began to fear for the man's sanity. "When the stars are in their appointed places, then shall Dagon lead his servants to the living tomb of the One before whom even he is as nothing and less than nothing, and there they shall remove the seal that binds him, and he shall rise in all his majesty and terror, and open the cosmic gate to the unspeakable and unknowable things that lurk outside. Cthulhu! Great Cthulhu! See here, here! The words of Dashwood Morley, as he writes of the return of the terrible Priest-God."

I stared at the passage to which he pointed, one of Morley's "revisions" to old de Lacy's book. So startled was I that it was several seconds before I could comprehend the insane words.

> He knoweth *Them* but dimly, yet is His the most urgent task of all, for when the stars shall be in their set places, and the times between be as the times that were, and are, and shall be, then shall He be awoken, and the prisoning Seal be lifted. Then the Deep Ones shall be as one with their Masters, and *They* outside shall be freed once more to possess Their especial Realm. After day cometh night, and after night, day. Lo! Their day shall be your night. They sleep now, but where you are, *They* were, and where you are, *They* shall be.

"For many untold aeons," said Warden, breathlessly, "Cthulhu has lain beneath the Seal of the Old Ones, far under the ocean, sleeping and dreaming foully, but the stars are approaching their proper positions, and the god is restless. The Deep Ones have not been idle in preparing his way. I give you warning!"

The old man gulped, and peered around him nervously. Then he steadied himself, but I could see that there was a twitch or tic affecting the lid of his protuberant left eye.

"Witchcraft, I said, and witches they are, but in Wrabsey they worship a darker devil than ever that fool James could have imagined! They that dwell in the Depths may, perhaps, be considered as a parallel development to mammalian life. For centuries, our sailors have told tales of intelligent life in the sea. Nonsense! said some. Mermaids, said others. Mermaids! Hah! If only they knew....

"The Dwellers in the Depths, you see, have interbred with human beings."

"My dear sir!" I protested. "This is outlandish! Quite absurd. Mere superstition."

"No, no!" he replied, warmly. "It is truth, sir. Truth! Oh, it has happened in many places — in islands of the warm southern seas, and in the civilized world, too. In England, at Gate's Quay, and at Wyvern, and here. Hah! Yes, here, at Wrabsey! Here!"

He was working himself up now, sweating profusely, and the twitch was more marked. Now that it was wet, his crusty skin seemed somehow curiously scaly, and his eyes bulged horribly. I was too taken startled to interrupt him, and he continued, stammering rather.

"Back — oh, hundreds of years back — in the early seventeenth century, the books say... The people here don't remember *when*, you see, but they remember *what*! The thing that Jabez Martyr brought back with him from beyond the Indies — *the thing that he called his wife*. Why were the sailor's children not seen again when they reached maturity? It was then, I tell you, then that the decline set in! Oh, yes, this town had been an important maritime centre; it was a chartered borough, but where is its glory now? Gone with the coming of the outsiders! Fish, fish became the support of the people of the town. Fish, that the men of Maldon and Lowestoft could never match. But they didn't sell it, you see; they ate it. And they kept themselves to themselves. Hah! Do you know why the men of the marshes shun Wrabsey, as they have done for centuries? And what goes on in that Hall of Dagon, while the church is empty? *I* know!

"*And why do the townsfolk look only half-human?*" The old man seemed near to collapsing with his insane exhaustion. I was alone with a madman in the darkness of a winter night, and I shuddered at the thought. He noticed, and smiled grimly. "Look at me!" he commanded. "*Look at me!* Am I not living proof of hell here on earth? Oh, Father Dagon! Why hast Thou delayed so long? Why torment me, when whether I will or not I must soon go to join my brothers beneath the waters and prepare for the triumph that is to come?" He was racked suddenly by uncontrollable sobs; tears filled his huge eyes, and his narrow shoulders shuddered. The man was mad! Utterly, incurably mad!

Then he saw the expression on my face, and his own showed anger. "You don't believe!" he cried. "Hah! I'll show you! I had my pride once, and why do you think I have so much hair on this venerable head, when I could not grow a beard ever? See, see, unbeliever!"

Shockingly, inexorably, he demonstrated the very truth of the insanity of this world. We live our lives in a mist, and when it is lifted, be it only for a second, stark horror is revealed. When I saw what I saw, I fled in awe and disgust from that haunted house in that haunted town. I ran, stumbling and tottering from Wrabsey, until I reached the outskirts of Maldon, and there I collapsed, exhausted, and lay under a hedge until daybreak, when I might catch the first train home to London, safety, and sanity. Even now, I can feel only fear and horror for the creature that I left, collapsed, twitching and moaning, as in a fit, in that house on Murrell Hill, for what I saw was this:

Aliah Warden put his hand, his webbed hand, to his head, and *lifted off* his benevolent mop of white hair. I hardly heard him as he muttered, "I had my pride, and I was human, once..." For I saw, and realized horribly, that *the grey, bald skin of his head was closely covered with coarse, icthyic* scales, *while behind and below his little ears were two rudimentary growths that might or might not be gills.*

Afterword

This story dates from over forty years ago, though I expanded and almost completely rewrote it when Jeanne Youngson asked for a contribution to *The Count Dracula Fan Club Annual* H.P. Lovecraft special issue. It's very basic Yog-Sothothery, but I hope it conveys something of the wonder and fear that Lovecraft himself achieved. You'll recognise the influence of "The Shadow over Innsmouth".

I've tried to devise a British milieu to echo Lovecraft's New England setting, though only Wrabsey actually features in the stories so far. I imagine the little town as like Maldon, seen in a distorting mirror.

De Potentiae Deorum Antiquorum is my contribution to the extensive list of occult volumes that began when Lovecraft created the *Necronomicon*. It's conventional to claim that the unwary reader of such a book is likely to lose his sanity or even his life, but I'm inclined to follow the lead of Robert A.W. Lowndes, whose imaginary grimoire is *The Song of Yste*: he suggested that the main danger to the average reader would be from sheer boredom.

"Aliah Warden" was reprinted in Robert M Price's 1996 anthology *The New Lovecraft Circle*.

THE DREAMING CITY

Mordecai Howard was mad. That much is agreed, at least by those who attended him upon his return from the East. Of course, an archaeologist must have imagination, but surely only a madman would seek for a lost city with no more basis for his search than scraps of ancient magic and the vaguest of legend.

It was true that Howard had made some particularly important contributions to the scholarship of the monumental ruins at Great Zimbabwe, but his allusive references to "the ancient texts" and his suggestion of still-extant cults as a source for his thesis were simply passed over by the archaeological establishment. Only with the eventual publication of his journal of the Eastern Expedition did it become clear that this was no mere occultist aberration, but the very foundation of his scholarship. The result, of course, was to cast doubt upon all his work, which is unfortunate, both for his own reputation and for the advancement of knowledge in the field. I am certain that the Expedition did uncover something remarkable, though whether it was quite what Howard himself believed can only be conjectured.

It began in 1924, with the return from Shanghai of Howard's friend Philip Wendigee, who in his day had been an archaeologist of some repute, particularly in his native Holland. At this time he was in his late sixties, and was employed in an unspecified capacity by the Dutch government. That latter fact is relevant only in that his journey to China had a semi-official basis. The conversation between the two men following his return made no reference to international politics, a subject that held no interest for Mordecai Howard, but turned instead to the younger man's conviction that the dry wastes of the Gobi hid some remnant of a city that predated by centuries — perhaps by millennia — the coming of the present nomadic inhabitants.

This notion had been acquired from his reading of certain obscure volumes of occult lore, books to which few reputable scholars have attached any importance except as evidence of the eccentricities of the human imagination. Nevertheless, Howard appeared to take them seriously. He had spent many hours in the British Museum, consulting Ludwig Prinn's *De Vermis Mysteriis*, the *Necronomicon*, and even the notorious and highly dubious *Liber Ivonis*. This last, he informed the sceptical Wendigee, he regarded as particularly important, since it purported to date from almost the same inconceivably remote age as the hidden city itself. It was, indeed, from the mage Eibon — otherwise *Ivonus* — that he learned the name of the city: *Ishtaol*, translated as "The Mighty". Further details could be gleaned from the cryptic text of the poet El Hazred, whose *Necronomicon* refers to an immeasurably ancient and long-abandoned city in the Sandy Desert, to which he gives the unexplained and alien name of *Sath'gon-Thargn*. That this was the same place was made apparent by allusion to the patron god or demon of this city: the name given by the Arab to this being is *Ib-steoll*, which is clearly the same as Eibon's "Ishtaol".

At length, Howard thought to consult an old volume that had sat unopened upon his own shelves since he had acquired it at auction with the contents of a private collection. This was the 1843 edition, in English, of *De Potentiae Deorum Antiquorum*, written in the mid-twelfth century by that elusive figure Sir Geoffrey de Lacy, and translated — and considerably expanded — in the 1760s by one Thomas Dashwood Morley, who called himself *Frater Mednamae*. Since de Lacy's original is now lost, it is impossible to be sure how much of the present text is interpolation, and of course it is entirely possible that the references that Howard found to "Ishtaol" were derived by Morley from his own readings of Eibon's grimoire, with which he is known to have been familiar. Still, whether it were truth, legend or fiction, the equivocal tale that Howard read, of how old de Lacy had actually journeyed to the fastnesses of the great desert, and there found the aeon-haunted ruins of the Mighty City, excited him strangely.

It could not, he thought, be all the spawn of imagination, and even if the old man merely repeated legend — why, had not Homer done the same? And did not Homer's epic tale, so long dismissed by scholars as "only" myth, lead Heinrich Schliemann to discover the very walls of Ilium?

Even while he disregarded de Lacy's circumstantial account of the spells and sacrifices employed to disclose the wonders of lost Ishtaol, preferring to rely upon his own ability as a skilled and seasoned archaeologist, his inner eye saw him returning to England in triumph, the discoverer of something as important as Schliemann's Troy, and immeasurably more ancient. The truth of the elder texts would be confirmed, and the scholarship of history turned upon its head. All things would be his for the asking . . . Dreams! Ah, dreams!

"The Dreaming City": that was what the unsavoury Ludwig Prinn called it, deriving the name from the Arab's allusions to "Sath'gon-Thargn". Information from certain dubious occult sources had persuaded him that, after many centuries of prosperity under the aegis of the god Ishtaol, the human dwellers in the city (Prinn stressed their humanity in a curious way) had undergone a sudden and disturbing change. The Mighty God had died, by what means none could tell, and with him died the might of the Mighty City. Prosperity vanished, and in its place came delusion, madness and dreams.

Prinn's account, here as elsewhere in his magnum opus, is so cryptic that it is hard to be sure of his meaning. Howard understood that, at the least, a devastating mental disturbance came upon the citizens of Ishtaol. Those who did not succumb utterly to madness fled, until only the stones, the riches, and the god — or his effigy — remained to mark the resting-place of the countless tortured dead. Whether the exiles were absorbed into other communities of that then-flourishing region, or whether they perished as shunned outcasts, is not made clear. It is certain, however, that the city itself was sedulously avoided, for experience proved that the plaque of nightmare delusion still infected the abandoned metropolis. No longer the Mighty City, it became known and feared as *Sath'gon-Thargn* — the Dreaming City.

Philip Wendigee listened to this tale with a sceptical amusement that rapidly lessened, for he had heard something of this before, and recently.

"Shortly before I left China," he said, "my business took me north to Tientsin. Here, my host, knowing my personal interest in the exotic and the outré, introduced me to another guest of his, a Mongolian merchant who dealt principally in the sturdy horses for which his country is famous. The social disorder following the recent death of the ruler, the Living Buddha of Urga, had made it inadvisable for this man to return immediately to Mongolia.

"Well, to be brief, my merchant responded most cheerfully to my questions about the legends and superstitions of his land, telling me a little that I already knew, and much that I did not. One thing he said puzzled me greatly. He spoke of an area within the great Gobi that is shunned by the nomads of the desert — an area which they regard as sinister, because they say it "affects their dreams".

"That is what he said, according to my host, who had to act as interpreter. You will understand that it was most frustrating for me not to be able to question the man directly, for, even though he could tell me a little of this bad place, what he did say was so vague and improbable that at times I thought the translation must be at fault. He told me, for example, when I asked just where the shunned place was, that he could not be certain, for accounts differed strangely. Indeed, one old fellow, whom he suspected of not being entirely compos mentis, averred that the area of bad dreams actually moved, so that one man might stumble across it in one location, and another — well — elsewhere. A patent absurdity, of course, but curious nonetheless."

"Curious indeed," said Howard. "Convincing, too. It must surely be the place referred to in the ancient books. Why, man, this is the key! Did your merchant tell you whether the bad place had a name?"

"Indeed he did. And this again is odd, for the name he gave it was *Tse-Quong T'ang* or *Tse-Quong Tao*, which seems Chinese rather than Mongolian. Yet, despite that apparent reference to the eternal truths of Tao, I am assured that the phrase has no meaning at all in either language. Mere nonsense, in fact. And yet — "

"And yet," Howard concluded triumphantly, "this meaningless name bears a singular resemblance to El Hazred's 'Sath'gon-Thargn', which Prinn translates as 'the Dreaming City'. Beyond doubt, my friend, this is nothing less than a survival from the unthinkably ancient days before even the Mongol herdsmen came to the Sandy Desert. Before, in fact, it was desert at all! Can you doubt now that something is there to be discovered?"

The Dutchman paused before replying. "No," he said at last. "Something is there, to be sure, but I hesitate to suggest that anything material might have survived the ages. Should you carry this plan through, as it seems you are determined to do, then I fear that you will find only a lingering and malign psychic influence. You are prepared to credit the one aspect of the Mongolian legends; do not neglect the other!"

But the younger man's enthusiasm had raised him beyond the reach of warnings. What he wanted now was help and advice, of a purely practical nature, and these, at last, he received from his friend. Together they studied the ancient texts, collating the little information that appeared to be sound and rejecting the far greater amount that did not. Indeed, so many of Prinn's and de Lacy's references were ambiguous, of merely vague, that they felt justified in ignoring them utterly, while the tales attributed to Eibon of Mhu Thulan were so outrageous as to be manifestly the product of a deranged imagination.

Wendigee offered to contact the Mongolian authorities, but the dearth of information he received merely confirmed his fears that the pragmatic thinking of the newly established People's Republic had no time to concern itself with anything so reactionary as peasant superstition. Maps were obtained with great difficulty, bearings taken, and routes plotted. Permission to enter the country was somehow gained, and at last, in the spring of 1926, Mordecai Howard assembled a small team to accompany him on his expedition.

It must be said that this team did not meet his fullest hopes, for many of the most reputable members of his profession had refused to associate themselves with such a wild venture. Still, the two archaeologists who did agree to come had proved themselves to be both competent and enthusiastic, and Geoffrey Challenor, the elder of them, had gained some distinction by his participation in the first of Francis Luttrell's major earth-boring investigations in Western Australia. Less was known about the capability of his colleague Julian Hardwick, but certainly nothing could be said against him. The photographer, Ian Dakin, had accompanied two previous expeditions to central Asia, and the resulting work had been very well received, both by the cognoscenti and by the public at large.

Howard's journal describes very fully the difficulties encountered in his search for the ruins of Ishtaol, but there is no need even to summarise them here. A single note in the journal states that calculations based upon the Trone Tables had been invaluable in enabling him at last to locate the forgotten city, but there is no further reference to this particular work. However, three days later, on the fifteenth of May, an entry triumphantly records that the city had indeed been found, in the form of gigantic blocks of a whitish stone whose regular shapes could be discerned beneath the all-covering sand.

The camels were tethered, the tents were pitched, and a small celebration was held — which is to say that a bottle of whisky was broken open and shared between the four men before they retired. The following morning's entry in the journal begins with the happy observation: "All slept soundly. No bad dreams at all. What price superstition, Wendigee?"

Howard had drawn up a conjectural plan of the city, based upon Geoffrey de Lacy's account of his own visit to the haunted spot, but he found great difficulty in relating it to the waste of immense masonry that his little team was uncovering. Most of the great stones, though plainly artificial and still bearing vestiges of incised decoration, seemed to conform to no pattern that he could discern, and as the excavations proceeded he was disturbed to find that he was becoming subject to rather curious optical phenomena.

Angles seemed to behave wrongly. He would glance from a distance at an apparent vast jumble of separate and unrelated blocks, and instantly see them connected in a clearly intentional way; yet when he approached, he found the connection lost. The independent megaliths were now merely that.

At first the journal tells only of Howard's own susceptibility to this disconcerting effect. Perhaps he did not speak of it to the others, not wishing to arouse suspicions in their minds. It became evident, however, that he was not the only one to suffer from these illusions, for on the twenty-fourth of the month Challenor and Hardwick reported a most singular occurrence. It had seemed to Hardwick that two great blocks, roughly cubic and measuring some five feet by six, belonged together, since each bore a part of a representational bas-relief — severely eroded, to be sure, but still apparent. Making strict measurements, he drew each design to a scale of precisely one sixth, and found that they fitted perfectly together. This picture, representing a creature apparently ophidian, but with disturbingly hominid characteristics, he showed to Challenor, who suggested that the two of them should attempt to move the two stones together so that the theory might be confirmed. This was achieved, with help from Dakin, the photographer, but, to the astonishment of the two archaeologists, the result was not at all what they had expected. When Hardwick measured them, the two blocks had appeared to be within a couple of inches of the same size; now it was apparent that one was fully a foot shorter than the other on all sides. The relationship that had unified the two sculpted designs was quite lost. Yet there remained Hardwick's drawing to show that to him, at least, it had existed.

Conversation naturally arose about the disturbing optical effects that were an apparent property of this strange place, and it was now that Ian Dakin confessed that he too had been plagued by odd phenomena. He showed the archaeologists a number of photographs that he had taken, and made the curious remark that the pictures did not show precisely what he had seen. Where only a disconnected confusion of stones had been apparent to him, the photographs showed evident relationships between the stones. He had not liked to mention it before, because —

Strangely, perhaps, it was Dakin's photographs that proved to be the key that unlocked the mystery of Ishtaol. Howard and the others took to using the pictures as a guide, and found that the pattern observable in them matched very closely the plan he had derived from old de Lacy's description. It was certainly the strangest method of working that any of the archaeologists had encountered, but in the end it proved effective, and much was achieved. By digging at the points indicated, they were able to place precisely a number of the major structures of the city. None of them was complete, of course, though at least two were in a quite astonishing state of preservation, and identification was as certain as it could be.

It is at this point in the journal that Howard mentions an extension of the disquieting visual effects. At various times, all the members of the party — with the exception of Ian Dakin, who seemed to be growing more withdrawn and uncommunicative — reported the strange impression of seeing one or more of their fellows in places where they were not. Frustratingly, these were never more than indistinct glimpses, though occasionally two of the men would seem to see a third — always in conditions that made it impossible to be certain of his identity. They would hail him, and be answered by a call from a different direction. Once, Howard, Challenor and Dakin were together when the two archaeologists caught a most disturbing half-sight of two other figures. Whether the photographer also saw them cannot be established. Needless to say, Hardwick was not even near the spot where the figures had appeared to be.

Two important discoveries now took place in quick succession. On the seventeenth of June, the lifting of a large, roughly triangular stone revealed a similarly shaped hollow beneath, to which it had served as a lid. In this space were two human bodies; they were no more than skeletons coated with skin, and over the next few hours they disintegrated completely. Howard says of the cadavers that they were unmistakably those of a woman and a man, and that the shape of the skulls proved them to be of a quite different racial type from the present-day Mongolians. He adds further that the bodies gave the curious appearance of being "elongated", amplifying this word only by the addendum: "not tall as we understand it, but stretched." His vagueness upon this point is typical of a regrettable lack of precision that becomes more and more evident in the journal.

The second discovery was yet more momentous. The principal building of the city, from its earliest days, had been the temple of the god Ishtaol, and it was this that the party finally located, upon the twenty-fifth of June. "Building" is not actually the right word, for the temple, as de Lacy had made clear, was entirely subterranean. Howard's account again is not all that one could wish, but it is apparent that he himself, with the assistance of Dakin's photographs, identified the enormous block whose almost obliterated carven device of a single non-human eye proved it to be the doorway to the temple of Ishtaol.

The journal mentions "the pit of the six thousand steps", but this appears not to be a reference to the temple itself, for a little later Howard gives the number of the steps down to the great vault as precisely sixty-three. The relevance of "the pit", in fact, is left unexplained.

By means of some mechanism, unthinkably old but still functioning, the immense trapdoor could be swung open with surprisingly little effort. Howard says nothing about the quality of the air thus released, which suggests that it was not utterly stale, as one might have supposed. The hole revealed was a good twenty feet square, and the steps leading down into the blackness appeared to be in a state of perfect preservation. Leaving the photographer to guard the door, the three archaeologists started down the steps. These were shaped from the same whitish stone as everything else in the city, and were arranged in a rather curious fashion. There were six steps, very approximately eighteen inches from front to back and twenty-five inches high, and then a level platform ran forward for about five feet, after which six more steps led downward, and so on to the bottom.

The vertical faces were carved with designs whose clarity of outline contrasted utterly with the all-but-eroded incisions and bas-reliefs of the stones upon the surface. Of the designs themselves Howard says little, beyond noting an occasional slight resemblance to the Babylonian. Generally, they appear to have been quite unrelated to anything that survives elsewhere.

At the foot of the mighty staircase, the floor ran forward for about thirty feet to an immense monolithic portal, some twenty feet high. The electric torches revealed that, in contrast to the profuse decoration upon the steps, this great entrance was utterly unadorned, save that over it was repeated the symbol of the single eye. Within the huge vault beyond was the first touch of colour that the men had seen in this ancient metropolis: the floor was paved with mosaic tiles in sombre greens and greys, laid in an apparently random fashion. This was not immediately noticed, however, for the thing that stood or squatted in the centre of the floor compelled the attention of all. It was nothing less than a statue, or idol, of the god Ishtaol, and it was as totally alien as the carvings of its eye had suggested.

In shape it resembled nothing so much as an immense lump of white clay that had been allowed to settle into a rounded, bulbous cone, some ten yards across and six high. No individual features could be discerned, except for a dozen or so globular bulges freely arranged towards the summit. The material of which it was made appeared to be a peculiarly hard stone, differing from any in the city above ground in that it was pure white. Howard draws a comparison with a monstrously mis-shapen maggot, and this may give a clue to his state of mind, since he is known to have had an unreasoning horror of maggots. Perhaps the most remarkable feature of the idol is that the flashlights disclosed no sign of joints anywhere: the thing appeared to have been carved from a single block.

Nothing is recorded of the size and shape of the sunken temple, nor of any mural decoration. This may mean that there was nothing of note to be seen, but it seems more probable that the three men were so awe-stricken by the vast blasphemy before them that they had no mind for anything else. They spent no longer than ten minutes in the vault before Hardwick, who was not noted for nervousness, abruptly turned and left. The others followed immediately.

At the top of the staircase they were shocked to find that the great stone slab had swung shut, though no sound had penetrated to the depths beneath. To their unspeakable relief, the door was opened as easily from within as from without, but its opening disclosed tragedy. Ian Dakin was dead, his head crushed to pulp. It seemed that he had been leaning over the edge of the pit, looking downwards, when the mighty slab descended. They could only hope that he had died instantaneously.

Hardwick, who seemed to have been the worst affected by the exploration of the temple, now showed clear signs of a nervous breakdown. He was of no practical help in the gruesome business of interring the body — for transporting it home to England was out of the question — and his behaviour became distressingly erratic. Howard and Challenor had themselves been severely shaken by the photographer's death, and now their equanimity was frequently disturbed by Hardwick's tendency to wander aimlessly among the cyclopean ruins, quietly declaiming scraps of verse from the metaphysical poets.

As his behaviour deteriorated, so did the nervous condition of his colleagues. Perhaps influenced by Hardwick's dark, gnomic mutterings — or perhaps not — Howard and Challenor separately became convinced that among the shadowy figures that occasionally impinged upon the edge of their vision was one that strangely resembled Ian Dakin.

For the first time, too, Howard's journal mentions his dreams. Although he had so proudly recorded upon that first day that none of the party had been subjected to nightmares, he now began to suspect that this had not always been so — that their conscious minds had in fact rebelled at remembering the visions of sleep. It seemed to him at last that his own ego was losing its strength to resist, and that some thing or some force within the city was determined to prove the truth of his Dutch friend's warning.

The journal is frustratingly reticent concerning the content of Howard's dreams — there are equivocal references to "the Dwellers in the Wheel", "the Swimmer in Darkness", and "the Silence of the Dragon" — but of their quality there can be no doubt. Each morning he would find it less easy to awaken to full awareness of his situation.

"My brain," says one late entry, "is merely liquid, and its every motion can be felt."

The entries become increasingly incoherent, except on the rare occasions when Howard makes an evident effort to analyse his own mental and physical condition. Even then, a strong vein of fantasy is apparent. Little more is said about Challenor, or even about Hardwick, until the final note. Towards the end, after a description of the unnatural and excessive wasting to which his body had become subject — a description that impresses the more because of its impersonal rationality — there appear such entries as: "Weather continues charming," and "There is talk of disruption upon the railways."

The last entry is headed the thirtieth of August, though of course it is impossible to gauge the accuracy of this date. I find something chilling in its very prosaic nature.

It says simply: "Hardwick is dead. Challenor has gone to the temple. I think that I shall join them."

———

On the fourth of September, a group of nomadic herdsmen arrived at the camp, accompanying a minor government official. It appears that one of this man's superiors had become aware of the permission so lightly granted for Howard's party to enter the country, and had decided that the presence of European imperialists was not, after all, in the best interests of the Mongolian People's Republic. The deputy had been sent, therefore, to see that the foreigners left Mongolia without delay.

Possibly he expected to find a group of capitalist spies; one cannot be sure. What he actually found were three corpses and one other — a man perilously close to physical death, and mentally dead already.

Mordecai Howard alone of his party had survived, reduced to a state that the horrified Mongolians assessed variously as lunacy and idiocy. At first they naturally ascribed the deaths of the others to the one living man, but closer examination of the bodies gave them reason to doubt this conclusion. One man, whose head had been thoroughly crushed, as if by a great weight, was buried in a shallow depression, from which the wind had blown most of the covering sand. Certainly he had died by violence, though the wound could not be related to any weapon that could be found. The other two had been stricken by some emaciating disease. The bodies were lying some hundreds of yards apart, but they showed identical symptoms; it was evident that they had not long been dead, and that the wasting had occurred before and not after death. Indeed, the same symptoms were already far advanced in the survivor. The report that accompanied the madman on his eventual return to England described the dead men's frames as being unnaturally attenuated or stretched.

The government official who drafted the report had evidently read Howard's journal, for he scornfully dismissed the notion of a ruined city in the great desert, calling it "a diseased fantasy". He did, however, mention the destruction by his junior of "certain shamefully fraudulent photographs".

If any reference was made by the nomads to *Tse-Quong T'ang*, the "bad place", the report did not acknowledge it. Perhaps the hint was taken.

Afterword

This is another very early, but extensively revised Lovecraftian story, influenced by "The Nameless City" and "The Shadow out of Time" — and by Basil Copper's splendid novel *The Great White Space*, whence come the references to "the Trone Tables" and to Francis Luttrell's earth-boring expeditions.

Robert M. Price included "The Dreaming City" in his 1999 anthology *The Antarktos Cycle*.

CUSTOS SANCTORUM

Wrabsey,
nr Maldon,
Essex.
13th Nov. 1832

to Mr Salter,
Wyvern.

Cousin,

You have asked me about the coming of a stranger to this town, of whose visit rumour only has reached you. One, as you have heard, claiming kinship with us of the Blood. Be sure, then, that none save Those who guard us may know the full truth, but that I, Their servant, can tell as much as any man. From me you shall learn what befell.

It was upon the second Saturday of last month that the man came to Wrabsey. His appearance should have been instantly noted, for strangers are few and unwelcome, as you (more than most) will appreciate, in this small town, whose days of market and fair are long vanished. Nevertheless, he was not remarked, it seemed, until he presented himself at my office in Fish Street and asked to have word with me. I beheld a person of middling height, slim but stooping slightly, plainly dressed, and with dark hair receding somewhat from a scalp whose greyish pallor matched that of his face and hands. His age, I suppose, was about thirty, but there was such a set of wrinkles upon his face, and his pale eyes bulged so hugely, that I could not be sure. In short, you see, he had about him that look which distinguishes us from the common rank of men.

His greeting was fair but brief. "Mr Martyr," said he, "I understand that you are the leader of the people of this town." I replied, somewhat wary, that to see the leader he should enquire for Amos Luckin, the Deputy, at the Moot Hall. "I know of the Deputy," he said, "and am persuaded that you, and not he, are the man I seek. Let me make myself known. My name is Walter Garlick, and I have come hither from Gate's Quay, on the rocky coast of Dorset. My home, if not my family, must be known to you."

The name of Gate's Quay was, of course, familiar to me, as it is to you, Cousin. "Then you come in the service," said I, "of Those whom we serve?" I spoke with caution, for one does not lightly utter the names of power, but my mind was set easy — in part, at least — by the instant assurance that Mr Garlick was a faithful adherent of C———. He had, he claimed, a mind to settle here in Wrabsey and so forge stronger links of friendship between two enclaves indissolubly bound by ties of blood and allegiance.

For the moment nothing further could profitably be said on so important a matter. I resolved to call as quickly as might be a meeting extraordinary of the Elect, and meanwhile to show all courtesy to this unbidden guest. Over a glass of good port wine, I commended to him the facilities of the Dolphin Inn, under the ownership of my friend Silas Choate, while he sought a proper dwelling in the town. "And I myself," said I, "may be of service to you there, for my small practice has mainly to do with property. A man must live in this world, you know, even while preparing himself for that other that we know of. There is a house but recently untenanted upon Murrell Hill, belonging to Thomas Warden, who is of high rank among the Elect. Surely he would be glad to see it occupied by a kinsman such as you."

After some further talk of this nature, I asked him how matters stood in his native town — for you know, Cousin, that I am of an enquiring mind, and hold that we who are so encompassed upon all sides by mere humanity do need to keep aware of the doings of our brethren, that we may better serve our Masters. To my questions he answered in straight but general terms, telling me nothing that I did not already know, but revealing an authentic knowledge of Gate's Quay and of the Blood. It was a pleasant conversation, though necessarily guarded upon one side (at least), for Walter Garlick, whatever else he might be, was an intelligent man and educated. At last, bidding my clerk to oversee the office until my return, I conducted Mr Garlick out into Fish Street and thence by way of Salt Street and Church Lane to the Hythe, where stands the Dolphin. As we passed St Mary's church he looked with an appraising eye and remarked, "It seems in good repair, friend."

"To be sure," said I, "for there are still in Wrabsey many of the common sort of humanity who cling to their fathers' faith."

"As we to ours," said he, "and with solid reason. But do you not find dissension between the men who attend upon Christ and the Chosen who swell the congregation of Dagon?"

"There has long been unease," I admitted, "but you may find this country somewhat different from your own. These marshlands, bare and bleak, that sever us from the rest of Essex, breed men to suit them. In this land that is not quite land, nor yet quite sea, the people are accustomed to uncover the secrets of both. They are, you may say, amphibious. Wrabsey is in England, but it is no more of England than is Gate's Quay, or Wyvern, or that place of wonders where our fathers dwell. No, the church is under the care of the Vicar of Tolleshunt D'Arcy, but those who attend know enough to keep their beliefs to themselves. They know that we, and not he, are their kin. Will it surprise you to learn that some of them — one a warden — are faithful servants of the Council of the Elect?"

Surprised he was, none the less. "It is not so in Gates Quay! Spies, are they?"

"It would be wrong to call them so. They are but men. Men who know which way this world tends, and suspect to whom it truly belongs. It is not from within that danger comes, but from without — ah! But here is The Hythe, and yonder the inn. Good day to you, friend. You shall be summoned as soon as may be to meet us formally and, I trust, to be admitted to the mysteries of the town."

Things are not done hastily among us, who have a sacred end in view. None the less, upon the very next evening, the Sunday, the Inner Council of the Elect was gathered within the great Hall of Dagon, upon Murrell Hill, ready to receive and appraise the newcomer. If I name names, it is so that you, cousin, may appreciate the utter trust which I repose in you, as a blood-kinsman of like rank within the Chosen. Present, then, were the senior members, as yet untranslated, of the senior families of Wrabsey — those who, between them, two centuries ago, had brought destiny from the East and from the Sea. Aye, destiny and glory and fear!

In full, the Council numbers twelve, but the Inner Conclave only four, viz. Silas Choate, Enoch Warden, Rahab Martyr, and myself, Israel Martyr, as Principal. On so solemn an occasion, naturally, we were garbed in the panoply of office bequeathed us by our fathers beneath the waters — such robes as would make the recognised Deputy of the town sweat with envy and fear.

While Walter Garlick sat in the antechamber, we four deliberated upon his fate. I had not spoken idly in asserting that danger might be expected from without our ranks, and what was he, if not an outsider? Still, his claim was to ties of blood and allegiance (allegiance to the Great Ones that we know of), and truly he had that look about him that spoke of such. Nothing must be done in such haste that we would regret it, though to be sure there remained one final test or protection that should make all plain. We in mortal state may be fallible, but our fathers who have undergone translation and who dwell in that other world (to which, C— grant, you and I are bound) are far from such. On their powers we may rely utterly.

At length it was decided to take the man Garlick, to appearances at least, upon his own word, and Silas Choate was dispatched to the anteroom to bring him before the Council.

This I must say in his favour: Upon entering from the severe blankness of the anteroom into the gorgeousness of the great hall he showed not the smallest sign of surprise. Even our own younger Brethren have been known to exclaim in wonder at first seeing the barbarous magnificence of the mural hangings (predominantly green, purple, and gold) which everywhere catch the eye, telling to those who have the knowledge and the intelligence of the wonders of that subaquarian world whence our fathers came to glorify mere mankind, and of that other, nearer realm where they now serve, awaiting the return of the great Dagon and his greater masters. And if Walter Garlick did not blink at this (but with such eyes, after all, he could not blink), how much more telling that he gave no start at seeing the four judges (for such we surely were) who sat before him! Our garments of green and gold, woven with fantastic designs, our diadems, whose richness the King of England himself could not but envy — these alone must have bewildered mere humanity. But what could mere man think when confronted with our own selves? Silas Choate and I have still some years — even decades — to go, but Enoch Warden is fast approaching the Change, and so must appear most monstrous to men, while Rahab Martyr (representing the cadet branch of that same ineffable family of which I am head) was so perilously close that she could not long bear to be away from the salt water. There was little left in her of the corruptible flesh of humankind, and even in this haven she was then rarely to be seen abroad in the daylight hours.

No sign of surprise showed upon the face of our postulant (if so I may call him), but only, if Silas interpreted correctly, the slightest expression of satisfaction. Here was one who had in part achieved his goal. Very good, then. Let us know whether he were fit to achieve it fully.

Yourself being a fully professed adherent of Dagon to the Third Degree will be aware of such questions as we thought it good to put. Had this Garlick subscribed to the first Oath, and could he repeat that Oath in full? He could, but so can many who are not of the Blood. Satisfactorily, too, he repeated the second Oath, but what of that? The supreme test would be the third and greatest Oath, and this test, also, he passed.

Supreme, did I say? In some places that would be so: in Gate's Quay, perhaps, and even in Wyvern. But here in Wrabsey we have yet a further ordeal, and of a very different kind, a kind that should not be revealed to the postulant immediately, for it occurred to us four (Rahab uttering thought in those indescribable tones that have already replaced mere human speech in her) that within three weeks, upon the last day of October, would be celebrated one of the two great Festivals of the Order, and that this occasion, no other, should prove the making or breaking of Walter Garlick.

In the meanwhile, we thought it well to tell him something of the history of our People in this place, and of their practices. From him, too, we might learn of how things were done in Gate's Quay. Similarities there must be, for our greatness all derives from a common blood and a common revelation, but for the rest we have also humankindness in our veins and are prone to fallibility and change.

We discoursed, therefore, of that great voyage of Jabez Martyr (my own great-great-grandfather) to the Indies and beyond, where he encountered those strange dwellers upon unknown isles and in unknown seas, whose form was not as the form of men and whose worship was not as the worship of men. Of how Jabez and his fellows (Ambrose Choate and Marcus Warden among them) embraced wholeheartedly the wealth of gold and fish that the strangers offered, and with them the new faith (new but aeon-old) that was demanded in return. Of how, in 1629, the ship Sea-Unicorn returned to Wrabsey, with but half her crew on board, and that half having taken wives from those lands beyond the Indies. Of the treasure brought as dowry by those wives, and of the Charter of Regulation that Jabez had drawn up upon the instruction of his own wife, the Charter which for two centuries, in despite of the Deputy and his officers, has truly been the pattern for life in this town.

"On the thirty-first of the month, friend Walter," said I, "on that eve that the Christians call Hallowmass, the Chosen of Wrabsey will meet in full. Supplications will be made and sacrifices offered. Doubtless you have attended such gatherings in your own native place, and as a full member of the Order of Dagon. Here, we shall be pleased to welcome you as such. Until that time, you may come and go freely as you will, provided only that you stay within the town. You have our full permission to converse with the People of the Blood, but do bear in mind that they may not wish to converse with you until they know you fully. You may also converse with those townsfolk who are not of our kind, but you will, of course, refrain from speaking of matters which do not pertain to them. Go in peace now, and return upon the appointed day."

I saw but little of Walter Garlick during the days that followed, though twice he called into my office to pass an hour or so in the most innocuous fashion. For the rest, I have heard that he was betimes to be seen wandering down by the waterfront, among the boatyards, the cocklesheds, and the fishermen's huts. If the odour offended his nostrils (as I have heard that some men complain) he gave no sign of it. Altogether, he seems to have conducted himself with great circumspection, speaking but little to any of the townspeople, of whatever sort, and apparently neither prying where he should not, nor asking importunate questions. Of his behaviour, save for the long hours during which he confined himself to his rooms at the Dolphin, I have some measure of certainty, for I had taken pains to have him watched. If he did not spy, at least he was spied upon, both by some more agile members of our Order and by some of those faithful servants whom I mentioned before.

His thought, as I should judge, was simply to let himself be seen, so that the folk of Wrabsey might come to recognise him and become accustomed to the fact of his presence. They might, so insular are the men of these marshlands, forever scorn him as a foreigner, but should he prove true — should he actually settle and marry here — then his position would be secure. I could only admire the soundness of the ploy. And in the meanwhile the execution of it gave me no cause for worry. Besides, the eve of the Festival would tell all.

Time came, and with it Walter Garlick. He took without demur the seat specified for him among the congregation in the Hall of Dagon, as one who has no reason to keep within the shadows. And if he showed some hesitation in response and gesture, what of that? The end may be the same, but doubtless the form differs somewhat between Wrabsey and Gate's Quay. Not even our most respected Elders can claim perfection this side of the Water.

It is said that spies before now have betrayed themselves at our great ceremonies by their reaction at the moment of sacrifice, but that night Walter Garlick's face and posture remained utterly calm and inscrutable. Even when our congregation was blessedly swelled by the presence of two of our Fathers from the Sea, now grown quite beyond human semblance, I could read in his face neither fear nor horror, but only wonder. Here, said I to myself, is surely a true Brother of the Blood. There remained but the one final test.

The symbolic feast concluded the ceremony, after which, with the golden wand bequeathed to us from the Indies, I made the sign of the Sun Wheel in true blessing, and gave permission for those who could to make their way out into the salt waters, there to commune with those who had gone before. For Rahab, my cousin, this was, indeed, to be her last farewell upon land. Henceforth we would meet only in our natural and final element. I was greatly touched, not with sadness, but with the hope that but few more years might pass before I should join her. In spirits high but tranquil, then, I summoned Walter Garlick to remain within the hall, and to join the members of the Inner Council upon the dais. (Knowing that Rahab was so soon to leave us, we had already appointed her younger sister, Zillah, so that our number remained at four.)

"Friend Walter," I said, "the final stage of your initiation into the mysteries of Wrabsey will be conducted shortly. I shall not ask whether you wish to proceed, for you must do so. Your choice, as you will recognise, is to proceed or die. Perhaps to proceed and die, but if so the matter is not within our hands. Very well. Before we withdraw to the Inner Chamber — to what I may call the Sanctum Sanctorum of this our Temple — you must know the history and the purpose of this final stage.

"Learn, then, that this Hall of Dagon in which we sit was builded nearly a century and a half ago by my own great-grandfather Japhet Martyr, son of that Jabez of whom you have heard. There had been a house, among other houses, here upon the hill, where dwelt Jabez and his wife from the sea, and their children also. But in time a wonder occurred, for the wife lost her human semblance to take on that of the very gods whom Jabez and his fellows had learned to serve. Who can tell what emotions were in the old sea-captain's breast as he realised that the same divine blood ran in the veins of his children, and not in his own? Doubtless he conferred much with the men who had returned with him from that fateful voyage. Some, we know, perfidiously foreswore their solemn covenant, but what became of them we know not, only that their wives and children survived. Jabez himself remained faithful and was admitted to full counsel with those of the Blood. Truly he could never be of their kind, but he had been the willing means of bringing them to this land.

And so, being merely mortal, Jabez Martyr died, having seen with joy his wife return to the sea, which was her first and last home. Full of years and honour, he was buried in the churchyard of St Mary's. His children, meanwhile, and those of his crew members, were grown to adulthood, and in their features could clearly be discerned the mark of their mothers. Numerous they were, and glorious, strong enough already to resist any bar raised against them by the children of men. And they coupled, with each other or with the townsfolk, for the Blood is not made less strong thereby. Not wishing to draw the attention of the world to this little town, they made no interference with the Corporation, and since then the office of Deputy has never been held by one of the Chosen. But it was by that generation that the Council of the Elect was fully established, which is the inner life of Wrabsey. And being an organised body, the Council needed a meeting place of proper dignity. Hence this hall.

"The design was laid down by Japhet himself, and was inspired, so I understand, by that of one of the London churches. Myself, I have never travelled so far inland, so cannot tell, but I think you will admit the majesty of that Doric facade, whose pediment bears the name of Dagon in letters both discreet and imposing. You must confess too the very striking nature of this great chamber of worship, but there is more to the hall than this, for, acting upon the commands of his mother, Japhet constructed also an inner chamber, a Holy Place. Thus far, friend, the story will be familiar to you, for surely the Chosen of Gate's Quay have also a hall of worship, but of such a Sanctum Sanctorum I have never heard tell elsewhere. It is protected, friend Walter, guarded by one who is beyond fear or corruption.

"None may guess with what anguish Japhet Martyr laid the first stone of the Holy Room, for below it he had interred the small body of his own first-born child, slaughtered in most decorous and ritual fashion by himself at the stern decree of his mother. Think! A child that should have grown to be a prince among the People of the Sea, and yet who now serves in a different fashion Him Who is to Come, for it is the soul — the essence — of that child that is the supreme guardian of the Faithful of Wrabsey.

"There may enter the Sanctum in safety only those of true Blood and true Allegiance. All the Elect of the town, upon coming of age, must pass the test of that room, and since you, Walter Garlick, desire acceptance among the Elect, then you also must pass the test. Are you prepared for the ordeal?"

No sign of fear showed upon that impassive face, but he ventured a question: "Of what manner, Master, is this ordeal?"

"Alas. Of that I may not speak." And nor, indeed, could I, for within my own long lifetime none had failed to enter the room with utmost safety, though I had heard of one in my father's time, a faithful servant but not of the Blood, who had reasoned to herself thus: I have sworn to the highest Oath of this Order and am as true an adherent of C— as any in this town; why may not I with impunity enter the Holy Room? And against dissuasion she entered in. What became of her, my father declined to tell. Certain it is that she did not return alive, although no man laid hands upon her. But of this I did not speak to Walter Garlick.

"I am prepared," said he, at length, and at my sign Silas Choate drew back the great and gorgeous curtain that hung behind the dais. It is fitting, cousin, that this curtain should conceal the entrance to the Sanctum, for upon it is depicted in most fearful majesty the image of Him who lies dreaming, and whose coming we are destined to precipitate.

With that key that hangs always upon a chain around my neck, I unlocked the great door and pulled it open. "Come, brother," I said. "Stand here at the portal with me and tell me what you see within."

Still his features showed no emotion other than calm self-assurance as he gazed steadily through the doorway into the chamber. Instead, it was I who felt an insidious unease as I heard his pronouncement: "Why, Master, I see naught but darkness. No — darkness and water! Master—" (he turned his face to me for a moment, and at last there was true expression there, of joy and wonder) "— this is indeed a great mystery! For surely within this room, within this hall, situate as it is upon a hill, is the sea!"

I trust that my own face betrayed nothing, though my heart within me was heavy, as I said, "Very good, brother. Now, do you remain here while we enter the chamber, and then you shall join us, no man forcing you."

"Oh, willingly!" said he. And at that my heart sank further, for it seemed, to his own loss and ours, that he was in all things sincere. But the Charter must not be transgressed, and the farce must be played out. Together, then, Silas Choate, Enoch Warden, Zillah Martyr, and I entered, as we had done many times before, the room which we knew and saw to be a plain, square, unfurnished chamber. It measures fifteen feet in each direction, the walls and ceiling being quite bare, and the floor set with marble squares of green and gold, in a pattern that will be known to you.

Having reached the farther wall, we turned, and I said, not loudly, "Brother Walter, you may enter now."

Each of us bore a lantern, and the light fell full upon him, yet his expression was that of a man in darkness. He peered this way and that, and called out with some attempt at his former confidence, "Master, I can scarce hear you!"

Again, I summoned him, but more loudly. His own reply sounded very loud to my ears: "Enter, Master? Oh, yes, I shall enter. But oh! this is a terror and a wonder! In the name of our fathers, if only I could see you!"

My heart a stone in my body, I watched him, plainly gathering his courage and then taking a bold step into the room. Then I saw happen what I suppose my father must have seen all those years ago, and what I hope never to see again. He was throughout like a man blinded, stretching his hands before him to feel his way (in that bare and well lit room!) and, cousin, I swear to you that as he progressed the sound of his voice grew fainter — and as for his footsteps —

He approached us for perhaps four feet and was then brought up sharply by some obstacle invisible (and indeed intangible) to us. I heard him mutter, "Most strange!" as he felt with his hands this apparent wall — up, down, to left and right. At last he turned to his left, feeling the wall along his right hand, until he encountered a wall that was indeed visible to us, for it was the northernmost wall of the room. At that he paused, considering, and then retraced his path, keeping the invisible obstruction now upon his left. A little more than two thirds of the way across the room, his outstretched left hand suddenly encountered — nothing. Either this putative wall took a turn here, or else there was a gap. Walter Garlick made some small hesitation here, and then plunged boldly forward.

My account now must retain its utter precision, for all that it resembles the merest fantasy. Cousin, within two or three steps Walter Garlick's path began to descend — and this on a level stone floor. I cannot explain it, but only marvel at the subtlety and efficacy of our protector. It was not at first noticeable, for my attention was fixed upon his face, and plainly he felt nothing more strange than his already strange experience. It was Zillah who grasped my arm and pointed wordlessly to Walter's feet — or rather, to the floor where his feet should have been visible. They were not. In macabre fashion, he seemed to stand upon the stumps of his ankles. And then we saw one foot raised, as it seemed, through the solid stone of the flooring. Gradually he proceeded and descended, his steps becoming more and more laboured, as if he were in truth wading through salt water. Not once did he come near to any of the walls that we could see; his way took him this way and that within the room, often moving where he had moved before, but ever descending, until at last only his head remained visible above the stones, the eyes bright with fear and wonder. And never, though at the last we could distinguish no words, did he cease to speak:

"This is a great and holy thing!"

"I am daring much to be accounted worthy!"

"Master, shall I be with you soon?" — and the like. And at last he was gone, with never a sign in the room to show that he had ever been.

It was with most solemn hearts and minds that we four left the Holy Chamber, and with no obstacle (need I say?) to bar our way.

No word was spoken as we closed and locked the door, redrew the curtain, and departed the hall, each to our separate home, but I know that we thought to see no more of Walter Garlick.

In that we were mistaken, however, for upon the following morning I was woken early by that churchwarden of whom I have spoken, a bearer of strange news. The body of Walter Garlick had been found lying dead within the churchyard of St. Mary's, beside the grave of my own ancestor and founder of the town's fortunes, Jabez Martyr. There was an ironic appropriateness in that, I suppose. But stranger still, examination proved him to have died of drowning — which is all but unheard of in people of our kind. And, yes, cousin, I have to report that examination proved beyond a doubt that he was indeed of the Blood. (Naturally, I ensured that the matter was taken in hand entirely by my own office, so that knowledge should be confined to those who ought to know.)

Questions no doubt occur to you, as they occurred to me — and, alas, I cannot answer them. If Walter Garlick was of the true Blood, why did he fail the final ordeal? Was he, perhaps, apostate — that danger from without of which I have spoken? Or could it be that the Guardian accepts only those born of the faithful of Wrabsey? I do not know. But this I do know: As long as the hall and the Sanctum Sanctorum survive, then the future of the Faith in Wrabsey is secure.

In the name of Him who Dreams,
I am yr. affect, cousin,
Israel Martyr.

Afterword

Stories about the Deep Ones have tended to concentrate on their alien wickedness, but these tales are mostly told from the viewpoint of an outsider to the community. Surely the Marshes, Gilmans and Waites of Innsmouth didn't see themselves as evil! Over the years, they would have developed their own establishment, in parallel to that of the land-dwellers, recognising that they were outnumbered, but confident of their eventual destiny as the true lords of the earth. I hope I've been able to convey a sense of the wonderful amid the commonplace.

"Custos Sanctorum" was published in *Deep Things Out of Darkness* in 1987, and reprinted by Bob Price in his 1998 anthology *The Innsmouth Cycle.*

ISHTAOL

"Tell me of this latest journey," I said.

My host waved his left hand towards the spirit-case, "Very well. Pour us both another whisky, if you will, and I'll tell you about the journey, and about this."

He stretched towards me his right hand, or rather what remained of it. The fingers were entirely gone, and only a stump was left of the thumb, yet the wounds were already so thoroughly healed that it might always have been the mere lump of flesh that I saw now. After taking a sip from his glass, my host gestured towards the many shelves of books that surrounded us in the study.

"What do you know of *Ishtaol*?" he asked.

"The name strikes only the most muffled chord, and yet — " I considered for a moment, and then: "Wasn't there something about Mordecai Howard, thirty or so years ago? Of course! Howard had the notion of a long-lost city, somewhere in the far east, and he called it 'Ishtaol'. But surely Howard was mad?"

"Agreed. At the end, Howard was certified insane, and the world said that his search for the hidden city was merely a result of his madness. So I thought at one time, but now I know that the reverse was true: the quest was the cause of the madness. I am utterly certain now that Mordecai Howard achieved precisely what he claimed to have achieved — he found, and lost again, the long-buried ruins of Ishtaol, the Dreaming City. My uncle, you know, was Howard's mentor, Philip Wendigee, and from him I inherited all Howard's papers.

"Believe me, I made a more thorough and more sceptical investigation of the whole business than even Wendigee himself before I became convinced of the truth of it. After reading Howard's notes, I then went on to study in depth all the sources upon which his claim was based: scientific report, legend, folklore, occult texts. There was more, too — works of which he was apparently ignorant. Yes, he must have been unaware of them, or he would never have gone about things as he did.

"The fullest and clearest account is in old Geoffrey de Lacy's *De Potentiae Deorum Antiquorum*, but since only Morley's revision now exists one can't be sure how much is original and how much interpolation. At all events, de Lacy claims to have made what he terms a pilgrimage, from Arabia through India to the wastes of the Gobi, in search of the Dreaming City. It must have been a journey of almost incomprehensible difficulty and danger; yet the old man not only accomplished it, bur brought something back with him — something of immense age and quite incalculable value. I don't know whether Mordecai Howard understood this reference, or whether he simply ignored it. The latter, probably, for his interest was mainly archaeological.

"Nevertheless, it was the thought of de Lacy's prize that inspired my own expedition.

"Oh, the hours — the days and weeks — that I spent in reading those books! All this, I should say, after many months taken up in gaining access to them, for some are quite fabulously rare. I was obliged to travel great distances before I could even begin the research for my principal journey.

"What shall I say to you of the books themselves? Some of the titles may be familiar to you. There are hints of the matter in Harold Sprague's *Geographica Antiqua*, in *De Vermis Mysteriis*, and even the occasional allusion in the *Necronomicon*, confirming a brief reference made by old de Lacy. At the end of it all I was torn between the desire to mount a full-scale expedition immediately and the wish to dismiss it all as unwholesome, morbid lunacy. Of course, I did neither. In fact, I secluded myself for a full two weeks and considered the matter carefully. By the end of that time, it was clear to me that there was at least a majority of truth in it all, and that such a — treasure-hunt, shall I call it? — would need all the courage that I could muster and knowledge that could only be gained through much further research.

"Ishtaol exists. Be in no doubt about that. Over the millennia, ruined and devastated, the city has survived. But it is guarded — and guarded by the very thing that I must seek. The city is almost unbelievably old — pre-human, certainly, if one may believe such unreliable texts as the *Liber Ivonis*. Yet its guardian is older still.

"This is not a time for theological debate. I shall mention only that the gods of our own people — and I am thinking back to the Teutons, the Celts, the Greeks and Romans — are all essentially anthropomorphic. As you dig more deeply, however, you will find that it was not so in the long-vanished past. The beings worshipped then were not merely un-human, but literally unearthly. Most of mankind is only now beginning to realise this as a possibility, but I tell you that it is fact, and that I have seen one of these ancient gods, one of these *dei antiqui*."

"You mean — ?"

"I mean *Ishtaol*. For the god or demon that guards the city is also known as Ishtaol. It was worshipped and propitiated by the original inhabitants, the unknown creatures that built the place, and later by the first human beings who dwelt there. In time, however, over many thousands of years, a lassitude came upon the god, incomprehensible to its human worshippers, and an appearance of death. I put it like that because I am certain that Ishtaol did not die, but merely entered a phase in its all-but-eternal existence that could be compared to the sleep of mortals. A prosaic, but not, I think, inapt simile, for the sleep gave rise to dreams. And as the god dreamed, so did the denizens of the city; and, being merely human, their minds could not comprehend the dreams of a god. Those who did not go mad deserted the place, and went to live among the other peoples of that then-flourishing region.

"As the ages crept onward, so the abandoned city lost its reality in the world of men. It became known as *Sath'gon-Thargn*, which means no more than 'the Dreaming City', and passed into legend before becoming almost wholly forgotten. That fertile area of east central Asia was in time lost to men, save for the nomadic Mongolian tribes. For millennia now it has been *Gobi* or *Shamo* — the Sandy Desert. But the city survives, and the dreams of its god have complete sway.

"I studied, far more deeply than poor Howard did, the ways of finding the city and the means of protecting myself while there — for, as his case shows too clearly, no unprepared man is proof against the devastating delirious impact of the dreams of Ishtaol.

"From intimations made by Alhazred and by Ludwig Prinn, and from fuller directions left by Geoffrey de Lacy, I eventually assembled a psychic armoury of both incantations and physical objects that I believed would shield me from the worst harm."

"One moment!" I said. "You speak of 'ways' of finding the city. Howard's way seems to have been straightforward enough, and he did find it — or so you imply ..."

"Howard was lucky — though you should bear in mind that luck may be good or bad. I mean just what I say when I refer to 'ways'. There are aspects of Ishtaol that Howard did not know, or did not understand. You must realise that the millennial dreams of a god have had a far deeper and more devastating effect upon the city than poor Howard imagined. It cannot, I think, be explained in terms of our present-day science, but you may take it as fact that Ishtaol no longer exists entirely in our world. It has gradually slid, or been pushed, into a crack — a fissure — between this world and others.

"Howard, I say, was lucky. He saw the ruined city, and there it was. But not every man may see Ishtaol, and not every man may find it where it is seen. Understand: I do not speak of mirages, which are a property of the desert. This elusiveness is a property of the city itself, or of its god. Hence the absolute need for my intense research.

"I learned much from de Lacy, more from Alhazred, and most — surprisingly — from the mage Eibon, who claimed to have encountered such things himself, in lands long since vanished.

"Mordecai Howard's was a scientific expedition. His way, as you have rightly said, was straightforward, but it was not my way. Like Geoffrey de Lacy, I went upon a pilgrimage, and I went alone — though at no time, until I was within twenty miles of the spot where I knew the city to be, did I eschew the help of native guides. My preparations had been long, exhaustive and often tedious, but they were necessary. Unlike Howard, I returned alive and sane — without my right hand, to be sure, but with a treasure that Howard could not have conceived.

"What shall I say of the city? Imagine vast, dreary, windblown wastes of sand, stretching to the horizon and endlessly on. That desert is relieved only be the almost completely buried shapes of huge stone blocks, whitish in colour, which even the passing of ages has not rendered entirely smooth. The keen eye sees at once that they are artificial, and a closer scrutiny reveals almost obliterated incisions and low reliefs, some bearing a vague resemblance to the Sumerian, though others seem totally alien. It must be hard for you to comprehend — as it was for me — the immense, almost incalculable age of those great megaliths. I should have been quite prepared, but as I gazed upon that scene of utter desolation, the stone gleaming sliver in the moonlight, I felt such awe as I had thought I could never experience and live.

"Even with the example of Geoffrey de Lacy to follow, I found it difficult to relate this apparently random debris to what I knew of the ancient city, and many were the hours and days that I spent in clearing that infernal sand from the stones, searching for some sign, some slight indication that would lead me to the very heart of the city, to the subterranean temple wherein was Ishtaol himself.

"A formula from John Dee's *Necronomicon* proved of great help then, for, if used in conjunction with the burning of certain substances, it would cause things long hidden to reveal themselves. Only small things, mind, and only for a second, and I dared not use it more than three times, for the power that it consumed came from within myself. Still, in the end it was sufficient. I located the immense block, still recognisably engraved with the device of a single ab-human eye, which covered the entrance to the sunken home of the god. I found that its balance still held true, that it could be opened with little more than the touch of a hand — and I opened it.

"I had expected the air thus released to be stale, even noxious, but it was not. To my ungovernable surprise it was sweet, with something of the acid sweetness of citrus. What was the cause of this, I could not tell, and nor do I know now. I merely state it as fact. Being warned by something that de Lacy had said, I did not at once venture into the great chasm that opened before me. Instead, I first, with more strength than I had believed possible, manhandled the nearest great slab of stone towards the trap-door, so that it might serve as a kind of prop. It was not to hold the door open, but merely to stop it from closing. That would suffice, for unless it was completely closed it could not lock.

"Don't ask me to explain the lock. All I can tell you is that although a man might open the trap from the outside, he could not always do so from within. I had no wish to take more chances than necessary.

"Next, I ensured that a number of small packets, containing items that I believed would afford me some measure of protection, were in place about my person, and that the paper bearing a certain incantation was ready to hand. Only then, clutching my electric torch, did I descend into the abyss.

"When I had taken my prize, I retreated as quickly as I possibly could, pursued by mental or psychical projections of such appalling power that I truly believed my brain would burst, and I would become as mad as poor Howard. But my protection held, And the only lasting harm I suffered was purely physical — the loss of my hand. When I reached the summit of those many steps, I was horrified to see that the mighty trap-door had all but crushed my three-foot slab of stone — crushed it to dust. If I had delayed but another minute ...

"You are eager, of course, to see what it was that I sought with such determination: the prize that cost me my right hand. You will find it in the wall-safe behind you, wrapped in a cloth. Here are the keys."

Inside the safe there was but one object, spherical and about the size of a basketball. I took it out and carried it to my host's desk. The cloth, which I had supposed would be a rich silk or damask, a fit covering for a great treasure, proved to be a simple bag or sack, made apparently from a cheap blanket. The object was surprisingly heavy for its size, and my mind turned happily to thoughts of solid gold. I handled the thing with great caution.

"Oh, don't worry about breaking it!" my host exclaimed. "That cloth isn't intended to protect the thing — on the contrary, it's to protect us. Yes, you may well look surprised. The fact is that it's not safe to look at it for more than a few minutes at a time. The drain on one's psychic resources is too great. The battery needs time to recharge.

"Well, don't stand there, man! Take it out of the bag. I assure you that you are quite safe for the short time that I shall allow you."

Wondering, I obeyed him. The object was indeed a perfectly regular sphere — not, as I had suspected of gold or any other metal, but apparently of glass, like a clairvoyant's crystal ball.

My disappointment must have shown in my expression, for my host remarked, "No, it isn't glass. Didn't I tell you that it was unbreakable? You can test it if you wish — no, don't drop it on the floor! It's so heavy that it would probably go right through the into the room below. Look, isn't that a diamond in your tie-pin? Very well, then. Just try to scratch that thing with it."

I tried, but to no effect at all. The diamond, the hardest natural substance known, merely slid off the surface of that strange sphere. Whether or not my host's story was true, the object before me was incontrovertibly alien to the prosaic world I knew. As I picked it up again, something about it impressed me.

"Why," I said, "it is surely hollow!"

"Indeed it is. Hollow, and partially filled with a clear liquid. See how it swirls as you move the sphere! But look at it more closely. Concentrate upon that liquid. Clear, I said, and so it is, but not quite as colourless as it seemed at first, eh?"

It was true. What had appeared to be a pellucid, viscous fluid, rather like pure alcohol, seemed now to be composed of infinitely many colours and shades of colours — and not colours merely, but shapes. As I gazed, fascinated, I found that I was looking at a scene, evidently in the open air, which was utterly unknown to me. It was almost as if the sphere acted as a *camera obscura*.

The picture clarified, became solid: the entrance to a walled town or city — though the style of architecture was not one that I recognised, consisting as it did of sinuous, serpentine curves and waves, with not a single angle or straight line visible anywhere. Equally baffling was the material of which the buildings were constructed. Not wood, and not stone. It looked for all the world like *ivory* — but surely that was impossible?

Now I saw movement, as first one human figure, and then another, and then many, ran pell-mell through the gateway towards me, scattering here and there in evident panic, their images growing rapidly bigger as they approached. Their movements, and what I could distinguish of their light-brown faces, spoke of an overpowering fear — a fear that somehow was instantly communicated to me. The refugees came ever on, and the whole picture seemed to expand, threatening to engulf me.

What was the cause of their terror? And — God help me! — should I be forced to confront it myself?

Unable to avert my eyes, I watched in growing dread as something shapeless and translucent, wet and glistening, forced its way through the arch towards me, moving with a quick and horrible ease. Still it came, pouring out, seemingly guided by an unimaginable intelligence. The brightness of the sun began to show the dull, alien hues of the rope-like organs that twisted and throbbed upon the surface, pulsating and oozing with slime. For an instant I thought I glimpsed what might have been an eye, utterly non-human, far beyond the arch, but approaching, and growing, and swelling ...

"That's enough!" With a practised hand, my host enveloped the sphere once more in its coarse cloth bag. "I'm sorry. Perhaps I shouldn't have let you — "

For a moment his words meant nothing to me. I felt drained, and sight and sound were nothing more than the unwelcome impressions of dreams. Reality, somehow, was within that damnable crystal sphere. With less difficulty than he had implied, my host opened the decanter and poured out a good dose of whisky. He pushed the glass towards me.

"Here," he said. "Drink this. It will help to restore the psychic balance.

"I had forgotten how bad it can be the first time," he continued. "Eventually, with preparation, you become just a little used to it. Never wholly, of course — we're only human, after all — but although I've seen worse things than that in the sphere, it isn't all bad, by any means. Alien, yes — nearly always alien, but not always bad."

"But what is it?" I demanded. "What have I seen?"

"The dream of a god," he answered, soberly. "And man cannot share such dreams for long."

"And this — this thing? You haven't yet told me just what it is. Nor — " (I turned my gaze to the lump of flesh at the end of his right arm) " — have you told me how that happened."

"True, true. Well, I did tell you of my conviction that the god Ishtaol had not died, but had merely entered a different phase of its inconceivable life-cycle. I believe that, during this period — which may last for countless millennia yet — during this period, I say, its metabolism has slowed to such an extent that merely to move a fraction of an inch may take many hundreds of years. Imagine a sentient mountain. Picture to yourself how slowly it must live, compared even to the trees that grow upon it, and you may have some conception of my meaning.

"Physically, then, I knew that I was quite safe in confronting Ishtaol — unless I planned some such act as was actually in my mind. Spiritual and mental danger was another matter, but I had prepared myself against that.

"It is not hard to describe the god to you, but it would take greater powers than mine to convey its utterly unearthly nature. It looks like smoothly carven white stone, in the amorphous form of a mere lump of dough, resting upon the tessellated floor of its temple. Howard, in his journal, describes a monstrous statue of the god, but it is my belief that no effigies were ever made, and that he saw, but failed to recognise, nothing less than Ishtaol itself. As I found it, it must have measured some thirty feet across and twenty high, in a roughly cone-shaped mound.

"The slick smoothness of its surface made it very difficult for me to climb to the top, but I did achieve it, and found, as I had expected, no fewer than fifteen crystalline globes clustered upon its summit, and two hollows to show where more such globes had been. These, I take it, were left when Alhazred, and after him de Lacy, took their prizes.

"I likewise took mine. I had to use a very special blade, and even so, the fluid that oozed from the cut actually burned off the fingers of my right hand, so that I was close to fainting with the pain. But I had what I sought, and I emerged as you see me.

"It cost me the use of my hand, but I think that the sacrifice was worthwhile. I did not seek wealth, nor do I want power. It is *knowledge* that fascinates me, and any man so desperate for knowledge may do as I did. Fourteen remain for those who go properly prepared.

"As you can bear witness, strange things may be seen in the eyes of Ishtaol."

Afterword

I thought that the theme of "The Dreaming City" would bear elaboration: hence this story, suggested by Brian Lumley's "An Item of Supporting Evidence".

My friend Jan Arter thinks that there should be a Society for the Prevention of Cruelty to Gods — perhaps she's right.

"Ishtaol" was first published in *Deep Things out of Darkness*, with a striking illustration by Dallas Goffin.

FROM THE DESERT

I cannot explain it. I can but tell my story, and you must judge for yourselves.

I had fallen in with a group of merchants, rich men and jolly, dealers in fine silks and rare gems. Far in the heat of the desert, our caravan was set upon by robbers, and all save myself were slain. Our beasts and chattels they took, and me they left for dead. When I recovered my senses, it was in the shimmering, searing heat of noon. I was alone, many leagues from humankind, and I knew that I was doomed. Pain burned in my left leg where a knife had cut deep, and my own blood soiled the white sands about me. Nonetheless, the will to live is a fierce thing in man. I fashioned a dressing from my tattered garments, to stem the flow of blood, and slowly I pulled my aching body from the defile wherein we had suffered attack.

I do not know whence came my strength, but I moved painfully onwards, until I came at length to a mighty rock, *solus* amid the white and fiery sands, as though it had been cast from out the heavens. In the shadow of this great stone I rested, and fitfully slept until after the coming of night, when, with thirst raging through me, I awakened, to find that — strangest of strange things! — a camel stood by me, patiently waiting upon my return to sensibility. On its back was a saddle of fine-grained leather, sewn with silks, and stamped with gold in fantastic designs, as had it been crafted for some great and mystical Lord of the Desert. Weak though I was, I yet contrived to seat myself upon the back of the beast when it knelt, and shortly was borne away through the soft coolness of the desert night — I knew not whither, nor cared at all.

When morning came, the heat of the daemon sun provoked within me a thirst that parched and seared, and would not be quieted. Alas! I *could not* quiet it. I recall little of that terrible day, save the heat, the blinding brightness of the hideous sands, and the monsters that my mad thirst conjured before me. I beheld whole caravans whose members were but the whitened and gnawed skeletons of camels, their trappings ragged and bleached, their riders stern-faced liches, whose yellow skin clung obscenely to their naked bones. Djinn there were, horned and fanged, with eyes that bulged grotesquely, and thin, knobbed hands that clutched at the air, as if in expectation of — of I know not what.

Strange things, they say, are writ in the ancient books, and Alhazred had cause for his madness; but have I not also cause for mine? I have seen the timeless Guardians of the Desert, the Afrits that gibber and howl unceasingly beneath the white flame that is the sun. They stretched out their thin arms to me, and laughed as they implored me to join them in their insanity.

Mirages also I saw: blue lakes and green trees, pools of sapphire and palms of emerald; luscious fruits and cool, lucent water, shimmering always at an unconscionable distance, for ever inaccessible. Sometimes these visions merely faded; sometimes they vanished suddenly; and sometimes they grew to vast proportions as we neared them, so that it seemed as though the entire yellow sky were replaced by a waste of azure water, and the firmament were painted over with ineffable colossi — *upsidedown.*

At length, toward evening, I beheld the image of a city, a place of immense white palaces, golden-roofed, many-towered, and resplendent. My brain was numbed, or I should have recalled that in that region of the great desert no city had stood since before Iskander himself was conceived.

And yet the city appeared there, and in truth I saw it. Among its structures of richly gleaming white stone I could shortly descry others: tall, monolithic, and seemingly carven of onyx, their shade the shade of deepest night. Light glowed blood-red through round windows in these black towers, and from them, methought, issued forth a dark and ineluctable malignity.

As we neared the unknown metropolis, it seemed to me that the camel was deliberately making its way thither, as though it too saw this strange place, not merely seeing it, indeed, but knowing it. Half-mad as I was, I yet felt uneasy, for I dared not leave the beast while we were yet amid the endless sands of the desert; but also I began to be afraid for my soul of that mysterious city. I peered through the spaces between the buildings, and I beheld things that *should not* have been there. It seemed to me, moreover, that the golden spires, which before I had thought so magnificent, were yet in some way evil: some subtle wrongness of proportion, some weirdness of character, conveyed a sense of dream-like terror to my disordered mind.

The camel moved pitilessly onward, and, in seeming near, the strange city seemed also to wax hideously vast, even as the mirages that I had previously beheld. And yet — it *was* of itself vast, for I was at length able to discern some of its denizens, and they appeared infinitesimal among those colossal structures. I could not yet descry any detail of these inhabitants, but it seemed to me that there was something delicately *wrong* about their shape and their proportion.

As I strained my weary eyes, inexorably we drew nearer, and still the slender black towers and the insidiously beautiful white blocks, with their twisted golden roofs, became rapidly more huge. Gigantic now they seemed, blocking the red sun with their immensity, and piercing the very sky. Their outlines quavered, shaking with a mighty thunder, as though they would fall and crush me. And now — dear God! — *now* I saw clearly the denizens of that hellish place: *their bodies that were less than animal and their faces that were not faces.*

God preserve me! They were not *human*, nor ever had been.

Daemons I had seen — Djinn, created by my own fevered brain — but these were not they. These were worse. Mad, evil — with an evil that was of the soul and the body!

Forgive me. I *cannot* describe them.

I dare not try.

It seems that I swooned, through weakness and loss of blood, through thirst and fever, and through madness. A group of Bedouin found me on the evening of the next day, and there was no city at all. The camel that bore me upon my strange ride had likewise disappeared.

Afterword

Yet another plot derived from a note in H.P. Lovecraft's Commonplace Book, though Jeff Dempsey and David Cowperthwaite perceptively noted that "From the Desert" is less like Lovecraft than Clark Ashton Smith. The title deliberately echoes Smith's "Told in the Desert".

THE FOOL'S TALE
being the narrative of one who journeyed to the City called Mighty and there found its Guardian dead and its People dispersed

In dreaming, it seemed to me that I stood within a dark place, heavy with the velvet blackness of night. Yet it was not within any house of the Mighty City that I stood, for the floor was rough and cold beneath my feet, and the air was chill. It came to me that I was in some strange and massy pile, builded of cold and harsh rock.

Feeling my way gently, lest there should be some pitfall or stumbling-block, I walked forward into the darkness, and at length encountered a wall of crudely carven stone blocks, stretching up higher than my hand could reach. After much deliberation, I resolved to follow this wall to the left as far as I might. moving gingerly and touching the barrier with my right hand, that I might be aware should it break off. After a short while, it seemed to me that I progressed along a narrow corridor — and so indeed it proved, for upon stretching out my left hand I felt again the rough, hard dampness of just such another stone-built wall. I began to feel somewhat afraid, knowing not whither this enclosed alley might lead me, for I am a man not noted for courage. I was besides quite unarmed, even as when I had lain me to sleep.

In time I came to a staircase, narrow and winding, formed of blocks of the same chill stone. The steps, as I could feel, both mounted and descended, so that it was a puzzle to me to know whether I should venture up or down. I decided at last to climb upwards, in hopes that I might reach some part of the castle — for castle it surely was, though strange and barbaric in truth — wherein light shed its grateful beams.

In this I was well-advised, for I had not ascended far, turning ever widdershins, upon this flight, when a dim glow became apparent — not yet a light, but rather a mere lessening of the darkness, though holding a barbarous yellow tint. I saw now that the stones of this castle were indeed massive, rough and pitted, grey, and running with a chill moisture. The illumination, as I shortly discerned, came from a primitive torch, fixed to wall by a corroded metal bracket. Below this, huddled upon the stone flags in apparent slumber, was a man, clad in a clumsy armour of interwoven metal rings. His leggings, and the helm that lay beside him, were of beaten iron, and over his mail tunic was a white surcoat, bearing as emblem a single blood-red cross. In his belt was a metal dagger, and his right hand clutched the hilt of a longsword. A shield rested against the wall next to him, charged with that same symbol of the crimson cross upon a field of snow.

Whether this sleeper were friend or foe I could not tell, wherefore I edged past him most stealthily. Higher up the staircase, yet more flamboys cast their uncertain yellow glow, and under each slept an armed man. It seemed that the guardians of this strange fortress had suffered the enchantment of some necromancer, for assuredly all slept as if in the long sleep of death. Yet dead were they not: that I know, for one as I passed turned his iron-clad head and muttered a few words in a language not of our world, a most singular harsh tongue, which in my dream I could yet comprehend. The import was this: *The Beast must have its due.*

As I mounted ever higher, wondering upon what I had seen and heard, it seemed to me that the light ahead differed in essence from that shed by the fiery flamboys, being colder and greyer in tone. The reason for this I soon discovered, for upon rounding a turn of the stair I saw before me a narrow window, a mere slit in the dense stonework, through which appeared a strip of sky, grey and sullen. Beside the aperture lay another soldier, who clutched in his hand a longbow, crudely but strongly made. I stepped cautiously over the recumbent figure and gazed out of the strait, stone-bound slit to see what lay beyond the walls of the castle.

Before and below me — more than a dozen ells below — there was extended a vast and dreary plain, whose growth was nought but scorched grass and low, stunted trees. Upon this dismal heath a battle progressed between two armies of men, all borne upon strong horses and clad in unwieldy metal armour. Their weapons were long lances and mighty swords; for defence they carried such shields as I had seen, and by the devices upon these shields alone were they distinguished, for no faces could be seen beneath the enveloping iron helms. The one party — that of the lord of this castle, plainly — had as symbol a single crimson cross upon a white field, while the foe was marked by a most curious emblem: the creature emblazoned in red upon the yellow surcoats and bucklers was a Serpent, and it resembled most terribly the Silent Dragon of the Endless City.

The clash of weapons was a most awesome sight, as the steeds plunged across the barren ground and the men swung their mighty swords, or attempted with their spears to spit their opponents. A few carried great spiked maces, which they wielded with violent precision. The bodies that lay scattered upon the field bore mute witness that fully half of the original combatants were slain or grievously wounded, and the greater number by far were Knights of the Cross.

Their living fellows by now were hopelessly outnumbered. The clash and clang of steel against steel, the desperate whinny of a horse, the dull shock as another man was felled — these were the only sounds that reached my ears from this heroic spectacle. It seemed that the sun was setting behind the castle, for a red glow was reflected weirdly in the polished arms and armour of these strange antagonists, while the firmament above them grew darker and heavier, and stars became apparent, grouped in constellations unknown to me.

Engrossed as I was in the epic combat before me, it yet occurred to me to wonder where — and, indeed, when — I might be, for all about me was most strange and foreign. But even as I had comprehended the uncouth words of the slumbering soldier, so now I understood that this cataclysmic battle was being waged in a land yet unborn in our own age, a land that would lie at the very edge of the known world, in a time that my waking self could not possibly live to see; a land where noble warriors would wear just such primitive defensive garb, and wield just such barbarous weapons, and proudly don that same device of the blood-red cross, in deference to their protector, the holy Georgius.

But who were these others, these strangers, who so overwhelmingly threatened my own land? Aye, my land, I say; for I was myself, as it seemed, a man of this nation, so far in space and time from the Mighty City. A man to whom the outcome of this battle must be vital or mortal, and yet one who could neither help nor hinder those who contended. I stood high within a grim and mighty stronghold, and could but watch powerless as there unrolled before me a most desperate struggle between the men of my own nation and an army whose totem and symbol was that most feared and abhorred of all creatures, the Red Serpent.

There was, I knew, a people allied to mine own who claimed the dragon for their protector, but these were not they. These were an alien host, arisen from unknown gulfs of night. I watched, and wondered, and was afraid.

With a stately and painful slowness, the warriors strove. Mightily they smote and parried with their great blades, and even as I watched, within the space of a few minutes, fully seven of the Knights of the Cross were slain, for the death of but one of the foe. This one, pierced through the heart by a lance, remained upright in his saddle for several minutes before at last toppling, infinitely slowly, to the ground. Steel struck upon steel, clashing lustily, and while the dying gasped and groaned, the living cried aloud: *God for Saint George!* Thus the Knights of the Cross. Their foes, they of the Serpent, said nought, but remained most strangely and terribly silent, uttering no sound, neither in fighting nor in dying.

The chief of the defenders stood out from the rest, not alone by his great stature, but by virtue of the dully gleaming fillet of gold that encircled his helm. Looking upon him, I knew that I beheld a great warrior and a great king. Yet among his opponents was one who was fully his equal in height, and who wore a coronet of polished steel around his helm. The Serpent upon his shield was shown coiled around a princely crown.

At length, as must happen, these two mighty men came together, face to face, whereat he of the Cross reined in his mount and raised his sword on high over his steel-clad head. Upon the instant, the fray ceased, and silence fell upon the field. Men let fall their sword-arms and halted their horses and turned to face their lords. The two giants sat in momentary silence, each seeming to gauge the other's strength. Then spoke mine own countryman: *Come you the captain of this hellish legion?*

The other spoke no word, but with slow majesty bowed his head in acknowledgement.

Then said the Prince of the Cross: *Now let single combat decide between us, for I will not sacrifice more noble lives.*

There was a brief and terrible pause, and again the Lord of the Serpent slowly nodded. At this the other warriors expeditiously retired behind their masters; by some chance the defenders now faced the very fortress that was their charge, so that I could fancy that they saw me even as I watched from the high window.

The two princes now stood alone in the midst of a great circle of men. Almost as one, they first raised their lances in salute and then lowered them in readiness to charge; and as they galloped towards each other their horses hooves pounded upon the black and blood-soaked earth, like the rolling of infernal thunder. The champion's weapon struck his opponent's shoulder as they met, but merely glanced off again, almost throwing him off balance. The challenger's lance was caught by his shield and shivered to fragments.

The two men wheeled their horses round and turned again to face each other. Seeing his opponent's loss, the Knight of the Cross raised his own lance and contemptuously threw it upon the ground. Both drew forth their longswords and prepared to meet again.

More warily now it seemed, they came together, swinging and cutting mightily. Almost as one they struck, the blades biting savagely into the shields, battering, denting and cutting, with slow, powerful strokes. Implacably, inexorably, they smote and smote again, while their steeds circled around, seeming to follow the pattern of the blows, so that now one warrior faced me, and now the other. Still those deadly blades gleamed fiercely in the bloody light of the dying sun, and still each man majestically parried the other's blows, so that neither gained the advantage. Never have I seen so fairly matched a pair of heroes. They might have continued to cut and strike and ward for days, until their strength gave out.

But something — I know not what — distracted the champion's attention. For an instant he gazed fixedly at some point above me, and numbly lowered his guard a fraction. With vicious speed his foe struck out, but the Knight of the Cross hastily thrust his shield upwards, and was able to deflect the blow before it should sever his head from his body. Even so, the hard steel sheared through the soft metal of his royal coronet, and all but cut the crest from his helm. Seeing his enemy take so unjust an advantage, he became greatly enraged, and cut and thrust yet more strongly, but not wildly, so that his opponent was much disconcerted.

Fierce and continuous were the champion's blows, and at last a fateful cross-stroke passed the challenger's shield, cutting cleanly through the steel headpiece, shearing the visor from it. From my high post I could not see what manner of face was thus revealed, but methought it must be devilish indeed, for the Lord of the Cross ceased his fury of a sudden and let his sword fall unheeded to the blasted and bloody earth. For full half a minute he gazed at the revelation before him; then he turned his head to see what reaction his men made.

One, sorely wounded, had swooned, and fallen from his horse. Two others had hastily averted their eyes. The rest looked on in blank amaze, and all had swiftly traced upon their breasts a cross, as though for protection against some monstrous evil.

While the Prince, his head turned, gazed thus at his knights, the foeman had wheeled his horse slightly, and now stood directly facing him, and thus with his broad back to me. Reluctantly, the guardian of the castle directed his eyes again to this strange enemy, and, like his men, crossed himself. The Lord and the Host of the Serpent stood unmoving. For some seconds of eternity there was a pause, pregnant with fear and mystery, and then, with characteristic slow and impressive dignity, the enemy lord raised his iron-gloved hands and lifted off his helmet.

Suddenly I understood why they of the Cross were so astounded and so afraid. This was no monster, no freak of birth or breeding. This was the very essence of madness.

No head was revealed.

As I and the defenders looked on, awe-struck, this being — this spirit — this daemon — drew off his iron gloves, and with an easy contempt cast them to the ground.

He had no hands.

Then, somehow, a great mist arose, red with the blood of the dying sun, and it seemed that the enemy warriors and their steeds — aye, and even their slain — became themselves mere figures of mist. Certain I am that ere my vision was wholly obscured there remained upon the field only the Knights of the Red Cross.

The mist thickened and darkened, at first a violent crimson, and then a black like the blackness of the tomb. For a moment I saw nothing, heard nothing, knew nothing. But then the gloom was lightened; the blackness became red again, and then grey; and at length I could see.

And before me I saw — the massy stone pile of the castle, black against the crimson of the sky. About me stretched the barren and blasted plain, rich now with blood and bearing the bodies of a hundred of the defenders, slain in battle against that daemon foe. I felt the pressure of thick padding upon my flesh, saw the slitted visor before my eyes — realised the change in my *position* — and knew that I was myself the Prince of the Cross, upon the field of battle, mounted.

I now saw that the gaze of my knights was fixed upon something in the heavens, above the castle's lofty towers —

something that had struck them numb with fear and wonder. Not knowing, but myself fearing, I raised my head and looked also, to see that which made my heart grow heavy within my breast. The enemy, I knew now, though defeated, was not defeated utterly. It — he — they — had merely retired, to lick their wounds and to plot. England survived, as, please God, she should long survive, but she must yet face further onslaught from the same dark power, from whatever vile corner of Earth or Hell it came. And at the end, methought, must come the final conflict, whose outcome no man can tell.

What I saw was nought but a peculiar concentration of fantastic clouds, above the highest battlements. It was cloud, I say: nothing more — and I have seen strange shapes in the clouds before. And yet — that *shape*! And that *colour*! In the crimson glow of the setting sun, as dark and red as blood, I saw a mad likeness, a blasphemous effigy, of a vast *red serpent*.

Afterword

The narrative of this story is taken from one of Lovecraft's dreams, as described in his Commonplace Book. (I should have dreams like that!). I wrote "The Fool's Tale" a very long time ago, but revised it when I realised that the theme could be tied in with the "Dreaming City" stories.

THE MAN WHO INHERITED THE WORLD

Thale:
    Mother, must the Dynasty die only because you are bored?
    Only a word from you, and the Black Stars would rise again.

                     The King in Yellow, Act One, Scene One

Arcana, esoterica, secret knowledge — call it what you like; it may be a delight or it may be a burden. Paul Chesterton rejoiced to know that he was the rightful owner of the world.

Much has been said and written about his state of mind during those last months, but no one, I think, has mentioned what seems to me a peculiarly interesting fact: namely, that Chesterton had read the *Necronomicon* and certain other rare and cryptic books before he ever encountered *The King in Yellow*.

I knew him only slightly; I was his closest living relative, but the connection extended through several others, all deceased. We met on just two occasions, once when I was a child, and again some eight months before his death. At our first meeting he impressed me as the complete man of action. I heard with joy his tales of exploration in the deserts of central Asia, in the deep forests of Brazil, and in the desolate islands of arctic Canada. That I did not comprehend all that he said or hinted is perhaps not surprising. Later, having learned more of his life and work, I realised that he was a rare and wonderful amalgam of action and contemplation.

The second and final meeting took place in the autumn of 1936, at his house near the Essex coast. From the window of the library one could see the spot, at the foot of a shallow mound, where Chesterton would shortly build his eccentric brick tower, that tower whose significance has been so much disputed. Little enough was said, but fortunately Chesterton had from childhood been a compulsive diarist. Perhaps even then he had a premonition of destiny. The diaries were found *post mortem* in the study at Murrell House. There were calls from some quarters that they be destroyed, but that I could not allow. Without the diaries and the long letter addressed to me (and marked with the instruction that it was to be opened only in the event of his death or disappearance) the world would still be ignorant of the facts and the fancies that had spurred Paul Chesterton's life — and, so to speak, ended it.

I have noted that Chesterton was familiar with various books of rare and ancient lore. The diaries mention the *Necronomicon* in John Dee's English translation, *De Potentiae Deorum Antiquorum*, ostensibly by Sir Geoffrey de Lacy, the Bridewell Press edition of Friedrich von Junzt's *Black Book* — considered by many scholars to be severely flawed — and a much-censored eighteenth century printing of Prinn's *Mysteries of the Worm*. No other titles are specifically named, but it is clear that his reading was not limited to these. As in the case of Mordecai Howard, with whom he seems to have been unacquainted, my cousin went his own way, scornful of, and rather scorned by, the scientific establishment.

I have myself read de Lacy's book, in the only surviving version, first published in 1763, translated and revised by one Thomas Dashwood Morley. Alas, I found it confusing, frequently tedious, and always frustrating. Those concepts that are stated clearly are too outrageous for the rational mind to take seriously, while those — the greater number by far — that are merely hinted at are just too nebulous to be grasped. Yet Chesterton, it seems, found something in this gibberish that inspired him, leading him to mount the expeditions of which he had told me. He somehow discerned an ulterior or interior purpose to the world, a destiny that was intimately bound up with his own life. He was, he thought, intended by fate to be recognised as a great discoverer, whose name would be recognised and acclaimed with those of Galileo, Newton and Einstein.

And yet Paul Chesterton was no scientist. He saw himself as something more akin to the great philosophers of ancient times, men whose minds encompassed both certain physical fact and the wonders of metaphysical speculation. He would quote with derision the story of Hegel, who in the year 1800 elegantly and irrefutably demonstrated that it was impossible that more heavenly bodies could exist than were already known. On the first day of the following year, Ceres was discovered, the first of the asteroids. To Chesterton, the philosopher or philosophy that could not cope with such an outcome was unworthy of the name. On the other hand, he admired Bertrand Russell, though he deplored Russell's atheism.

It was fortunate that his income was generous. Even though he had been obliged to sell much of his estate to pay the debts accrued by his late father, more than enough remained. Murrell House, built in the middle years of Victoria's reign in a rather heavy version of Greek Ionic, was not particularly large, and was furnished rather frugally. The most valuable feature of the house in Chesterton's time was the library, and he did not consider that to be a luxury, any more than he regarded his travels as relaxation. They were his work, and eventually he would make the ultimate discovery for which he was destined.

He was in his vigorous early sixties when the idea came to him that he had been looking *in the wrong place*. He tried to explain this to me when I visited him, and I fear that I was slow to comprehend.

"You told me," I said, "that in all your journeys you were inspired by some statement or hint in one of these books." (I could not, even yet, bring myself to realise their importance.) "Do you mean that you have misinterpreted what they say?"

"No," he said. "It is not that. All — nearly all — of my quests have revealed something of importance. Even the Royal Geographical Society cannot deny that. I have added to the world's knowledge of anthropology and comparative religion. I have shown, could the timid folk bring themselves to admit it, that intelligent life is far older than humankind. What would they know, if not for my work, of the Feast of Druphak and its ritual? Of the Thirteenth Covenant? Of the Dwellers in the Wheel?

"Yet there remains the great discovery, the ultimate revelation. I wonder if, perhaps, I have at last served my apprenticeship. I have read the writing that is carved upon vast rock-faces in Yucatan. I have witnessed the worship of entities that are old beyond our imagining, and I have seen what will come if it is correctly called. I have — not twenty miles from here — spoken with men who are not *human*, not in our petty sense of the word. Now I feel that my destiny awaits beyond and above these things."

This was beyond my understanding, but that is not to say that I dismissed it as the rambling of a lunatic. I had too much respect for my host to make so glib and facile a judgement.

Chesterton sighed. "I must be constantly aware," he continued, "keeping my mind and my senses keen. I shall know. At the moment I have only the merest whisper of a thought. We shall see."

Then, during the pause that followed, there did indeed come a discovery. By a singular irony, I myself made it, and made it by chance. Among the books on the highest shelf behind my host — that is, to the right of the great fire-place — was a volume that I did not recall having noticed before. It was bound, apparently, in the mottled yellow skin of a serpent, and it seemed, despite its slim rectangular form, to have a certain sinuous ophidian quality. It was too high for me to read the pale lettering on the spine. I drew Chesterton's attention to it, but he too was unable to discern the book's title in the uncertain light.

"This is most odd," he said. "Of course, there are many volumes here that I have not read, and a number that I have never opened — books that belong to the house, as you might say, rather than to me — but I would surely remember such a thing as that. Wait, and I shall fetch the library steps."

Having mounted the steps, he glanced first of all at the title so palely inscribed upon the snake-skin binding, and then, deaf to my questions, he opened the mysterious volume. His expression of puzzlement deepened, and he seemed engrossed. It was only by grasping his elbow and shaking it firmly that I was able to attract his attention again.

"What is it?" I asked. "What is the book?"

He closed it gently and descended the steps. Not until he was again seated did he reply.

"It is," he said with deliberation, "*The King in Yellow*. How it came here — no, I am at a loss to explain. I had thought that there were no copies left in this country. There was only the one edition in English, you know, and that was printed in the United States of America. The Lord Chamberlain refused to allow publication here.

"The play has never been performed, of course. At least, it has never been performed in full."

This meant nothing to me, save that Paul Chesterton had evidently found something of quite extraordinary interest to him. Apparently oblivious to my presence, he again opened the book and was instantly lost in it. There was no more than a vague murmur in reply to my eventual farewell. Perhaps, I thought lightly, he has found the guidance that he sought.

We were not to meet again. It was only from the letters and the diaries that I learned the significance to him of *The King in Yellow*.

Within the hour, he had read and re-read the book. It held for him, as for others over the years, a fascination that is difficult to define. The words "hypnotic" and even "magical" would not be out of place, but neither is strictly accurate.

Paul Chesterton had found, in the stultifying confusion of Dr

Dee's *Necronomicon* and in some other works of a similar kind, an inspiration and a stimulation that were and are completely lost to me. Their apparent anticipation of de Sade's joy in the infliction of pain might have justified the action of authority down the ages in restricting and even banning such books. One could perhaps understand how their denial of any sort of monotheism would render them abhorrent to the church. But the very wildness of their assertion of ab-human intelligences, "vast, cool and unsympathetic", of powers beyond the imagination of humankind, together with their often chaotic incoherence, render them pathetic rather than dangerous — or so I thought.

The King in Yellow is another matter altogether.

The fact that Oscar Wilde was forced to defend *The Picture of Dorian Gray* seems absurd to us, since it is above all a moral fable, but there is nothing moral in *The King in Yellow*. The anonymous writer's skill is astounding. The very simplicity of the first act makes the impact, mental and emotional, of the second yet more devastating. The style is undeniably that of a poet, but there is neither magniloquence nor obfuscation. The straightforward language is pitilessly effective in conveying the author's strange and wicked philosophy to even the dullest mind — and yet it would take a very sharp mind indeed to define that philosophy. The book's tendency, as the lawyers say, is to corrupt — and yet Chesterton believed that a strong mind might learn from it without succumbing. Who shall say that he was wrong?

There was a deliberate coolness in his first notes on the subject, but the apparently forced restraint gave way to a rational enthusiasm that remained the dominant tone until the final days. He seemed to see this new discovery initially as simply clarifying certain important aspects of the lore expounded in the *grimoires*.

"One must always be wary," he wrote in his last letter, "of the seductiveness of such writing. I in particular must bear in mind the tragedy that befell young Castaigne back in the eighteen nineties (he was, I think, some sort of cousin to my father). Equally, it does not do to forget that Castaigne's mind was already unhinged when he first read the book — so much so that his very conception of time had become distorted. It is essential not to confuse fact and theory."

The first significant note in the diaries is this, written on the 28th October: "It is evident that the nature of *Hastur* (the entity, not the city named after it) has been grossly misunderstood, especially by von Junzt, who repeatedly refers to it, or him, as 'the Unspeakable' — *die Unaussprechlichen* — though this is clearly a misreading of the Latin *Innominandum:* that which must not be named. He who watched with indifference as the two suns sank into the Lake of Hali, who sounded the mystery of the Hyades, whose mind encompassed the stricken Cassilda — he is certainly something other than the daemon pictured in the old books. Even the Arab's word 'god' seems wrong, though it does hint at the immense age and power that are his attributes. (Incidentally, the word 'indifference' is wrong too, in so far as it seems to imply humanity, but I cannot at present think of a better.)

"Now, if this is true of Hastur, may it not be equally true of other beings? But one must keep an open mind. It has been argued that *Nyarlathotep* and *Azathoth*, for instance, are no more than symbols for natural or præternatural forces, and indeed the notion has a certain specious attraction. I wish sometimes that I could believe it, but, except in the sense that all reality is merely symbolic, it has no validity."

I was aware of Chesterton's conviction that much of the strange lore contained in those once-forbidden books was literally true, but this considered emphasis on the actual existence of beings from nightmare realms beyond man's imagination — this was new and rather disturbing.

Referring to Hastur again, he writes on the 4th November: "The philosopher called him "God of the Shepherds", a phrase that one might take to suggest a bucolic tenderness. Great Pan also was the God of the Shepherds, however, and we should not forget what *panic* truly is."

A later note, dated the 9th November, is more cryptic, one of several that seem to need more explication than I can give: "It would be a wonderful thing to see — maybe even to visit — that place where the black stars hang in the heavens over the glassy surface of the lake, where the shadows of men's thoughts lengthen in the afternoon, where the towers of Carcosa rise behind the moon. If only one could be sure of comprehending Truth!"

There is mention too of "resistance", from people or forces that are not defined. A psychiatrist has suggested that there was actually a struggle within Chesterton's own mind — that some, perhaps unconscious, part of him was trying to hold him back from a venture into madness. Certainly it is difficult to imagine from what quarter external resistance might come, since all the evidence suggests that for weeks before making this entry Chesterton had neither left Murrell House nor held communication with any person outside.

Eventually, it seems, he reached the conclusion that he should shake off this reclusiveness. He made trips into nearby Colchester, and once even into London, where he spent some time at Somerset House. He wrote to a number of specialist booksellers, though the diary entries carefully neglect to specify which volumes were the subject of this correspondence, and neither his letters nor any replies are still extant. He paid the occasional visit to the small and ill-regarded town of Wrabsey. He asked for estimates for building work.

And all this time he did not cease to make notes in his diary, though, as before, they were a tantalising mixture of the gnomic and the explicit. Allusions to "the secret parable" and to "the cosmic reality of silence" are quickly followed by the announcement of what must, even to Chesterton the explorer, have been the most momentous discovery of his life. He expanded upon the matter in his final letter, and it is that which I quote — though it is, perhaps, significant that the letter, begun in early November 1936 and added to over the following months, was not intended to be delivered during the writer's lifetime:

> "At that last meeting of ours, I fear that I was uncourteous to you. I beg you, my dear boy, to forgive me, bearing in mind the stupendous nature of the thing that I had found — no, that *you* had found — upon these bookshelves. *The King in Yellow* has opened my eyes, my mind, my very soul. You will recall, no doubt, my expression of frustration, my conviction that there was somewhere a key that would unlock the gate to a destiny further and higher than any achievement I had yet made. It was you who placed that key in my hand.
>
> "I have checked and checked again, and there is no doubt in my mind. For all his insanity, there is more than a kernel of truth in Hildred Castaigne's statement. If it were not occluded by the delusions that resulted from an injury to the brain when he was thrown from his horse (yes, *that* was real enough) it would have been noted and investigated long before now. The poor fellow imagined the strangest things — war between the United States

and Germany, caused by the latter's invasion of Samoa; the encouragement of euthanasia in America; that he, who was to die in 1894, actually lived until the early nineteen twenties. Hallucination, perhaps. Delusion, no doubt. Madness, certainly. But one thing he did *not* imagine: he was, after his cousin Louis, the true heir to the world, under the King in Yellow.

"I have, of course, known for many years that the Chestertons of Murrell House were originally named *Castaigne*, being a Huguenot family that fled to England after the repeal of the Edict of Nantes. Further, I have established beyond doubt that the direct line of Louis Castaigne is now extinct, and that — cousins in the United States notwithstanding — I am myself the rightful heir.

"My boy, can you imagine my feelings when this fact became manifest? Perhaps you can, once you are able to shake off your own astonishment and remember that you, as my closest living relative, are next in line! Indeed, if you are reading this, it can only be because I have either died or disappeared, and in that case, my dear boy, the glory is already yours. We must remember, though, that to rule in such case is but to serve, and that our master is a King who will not, cannot, rest until he controls the thoughts of mankind from the very womb. There is glory, but there is peril also, and it is in full knowledge that I embark upon this greatest expedition."

In his diary, on the twelfth of November, Chesterton again expresses a yearning to see the black stars as they hang in the heavens, the cloud-waves as they roll and break upon the shores of Hali; to hear the mournful song of Cassilda, echoing through the empty halls of the palace. There is a sense of expectancy, even of urgency, to this entry. He seems almost to have realised that he stood upon the brink of a second momentous discovery.

There follows the brief record of a conversation with a man named Martyr at Wrabsey, and for the first time a name is given to the "resistance" alluded to in earlier entries: "M. claims quite bluntly that only he and his kind are the true servants of Him Who Dreams, that theirs alone is the right to open the gate to the final age, and that I should not meddle. I told him that it is not my intention to meddle, but that I do mean to claim what is mine by my right in Hastur.

"These folk of the water shall not receive the Yellow Sign. Perhaps it would be as well to call down upon them the power of Thurgha, whose essence is fire. I cannot afford to tolerate opposition."

The mention of *Him Who Dreams* again brings into question the nature of certain beings or entities. This elliptical mode of reference was apparently usual among those who dwell in Wrabsey and in some other maritime settlements, both in Europe and elsewhere. There is known to be — or, rather, to have been — a certain traffic between this obscure Essex town and a once-flourishing port in Massachusetts, and between both and various islands "beyond the Indies". The designation, as I understand it, hides the reality of an entity, powerful beyond human understanding, yet not itself a god in any true sense: a being whose purpose is to guide the dreams of sentient life and to unlock the gates to the Great Ones from outside at such time as the stars are right. As to *Thurgha,* there is no connection, I am sure, with the Hindu deity Durga, the wife of Shiva: this spelling, rather than "Cthugha", is that preferred by Thomas Morley, and may represent a closer approximation to accuracy in pronouncing a word that is essentially non-human. Only one thing is beyond dispute: the name in its several variations has always been associated with all-devouring flame.

The letter explains that puzzling record of having requested estimates from local builders. Chesterton's life at Murrell House was simple without quite being austere. There was no need for repair or extension to the building, he kept no horses, and the notion of a summer-house or gazebo was quite out of character — especially as he seemed to be almost obsessed with this idea of exploring new territories, however phantasmal those territories might be, and of claiming what he spoke of as his rightful kingly power. The letter makes matters clear, or at least it makes Chesterton's plans clear.

He was making a road, a tunnel — a way through the dark dimensions to that very world where the King in Yellow himself may be glimpsed among the towers of Carcosa, rising behind and beyond a moon that hangs low over the rolling cloud-waves and drips with spray.

He had discovered in the *Necronomicon*, which he regarded

as marginally the least untrustworthy of the *grimoires*, a formula or pattern, hidden within a parable. In his usual careful way, he combed the other "magical" texts for any corroboration, even going to the length, as I have mentioned, of attempting to gain access to yet more material, writing to antiquarian dealers and specialist libraries. *De Potentiae Deorum Antiquorum* contained the clearest confirmation, though, as Chesterton wryly noted, "in all conscience it is nebulous enough." At all events, it was sufficiently clear for him to embark upon his strange project.

"Road" is merely a symbolic word in the circumstances; "tunnel" is only slightly more accurate. What he was actually constructing was a tower, rooted in our own world, but whose pinnacle, somehow, would stretch into another. I do not pretend to understand this, and can only fall back on the recent statement of a popular writer, that any sufficiently advanced science is indistinguishable from magic. That thought enables me to retain such hold as I have upon my sanity, for I cannot now doubt that Paul Chesterton did indeed travel to a world beyond ours.

I saw the tower once before it was demolished. It appeared to be no more than a thin cylinder of coarse red brick, some seventy feet tall, windowless, but with an unprotected opening at the base. There was a plain but serviceable spiral staircase around a central pillar, also of brick, leading to a flat concrete roof. I recall no other features. More than anything, the structure put me in mind of Bull's Tower at Pentlow, on the Suffolk border, but where that folly wears an almost palpably malign aura, there was nothing in the least intrinsically atmospheric about Chesterton's tower.

It is evident that there was more to his project than this simple building, but the documents contain only unexplained references to "the calling", and I cannot make sufficient sense of the old books to identify his source. Perhaps it is as well, though at times I think otherwise, when I recall the tantalising nature of Chesterton's hints about that other world.

He writes of the acid sweetness of the spray, of "the elegant attenuation" of the minarets — but also of the menace that seemed to crawl just beneath the surface of the lake, and of the anguished cry of Cassilda: "Not upon us, oh King, not upon us!" Beauty there was, and power, but great danger also.

He wrote too of "those who oppose, for reasons all too plain." Being convinced of his own lawful cause, he was very bitter at the thought of resistance. "Of course," says an entry in his diary, undated but apparently written in February 1937, "one must expect confrontation with the merely temporal despots, but they are mortal and rational. More worrying are those that are beyond mortality and reason; to them life and death are the jest of a moment." His greatest concern, if I have correctly read his meaning, was awakened by those whom he called "the folk of the water" or "the deep ones". His writing on this subject is frustratingly obscure, but it seems probable that these are the people mentioned in certain dubious books as followers of great Cthulhu. Nowhere does that outlandish name appear in full in Chesterton's diaries or in the letter, but his occasional references to "C" do not seem to allow of any other interpretation.

Whether this is so or not, it is plain that both the entity and its followers aroused in Paul Chesterton strong emotions of hatred and fear. Again and again he writes of summoning against them "the power of flame", and an initially cautious tone quickly gives way to a certain obsessive conviction that might even be called arrogance. An early passage in the diary begins: "If the King thinks me worthy to wield the power as his servant . . ." but by the time, the day before the end, when he completed and sealed the letter, he had the sublime confidence to write: "Soon I shall seize the crown, and then let my foes beware!"

A second time he made the unimaginable journey to that other world, and again his subsequent notes are tantalisingly obscure. "It must be so," runs one, "for the King wills it." But then creeps in a note of uncertainty: "What thoughts are hidden by the Pallid Mask? Could I only be sure of my strength and my weakness!" Such doubts were quickly dismissed, however, and he prepared, as the letter explained, to travel for the third time, and perhaps the last, to the realm of the King in Yellow, there to gain the crown and the power — a power which he fully meant to employ.

What happened can only be conjectured. The final passage of the letter, in which he stated his intention, was written upon the fifteenth of May 1937. At about twenty past three on the morning of the sixteenth, according to the unanimous report of a number of early risers at neighbouring farms and in nearby villages, the night sky, for one astounding moment, seemed to be a searing sheet of light. Witnesses facing Murrell House were temporarily blinded. Those who were fortunate enough to have been facing away from the phenomenon waited tensely for a thunderclap that never came. Then, aware that something quite extraordinary was happening, they turned, and saw what the others could not.

Against the velvet blackness of the night, a funnel of bluish-white flame danced in the sky, like a cyclone, its eye focussed with a steady and seemingly mechanical precision upon one particular spot. Only Samuel Blanks of Montpelier Farm was standing in the right position to see that the fire was concentrated upon Paul Chesterton's brick tower. It appeared to enter the opening at the top of the structure, forcing its way down, to spill glowingly out from the archway at the foot.

Blanks, like his unknown fellow-witnesses, stood as though transfixed, held by the spectacle and unable to consider its cause or its consequences, until, after a matter of mere seconds, there came a sharp, loud hissing sound, and the flame simply vanished, leaving a stark after-image on his retina. Not until minutes had passed did it occur to him that his help might be needed.

He went first to Murrell House. Receiving no answer to his frantic hammering on doors and windows, he rushed onward to the tower, reaching it almost simultaneously with the village constable of Peldon, P.C. Jack Forbes. It is important, I think, to bear in mind that there were thus two witnesses to the macabre climax of the whole strange affair, and that the authorities, though they might — and did — eventually dismiss the two men's testimony, could never shake it. It was the proof that the essence of Thurgha is flame indeed, and that a god is not to be summoned at will, like a slave.

Lying mostly outside the entrance at the base of the tower, with just its head on the concrete floor within, the body of Paul Chesterton was black and burned. The features were intact and clearly recognisable, and the expression on the face was not good to see. The interior of the building was scorched, but still sound. The fire, it seemed, had been so sudden, so intense, and so precisely concentrated that it had transformed a human being instantaneously into mere charcoal. There was hardly a trace of odour in the damp air, but, as Forbes leaned forward and touched the corpse, it crumbled, leaving only a scattering of black ash upon the ground.

Both Forbes and Blanks swore upon oath that their account was accurate and complete, and, although the coroner had some sharp remarks to make, he let the testimony stand. He did, however, order one statement to be struck from the record of the inquest: this was Forbes's assertion that he and Blanks had seen upon the dead brows of Paul Chesterton, strangely and elegantly shaped, though blasted like the body itself, a head-piece that could be nothing but a crown.

That information came to me directly from Samuel Blanks, and I see no reason to doubt it, since neither man had anything to gain by lying. Sadly, by the time of the inquest, the tower had been demolished, according to the terms of Chesterton's will. Even had he not given that instruction, I am sure that those same timid persons who demanded the destruction of his papers would have forced the issue. I saw the tower just that brief once, and could make no sense of its supposed transcendental properties.

And now I find myself in a state of almost intolerable frustration. Without Chesterton's immense scholarship and experience, I cannot hope to find in the mind-numbing pages of the *Necronomicon* the formula by which he reached at last that beautiful and perilous realm. And yet — and yet —

I have checked and re-checked the genealogical tables. I have read and re-read that wonderful, damnable book. I *know* that Paul Chesterton was right. He was indeed the heir to the world, under the King in Yellow. Now he is dead, and the inheritance is mine, by my right in Hastur.

But how am I to claim it?

Afterword

Robert W Chambers (1865-1933) was a talented artist and a hugely popular writer of historical and romantic fiction — most of it entirely unread today. His reputation now rests on the four short stories and one poem that constitute the core of his early collection *The King in Yellow* (the book also contains six unrelated stories), in which he creates a world of fear and wonder quite unlike anything published before. Curiously, although Chambers occasionally returned to weird fiction, he never revisited the universe of the King in Yellow.

In the last quarter of the twentieth century, a good many horror stories were inspired by Chambers' work, thanks largely to the creators of the rôle-playing game "Call of Cthulhu". The tendency of these tales — in the popular *Delta Green* series, for instance — is towards confrontation, physical horror and brutality. I wanted to see if I could achieve something closer to the rarefied quality of the original stories.

IN MEMORIAM
(by Roger Johnson and Robert M Price)

"We are each our own devil, and we make this world our hell."
— Oscar Wilde: *The Duchess of Padua*

There was a weariness in the eyes of the recluse as he observed his guest, and a wariness in his voice as he spoke.

"I am afraid, my lord, that this visit is a waste of your time and of my own. It is clear to me that you believe neither in ecstasy nor in the reality of sin, whereas I believe in nothing else."

Lord Henry Wotton's features, smooth and handsome at fifty, expressed only a mild courtesy at the old man's words, but then his lordship's face was as much his servant as any of his household staff.

"There is no sin save boredom," he said, with a lazy movement of his hand, which subtly suggested that he might not be wholly serious. He did not add, for he was a gentleman, as the devil is supposed to be, "We may forgive those who bore us, but never those whom we bore." The sentiment was true and beautifully expressed, but it was not, alas, original. He would save it for less erudite company.

"The evening has not been wholly wasted," he continued. "You have been both clear and eloquent in expressing your belief, and for that alone I must thank you, since clarity and eloquence are rare partners. Besides, in rejecting your credo I find myself confirmed in my own. The senses are the key, and consequently sensation is the only reality. Come, Adrian."

Nodding languidly to the recluse, and somewhat less so to the friend who had accompanied him to this decaying house in an obscure street, he took his hat and stick and stepped through the front door into the mystical air of Barnsbury.

The night was mild and clear. Turning southward, towards the Pentonville Road, Lord Henry and his friend saw the lights of London scattered before them, like gems upon a black velvet cushion. In daylight they could easily have singled out the different quarters of the city, each with its own personality — maritime London, commercial London, industrial London, literary London, hotel London, theatrical London, fashionable London — but at night they could only guess where one ended and the next began. It was mysterious and rather beautiful.

"There is so much to this city of ours, Harry. It could be a man's life work to know it all, and at the end there would still be some street, even some whole district, that remained a *terra incognita*. One might be frustrated, but one should never be bored." The younger man spoke diffidently, being rather in awe of his companion. Momentarily he saw the bland expression harden, the jaw tighten, and unaccustomed lines appear on the brow, but then came a brief sigh, and he knew that Lord Henry had not taken offence.

"No doubt you are right, Adrian. I shall make you my confessor, for heaven knows I have sinned! *Peccavi, pater.* There is no sin save boredom, and, o my dear boy, I am bored! The *ennui* set in with the death of dear Dorian, and now there is no stimulus to my senses. I had hoped that our funny old host this evening might be able to explain me to myself, but it seems that my nature is too simple for his subtle mind to comprehend. The only person who truly knew how to relieve the tedium of life is gone and might never have been. He is one with the cities of the plain."

Lord Henry seemed to withdraw into himself, brooding in a way that Adrian Lee had noticed in him only within the past three months. As they walked on in silence through the void and desolate streets, deserted as those of Pompeii, towards King's Cross, where they might, even at such an hour, expect to find a cab, Adrian reflected upon the strange case of Dorian Gray.

II
"His eye fell on the yellow book that Lord Henry had sent him."
— Oscar Wilde: *The Picture of Dorian Gray*

It began, so far as the world was concerned, with Lord Henry Wotton, who had more than once expressed his belief that the only art worthy of the name is the moulding of another human being. Two decades before, he had met Dorian at the house of the painter, Basil Hallward, and, being entranced by the lad's youth and beauty, had taken it upon himself to shape his life and his character. Hallward, whose sudden disappearance some years ago caused, at the time, much public excitement, and gave rise to many strange conjectures, was an artist of great talent, but the picture of Dorian Gray proved to be the zenith of his art, and possibly his one work of true genius. Harry Wotton had fallen in love, in so far as he was capable of such emotion, with Dorian Gray, and Dorian Gray had fallen in love with his own likeness.

Over the years, while Lord Henry aged gracefully — or disgracefully, in the opinion of some, who perhaps knew better — Dorian, to all appearances, did not age at all. Like his mentor, he developed a deep and hungry appetite for the gratifying of his senses, and many equated this with that appetite for life that can keep a man young. It could not, however, account for the unchanging youth of his appearance, which seemed, the more one came to know him, like a beautiful pallid mask, hiding a multitude of experiences, good and bad. It would have been interesting, thought Adrian, to compare the two Dorian Grays, the living man and the painted image, but that had not been possible. For some reason, a couple of months after the artist had completed it and given it to the sitter, the portrait had been banished to a disused room on the top floor of Dorian's town house and had not been seen by any other eye until its owner's shocking death just a quarter of a year ago.

Shocking indeed, and mysterious. When the servants broke into the little room, they found hanging upon the wall the splendid portrait of their master as they had last seen him, in all the wonder of his exquisite youth and beauty. Lying on the floor was a dead man, in evening dress, with a knife in his heart. He was withered, wrinkled and loathsome of visage. It was not till they had examined the rings that they recognised who it was, but they could not explain how Mr Gray's appearance had so suddenly and horribly changed. Lord Henry was called to identify the body and agreed that the dead man was indeed his friend; if he knew how the terrible transformation had come about he did not say, but he was, as Adrian well knew, adept at concealing what he did not wish to reveal.

Adrian himself, who had not seen the corpse, was inclined to agree with the doubters. Dorian Gray had been known to disappear from London and from Society for days, and sometimes weeks, on end. The dead man might have been an intruder who had engaged him in a fatal quarrel, upon which he had incontinently fled — a burglar, perhaps, or even a blackmailer. There were stories enough about Dorian to make even the latter notion credible. Not everybody had felt sorrow at the announcement of his death. Some — the Duke of Berwick, Lord Kent, and Lord Gloucester, to name but three — had openly rejoiced. It was a puzzle, and it occupied

Adrian Lee's uncomplicated mind during most of the journey to Lord Henry's house in Mayfair, where the two men sat in the little library, each with a brandy and soda, for fully twenty minutes before his lordship broke the silence.

"I must arrange for a memorial to dear Dorian," he said. "Not a thing of stone, with pious inscriptions that few will read and fewer still believe. It would not be suitable."

Adrian coughed gently, and turned to indicate the wall behind him. "There is the painting, of course," he suggested.

"I had thought of exhibiting the painting, but it too is dead since its original died. It is only a mask with nothing behind it — not even a phantom. No, the painting shall remain here, where I can regard it as one of the most wonderful and most mysterious of my books."

"I wonder," said his guest, "I do wonder — "

"Yes, Adrian?"

"I wonder just why Dorian hid the picture away for so long. Do you know, Harry?"

Lord Henry smiled, showing very white, even teeth. "I can guess," he said, "and some day I may describe my guesses to you. But your suggestion confirms a part of my intention, at any rate: we shall not make a public memorial for Dorian. No, it must be private, and known only to the select. In fact — yes! Why not? Why not, indeed?" He rose and crossed to the wall where the portrait now hung, and his features were more animated than Adrian had seen them in many a month. For a few moments he regarded the beautiful painted face, the finely-shaped red lips, and the blue eyes, almost arrogant in their innocence. Then he turned to an exquisite rosewood book case, whose door he unlocked with a small key that hung upon his watch chain. He opened the right-hand door wide and took a slim yellow-covered volume from the very end of the shelf. "I keep it there because with the doors closed it cannot be seen," he said. "It has been a privilege to help shape Dorian Gray's life and yours too, dear boy, but I decline to take the same responsibility for my servants. Here, Adrian. This is how we shall celebrate Dorian." And he handed his friend the book.

Adrian Lee recognised it immediately, for he had read it several times, spurred at first by Lord Henry's suggestion and then by a fascination that combined awe and dread in equal quantities. The front cover bore in serpentine letters the simple words, *The King in Yellow*. He placed the book on the little table before him.

"I should remember," said Lord Henry, "the first time that I read that beautiful, accursed book, and yet the memory has become uncertain. That first reading has faded into the many subsequent ones until only the book is real, and not the memory. But I do recall with great clarity how casually I introduced Dorian Gray to the crystalline delights and the gem-like terrors of *The King in Yellow*. He told me, much later — and I fancy that you said something of the sort yourself — that I had poisoned him with the book, but of course that is nonsense."

"And the notion of sin?" said Adrian, almost without thinking.

"Adrian, you disappoint me! You paid too much attention to that funny old man in his crooked house in Barnsbury. Our first duty is to ourselves. To realise our own nature perfectly — that is why we are here. If we cease to do so then we sin. That is what I meant by saying that the only sin is boredom."

"And yet — forgive me, Harry — *The King in Yellow* has been denounced, as you well know, in England, in America and in France. Both press and pulpit have claimed that it spread like an infectious disease, from city to city, from continent to continent, barred out here, confiscated there, censured even by the most advanced of literary anarchists."

"How innocent you are, dear Adrian! It is your chiefest charm, I think. You will admit that no definite principles have been violated in those pages, no doctrine promulgated, no convictions outraged. Quite simply, the book cannot be judged by any known standard, and even its severest critics acknowledge that the author has struck the supreme note of art."

"But all art is quite useless," said Adrian. "You told me that yourself."

"So I did, and I meant it. Art has no practical purpose, or it would cease to be art. None the less, it is essential to humanity, for without art man would be a brute beast, or worse — a scientist. Now, may I offer you another brandy and soda?"

Adrian laughed and held up his hands in surrender. "Thank you, Harry," he said. "That would be charming. But do you really intend to perform *The King in Yellow* in memory of Dorian Gray?"

Lord Henry tapped the book with a slender forefinger. "It would be fitting, don't you think? Dorian dared to do things that none had done before him — " He glanced quizzically at his young guest, but there was only the briefest nod in response, and he continued, " — and we shall perform a play that none have yet dared to perform. It will not be a public performance, of course. Some dozen of Dorian's friends shall act, under my direction, and perhaps the same number shall constitute the audience. My dear boy, it will be perfectly delightful. Now, what rôle should you play, I wonder?"

III
"There were moments when he looked on evil simply as a mode through which he could realise his conception of the beautiful."
— Oscar Wilde: *The Picture of Dorian Gray*

The following afternoon Adrian Lee called again at his friend's house, where he found Lord Henry in the little library, compiling a list of people whom he wished to take part in his unique memorial production. He looked up as Adrian entered.

"It would have been amusing," he said, "to invite Sir Henry Ashton's uncle, and Lord Staveley, and the Duke of Berwick, but it would also have been cruel, and I am never cruel without purpose."

Adrian's face grew momentarily grave. "I am glad that you resisted the temptation, Harry," he said.

"And so am I. It entitles me to yield to another more pleasurable one. Please sit, Adrian, and look over my list."

His visitor took the sheet of foolscap and perused it carefully. "Hum. Geoffrey Clouston — yes. Adrian Singleton? I don't think I know him. Lord Grotrian. The Duke of Perth. The Duchess of Monmouth — is that wise, Harry?"

"The little Duchess adored Dorian," said Lord Henry, with a characteristic wave of his hand. "I think she would be ideal for Cordelia. She need only look beautiful and sing sweetly."

"And appear mad."

"True, true — but much of the madness is expressed in the song, and her voice is as pretty as her face. Lady Gwendolyn will happily play Cassilda."

"Your sister?"

"Just so. I have not yet made up my mind about Camilla. I myself shall be the King, and I should like you, my dear boy, to play Corydon. It is the rôle that would best have suited Dorian, but you will fill it admirably, I am sure."

The idea appealed to Adrian's quite genuine passion for art. As Lord Henry had said, the play was supremely well written. One critic had both condemned and praised what he called "words which are clear as crystal, limpid and musical as bubbling springs, words which sparkle and glow like the poisoned diamonds of the Medicis!" The young man also felt an unaccustomed excitement, in which he was startled to recognise the charm of danger. He was not sure that he had ever truly liked Dorian Gray, but he had, he thought, come perilously close to worshipping him, and the attraction had not greatly diminished. "I should like that, Harry," he said. "But what of the Stranger — the Phantom of Truth?"

"Ah! You must not ask me about him just yet. I have an actor in mind, and that is all I shall tell you at the moment. Now, have you your own copy of the book? Capital! If you will dine with me at Verrey's on Monday we can discuss things further. There is no place like a good restaurant for observing Society. I have often thought that the really interesting thing about people in good Society is the mask that each of them wears, not the reality that lies behind the mask."

IV
"There were poisons so subtle that to know their properties one had to sicken of them."
— Oscar Wilde: *The Picture of Dorian Gray*

Adrian Lee spent much of the next two days reading and re-reading *The King in Yellow*, and once again found that the delicious hunger that the book inspired was never quite satisfied, for each reading seemed to demand another. The heavy odour of incense seemed to cling about its pages and to trouble the brain. The mere cadence of the sentences, the subtle monotony of their music, produced in his mind a form of reverie, a malady of dreaming, that made him unconscious of the falling day and creeping shadows. There was nothing, he realised, of the decadent or the *symboliste* in the style; only in the songs was there even a hint of literary preciousness. The anonymous author used no words that could not be understood by the ignorant as by the learned, and yet he, more than any *symboliste*, was successful in conveying a staggering wealth of strangeness and — Adrian chose not to be too precise here — of the seductive power of sin. There was, he thought, some Gallic flavour to the play. Was the unknown author

French, perhaps? Some said so, but Adrian thought he remembered talk of an edition translated into the French language.

Such speculation, though intrinsically unprofitable, led his thoughts to the drama itself, and, in daydream or waking nightmare, he stood beside the lake, watching the black stars as they hang in the heavens, and the cloud-waves as they roll and break upon the shores of Hali. In his mind he heard the desolate song of Cordelia, echoing through the streets and piazzas of lost Carcosa, and glimpsed the swirling, many-coloured tatters of the cloak that marks the King himself. He imagined himself at the ball, unmasking, and the climactic moment when the Stranger is recognised as the herald of the King in Yellow . . .

It was clever of Lord Henry to reserve the rôle of the King to himself: the character appears only at the end of the play, but his impact is literally tremendous. His lordship would be able to have direct command of the other actors almost throughout the passage of the drama, and the audience would leave the theatre convinced that he had dominated throughout.

The theatre! Just where, after all, did Harry propose to mount this production? And whom had he chosen to portray the Stranger?

V
"Those who want a mask have to wear it."
— Oscar Wilde: *De Profundis*

Adrian's questions were answered in the conversation over *filets de boeuf à la Rossini* at the Regent Street restaurant. Having approved the Beaune, Lord Henry said, with unaccustomed diffidence, "Are you familiar with the Standard Theatre, Adrian? It is in Shoreditch."

"Shoreditch, Harry? I am not sure that I have ever been there."

"No." said Lord Henry. "No, I don't suppose you have. Shoreditch is not a stopping place on the way to anywhere else, and goodness knows it has few attractions of its own. Whether the theatre qualifies as an attraction you must judge for yourself. None the less, I have chosen it for our production of *The King in Yellow*. Don't look surprised, Adrian; I assure you that there is a very good reason. Years ago, you know, Dorian Gray was engaged to be married, to a charmingly pretty young actress. The *affaire* was doomed, of course — nothing kills love like an overdose of it —

and the silly girl killed herself when she realised that. But it was at the Standard that they met, where she was playing Rosalind."

"And afterward?"

"Let us not talk of what happened afterward. The important thing is that the Standard is the right place for our production. By some remarkable chance the same man is the proprietor, a Mr Isaacs, as gorgeous and obsequious and unsuccessful as he was nearly twenty years ago. It was not hard to persuade him to let the theatre for an afternoon, with the staff necessary for a full-scale performance,"

"Very good," said Adrian, "but what of the Phantom?"

"Ah! I told you that I had an actor in mind, didn't I? No doubt you know Aubrey Manners?"

"Manners? We haven't met, but I have seen him act, of course. He is currently appearing as Ingomar at the Imperial. Was he a friend of Dorian's?"

"No, but he is an acquaintance of mine. He is a baronet, you know — or will be when his father dies. Manners is a stage name, but that is by the way. The important thing is that he owes me a favour, and I have persuaded him to take on the rôle of the Stranger. He has great presence, as you know, and a magnificent commanding voice. That is essential, since the character wears the Pallid Mask throughout. It is an actor's job to lie, of course, but it is harder to lie successfully without using any facial expression."

Aubrey Manners! This was exciting news indeed. Adrian had enjoyed some acclaim in country house dramatics, and the thought of sharing the stage with a distinguished professional actor was very attractive. Lord Henry followed his thoughts with ease. "Yes, I thought that would please you," he said with a smile. "I am rather glad that the Stranger leaves the stage before the King enters; otherwise the competition would be too much for me. Manners will not be able to attend our rehearsals, unfortunately, but he is familiar with the play and he has assured me that he will be at the Standard in good time for the performance. I trust him to know his lines and his cues, of course, and his movements are clearly indicated in the stage directions."

Adrian mused upon this information while he ate. At last, as the gooseberry charlotte was brought to the table, he asked, "Whom have you chosen to play Camilla, Harry?"

"Victoria Waterlow. You know, her, I think, Adrian — a charming woman, who has somehow managed to stay twenty-one despite the recent passing of her thirtieth birthday. She was very fond of Dorian. Young Lord Poole is to be Uoht, and Perth will be Thale. I have induced Lord Grotrian to take the rôle of Naotalba — his portentous manner will suit the character well. As for the rest, you shall know at the first rehearsal, which will be at my house at eight o'clock on Friday. For once, my dear boy, I must insist upon punctuality. Few things in my life are really important to me, but this memorial to Dorian is one of them."

"You have not yet told me when the performance is to be."

Lord Henry smiled quizzically and stroked his pointed beard. "I have engaged the theatre for the afternoon of the thirteenth of next month." he said. "It is a Friday, which seems somehow appropriate. But now it is time for coffee and liqueurs. Let us drink to the success of our production."

VI
"In a very ugly and sensible age, the arts borrow, not from life, but from each other."
— Oscar Wilde: *The Decay of Lying*

Adrian indulged his curiosity so far as to take a cab the next day to Shoreditch High Street. He was surprised to find how close it lay to the City, which — or parts of which — he knew well; and yet the contrast was startling. Here were no banks, no classical churches, no monumental office buildings. The grimy houses with their smeared and broken windows looked uneven and frequently unstable. The shops were mean and garish, and the people appeared either truculent or cowed. Adrian remembered something that Lord Henry had once said: that the poor folk of London seemed sadly unaware of their own picturesqueness; but there was nothing of the picturesque about the people of Shoreditch.

He was inclined to change his mind, however, when he came to the Standard Theatre. In the daylight its honest vulgarity held much of the charm of a country fair. Adrian gazed with something like admiration at the gaudy posters that promised *The Colleen Bawn*, *Hoodman Blind*, *Jim the Penman*, and other thrilling melodramas. At night, he thought, with the gas-jets blazing, the theatre must be perfectly delightful.

His thoughts were interrupted by a servile cough, and he turned to see standing beside him a fat, elderly man, evidently Jewish and dressed in quite magnificent bad taste. Adrian had never seen anything quite like the waistcoat that seemed almost to shimmer and glow before his eyes. This amazing old man doffed his homburg hat and spoke:

"You have come too early for the first house, I am afraid, my lord. At six o'clock we shall stage today's first performance of *The Silver King*, an old favourite. Or if you prefer to come later, the second house is at half past eight. I can offer you a box for either. We provide only wholesome and uplifting entertainment at the Standard, my lord, and we are proud of our reputation."

Remembering what Harry Wotton had told him, Adrian asked, "Are you Mr Isaacs? I am a friend of Lord Henry Wotton's, and I shall be taking part in his private production here next month."

The old man's smile threatened to split his face in two. He seized Adrian's elegant hand in his own fat paw and pumped it vigorously for quite ten seconds. "Any friend of his lordship is a friend of mine!" he declared — a statement that his visitor took *cum grano salis*. But the talisman that was Lord Henry's name had unlocked the door. Adrian could and did refuse a box for either of the evening's performances of *The Silver King*, but he accepted old Isaacs' invitation to look over the theatre.

Within it was even more wonderfully garish than without. There were anatomically improbable *putti* and caryatids, interspersed apparently at random with cornucopias and an occasional unexpected satyr's head, all in fading shades of green and gold. The stalls and the dress circle were upholstered in what might once have been a rich burgundy but was now nearly black. The little private boxes, one on each side of the stage, were clean but shabby. Yet Adrian could sense the vigour of the drama here: the many plays — good, bad or merely adequate — that had been performed upon these boards had, each of them, helped to instil life into the building. Every theatre has a soul, and Adrian was pleasantly impressed by what he sensed of the Standard's. He looked forward more keenly than ever to the memorial performance of *The King in Yellow*.

In the meantime, however, there would be rehearsals.

VII
"Things of which he had never dreamed were gradually revealed."
— Oscar Wilde: *The Picture of Dorian Gray*

Adrian was almost surprised to realise, as he was greeted by Lord Henry's manservant on the Friday evening, that he felt nervous as well as excited. Even though he had obeyed his friend's instruction to be punctual, he found that the rest of the cast — with the exception, of course, of Aubrey Manners — were there before him. The furniture had been moved away from the centre of the large drawing-room, leaving an empty space that would serve for the time being as the stage. Within this space a dozen or so people had gathered into small groups. Most were conversing quietly, but one or two were diligently reading their copies of the play, and one at least appeared to be reciting his lines *sotto voce*.

As Adrian entered the room, Lord Henry clapped his hands together just once and said, "My dear friends, we are all met to prepare our own special tribute to Dorian Gray. More years ago than seems reasonable I introduced him to *The King in Yellow*, and he told me later, on several occasions, that the book had changed his life. Of course, that is what I had expected when I gave it to him, as you will appreciate, since I introduced most of you to the book as well. It is fitting that our memorial to Dorian should be a performance of the play that meant so much to him.

"In my dreams I too have sat in the palace of Hastur, gazing at the haunted city of Carcosa, far across the lake. I have seen the moon dripping with spray, and the towers of Carcosa rising impossibly behind it. I have heard the bitter cry of Cassilda: "Not upon us, oh King; not upon us!" — and the terrible response of the King: "Did you think to be human still?"

"As far as I am aware ours will be the first performance of *The King in Yellow*, and decades may pass before any are bold enough to mount another. For Dorian's sake and our own, we must ensure that it is perfect. Before we read through the text, however, I should like to hear the two songs, Cassilda's and Cordelia's. Adrian, you play charmingly; will you please accompany Lady Gwendolyn?"

Adrian seated himself at the piano, where the music was already open at "Cassilda's Song". Fortunately he was a more than competent sight-reader, and he soon found that the melancholy strains seemed to take on a life of their own, weaving a baroque pattern around Lady Gwendolyn's low, rich voice:

> "Along the shore the cloud waves break,
> The twin suns sink behind the lake,
> The shadows lengthen
> In Carcosa."

At the fourth and last stanza there was quiet applause. "Excellent!" said Lord Henry. "My dear Gwendolyn, it could hardly be improved upon. Adrian, your playing was capital. Did it come easily? Yes, I thought so: I have rarely heard you play better. I have engaged a string quartet for the performance itself, and they will be with us at the next rehearsal, but for this evening we are most grateful to you. Now, where is our little Duchess? Ah, yes. Gladys, my dear, have you prepared your song?"

"Of course, Harry," said the Duchess, rebuking him with her wonderful eyes. "Mr Lee, are you ready? Then please begin."

There is melancholy also in "Cordelia's Song", but, as Adrian quickly discovered, it is in counterpoint to an almost mischievous dreamlike quality that never quite dominates it. The notes seemed to flow naturally from his fingers, and he listened entranced to the Duchess's pure silver voice:

> "The moon shines whitely; I shall take
> My silk umbrella, lest the moon
> Too warmly fall upon the lake
> And cause my bridal flowers to swoon."

The applause that followed the final stanza, Adrian felt, indicated more than just approval of this single performance of a song. It was as if, for the first time, all present realised that the production of *The King in Yellow* could and would be successful. The look that the Duchess exchanged with her brother, Geoffrey Clouston, spoke of something close to awe. Lord Poole stood open-mouthed, and Victoria Waterlow appeared almost ecstatic. Only Lord Henry Wotton seemed unmoved. Adrian's thoughts turned momentarily to the mouldering house in Barnsbury and its reclusive occupant, but he was brought back sharply to the present.

"Splendid!" said Lord Henry. "Now let us read through the play. You are all familiar with it, so I shall expect everybody to be fluent. Please observe the stage directions as far as you can. I shall make notes as we go, but I shall save them until the end."

"What of the Stranger?" asked the Duke of Perth. "I understand that Aubrey Manners cannot be with us for the rehearsals, so who will deputise for him?."

"I shall. Please regard me as his understudy. Now, Cassilda, you and Naotalba are discovered on the stage. Camilla and Corydon, be ready to enter.

"My lords, ladies and gentlemen, the curtain is rising . . ."

VIII
"And yet the thing would still live on. It would be always alive."
— Oscar Wilde: *The Picture of Dorian Gray*

When he thought of it later, Adrian was astonished at the ease with which the cast seemed to inhabit their characters and the fluency and conviction with which they spoke the words. By the end of the first scene, when Cassilda declares: "There will be no other king in Hastur till the King in Yellow!" he felt curiously invigorated, even inspired, as if he were in truth Corydon, witness with his fellow citizens of Hastur of events beyond the understanding of Earth's children. Glancing at the other actors, he seemed to see in their eyes souls that were not their own, though he knew and could name each face. The words, too, sounded as if they were framed by alien tongues, though he knew and could name each voice.

Lord Henry alone seemed unaffected, but he had not yet been called upon to act, for the Stranger does not appear until the second scene. When Adrian did hear his voice in character he was disconcerted to realise how little character there was in the voice. Even in the Stranger's most notorious exchange, in the conversation at the ball with Cassilda and Camilla, Adrian was mildly disappointed to hear only the words, with no feeling to give them life.

Camilla   You, sir, should unmask.
Stranger   Indeed?
Cassilda   Indeed it's time. We all have laid aside disguise but you.
Stranger   I wear no mask.
Camilla   *(terrified, aside to Cassilda)* No mask? No mask!

The Stranger's lines continued to be delivered with an efficient lack of expression, in notable contrast to the vitality that infused all the rest of the *dramatis personae*, and at length it occurred to Adrian that Lord Henry's stolid reading was deliberate — that he was in fact leaving the inspiration of life to the actor whose rôle it truly was, Aubrey Manners. At length came the last brief scene; Lord Henry assumed his own chosen character, that of the King in Yellow, and his delivery was magnificent. Adrian knew then that his surmise was correct. The King spread wide his tattered mantle, and over the fallen body of Cassilda he intoned the words, "It is a fearful thing to fall into the hands of the living God!"

There was no applause, for all the actors were, spiritually if not physically, exhausted. After a moment, Lord Henry broke the mood with an ironic bow and said, "All of you have adopted your characters quite admirably. We shall not, I think, need more than two more rehearsals. I am grateful to you all — and so, I trust is the shade of Dorian Gray — for your diligence and your determination. We are bold to perform a play that some have said could never be performed; but that is something that Dorian himself might have foreseen. We shall perform it moreover in a flea-pit of a theatre in a depressing, shabby Gehenna that no cultured person would recognise as a limb of the greatest city in the world. That, I assure you, will make our achievement the more remarkable. The theatre-goers of today think that they have a monopoly of sensation, but we, my dear friends, shall experience such sensation as they could not even recognise. The senses are the key to life, and one can never pay too high a price for true sensation."

Although the hour was still, by civilised standards, early, no one save Lady Gwendolyn and Adrian himself seemed inclined to stay. Adrian was at first somewhat in awe of Lord Henry's sister but he found her company both amusing and invigorating. It was, inevitably, her brother who asked, "Well, my dear boy, what do you think of the Standard Theatre?"

Adrian had known Lord Henry long enough not to be surprised. "How did you know I visited the theatre?" he asked.

"Oh, that is elementary: I went there myself yesterday to have a word with old Isaacs, and he told me of your visit. But seriously, what do you think of it?"

"It is quite delightful, Harry; its very artificiality is natural and honest. But do you really think it is the right setting for a tribute to Dorian Gray?"

"Most certainly. Dorian quickly got over the death of his actress — after all, his love for her had already died — and I think that he too would now have enjoyed that charmingly pretentious little playhouse for what it is."

Lady Gwendolyn laughed briefly and said, "Now I am more eager than ever to see the theatre. I am interested, you know, in anything that Dorian Gray would have liked. And, Mr Lee, I have not thanked you properly for accompanying my song; your playing was wonderfully sympathetic."

There was, Adrian thought, a brightness in her eyes that was not altogether natural, but considering the remarkable intensity of the rehearsal, perhaps that was not surprising. He murmured an appropriate compliment about her singing, and added, "But really, Lady Gwendolyn, everybody's performance was quite extraordinarily good. I have never known a first rehearsal so full of promise. I feel quite intoxicated!"

He meant the remark as a metaphor, but as he spoke, he realised that it was literally true: he did indeed feel intoxicated. A thought flashed momentarily across his mind and was gone. Lord Henry regarded him with an indulgent smile and said, "Dear me, Adrian! Early as it is, perhaps I should instruct my man to call a cab for you. No? Then I suggest that the three of us have a light supper and end the evening agreeably by congratulating each other."

IX
"Dorian Gray had been poisoned by a book."
— Oscar Wilde: *The Picture of Dorian Gray*

In the morning Adrian was mildly surprised to discover that he still felt pleasantly inebriated, although he had not drunk more than half a bottle of Lord Henry's excellent Médoc with the cold game pie. As he breakfasted the thought that had eluded capture the previous evening returned, but he dismissed it immediately: it was simply that the root of the word "intoxication" is the Greek *toxikon*, which means "poison".

For Adrian the days seemed to pass almost in a dream, and it was a dream of *The King in Yellow*. The slim yellow book constituted his only reading matter. At a recital, the music that sounded in his ears was the desolate song of Cassilda. Gazing across the Park towards the faery-like domes and turrets of Whitehall, he saw the fantastic attenuated towers of Carcosa, piercing a sky where black stars hung and the moon was an amber mask. When friends addressed him, he heard the words of Cordelia, or Naotalba, or Aldones. He imagined, with a thrill of anticipation, the rich, golden voice of Aubrey Manners declaiming the lines of the Stranger: "I am Truth. Can you not accept the truth?"

At the two remaining rehearsals, Adrian witnessed a reality that was becoming more and more solid, while the world outside grew more tenuous by comparison. Even at the first rehearsal the actors were all word-perfect, and by the second they knew their movements thoroughly. By now, however, that did not seem remarkable. If Adrian thought about it at all, he ascribed the phenomenon to the play rather than to the players. A mind less obsessed might have wondered why no one had thought it possible to mount a production of *The King in Yellow* before, but the question did not even cross his mind.

The string quartet played quite superbly. At first Adrian felt a slight pang of jealousy, wishing that his could be the hands from which flowed such exquisite melody and counter-melody, but envy was quickly overcome by the fascination of hearing how perfectly the music complemented the two singers. The musicians also played the overture and the incidental music, which at the performance proper would be performed by a small orchestra, of which they would constitute a part.

The second and final rehearsal was held at the theatre itself just two days before the performance, and it would have been natural for the performers to react to the vulgar little building, with pleasure or horror, each according to his nature, as Adrian had done upon his first visit, but all were so entirely engrossed in the play that they barely noticed their surroundings.

The costumes, appropriately Greek in inspiration, were ready for that second rehearsal. If the world of *The King in Yellow* were indeed becoming the actuality of which all else is shadow, the clothing of the characters was vital to the transformation. There remained only the scenery — and the Phantom of Truth. Adrian lived now only for the performance. He could see by their faces, especially the eyes, that the same was true of the other actors — yes, and the musicians, and even the backstage crew. They were all caught up in this amazing work, that had begun simply as a tribute to Dorian Gray but had taken on a vitality of its own. This, he thought, *this* is life. Here and only here are thought and feeling. Here is humankind, with all its ambition, its soaring nobility and its crushing vileness. Here alone is Truth!

As before and throughout, only Lord Henry Wotton was apparently unaffected. His gentle smile seemed permanent on his handsome face, and there was, though Adrian did not recognise it, a sort of bland mischief in his dark eyes. "My dear, dear friends," he said, as the final curtain fell to a silence that was more fitting than any applause, "in just two days' time we shall have accomplished what no one has accomplished before us. We shall have given life to one of the most remarkable books ever written, and in doing so we shall have celebrated the life of Dorian Gray, whom we all, each in his or her own way, loved. There will be just the one performance of *The King in Yellow*, and with the essential participation of Mr Aubrey Manners, that performance will be perfect! Go now, and return to this improbable and fantastic sanctum on Friday the thirteenth."

His farewell was strangely like a benediction.

X
"It was perfectly true. The portrait had altered."
— Oscar Wilde: *The Picture of Dorian Gray*

Throughout the next two days phrases from the drama wove themselves in byzantine patterns through his dreams, both sleeping and waking, and Adrian happily let them. An observer might have said that he was drugged, but he had imbibed nothing stronger than hock and seltzer for nearly a week. The true drug was *The King in Yellow*.

"Carcosa is a myth . . ."
"You all have the mists of Hali in your brains . . ."
"The messenger of the King drives a hearse . . ."
"Have you found the Yellow Sign . . . ?"

The Phantom's urgent question was loud in his ears as he awoke on the Friday, and the voice of his dream was familiar, but it was not, he thought, the voice of Aubrey Manners.

XI
"In art good intentions are not the smallest value."
— Oscar Wilde: *De Profundis*

After a light lunch at his club, Adrian took a cab to Shoreditch, where he was welcomed effusively by Mr Isaacs, who again called him "my lord" — his customary mode of address for any patron who appeared to be in some degree a gentleman. The old man's waistcoat had been exchanged for an even more remarkable one, and a large diamond gleamed and twinkled in the centre of an unexpectedly clean expanse of shirt front.

Behind the scenes, Adrian found Lord Henry and most of the others preparing to change and make up. The scenery for the first scene, made and painted to Lord Henry's instructions, was in place, its elegance in sharp contrast to the overblown baroque decoration of the auditorium. One might have expected the usual backstage nerves, with people running over and over their lines, or indulging in the sort of personal talismanic actions that amateur thespians are no less prone to than the professionals, but in fact all was smooth and smiling efficiency. Adrian himself failed to touch the handle on his dressing-room door three times with each hand, his invariable practice on such occasions; it simply did not occur to him to do so.

He had been allocated a room — fortunately a reasonably large one — with Lord Poole and Adrian Singleton, who had been cast as Aldones. Poole, whom he knew quite well, was normally a cheerful, talkative young man of limited intellect and even more limited imagination, whereas Singleton's natural disposition, so far as Adrian could gather, was terse and unsmiling. On this Friday the thirteenth, however, all three men were calm and gentle, uttering little beyond the occasional anodyne cliché. There was nothing amiss with their sight — each of them unerringly costumed himself correctly and, in the way of amateur actors, made up his own face — but an observer would have said that their eyes were attuned to something beyond the room, and perhaps beyond the mundane world.

They waited in companionable patience until, after a quiet, perfunctory rap on the door, Lord Henry entered and said, "Overture and beginners, gentlemen; I believe that is the correct expression. You will be pleased to know that all our spectators are now seated in the stalls. It is a select audience, and I like to think that Dorian would approve. Adrian — that is, Corydon — you should take your place in the wings now with Camilla, and be ready for your entrance."

As Adrian accompanied his friend from the room and along the dim corridor, he asked, "And where will you be, Harry? You need not even put on your costume until near the end of the second act."

"I shall secrete myself in one of the boxes and watch the play, of course."

"But where is Aubrey Manners? He should be here soon!"

"And he will be. Don't fret, there's a good boy. Now I shall leave you with your Camilla. Victoria, my dear, you look quite enchanting. You will break a heart or two this afternoon, I think."

The orchestra began to play the overture. At first one heard the quietest of prolonged notes on the cello, that gradually became more audible, and was joined by a single violin, and then a rippling glissando on the harp. In time the other instruments entered, adding their harmonies to the melody of the violin. Neither Adrian nor Miss Waterlow had heard the overture in full before, and they were entranced with the silvery, unearthly quality of the music. So too, it seemed, were the members of the audience. There was a silence of nearly ten seconds after the last, almost inaudible note had faded away, and then a collective exhalation of breath, and enthusiastic applause, which was prolonged as the curtain rose upon Cassilda's balcony overlooking the lake of Hali.

The play proceeded with the same dream-like tempo and rhythm that had marked the rehearsals. Cassilda and Naotalba discussed the reality or otherwise of the city of Carcosa, and there was reference to the Phantom of Truth. Corydon and Camilla spoke of the future of the imperial dynasty. Cordelia entered, and there was more mention of the Phantom, including the well-known exchange:

Corydon	Then, sister, you have seen the face of Truth?
Cordelia	Glimpsed — only glimpsed. For just one moment the Mask slipped, and I gazed upon the void. I knew then I was lost. Ah! lost indeed — lost in Carcosa! But the King opened wide his tattered cloak and took me to him.
Camilla	*(urgently, to Corydon)* She is mad — mad! O, let us be gone!

Cordelia's song received heartfelt applause, which was no more than its due, and all too soon, as it seemed to Adrian, the first scene was over, and the curtain came down. He had stolen an occasional glance to the sides of the stage, and had been reassured by the sight of Lord Henry in the right-hand box, smiling benignly. As to the audience, their faces bore that strange expression that one sees in those who are absorbed in a play when some great artist is acting. It was neither real sorrow nor real joy; it was the passion of the spectator.

XII
"Can they feel, I wonder, those white silent people we call the dead?"
— Oscar Wilde: *The Picture of Dorian Gray*

While the scenery was shifted for the second scene, the orchestra played a series of variations on the main theme of the overture, and again Adrian listened, rapt, as strange visions passed before his inner eye. He did not leave the wings, for Corydon's first entrance is early in the scene. The music died away, and the curtain rose on Camilla and Uoht, discovered in the ballroom of the palace, to be joined within a few lines by Corydon and Thale, who discussed with them the masked Stranger and the nature of Cordelia's madness. Glancing momentarily away from the Duchess and up at the box, Adrian observed that the old proprietor stood beside Lord Henry's chair, apparently in the act of handing him an envelope.

It was at this point that the Stranger himself entered from the left of the stage. Unable to see him, Adrian was startled by the gasp, both from the audience and from the other actors, that greeted the character's appearance. He looked quickly up at Lord Henry's box and was puzzled to see a frown on the smooth, handsome face. Without apparent haste, he turned to face the newcomer, and had the greatest difficulty in suppressing an exclamation at what he saw.

The Stranger's costume was as prescribed in the directions for the play: a hooded white cloak, with the Yellow Sign emblazoned on the left breast, and white gloves; but the Pallid Mask was not the blank featureless thing that he had expected. Instead, the face of the mask — exquisitely beautiful, but bloodless and dead — was the face of Dorian Gray.

For a moment he was angry with Aubrey Manners, but reason quickly asserted itself, and he realised that Manners would have had no reason to do this strange thing. No, it was Lord Henry Wotton who had conceived this production of *The King in Yellow* as a memorial to his idol and protegé; it must have been he who had caused the mask to be made, and instructed the actor to wear it. Adrian glanced again at the box, but saw no smile on his friend's face. He looked back at the Stranger, who uttered his first line in a loud whisper that sent a trickle of excitement coursing down Adrian's spine: *"Have you found the Yellow Sign . . . ?"*

The voice was familiar, but it was not, he thought, the voice of Aubrey Manners.

Their astonishment quickly subsided, and the actors were able to continue the scene, initially with questions directed at the Stranger, whose answers seemed deliberately unclear. His voice became progressively less hoarse and more resonant, but Adrian could not remember whether that was an attribute of the character in the play.

Looking again at the mask he recalled a stanza from the *Variations sur le Carnaval de Venice* of Théophile Gautier:

> *Et j'ai reconnu, rose et fraiche,*
> *Sous l'affreux profil de carton,*
> *Sa lèvre au fin duvet de pêche,*
> *Et la mouche de son menton.*

The Stranger's mask could not, save for its lifelessness, be called frightful, but Adrian wondered, perhaps unreasonably, just what sort of face it concealed.

The actors on stage were joined before long by the rest of the cast for the masquerade. All wore blank white masks, which created, as intended, a strange sense of uncertainty in the spectators, not dispelled by the elegance of the costumes or the stateliness of the dancing. And so they came inexorably to the revelation of the Stranger's true nature.

As the clock struck twelve, Adrian found that he was awaiting the moment with inexplicable unease. There was a brief pause, and the major-domo Naotalba announced that the time had come to discard the masks. Amid a rather forced gaiety, everybody did so

— everybody, that is to say, except the Stranger.

The dialogue here is probably the most celebrated in the play, but it did not run quite as Adrian remembered it.

Camilla   You, sir, should unmask.
Stranger Indeed?
Cassilda Indeed it's time. We all have laid aside disguise but you.

But, to the consternation of all, instead of replying "I wear no mask!" the Stranger said, in a voice that could not now be mistaken, "So be it." He moved to the centre of the stage, and with his beautiful dead eyes surveyed the audience, finally resting his sightless gaze on the box where Lord Henry Wotton sat. Then, very deliberately, he removed the cloak, to reveal curiously soiled and crumpled evening dress, and at last stripped away the mask.

The face revealed, withered, wrinkled and loathsome as it was, was yet recognisable as the face of Dorian Gray.

Adrian Lee recalled what his father had told him many years ago: "Sin is a thing that writes itself across a man's face. It cannot be concealed." He had not truly believed it until now, and for a sudden brief moment he knew that Dorian Gray was capable of any enormity.

Little incoherent sounds escaped his lips, and he tried to back away, but he could not move his gaze from the ghastly figure. Around him, the other actors, and the audience as well, were likewise transfixed. The horrible face peered this way and that with its dead eyes, and the hollow voice once again intoned the words: *"Have you found the Yellow Sign?"*

As they watched, the gloved right hand took from the waistcoat pocket a small black object, a polished stone, on which gleamed a curious symbol or letter in gold, which looked vaguely as if it might be Arabic or Chinese but was in fact neither. Nor, as the watchers well knew, did it belong to any human language. The figure held it aloft, so that all could clearly see it, and then, in silence, he began to fall in upon himself. There was nothing human, nothing solid at all, about the way that the creature collapsed. Within seconds there remained only the filthy clothes, the Yellow Sign, and a boneless thing that quivered and was still.

XIII

> "His beauty had been to him but a mask, his youth but a mockery."
>
> — Oscar Wilde: *The Picture of Dorian Gray*

The envelope that old Isaacs had given to Lord Henry contained a telegram from Aubrey Manners, expressing regret that the sudden death of his father prevented his participation in the play. No sooner had Lord Henry read the message than the Stranger had made his entrance, and it was, he thought, too late to take action — with what results we know.

In their varying degrees the friends of Dorian Gray were, with one exception, affected by the unexpected events of that afternoon. Lady Gwendolyn joined the Roman Catholic communion and in time entered a nunnery. The Duchess of Monmouth was not seen in London Society again for nearly a year; when she did return it was remarked of her that, although she occasionally smiled, no one heard her laugh again. Lord Poole moved very shortly to Naples, where he lived in seclusion for many years. Adrian Singleton cut his own throat, and the Duke of Perth died within a year of an overdose of cocaine.

Adrian Lee was discreetly committed by his family to a private asylum, where he was regarded by the staff with affection on account of his gentleness, and with pity on account of his youth.

The only person untouched by the drama was Lord Henry Wotton, whose soul was too small to be affected by either good or evil. At first he would pay an occasional visit to the asylum, for his own amusement rather than from any sense of duty, but at last he could no longer tolerate the monotony of Adrian's greeting. Every time, the sad, red-rimmed eyes would look imploringly into his own, and the plaintive voice would repeat, over and over:

"Have you found the Yellow Sign?"

Afterword

In 2006, Robert M Price was invited by Peter A Worthy to contribute to *Rehearsals for Oblivion, Act I*, an anthology of stories inspired by *The King in Yellow*. Having devised a cracker of a plot, he decided that I was a good person to write it. I was delighted and honoured to do so. "In Memoriam" is the result — a tribute to both Robert W Chambers and Oscar Wilde. I hope it's not unworthy of them.

ON DEAD GODS

The original poem (now lost) was in Arabic, and was attributed to the otherwise unknown *Achmet, called Al Ghul.* It was translated into Latin, supposedly in the year 1120, by Sir Geoffrey de Lacy, and included in his monumental *De Potentiae Deorum Antiquorum* — a volume that is likewise, alas, no longer extant. The would-be-epic doggerel given here is taken from page thirty-nine of Thomas Dashwood Morley's English version of de Lacy's book, published in 1763. Morley is known to have added much to the text and revised much more, so it seems probable that this is a free adaptation rather than a strictly accurate translation. Scholars will note that the final quatrain is not original, being copied from John Dee's *Necronomicon.*

"De Deis Occisis"

The *Ones* that potent were shall be again.
And nor shall They with petty plans of men
Confounded be. The *World* you think you own
Their orb-in-hand shall be, Their crown, Their throne.
Where you now are the *Old Ones* were before;
They do but wait till They return once more.
The *Day* that followed *Night* shall pass away,
And They shall come, with *Night* that follows *Day.*

They lurk now where you see them not. Ye blind!
Ye fools! They are not here, but lurk behind,
Between the things you know. You see them not.
They are not flesh as ye, nor doth *Time* rot
The *Ancients* as it rots man in his tomb.

Evil is dead! The *Gods* have seal'd Its doom!
Was once the cry of those who saw the Clash,
The Battle of the *Gods*, the cut and slash
'Twixt mighty Pow'rs of *Evil* and of *Good.*
They watch'd the Fray, and saw from where they stood
The Victory. The *Old Ones* overcome
Were sent to *Death*, to lie remote in some
Forgotten Realm in Earth or in the Stars.
Meanwhile the wise *Gods*, healing up Their scars

Of War, rejoic'd all in Their Victory,
And look'd about Them, happy not to see
The *Ancient Ones* oppress the mortal Soul.
They scarcely did observe within His Hole
The Shadow of the *Prince of Darkness* still
Brooding upon Hiss loss with thoughts of Ill.

The greatest Pow'r of *Evil* yet liv'd on,
And would His star-spawn'd Servants that were gone
Revivify, that in the Time to be
They should arise, and Men and *Gods* might see
The strength of *Darkness* fitted for the Fight,
And then the Battle, *Darkness* conqu'ring *Light*.

When comes that Time, the *Darkness* shall rise deep.
Then *Satan* shall awaken from Their sleep
His Minions, and Their rivalries within
Themselves shall cease, and They shall strive to win
The cataclysmal Fray, when Pow'rs of *Light*
Shall in despair attempt to halt the *Night*
That must come.

           Hoary *Nodens* and His Kin
Shall start awake, and see the Strength of *Sin*
Rise up. Then *Good* and *Evil* once again
Shall clash, amid the Groanings and the Pain
Of dying *Gods*. The outcome of that War
I know not: only what must come before.
The Stars into their places now are set,
Affording thus the Key that soon shall let
Great *Tulu* free. The Deep Ones at his call
(His Servants they) by mighty Spells shall all
The *Ancient Ones* awake, and there, and then
Their Might shall be reveal'd to *Gods* and Men.

From out the Earth doth black *Saddoqua* rise;
And Legions of *Ithaquus* fill the Skies.
Great *Hastur* from His pris'ning bonds releas'd
Within *Carcosa* (enmity now ceas'd
Betwixt Him and His Cousins) doth descend
Prepar'd to fight the Battle and to end

The Lordship of those mighty *Gods* of *Light*
That conquer'd Him and won the first great Fight.

Yog Soggoth, One-in-All and All-in-One,
Doth now before the Conflict is begun
Contract Himself. That *God* eternal is
And infinite, but now doth draw all His
Almighty Self into one Time, one Space,
More potent thus and stronger far to face
The *Elder Gods* of *Light*. Foul *Yigg*, the Sire
Of wise and ancient Serpents, doth wax dire
And strong with dreadful Strength. Lo! Hated *Zhar*
And *Loyggor*, from Their Prison in the Star
Where They did lie, to Battle now are freed.

Great *Azathoth* with all His hideous *Seed*,
Narlat Hotep, the Chaos out of Space,
And *Changa Faugn*, and others of Their *Race*
Make fight once more and thus avenge Their *Fall*.
The Vict'ry shall be final, Once for All.

Old *Nodens* under *Allah*, with His Kith,
Startled beholds the Evil *Gods* of Myth
Awaken with the Breaking of the *Spell*
That bound Them in Their Prison, which is *Hell*.
Then under *Satan* go They into War,
To such a Fight as never was before.

The Death of *Gods* the *Devil* might appal
If with the Years such Death be Death at all.
That is not Dead which can eternal lie,
And with strange Æons even *Death* may die.

Afterword

It really is doggerel, but it was fun to write, in an imitation of mid-eighteenth century style. "On Dead Gods" draws heavily on August Derleth's formalised version of H P Lovecraft's mythology. It was first published in the *Count Dracula Fan Club Annual* Lovecraft special issue, and reprinted by Bob Price in *Cthulhu Codex 11* (Lammas 1997).

"More Things in Heaven and Earth..."

THE SERPENT'S TOOTH

How the letter came into my hands is a matter of no moment. The original is in French, and was found among papers formerly the property of a lady once well-known in the world of letters. The translation here copied is in her own hand.

Biel,
Oct. 15th, 17—

My Dearest,

I rejoice to know that shortly you will join me for a. few golden days in this charming town. Nor need I tell you that my good cousin George also anticipates with pleasure your arrival here, for he has paid attention to my frequent descriptions of your beauty, our intelligence, and your sweet nature.

From George in return I received sad news, and yet strange, concerning his own uncle, one M. Leopold Meinster, recently departed this life. The gentleman, being the brother of my cousin's mother, was not truly related to our own family. Perhaps, therefore, I can relate dispassionately to you, my dear one, the curious and as I might say grotesque events which led to his demise. In reading, then, you shall read of a stranger.

Firstly, then, know that M. Meinster for some years occupied the position of professor of natural philosophy at the university of Besançon. His methods of researching and of teaching this subject, which he named the greatest of all the arts, aroused in his colleagues and superiors a considerable distaste, however, for they were based upon the texts of the alchemists and mystic philosophers of the age of superstition. Such ill-feeling was there, indeed, that in the year 17— the president of the university himself went so far as to confiscate and destroy a number of the books belonging to M. Meinster. Some of these volumes, the president avowed, were replete with blasphemy, while others wantonly defied the reason that places man above the brutes.

This most regrettable incident may have hastened the professor's retirement from the university, but such retirement was inevitable, for he had long determined to devote himself to a study of the mysteries of animation, to divine the undisclosed laws of nature, and uncover the means by which humankind exists. Our outward substance and our inner spirit were alike his target, and his inquiries were ever directed to both the physical and the metaphysical secrets of the world. On departing the noble institution, he roundly declared to the few that would hear him:

The proper study of Mankind is Man.

None can say whether he remembered the preceding line, *viz*:

Know then thyself; presume not God to scan.

Imbued with a fervent longing to penetrate the secrets of nature, M. Meinster worked alone in his old house, to all appearance becoming, like the building itself, more eccentric as the years passed. His reclusive existence did not go unremarked among his former colleagues, but they, like the *bourgeois* of the town, came in time to accept it. You may picture their astonishment, therefore, when, upon a day some two years ago, the *quondam* professor importunately interrupted a meeting of the academic staff at the university. All eyes turned upon him as he ran into the great chamber and climbed upon the president's own table.

"Gentlemen," cried he, "in past times you have derided both my thoughts and my deeds. Ah! do not smile! I know it to be so. I knew well that the principles of Cornelius Agrippa, Paracelsus and Albertus Magnus have been entirely exploded and that a modern system of science has been introduced which possesses much greater powers than the ancient, but I knew also that we have much to learn from the works of the alchemists, chimerical though their discoveries may be. I know, and shall prove to you, that you were the fools, and not I. All that I have worked for, through long and weary years, has come to pass: I have myself become capable of bestowing animation upon lifeless matter. You shall see for yourselves, gentlemen, that a man can indeed create another man, even as himself!"

At this astonishing assertion, there arose such a Babel of protest from the learned men of the university that the president was forced to call them to order When calm was at length restored, he addressed the wild and fantastical figure before him: "Are we to understand, then, M. Meinster, that you yourself have endowed with life that which was once dead?"

"That is so," replied the old man. "All here assembled are aware that my life has long been dedicated to studying the mysteries of animal life, that I might myself at last reproduce Nature's handiwork. Does my final success truly surprise you? But I am anxious to show to you this miracle, as should you be to see it. Time passes. I pray you, come with me now to my house!"

Wondering and doubting, the president selected a small party of the most learned of the sages, and they followed their former colleague through the narrow streets to the ancient building where he had lived and worked these many years. To what effect, they were soon to learn. M. Meinster himself, smiling and gesturing in his childlike excitement, hastened them down the winding stairs to the large cellar, for there it was that he had conducted his experiments and his operations. Recumbent upon a stone slab lay the body of a man. To be sure, its proportions were uncommonly large. Certainly its skin bore a dull, unnatural-seeming greyish tinge. It was true that about the neck and the joints of the limbs were a number of neatly stitched scars. Nonetheless, all the onlookers were no more convinced of M. Meinster's claim now than they had been before, for the eyes were closed, as were the lips, and no trace of life could be discerned in the body at all. Clearly, it was neither more nor less than a cadaver.

Leopold Meinster appeared at once amazed and crestfallen. "It lived, I tell you!" said he. "It lived and breathed, even as you and I. Alas! It has expired, while I was at the university,

The president approached the body and hesitantly touched the dead cheek. "M. Meinster," said he, "we are all men of learning. If you wish to persuade the gullible of your absurd claims of artificial animation, that is your own concern, but I must ask that you refrain from an attempt to deceive those who are your superiors in wisdom if not in erudition. Now, sir, I thank you for an amusing diversion from our more serious duties and bid you a very good day." And with that, the savants departed the house, leaving M. Meinster alone with the grisly results of his labours.

Those labours did not cease, however; indeed, they continued more urgently even than before, for Leopold Meinster was steadfast in his determination to succeed in his self-appointed task. At last, just one week ago, the president of the university received a note, delivered by a boy of the town, which read thus: "I beg of you, come to my house without delay and observe with your own eyes that I have in truth achieved my goal, for I have this day instilled life into a man-like body of my own making. I dare not leave it, for fear that it should die, like the other."

As you may surmise, this appeal was ignored, for the president and his colleagues were convinced that M. Meinster's previous attempt to persuade them had been a mere fraud. This, they were sure, could be no more genuine. On his return to the old man's house, the lad called out, to tell him of the president's unoourteous response. Receiving no reply, the he called again, and then proceeded cautiously to descend the narrow staircase to the cellar. In the dim charnel light he thought he could descry footprints upon the steps, but they seemed to his excited mind to be larger than the prints of human feet ought to be. On the lower steps, outlined in some oily fluid, the impressions were quite distinct, so that it was with considerable foreboding that the lad at last entered the vault.

His foreboding was vindicated, for the great room seemed to his horrified eyes to resemble a slaughterhouse. Two benches had been overturned, and the heavy stone slab was broken into three pieces. A number of bottles and flasks had been smashed, and their contents spilled upon the floor, so that the boy's boots crunched upon the fragments of glass. Then, appalled, he saw the body of Leopold Meinster, lying partly hidden by one of the upturned benches. The old man's skull was savagely crushed, and blood and grey matter were spattered among the various liquids upon the floor. About the body could be seen the impressions of huge naked feet.

Such, in brief, were the life and death of Leopold Meinster. A strange tale, do you not think, my dearest? In telling the tale to me, cousin George observed that it is, perhaps, as well that I was unacquainted with the old man, for had I known him I might myself have become engrossed in his passionate desire to uncover the secrets of life. I told him, as I tell you now, Elisabeth, that I hope as I live never to become so dangerously infatuated with the mysteries of existence as was the unfortunate M. Meinster.

But this rather macabre matter is, perhaps, too gross for your own delicate sensibilities.

I pray you to write soon and tell me when you expect to join me in Biel. I think of you constantly, and long for the time when we shall be together.

> I remain, always,
> Your loving cousin and fiancé,
> V. F.

Afterword

This story dates from my school days, when the English class was instructed to write a story on the theme of "The Boy Who Cried Wolf". In revising it for publication many years later, I have tried to approximate Mary Shelley's style, which is rather formal but rarely pompous. Real devotees will have noticed that I lifted three or four sentences, more or less complete, from her novel.

ENIGMA

There was no shortage of witnesses because the bar was crowded at the time. To be precise, thirty-four people were present, and they were forced, they said, to believe their eyes. The event was covered by the *Essex Chronicle*, the *Weekly News*, and the *East Anglian Daily Times*. It even made the national dailies, whose comments varied from the sober to the fatuous.

It happened in the public bar of the *Bell and Horseshoe* at Scrapfaggot Green, Essex, at 9.17 pm on November the thirteenth, 1977. People are still debating what it really was:

"A *thing* from outer space got into the beer." *(Then why was no one else affected?)*

"Someone slipped a new drug into his glass." *(We've never come across this drug since then.)*

"An unusual form of allergy to beer." *(He had never shown any signs of such an allergy.)*

"The bacteria decided to make war on man." *(And gave up immediately?)*

"A conjuring trick." *(Oh, come on!)*

"Mass hypnotism." *(Rather less improbable, but even so ...)*

"A witch put a spell on him." *(But he didn't just disappear.)*

"He himself was a witch." *(Um ...)*

"A chemical reaction between something in the beer and something in his body." *(This sounds like the allergy theory again.)*

"He himself was a ghost, and the beer was perfectly normal." *(But his life up to that time is well and reliably documented.)*

"There are more things in heaven and earth, Horatio... " *(And I reckon that's about the nearest we'll get to an explanation.)*

It took place nearly thirty years ago, and people are still trying to decide what really happened when Peter Francis Saltmarsh of Church Cottage, Scrapfaggot Green, was drunk by his glass of beer.

Afterword
I seemed to be remarkably prolific in my teens. This little joke was written a long time ago and published in *Deep Things out of Darkness*.

DESIDERATUM

People have gone to great lengths to contact the Devil, often without result. A waste of time and effort, they say, and so it is — but not necessarily for the obvious reason. The fact is that the Devil is just a little bit choosy. After all, when you've been around since the non-existent beginning of eternity, then you tend to develop individual tastes. The Devil is principally interested in people who really *want* to contact Him (or rather — let's not be sexist — It). And there's a difference between really wanting something and merely thinking that you want it. It's quite possible that you or I hold a deep desire to contact the Devil without being aware of the fact. Should the desire bubble up to the surface, though, we'd recognise it at once.

It didn't take James Summers more than a moment to get over the surprise caused by his unexpected visitor, even though the surprise was considerable. He was unused to entertaining visitors at all, and he had never expected (who has?) to entertain such a visitor.

It was indescribable. What Summers saw was an indefinable shape of an indefinable colour and an indefinable size. Also it gave off a quite indefinable odour. There was, literally, nothing that Summers could compare it with. Naturally, if that's the right word, the voice that accompanied the sight and the smell was equally indefinable.

The voice said, "**Well, what do you want?**"
For a moment Summers was lost for a reply, but the visitor seemed to be patient. It waited, shifting its shape, its colour and its smell to others no less indescribable, while he thought. At last he said, "If you are who I think you are, then surely you know what I want."

"Come now," said the voice. "**I am not omniscient.**"

"And yet you knew that I wanted to meet you."

"**Well —**" (the indefinable voice became, apparently, self-dismissive for a moment; though of course there was nothing that Summers could pin down) "**— we can sense certain feelings. Perhaps you have had the same experience yourself?**"

"Er..." Summers decided to try another approach. "Why are you here, anyway? I didn't call you."

"**There was no need,**" said the voice. "**You know now that you wanted to meet me, though you were unaware of it before. We come when we are wanted — really wanted. Most of those** who draw up the magic signs and pronounce the abominable words — well, they don't really want to meet me." There was a pause while the shape changed hue yet again, and grew momentarily vast. When it subsided, the voice resumed, in a tone that might almost have been nostalgic: "**Of course, we do sometimes appear to them — just for the hell of it, as you might say. But yours is a different case. Come now: what do you want?**"

"Just a moment!" Summers' curiosity was aroused. "Sometimes you say 'we' and sometimes 'I'. Just who are you, after all? And how many of you are there?"

The accent this time might have been mocking. "'**My name is Legion, for we are many.' No doubt you recognise the quotation.**"

"No doubt," said Summers, thoughtfully. If he hadn't expected such a visitor, still less had he expected such a visitor to be like this. More sternly he said, "It hadn't occurred to me that you would so cheerfully quote — "

There was a sound, which seemed to come from all around him, not entirely unlike laughter. "**Of course**," said the voice. "**I can quote it all if you really want. Would you prefer Hebrew, Greek, Latin, English...? No, no point really, I suppose. But you seem to forget that in this case it was the book that was quoting. We merely repeated ourselves. We often do that. It gives spice to our conversation. Now, tell me what you want.**"

Summers nerved himself. "Very well," he said. "Let me just say that I consider myself to have been unfairly treated by the world." (Was it a sigh that seemed to fill the air, or could it have been a groan?) "Unfairly treated, I say. I know I have it in me to be great — to do great things. Damn it, I'm intelligent, cultured, literate... I write — and write well, mark you! — I'm a first-class scholar, intelligent and imaginative. Yet here I am, stuck in this unprepossessing body. My tastes are too rarefied for the great unwashed, so that no-one wants to read my work or listen to my music (did I mention that I am musical as well?). I worked my way up from the lower middle class, which ought to be considered praiseworthy; instead I'm sneered at by the self-proclaimed intellectuals!"

All the bitterness that he had hardly realised existed came to the surface now, and it was plain why his visitor had come. For a moment Summers paused, but having begun he was determined to go on. "Not only am I frustrated professionally, but I have had the most humiliating of private lives. I am short and fat — no wonder the women prefer other men! But if they could only realise the intellectual and aesthetic pleasures I can offer! Instead they turn to men who are tall and slim, with flat stomachs — men with heads of solid bone..."

"I see," said the voice. "**So you want to be more attractive to women — is that it? Tall, dashing, debonair...**"

Summers' voice sounded small as he answered, "Oh, no."

"**No? You want to be professionally successful, then. Money, of course. Wealth begets wealth. Yes, much more sensible. Even if you were really ugly (and between you and me — well, no matter) that would bring the women running. Some women, anyway. And some men, I suppose...**"

For the first time, Summers felt that he had the upper hand. His self-assessment wasn't entirely unjust: he really was a clever man, and his visitor appeared to have rather a commonplace mind by comparison. Third-rate, thought Summers; positively third-rate. Well, well. Who would have thought it?

Aloud, he said, "That isn't it at all."

"**No?**" Perhaps there was something understatedly silky in the voice — but if so, Summers didn't notice it.

"No," he said firmly. "I've worked it all out, you see. Wealth can be lost on the turn of a card, the throw of a die. Fortune may come with wealth, but it will go when the wealth goes."

"**Hmmm...**"

"What I want — what I truly want - is knowledge."

"**Very well. But may we ask why?**"

Why? Surely even a simpleton could see why! "With knowledge, of course, I should be aware of the best way to make use of my talents. I could make money — acquire influence — gain friends... I could... " he stopped abruptly, to arrange the thoughts that were spilling over in his mind.

"You said," he resumed eventually, "that you were not omniscient. Well, that's exactly what I want to be! I want to know everything. All that will help me in life — help me to achieve the success that I know I am capable of. I don't ask for talent, because I have talent. I don't ask for sexual attraction, because — after all — I'm not actually hideous. What I want is to know how to use the qualities that I already have!"

"**And is that all?**"

"Well, hardly. There's so much more that I want to know! Some people crave power or wealth. I do not." (Don't you? said a voice that might have been inside or outside his head.) "It's knowledge that fascinates me. Can you understand? I *want* to know what song the Sirens sang! I *want* to know what name Achilles assumed when he hid himself among women! Oh, there's so much! If only I knew for certain that the world's approval wasn't worth having, then I'd be content in not having it... But I really *want* to know. To know everything."

The indescribable shape seemed to quiver, as if in consideration. "**Omniscient?**" said the indescribable voice, at last. "**You really want to be omniscient. Hm. You — er — you are aware of what happened to Adam and Eve when they sought forbidden knowledge?**"

"Adam and Eve!" Summers was scornful. "Mythical balderdash!" (The indefinable entity before him seemed indefinably to bridle.) "Very well. Accepting for the moment the truth of the lie — Adam and Eve became aware of the difference between good and evil. No more. And the entire human race has lived and flourished with that knowledge ever since. *It is not enough.* They thought that merely knowing of good and evil would make them godlike, but of course they were led on by — er... Well, it seems to me, anyway, that they didn't ask enough. I want to know what God himself knows. Yes, omniscient. I *want* to be all-knowing."

He concluded with a full resumption of the manly defiance that for some reason had momentarily deserted him. Who was this creature, anyway? What was it to deny him? It was one of the fallen; something inferior; something to do his bidding.

"**Omniscient,**" said the voice again. "**To know what God himself knows. Well, it makes a change from eternal life. Hard, though; very hard. Still, we are many, and between us it should be possible. Yes, it should be possible.**"

"Good! Now, what of my side of the bargain?"

"**Your side?**" The indefinable voice seemed indefinably surprised.

"Yes. Don't you want my soul or something?"

"**Oh, there is no bargain involved. It's quite straightforward: you get what you want, and we get what we want. No bargain. You have already committed yourself — your whole self.**"

But Summers was confident now. He knew what he wanted, and he knew how he wanted it. "I have not committed myself yet," he said, calmly. "All I've done is to tell you what I want. No agreement has been made — and, besides, I haven't said that I want it from *you*"

There was something like irritation in his visitor's voice. "**Quibbling,**" it said. "**Casuistry. Ho hum. No doubt you propose conditions upon your request?**"

"Not conditions. I just wish to ask you a question. Of course, I shall have to take your truthfulness on trust — "

The voice and its source seemed momentarily to engulf him. "**My truthfulness? Ha! Your species has a naive way of thinking in anthropomorphic terms, but I may say with pride that I have always been considered a gentleman.**"

"Pride," said Summers, sharply, "is a sin."

"**Of course.**" The voice quite calm now.

"Very well. I shall ask my question, and if the answer pleases me I shall ask you formally for the knowledge — the complete knowledge — that I want."

"**Ask away.**"

"As I said, you will certainly expect to receive my soul in exchange for granting my desire. Now, my belief in an afterlife, in the immortal spark, may have been rather sketchy, but your presence here compels belief."

Something not entirely unlike a yawn seemed to split the room, but Summers continued: "Just tell me whether there is a loop-hole — whether, having forfeited my soul, I can still retrieve it."

"**Oh yes.**" The voice sounded thoroughly bored. "**There is a way out.**"

"Then I agree!" said Summers, eagerly. "I now formally ask of you the total knowledge that I require, and in turn surrender to you my soul for all eternity, together with all its appurtenances, etc..."

"**Agreed,**" said the voice. "**You must be patient for a little while, though; these things take time. Oh, and now that you've committed yourself, I'll tell you something interesting about that loop-hole.**"

"Yes?"

"**Yes. Merely that we know what it is, and you don't!**"

Summers simply *had* to prick that gloating pomposity and watch it deflate. "You think you've fooled me — eh? You think I'm just another gull, so much more fuel for the fire. Well, now that you have committed yourself, *I* shall tell *you* something."

"**Oh?**"

"You have promised me the ultimate knowledge, the knowledge of God himself. And you cannot take me until you have fulfilled that promise."

"**Well?**"

"You are the fool! When I have that knowledge — when I know *everything* — then of course I shall know what the loop-hole is, and how best to use it! *You* are the fool."

"**Dear me,**" said the voice. "**Dear me.**" Perhaps its continued calmness should have made Summers hesitate, but in any case it was too late. "**Such is life,**" it said. "**Well, as you say, we are bound to keep our side of the deal. It will take a few minutes, but I am sure you can wait that long.**"

The soundless voice ceased. The formless shape and colourless hue seemed to dissolve, and for a moment Summers felt something like strands of cobweb pulling away from his face and body. Then he was alone. "At last!" he said, and he began to plan out his glorious future.

A few minutes, the visitor had said, and no more than a few had passed when omniscience came to James Summers. He alone of all mortal beings was possessed of the ultimate knowledge. He alone knew what God knew! It was a moment to savour.

Sadly, there was no time to savour it. There was time only for one thought: that the human brain is simply incapable of encompassing the knowledge of God.

James Summers just had time to realise that fact. Then his brain exploded.

Fortunately, there was little external damage, and the pathologist was able quite convincingly to suggest that death had been caused by the sudden growth of an unsuspected malignant tumour. One or two of the mourners at the funeral may have sensed an indefinable voice commenting upon the futility of things, but if so they ignored it.

"**Knowledge!**" said the voice. "**Pah! Solomon had the right idea. He asked for wisdom.**"

Afterword

I long wanted to write a "bargain with the Devil" story, and the idea for "Desideratum" came to me when I was asked to contribute to the second issue of a new magazine several years ago. Alas, *Close to the Edge* never made it beyond the first issue, so the story has had to wait until now for publication.

LOVE, DEATH AND THE MAIDEN

I'm getting old. It was something of a shock to realise recently that it's over fifty years since Valerie Beddoes died.
Fifty years. Just another unsolved murder case. And of course events took place shortly afterwards that rather pushed a single death to the back of the public mind. So why raise the matter now? Well, facts that I ought to have known about long ago have at last come to my notice and made some sort of sense of the affair. Some sort. If I'm right, then the whole business is even stranger than we'd thought back in 1939.
The relationship that Valerie and I shared is difficult to define. It's such a tedious cliché to say that we were "just good friends", but really that's about the truth of it. It was only after we'd said goodbye for the last time that some inkling came to me of why I'd been able to maintain a strong friendship with such a very good-looking girl without a sexual element in the relationship. We were — well, not like sister and brother, perhaps, but like close cousins.
And Valerie was an exceptionally attractive creature. Tall, shapely, blue-eyed and blonde — the Aryan fallacy taken to a perfect extreme; but one could hardly blame her for the looks she'd inherited from her Saxon forebears. And since she was intelligent and well-educated, I think that occasionally she found her beauty something of a disadvantage. Strangely, as it seemed to me then (at twenty-two I was naïve in many ways, but then my generation was like that), she found it hardest to get other women to take her seriously.
Margaret Pennethorne, for instance.
Playgoers under fifty are unlikely to know of Margaret Pennethorne. Even those familiar with her work may not recognise the name, since she didn't use it professionally, but she had a considerable reputation in the thirties and forties for strong historical dramas written under the pseudonym of Richard Border. *The Stone Queen* was the one that made her reputation — about Eleanor of Aquitaine — and although it hasn't been performed for years that particular play is still remembered because it also made the reputation of the young Celia Hesketh, who played Eleanor.
I was not a regular theatregoer in 1938, but I had recently seen the revival of *The Stone Queen* at the Arcadian Theatre, and when my cousin Jack Fellowes told me that he'd been invited to a

party at which Richard Border was to be present I begged him to take me along. I wondered at the time why his agreement seemed to hide a sort of secret amusement. When he pointed "Richard Border" out to me the reason became clear — at least, once I'd stopped looking for a man who might perhaps have been concealed in the corner behind the two striking-looking women who were chatting so earnestly together.

Somehow I got myself introduced to the author of *The Stone Queen*. Striking? Yes, she was, if not in any obvious way. Aged about forty, I suppose, dark-haired and with an expression of rather disconcerting amusement in her eyes. She was some inches shorter than her companion, but gave the impression of being the bigger personality. I found her then rather overwhelming. The companion, on the other hand . . .

The companion was introduced to me as "my secretary, Valerie Beddoes".

Well, you already have some idea of what Valerie looked like. After we three had chatted for a while about Queen Eleanor and her brood of kings, and my halting contributions had persuaded Miss Pennethorne that I wasn't just a celebrity-seeker, I was very pleased when Valerie took my arm and said, "Meg wants to have a word with Dolly Tappan about the design for her next play. Come along — we'll go and get another drink."

I remember trying to conceal my appraisal of her face and figure, blushing when I realised that she had caught me out. I remember joining in her delighted laughter as she said, "Like Cecily, I am very fond of being looked at. Well, by nice people, anyway. What about that drink?"

I had recently experienced a messy love affair, ending in a broken engagement. Will it surprise you to learn that I saw the lovely Valerie Beddoes not as a possible lover but as a sympathetic friend who would listen to my troubles? It seemed strange to me only in retrospect, after Jack and I had left the party, when there was only Valerie's picture in my mind. There was something about her presence that didn't allow thoughts of a sexual relationship. Odd. The very idea just didn't occur to me while we were together.

We became, as I've said, good friends. There were several interests that we shared: the music of Mozart, Thackeray's novels — other things too, including, of course, the plays of Richard Border. I visited Border's — Margaret Pennethorne's — house at Bray several times, though it was an experience that never quite pleased me because of the seemingly permanent sardonic amusement in Miss Pennethorne's eyes. She was always friendly, in a way that suggested some underlying motive, and I couldn't quite get used to the rather patronising way she would say, "I have work to do, I'm afraid. Val, why don't you two children settle down in the sitting-room and chat?"

Once she was out of the way, though, and we could hear the faint click of her typewriter through the study door, I felt more at ease. Valerie would produce cigarettes and perhaps a bottle of sherry, then she would sprawl elegantly on the couch while I took one of the big armchairs or walked restlessly about. I was young and full of serious ideas. Valerie, actually a year or two younger than I, somehow seemed more mature. She was certainly a wise conversationalist, able to listen and comment seriously on my profound political thoughts. I like to think that she was fond of me. I know that I've had no such good friends since.

We shared an interest in certain subjects, as I've indicated, but her near-obsession with the supernatural was something that quite escaped me. She had little time for ghost stories of the sort that appeared in the lurid magazines, but was fascinated (the word has lost most of its true magical force these days) by supposedly true accounts of the occult and bizarre. Perhaps it was this streak that made it inevitable that, at Margaret Pennethorne's request, Valerie should go to central Europe in search of the Bloody Countess of the Carpathians.

At that time I knew nothing of the Countess Elisabeth Bathory, though I have learned much in recent months. I was more concerned about my friend's safety in the uneasy atmosphere of a Europe that had so recently seen — how easily the word came to mind! — *Anschluss.* It was February 1939, and there was much to worry about for a sober-minded young idealist.

None of this seemed to matter to Valerie, though, nor to Margaret Pennethorne. I remember clearly how the news was broken to me when I called at the house in Bray, full of gloomy thoughts about the instability of the Munich agreement and the weakness of Neville Chamberlain. These ideas were quickly driven from me by Valerie's delighted smile and her words. "Darling! isn't it marvellous? Meg's got a new play on the boil, about a Hungarian vampire, and it's going to be even bigger than *The Stone Queen*—and I'm to do all the first-hand research for it!"

"A vampire?" I said cautiously. "Isn't that a bit outside her usual field?"

Margaret herself broke in here. The twinkle in her eyes seemed more metallic as she spoke: "Not really. I've always concentrated on the historical stuff — Eleanor, Barbarossa, Theodora — and this is really in the same vein. For heavens' sake, boy, I really believe you've never heard of Elisabeth Bathory!"

"Bathory? It — er — well, no..."

If there was something not quite sincere about the chuckle that greeted my reply, Valerie seemed not to notice. She took my arm and said, "I'll tell you about it. Come on. I've got coffee on the boil — and I'm sure Meg wants to be shot of us."

Still smiling, Margaret nodded and left. That smile seemed to be fixed onto her face.

[Elisabeth Bathory was a monster. Not physically, for she was held to be very beautiful, but mentally and spiritually. Her family, one of the most noble in eastern Europe, had intermarried for generations, and become marked by epilepsy, hereditary syphilis and madness. The madness erupted in this slim, dark, lovely woman.]

"I leave in two days' time," said Valerie at last. "Meg's fixed it all up. Boat-train to Dover, then Calais, Paris and across to Buda-Pesth. It'll be wonderful to get away — to be working on my own."

"Two *days*? That's a bit — "

"Oh, I'll miss you, of course, and a few other friends, but it's such an opportunity! And, you know — " (she lowered her voice a little) " — I shall be so glad just to get away from Meg for a while." She tossed a cigarette over to me, smiling at my expression. "I know it's sudden, but I think Meg's actually had the idea in mind for some time. You know how she likes to keep her work to herself until she's quite sure of it."

"Two days," I said again.

"This really will be big, you know. I told her I thought that the life of the Bloody Countess would make a stunning exercise in *Grand Guignol*. She said, 'Never mind *Grand Guignol*. This will be positively *Gross Guignol*.'"

[Elisabeth Bathory was a sadist. She is believed to have been directly responsible for the murders of more than six hundred and fifty young women, having them cut, slashed or burned so that their blood flowed. She would bathe in the blood of virgins in the belief that it would prolong her youth and beauty.]

"You're going alone? I suppose Margaret will provide the money, but how will you manage otherwise?"

"I'll be safe enough. Hungary may be rather unsettled, but I'm hoping also to get into Austria and Czechoslovakia. The Germans seem to have clamped down pretty firmly on crime there. Besides, my German is pretty fluent. I'll manage all right."

It was true that the private atrocities that had seemed to flourish in the uneasy Germany of the twenties had no place in Adolf Hitler's Third Reich. Peter Kürten, Karl Denke, Fritz Haarmann, Georg Grossmann — they were not part of the new German Empire. It was only rumour to us that private atrocity had given way to official atrocity, on a scale that made the activities of Elisabeth Bathory seem almost petty.

[Elisabeth Bathory was a devoted wife to her noble husband, the Count Francis Nadasdy, and a devoted mother to their children. She seemed to have no difficulty in keeping her domestic life quite separate from the bloodlust and magic of her darker nature.]

"What time do you leave Victoria?"

"The train's due out at 9.25 in the morning."

"Hell! I've got to go to Birmingham tomorrow and I shan't be back till Friday evening. I can't even come to see you off. How long do you expect to be away?"

"No telling. I'm to start at the state archives in Buda-Pesth and then, if I can, I go on to Elisabeth's castle in eastern Czechoslovakia and to Vienna, where she had a town house. There's a special research that Meg wants me to carry out besides just gathering details of the Countess's life. She's heard from a correspondent in Austria that a torture device made for the Countess may still exist. I'm to track it down if I can and try to buy it."

[Elisabeth Bathory had special torture rooms installed in most of her several houses and castles. She would also indulge herself in

private rooms when she visited friends or relatives. In the cellar of her mansion in Vienna was a spiked cage, in which her naked victim would be hauled up on a rope and pulley and prodded with hot irons until she impaled herself in her torment. The beautiful Countess, herself naked, stood beneath the cage bathing in the shower of fresh blood.]

"Good God! That's horrible."

Valerie shrugged. "Morbid, I agree, but after all, it's all in the distant past."

"You know as well as anyone that Margaret Pennethorne can make the past come alive. I suppose there's no changing your mind?"

"Not likely! I'm looking forward to this. It's a pity we shan't be able to meet again — but it isn't the end of the world, you know. I'll keep in touch, and we'll get together again as soon as I come back."

[After her eventual trial, at which in deference to her noble family she was referred to only as "a blood-thirsty, bloodsucking Godless woman, caught in the act at Csejthe Castle", Elisabeth Bathory was sentenced to lifelong imprisonment at that same castle. She was immured in a small room without doors or windows, and only a small hatch for food to be passed to her. In August 1614 she died, "suddenly and without a crucifix and without light". For three and a half years she had seen nobody and nothing.]

Two weeks later, I happened to meet Margaret Pennethorne in Hatchard's bookshop. Naturally, I asked whether she'd had word yet from Valerie. Her quizzical smile was unchanged as she shook her head.

"Aren't you worried about her at all? I mean, with Europe so volatile —?"

"Oh, no. She's a capable enough girl. She'll cope. Besides, just now I'm rather relieved to have got her off my hands. Protracted love-affairs become tedious, don't you think?"

Much later that day I understood her remark. A love affair. They had been lovers. Of course! The notion just hadn't occurred to me before (didn't I say that I was a very naïve young man?), but it explained one thing at least. In spite of her obvious and very feminine good looks, I had never been able to think of Valerie in terms of a heterosexual love. Now I knew what it was about her that had precluded such thoughts.

[Elisabeth Bathory was bisexual, and all her perversities tended toward the lesbian side of her nature. She began by mistreating the peasant girls on her estates, who were in a very real sense her own property. The Hungarian peasants' revolt of a generation before had been savagely crushed, and the peasants of Elisabeth's time had no rights — life itself was merely a privilege. Later she became convinced that only aristocratic virgins could provide the blood she needed. Her preferred victims were under eighteen years of age, blonde and buxom, in contrast to her own dark and slender beauty.]

A day or so later, the first letter arrived from Valerie, having taken four days in the post. My own feelings towards her were changed only in that they were now quite straightforward: she was and would remain the best friend I had. I read the letter with great interest.

She had succeeded in gaining admittance to the state archives in Buda-Pesth, and had obtained (helped no doubt by her own charm and Margaret Pennethorne's money) an abridged transcript of the trial records. This was in Latin, and she intended to spend some of the time while travelling in translating as much of it as she could. Meanwhile, she was now headed for what had recently become the independent state of Slovakia, to visit that same castle of Csejthe which had been the Countess Bathory's principal residence. All was going well, and she had encountered no difficulties of any sort. Everyone she had met had been kind and helpful. I must *stop worrying.*

There was a post-script: "I quite forgot to tell you just what the object is that Meg wants me to try and find. It's an Iron Maiden."

[The Iron Maiden was not a particularly common device even in the great age of torture. The most famous example was a bulky machine, very crudely shaped like a woman, and with a woman's face roughly depicted on the head. A section of the front was hinged like a door, and could be opened by means of a rope and pulley to reveal a hollow just large enough for a man to be placed. On the inside of the door were several long spikes, so arranged

that when the door closed the upper ones would pierce the victim's eyes and the lower ones his heart and vitals. *This was the Virgin of Nuremberg, destroyed during the Allied bombing in 1944. A copy of unknown age exists somewhere in a museum.]*

Unfortunately, Valerie didn't tell me where in Slovakia she would be staying, and I was unable to find Csejthe on any map available to me. Later events drove the question from my mind and it was only within the last few years that I learned that the place is now called Čachtice.

The next letter came about ten days later. Since the postmark was unreadable, I still had no clear notion of just where Valerie was, but somehow I felt reluctant to approach Margaret Pennethorne again.

The castle, long ruined, stands on a high green hill surrounded by level and fertile country. Sir Iain Moncreiffe described it as "like a land-girt St Michael's Mount" — which is more pithy and probably no less accurate than Valerie's longer description. If there was any local superstition attaching to the place, Valerie doesn't mention it; she seems to have had no trouble in finding someone to act as a guide. This woman, Anna, was presumably a native Czech speaker, but she had more than a smattering of German — of a sort... At least she was able, with little prompting, to show Valerie the very room in which the Bloody Countess had passed so many months in a living death.

[Elisabeth's family and that of her husband were Protestants, but they enjoyed the support of the Holy Roman Emperor. The estates at Csejthe were not subject to any interference from the Emperor or from the neighbouring Prince of Transylvania. Elisabeth herself was a Calvinist, a complete believer in predestination. As a noble with absolute authority, and a Christian already chosen for salvation, she had no cause to justify her acts to herself or to anyone else. Even when she turned to the devil for help — it was a sorceress who advised her that the blood of noble maidens was necessary — she remained a convinced Christian. One can only wonder whether John Calvin himself would have approved.]

Anna even told her that the Countess's house in Vienna had been situated in the Augustinerstrasse, near the Imperial Palace. As to the Iron Maiden — why, the *gnädiges Fraülein* could hardly expect a poor peasant woman to know much about that. Certainly it had existed at this castle, and she hadn't heard that it had been destroyed. Maybe it wasn't there when the authorities came at last to arrest the beautiful Countess. Maybe it had been sent away to one of her other houses. The house in Vienna, perhaps?

Fortunately perhaps, this fitted in nicely with Valerie's plans, since Margaret Pennethorne's reticent correspondent had also suggested that the torture machine might have been taken into Austria. As they said goodbye, Anna looked for a moment at Valerie and said (so Valerie thought), "You will find it, I think. You are the right sort."

[Elisabeth Bathory was given to torturing her young companions while making the long, slow journey from one house or castle to another. Later, unable to wait until she had reached her destination, she would kill the girls who travelled with her. The bodies were simply interred by the roadside, though in earlier years she had insisted upon a Christian burial for her victims.]

Even at the Austrian frontier, Valerie encountered no real difficulty. She had to be rather circumspect in writing from Vienna, but I understood that the passport officer, a true Nazi, had been most impressed by her evident Nordic beauty and fluent German. The only thing that slightly disturbed her was that more than once — at the frontier, and again a couple of times before reaching Vienna — she thought she caught a glimpse of the old peasant woman, Anna.

I never knew Vienna before the war. The only time I've spent there was in 1946 as an officer in the British occupation force. Even so, I doubt that my Vienna was any more unlike the city that Elisabeth Bathory knew. I try to put the great neo-classical and baroque structures of the Inner Stadt out of my mind but I find that there's nothing left. If I'd hoped for some sort of imaginative guidance from Valerie's letters, I was to be disappointed. A curious and disconcerting vagueness seemed to affect her — she who had always impressed me with the clarity and balance of her thoughts.

The accounts became at last almost dreamlike. I gathered that for at least a week after her arrival in the city she had more or less wandered around the Inner Stadt, admiring the Hofburg, the Opera House, the churches — and wondering, with a feeling that she couldn't quite define, whether she would meet Anna again. During these days, she must have passed many times the corner of the Augustienerstrasse and the Dorotheergasse. It didn't seem to occur to her, though, that there was anything special about the place.

[Elisabeth Bathory's mansion stood hard by the Austin Friary. As her blood-lust grew rapidly out of control, she abandoned nearly all rational precautions. The appalling screams of the tortured and dying were so loud that the good friars sometimes protested by hurling pots and pans at her windows.]

Almost every week brought a letter from Valerie — to which I couldn't reply, as, infuriatingly, she gave no address. Several times I tried to telephone Margaret Pennethorne, but there was no reply. Valerie knew that there was something particular she ought to be doing, something connected with a person she'd known in England. Or in Hungary. The letters would contain disturbing, almost surrealist, descriptive imagery of a city that was unlike any I had ever encountered. Yet, among these accounts, there were the names and descriptions of recognisable places. And then there were the people.

Soldiers, German and Austrian, goose-stepping, heel-clicking, saluting. The ominous *Heil Hitler* that seemed to have replaced the homely *Grüss Gott*. There was something in the eyes of the men that rather frightened her. All the men. The women, on the other hand . . .

It was never made clear whether she actually met Anna again but there were many references to her, brief and inconsequential, often questioning. Was her face in every crowd, or could it just be nervous imagination? Was she only one person? But there was no need to pursue that sinister line. Whatever hold Anna might have over her, she could always go to Dorothy for comfort. Dear old Dorothy, so solid and motherlike. Besides, if it hadn't been for Dorothy —

Dorothy. Dorothea. Something about the name. Something meaningful?

If it hadn't been for Dorothy, she would never have met —

She was here to find something. Someone.

— would never have met Mädelein.

There was that odd, stunted little man who often seemed to be near when she was with Dorothy. She didn't like the glances he gave her, but at least Mädelein treated him with scornful tolerance. She must do the same. Darling lovely Mädelein.

The very last letter — like the rest, it was undated, but it reached me on the 21st of June — contains one very clear statement. Valerie was in love. Irrevocably, over head and ears in love. With Mädelein. They had hardly even met — just seen each other in the street; and it was all so *proper*. Perhaps that was a part of the spell. Nothing that had happened in England (what *had* happened in England?) had been like this. How wise Dorothy had been to keep them apart at first. Not a word exchanged, but when Mädelein had smiled, showing those beautiful white, even teeth, and her eyes shining the clearest blue, then Valerie *knew*. She'd found what she was looking for.

Now, what was I to make of all this? I had been against the journey from the start. Not only was the journey itself unsafe, I thought, but the reason for it was plainly morbid and mentally unhealthy. Was I right? Something had clouded my friend's mind; I couldn't doubt that she'd become (the word repels me, but I must use it) insanely obsessed by her mad search and by the mad world in which she'd arrived. Her descriptions of Mädelein in no way eased my mind, for they were clearly descriptions of Valerie herself.

Again I tried to telephone Margaret Pennethorne. This time, at least, she answered, but it was with a brusque, "Oh, it's you. Well, you're Valerie's friend; perhaps you can tell me where the wretched kid's got to?"

"But for heaven's sake! Isn't she in Vienna?"

"You tell me. She's out somewhere spending my money, and I haven't had a word from her in weeks."

I was horrified. And somehow, I just couldn't bring myself to mention Valerie's letters to me, which were the reason why I'd called in the first place. I said something vague about passing on any news that reached me and I put the telephone down.

Fear for my friend inspired me to boldness. I wrote to the British Embassy in Vienna, explaining that I was very concerned for a young Englishwoman whom I believed to be alone in the city and possibly in some kind of trouble. If someone from the Embassy staff could find her and assure me that she was all right, I should be most grateful.

The reply came nearly two weeks later.

The body of Valerie Beddoes, identified by her passport and her belongings, had been found in her room at a small *pension* near the Rotenturmstrasse. The manageress, having been alarmed by a single dreadful scream from the room, had awoken her husband and one of the male residents and with much reluctance entered the room. When she had realised what the viscous liquid was that her bare feet were treading in, she had become hysterical and had to be sedated. The police were called at once.

Valerie Beddoes lay upon the floor of the little room, her spine broken and four ribs crushed. She was naked, so that the appalling wounds inflicted upon her could be clearly seen. Her breasts and genitals had been savagely stabbed with some sharp thick instrument like a chisel.

The police surgeon declared that he had come across nothing like it in Viennese criminal history. He could only compare it to the Whitechapel murders of 1888. Plainly it was *Lustmord*, the work of a sexual psychopath. The coroner was forced to agree. Despite the landlady's stories of visitors to the young woman's room that night, whom she was unable to describe in any detail — even to being unsure of their number — it was plain that these visitors were women, and neither coroner nor police could credit that this horrible act was the work of a woman. The verdict was: murder by person or persons unknown.

It was all so sad, said the landlady; the English girl had been a little vague, perhaps, but so sweet and so very pretty.

The person or persons remained unknown. As soon as I felt able to, I sent a copy of the letter from the Embassy to Margaret Pennethorne. I expected no reply, and received none. Nor did I hear again from Vienna.

On the 3rd of September, Great Britain declared war against Germany. My time and thoughts were occupied for a long while with other matters, and when I returned at last to civilian life I deliberately put Valerie's death from my mind, preferring to remember our friendship and the good times. The wound healed, though it ached horribly at times.

And now it has opened again, all because of a suspicious voice that will not be silenced.

Over fifty years ago, I considered Valerie's pursuit of a sadistic murderess to be morbid and unhealthy. I think so still. For that reason I made no attempt to research further into the blood-soaked career of the Countess Elisabeth Bathory. Only Valerie mattered, and Valerie was dead. My sole link with her had been Margaret Pennethorne, the enigmatic "Richard Border", and she was dead too, killed in the Blitz. So it was chance and not design that led me to realise that I'd made a false assumption all those years ago.

The Iron Maiden. The thing that Valerie had been looking for. Quite recently I discovered that the machine made for Elisabeth Bathory, to her own specifications (and which almost certainly was destroyed after her arrest at Csejthe), had been something rather different from the crude device that had existed at Nuremberg. It was made in the form of an attractive and shapely young woman, life-sized and naked, complete with full breasts and pubic hair. The blue eyes could open and close, and the pink lips part to reveal even white teeth. The flowing blonde hair was real and so were the teeth—they had been torn from the head of one of Elisabeth's victims. When the chosen subject, who must have looked like its living image, approached this hellish doll, its arms would enfold her in an embrace, at first amusing, swiftly bone-crushing. Meanwhile, from the genitals and the nipples, sharp spikes would spring to pierce the young woman's body.

I thought then that Valerie's mind had become clouded, and that "Mädelein" was merely a narcissistic projection of her own self. I think otherwise now, since I have discovered that "Mädelein", literally translated, is a diminutive of "Mädel" — a maid.

Valerie Beddoes did find what she was looking for after all...

Afterword

In 1978 I visited Czechoslovakia with the Dracula Society. From Prague, and the legend of the Golem, we went east in search of Elisabeth Bathory, her crimes, her trial and her death. Our guide here was the late Sir Iain Moncreiffe of that Ilk, a leading genealogist of the day, whose family is directly descended from the Bloody Countess and from several other participants in the drama. Thanks to him, the facts quoted in this story are strictly accurate.

A number of writers have incorporated Elisabeth into their horror stories, mostly connecting her with the vampire theme, like Raymond Rudorff's excellent *The Dracula Archives*. The most unusual — it doesn't even mention vampires — is John

Blackburn's superb novel *Our Lady of Pain*. I wondered if an equally different approach would pay off for me. It looks as if it did, because after the story's initial publication in *The Mammoth Book of Ghost Stories 2* edited by Richard Dalby, it was chosen by Stephen Jones and Ramsey Campbell for *Best New Horror 3*.

Margaret Pennethorne is a purely fictional character, but her career echoes that of the novelist and playwright Elizabeth Mackintosh, best known as the detective story writer Josephine Tey. In the 1930s she had great success with historical plays written under the name of Gordon Daviot. The most famous was *Richard of Bordeaux*; hence Meg Pennethorne's pseudonym, Richard Border.

ODDITIES INVESTIGATED: TALES FROM A HERO'S CASEBOOK

Few men in this world possess the courage, the intelligence and the moral integrity to earn their daily toast and pâté in combat with the terrible forces of the supernatural and the occult. Fortunately for him, John W Hero had a sizeable private income.

I first encountered him when he gave a lecture on "The Deaths in My Life" at the Oddfellows' Hall in Chelmsford. The audience were glued to their seats. Literally, as otherwise they would have left before the interval. The Hero's astonishing mixture of talent, charisma, self-confidence and a complete lack of understanding enthralled me, and I made a special point of visiting him the next day at his luxurious apartment, just over the road from the old Lion and Lamb *in Duke Street.*

"My dear!" he exclaimed. "Heavens! The stories I could tell you!"

And heavens! The stories he did tell me...

Were they fact or fiction? I have no hesitation at all in refraining from comment. I will just mention, however, that shortly afterwards I made the acquaintance of a charming young lady who had acted for some while as the Hero's personal assistant, secretary and bodyguard. She gave me a rather different angle on his exploits.

Readers may judge for themselves how much the following accounts have been influenced by the young lady's revelations.

1. The Hero Introduced

The sign on his door read:

JOHN W HERO, MD, DLitt, LLD, FRCM, etc.
Oddities investigated, Ghosts shot, Vampires Exterminated
(daylight hours only).

Inside his office he was seated elegantly at a rosewood desk, intently doing nothing. His pretty fair-haired assistant was also sitting at a desk, but hers was made of MDF, and she was working.

The tastefully rose-tinted telephone rang, and the Hero opened one eye. His assistant took the hint and picked up the receiver. She listened for a moment, then: "It's for you, sir," she said, brightly but not without reverence.

The Hero took the instrument. "Mm..." he said. "Yes, of course, my dears." And similar interpolations at appropriate moments. At length he replaced the receiver. "An assignment, my dear," he said. "That was the vicar of Waltham Abbey. He earnestly entreats me to come and deliver his flock from an inconvenient vampire that has come to light — the *mot juste*, I think — while workmen were laying cables under the floor of the north aisle. We shall have to hurry, my dear. The sun sets in less than ninety minutes, and you know what the traffic is like at this time of year."

The sun was on the point of setting as they entered the great romanesque church. The girl, following the masterful yet somehow absurd figure of her employer, carried a large hammer and a wooden stake. Their footsteps echoed softly between the mighty carved pillars, and the two adventurers could see where a streak of red light from the dying sun disclosed the resting place of the vampire. Quickly they removed the stone slab that covered the tomb and set to work breaking the seal of the ancient leaden coffin. But the sun was set now, and faint scratchings from within warned them that the blood-hungry fiend was awake.

The Hero decided to take a chance. Motioning his assistant to be ready with the stake and hammer, he kicked away the lid of the coffin.

Too late! The vampire, with a violent strength like that of three men, knocked the weapons flying from the girl's slender hands and grasped the Hero by the throat. White teeth champing, red lips twisted into a lustful smile, he fixed the Hero's gaze with his own hypnotic stare — and the Hero was paralysed while the steely fingers closed around his neck.

His assistant, as brave as she was beautiful, pummelled the monster vainly with her small fists. Gasping with an exertion she had not felt since her last session with Sven at the health club, she seized the vampire's shoulder and shook him, willing him to let go — and (*mirabile dictu!*) The vampire slumped back weakly into his coffin, leaving the dazed Hero to recover. "All right," he said. "I give in." And he lay back quietly while the girl hammered the wooden stake into his heart.

339

Then she closed the coffin-lid, replaced the stone slab, and assisted the half-conscious Hero out of the church and into the clear night air. He gagged a little and blew his nose. "You acted very competently there, my dear," he said, patronisingly. "I wonder what made the fellow suddenly give in like that? My forceful personality, I suppose." He wrinkled his nose and sniffed. Then he turned to his assistant, who was still panting after her gruelling experience. "My dear," he said mildly, "you've been eating garlic again. I do wish you'd lay off these filthy foreign habits. There's a good girl."

2. The Hero Strikes Again

It takes a special kind of courage to descend into the dark, evil depths of the sewers to rid a community of a vast horde of venomous blue spiders of a species hitherto unknown to science — to risk one's life utterly without thought of reward save the satisfaction of knowing that one has done one's duty. The Hero's courage was rather less special than that. He haggled with Chelmsford Borough Council for quite a while before they would agree to his fee.

If his intention was to price himself out of the market, he failed; and the Mayor was canny enough to withhold the cheque until the job was done. So, with as much enthusiasm as he could muster, the Hero entered the underworld and painstakingly destroyed the menace from the pit. He celebrated his victory that same evening by dining out at Amy's Bistro with his pretty assistant, who found it a pleasant change from Alf's Sandwich Bar.

The Hero did not offer her a cigar; the last time he had she'd been quietly sick over his new John Michael suit. Instead he launched directly into an analysis of the case. "Wasn't I intrepid, though, my dear?" he enquired, rhetorically. "Knew that there were about five million deadly poisonous blue spiders down there, but did I hesitate?" Tactfully, the girl said nothing, and after a short pause he continued: "Boldly I advanced on them, thinking of my country, my friends, my reputation...

"And my fee," he added. "It was a bit awkward, going to each spider in turn and stamping on it. My legs are aching, and my best Crockett and Jones brogues are covered in that filthy blue muck. But it was worth it! The town is free of the poisonous arachnids;

that's what matters. And I've got a nice lump sum from the Council; that matters too.

"The town's got a bit of peace, I've got the money, you've got me, and everybody's happy, my dear."

"Except the spiders," he added.

"Let's start dinner, my dear."

His assistant, enthralled though she was by her employer's daring exploits, had been indicating for some time by her wistful glances that she thought the soup might be getting cold. Eagerly, she took a mouthful, and discovered that it was not merely cold but chilled. To her relief she also discovered that it was gazpacho. The Hero meanwhile stretched out a graceful hand for the salt cellar.

Underneath it, glaring at him with an expression of baleful satisfaction, was a very ugly and very poisonous blue spider.

3. The Hero Heroic

In a way the Hero was glad that the venomous spider had taken a fancy to his pretty assistant rather than to him. It was unpleasant to lose such an efficient and decorative employee, of course, but then assistants are plentiful; heroes are not. On the other hand, he was rather annoyed with the girl for handing in her notice after he had crushed the spider with his soup spoon while it was ogling her. The emotional experience, she had said, was just too much for her.

So now here was John W Hero, left, temporarily at least, alone.

His latest assignment was a real puzzler. After successfully concluding the Affair of the Deadly Spiders, the authorities had commissioned him to find the source of the dreadful killer smog that was devastating the good folk of Chelmsford — and stop it! Those were his instructions. And now, with a few essentials at hand (an elephant-gun, his father's trusty old flintlock cigarette-lighter, and his new grown-up pipe), he was ready to think about the problem.

Undoubtedly there was a thick, acrid cloud that had permeated the town over the past couple of days. He walked about the streets for a while, but wherever he went he found the black smog, and heard the choking cries of invisible passers-by. He retired to his chambers in Duke Street, and playing over Bach's soothing *Toccata and Fugue in D minor* on his Bechstein grand tape-recorder, he set his mind to the problem.

But the smog had penetrated even into his private sanctum, and he found that he could not distinguish the keys through the thick, dark haze. He ensconced himself in a brown leather armchair that his father had borrowed from the Garrick Club in 1934 and forgotten to return, and, puffing away at his pipeful of Old Hobson's Curly Cut, he thought. An hour passed — two — three — and still he pondered. Then at last he leapt to his feet, overturning his ashtray onto a floor that was already ankle-deep, and he cried aloud, "*Ευρεκα!*" And for the benefit of the less well-educated, "I have it, my dears!"

He had it! The solution to the mystery was in his hands. He smiled happily. Then he blushed, and hastily he knocked out his pipe.

4. How to Be a Hero

The Hero was very pleased with his new assistant. She had been with him a week and had already proved that she was not only very pretty but very capable. However, rearranging his entire filing system so that he could actually find what he was looking for did *not* qualify her for a rise in salary. Absolutely not.

"My dear," said the Hero, as he reclined gracefully on his William Morris chaise longue, "do you really mean to say that you can't manage on fifty-seven pounds a week? Don't be ridiculous, darling. Just go and get on with your work. There's a good girl.

"Really," he mused, nibbling daintily at his mid-morning foie-gras pie, "the impudence of it! Dash it, it's so — so *un-English*. Maybe it's because she comes from Transylvania." He finished his snack, brushed the crumbs from his waistcoat, and moved to the wall-mirror, where he combed his hair and practised his Jane Fonda-style exercises. Then he went into the office to prepare for his new assignment.

The girl's long dark hair rippled attractively in the slight draught as he closed the door. "What is it today, sir?" she said in her charming accent. "A vampire?"

"No," he said. "We haven't had a vampire since before my last assistant left me." He smiled wearily, affecting an air of worldly wisdom. "Girls come and go, you know," he added, irrelevantly. "Today," he continued, "it's a werewolf, my dear. There have been reports of a wolf terrorising the chickens at the Sandon Egg Farms, and according to this morning's *Weekly News* it mauled the organist from the Cathedral. Terrible thing, terrible thing. But there have been no reports of wild animals escaped in the area, and we're too far from John Aspinall's zoo, so we must assume that the creature is a werewolf. Now we have to discover its human identity."

For a full four days he worked hard on the problem during his office hours of eleven till two, and he even devoted a few minutes of his lunch hour to it. Then, on the Friday, his assistant disappeared. Through three worried days he had hideous visions of her lithe body being bloodily crunched by the long red jaws of the wolf. "A dreadful situation," he mused. "It's such a shocking reflection on one's efficiency.

"Poor girl," he added, as an afterthought.

Then, on the Tuesday, a card arrived, postmarked Brasov, Romania. It read simply:

> *"Dear John,*
> *Please don't be angry. Circumstances beyond my control have forced me to leave, and much as I enjoyed working with you I shall not be coming back.*
> *"With love, etc.*
> *"P.S. You can drop the werewolf case now."*

It was another three days before he realised what she meant.

5. Portrait of a Hero

The Hero put down his copy of *Fabulous Monsters of Filmland* and pondered gently upon the ineptitude of horror films. Had any of these producers or directors ever actually come face-to-face with a werewolf or a ghoul? he wondered. He doubted it, strongly.

The door of his room opened softly, and an attractive young woman with fair hair and brown eyes peered in. His new assistant. "Sir," she said, almost pleadingly, "it's nearly four o'clock, and you haven't finished your breakfast yet. Oh, yes," she added, "and there's a telegram come for you. Something about a vampire."

"Oh, splendid!" said the Hero. "I'll be there directly, my dear."

As soon as the girl had gone, he leapt out of bed, dressed himself, and finished off his cold kedgeree, almost in one movement. Then he swept into his office.

"An assignment, my dear," he announced, after scanning the telegram. "The peasant folk of Messing are being plagued by a fiendish vampire, and they want me to exterminate him."

"Peter Cushing," he concluded, "has refused the task."

"You will be careful, sir, won't you?" said his assistant anxiously, as they descended from the 4½ litre Bentley at Messing Green.

"Of course, my dear," he replied nonchalantly. "You will be doing the dirty work, anyway.

"It builds character, you know," he added.

The two intrepid adventurers made there way to *The Old Crown Inn*, where, so the villagers said, the vampire lay by day. "There's the coffin," observed the Hero, stubbing out his cigarette on it. "I wonder if — yes! There his is, right enough." He flung back the lid of the wooden box, and the creature lay revealed before them. "Ugly-looking brute, isn't he, my dear? Have you got the stake ready? Jolly good. Now, I'm just going into the saloon bar (I hate the sight of blood) and... Oh! Good day, landlord! I'd like a White Lady, please — on the rocks."

But the elderly man who had suddenly appeared behind the bar did not seem interested in serving drinks. "Vhat is goink on?" he demanded, in a ludicrous attempt at a Teutonic accent. "Vhat are you doink to mein creation, hein?"

With dignity, the Hero drew himself up to his full five-foot seven. "We are about," he said coolly, "to exterminate this dangerous vampire."

"Vampire!!?!" shrieked the old man incredulously. "He is not ein vampire! Nein, not no vay! You see, *I* am Herr Professor Doktor Viktor von Glande, und *he* is the hideous und psychopathic semi-human monster vhich I have created. Ah, those veary nights robbink the graveyards und charnel houses of Essex! Und the laborious days workink in mein laboratory in the old vindmill at Tiptree!

"It is true," he went on, "that mein creature has been terrorisink the peasant folk of the countryside, but I do assure you that he is *not* ein vampire!"

And that, of course, was that. The Hero and his assistant closed the lid of the wooden box, collected their equipment, and returned to the car. They bade farewell to the old mad scientist and drove home to Chelmsford. When they reached the office, the Hero had a full report made out for the authorities, but that was all he could do. He did not want to be sued for wrongful extermination.

6. Mister Hero Esquire

"Be you Mr 'Ero?" said the old hag. She snickered.

"Yes, my dear. What can I do for you?"

"Oi've bin lookin' for yew, 'Ero," said the hag, harshly, "'cause yew done the dirty on moi sister."

Isn't she common, my dear! Thought the Hero. He had taken a dislike to her the moment she had ridden in through his office window. And she hadn't parked her broomstick tidily, either. "I've got it!" he exclaimed suddenly. "You must be Old Mother Boatpound's sister, Auntie Gutsache. And you're a witch as well," he remembered. "Oh dear." He didn't like witches.

"Thass roight, 'Ero," said the hag. She had an atrocious Essex accent, and she smelt of turnips and belladonna. "Oi've come to teach yew a little ol' lesson, 'cause Oi doesn't take koindly to them as gets moi sisters turned over to the fuzz. Heh, heh!" She cackled evilly. Then she disappeared.

The Hero was startled, because where she had been standing now stood a large and very unfriendly-looking wolfhound. He gulped. Where had he put that gun with the silver bullets?

He fumbled in his desk drawer, and the dog drew menacingly nearer. Then the Hero whipped out a rusty iron horseshoe from the drawer and held it out towards the dog. (He was not quite sure what a horseshoe was doing in his desk, but he remembered that cold iron is anathema to witches.)

The effect was startling. The great vicious dog became a small yelping cat, and then a tiny frightened mouse. After that there was nothing that the Hero could see.

Heavens, that had been close! The Hero put the horseshoe down and mopped his brow with his tasteful Bugs Bunny handkerchief. Then he looked at his watch. Bother. Another hour before he could breeze along to the Golden Fleece and find the place open. Oh, well. He would go to Dace's and browse through the classical records. Perhaps he would listen to a few and then say thank you, my dear, but he didn't think he'd buy them after all. Pensively, he left the office.

A few minutes later his pretty assistant came in. She noticed a flea on the floor. It seemed to be pulling out of a coma. Plucky little thing, she thought, and she crushed it with her heel.

And that was that.

7. The Hero at Large

"Hello, my dear," said the Hero, as he breezed into his office one afternoon shortly after closing-time. "What have we got today? A resuscitated Egyptian mummy?"

"No, sir," said his pretty assistant. "It's an angry pagan god."

"Oh, dear. Same old thing, day after day." The Hero sat down. "I think I'll go to the pictures," he said. "They're showing one of those splendidly down-to-earth kitchen-sink films at the Pavilion. *Doctor Horror's House of Terrors* or something."

His assistant pointed out that it was a school holiday, and the cinema would be full of twelve-year-old children. "Oh, bother," said the Hero. "Oh, well... What exactly is this pagan god angry about, my dear?"

"Well, sir," she said efficiently, "the Basildon District Council were laying a sewer through a wood near Billericay, and it appears that they dug through the foundations of an ancient Roman temple of Jupiter. And Jupiter became, so to speak, narked."

She was not a Latin scholar.

It was raining when the two investigators arrived at Temple Wood. In fact, Temple Wood appeared to have its own private rainstorm, with thunder, lightning and everything. The Hero carefully parked the Bentley just outside the rainy area and surveyed the scene. Reluctantly, he opened his umbrella, making a mental note to have his assistant charge the council for a new one. Then he strode magisterially into the wood. His assistant, water running down into her *décolletage* and her shoes, followed at a respectful distance. She felt that there was something odd about the storm, but she could not say what.

As soon as they reached the site of the temple, the Hero became uncomfortably aware of someone near him. Looking around, he was startled to see a tall bearded man standing by, as large as life and twice as natural. It seemed that the place was a nudist resort!

"Look here, my dear," the Hero said, in an agitated manner, "you can't go about like that, you know! I mean, you'll catch your death — "

"Quiet, please," murmured the bearded man, reprovingly. With an air of concentration, he lifted his right arm and pointed at a particularly fierce-looking cloud. Quite suddenly, there was a blast of thunder, and simultaneously a white bolt of lightning shot out from the cloud and struck the new sewer just where it entered the foundations of the temple. There was a dazzling flash of pure white, and the sewer burst open, with an unpleasant squelching sound.

The bearded man rubbed his horny hands together and looked pleased. "There," he said. "That's better. Now, what can I do for you?" He smiled pleasantly at the Hero and his assistant, who were busily trying to hide behind each other.

The Hero found his voice at last. "By Jove!" he exclaimed. "It's gone! Gone! By Jove!"

"By Jove!" he added.

"That's right," said the bearded man, and quietly he disappeared.

8. The Daily Hero

The Hero put down his pen and massaged his arm. He was writing a book, which he proposed to call *How to Win Friends and Influence People, My Dears*. He wouldn't publish it under his own name, of course: he would use a discreet nom de plume. Something like Dale Winton, perhaps. It was odd that no one had thought of it before. He picked up the pen and continued writing: "Politeness is all. The truly polite person is always respected and loved. Never use a rude or an unkind word."

Just then the telephone rang, and his pretty assistant answered it. "Rudeness can never be justified," the Hero wrote, but he was interrupted by his assistant calling to him: "Sir, a gentleman from the Maldon Town Council would like to speak to you."

"Oh, dash it all!" the Hero exploded. "Can't you leave me in peace for a moment, you rotten old bag, my dear?"

The girl burst into tears, and the Hero was sorry immediately. Now there would be tear-stains on those important reports. Bother. "All right, my dear," he said. "I didn't mean it. Hand me the telephone."

After a few minutes he put the receiver down and said briskly, "An assignment my dear. It appears that a *Gorgosaurus ingentissimus* has crawled out of the sea near West Mersea and bounced up the river to Maldon, where it has settled in the Marine Swimming Pool. It goes on daily excursions into the town, knocking down shops and things. And nobody knows what to do about it."

The Gorgosaurus, already dubbed "the Maldon Horror" by some of the tabloid newspapers, and "Bonzo" by some of the others, stood forty-three feet ten inches in its bare feet. It was, when the Hero and his assistant arrived, using those feet to trample its way back through the town after a shopping expedition. In its prehensile forefeet it held two Dutch cheeses and half a pig.

The Hero turned to the Town Clerk, the gentleman who had telephoned him. "I suppose you've tried cannon and tear-gas and all that sort of thing, my dear?" he asked.

"Well, er, no, actually, old boy," was the reply. "We haven't tried anything yet. Thought we'd leave it all to you. You're the expert, after all. Haugh!" he snorted.

The Hero said he needed time to think. He went off to the public library, found volume 10 of the *Encyclopaedia Britannica*, and opened it at "GORG". Then he went to sleep.

His assistant, meanwhile, went to have a look at the monster. She found it shuffling aimlessly around the Marine Parade, looking fed up. It had finished eating, and was looking for something else to do. It seemed to be a little sick of just wrecking things. The girl felt rather sorry for it. Perhaps it was lonely, she thought.

The Gorgosaurus saw the girl and shambled over to her. She held back an urge to run, and stood firmly while the great creature sat down very quietly beside her. Timidly, she patted its huge scaly ankle, the only part of it that she could reach, and for half an hour they stayed there together. No one knows what they said to each other, the brave young woman and the mighty antediluvian monster, but at last the Gorgosaurus stood up, patted the girl on the head in its clumsy fashion (it nearly stunned her) and started off down the river towards the sea. Those who saw it last, from Salcott-cum-Virley, said it looked as if it was waving goodbye, but they may have been wrong.

When the Hero emerged from the library, he was bewildered to find himself the recipient of a substantial cheque and an invitation to be guest of honour at a civic banquet that evening.

"What did I *do*, my dear?" he whispered fiercely to his assistant. "What shall I *say*?"

"Never mind," she said quietly. "Just be polite and never mind. You're the expert, after all."

9. Our Man Hero

The Hero's pretty assistant was taking the week off. She had said something about the strain getting her down, and had gone to spend a few days with her dear white-haired old mother at a night club in Soho. The Hero was lost without her, though he would never have admitted it. He needed a temporary replacement, and he was not going to take on just any old bag. Indeed not! He wanted a smart, talented old bag. And it was not long before a most attractive and accomplished young lady answered the advertisement he had inserted in the tobacconist's window. She knocked on his door at seven-thirty in the evening, because, she said, she had to look after her dear white-haired old mother during the day. The Hero refrained from commenting on the remarkable plethora of dear white-haired old mothers and hired the girl immediately.

"We'll start right away, my dear," he said. "First case tonight. I'm sure we'll get on splendidly." The girl smiled at him and fluttered her eyelashes coyly. "We have to go to Maldon," he continued, "and dispose of a ghoul who's been holding private orgies in All Saints' churchyard and disturbing the local residents."

The girl paled a little and swallowed hard; then she smiled bravely and accepted the job.

She clung very closely to him as they entered the old churchyard. The Hero found it awkward, if not exactly unpleasant, to have her hanging around his neck as he was trying to collect his equipment, but he put it down to her inexperience. The scene was fitfully illuminated by flashes of light from a wild party in a house on Cromwell Hill, and they soon espied the ghoul, loping around and chewing a bit of dead baby. Perhaps sensing their presence, the monster looked up curiously, tossed aside a small shinbone, and began to shamble gruesomely towards them.

The girl seemed to lose her head. She screamed, and started to plead hysterically with her employer: "He's going to eat me! He's going to eat me!"

The Hero, for once, was nonplussed. "There, there," he said gently. "The nasty ol' thing's not going to eat 'oo, den...

"Besides," he added, "ghouls only eat dead people."

The girl was desperate. "Do you think I don't know that?" she shrieked. "Don't you understand? *Why do you think I came to you after sunset* ?"

She grimaced, baring her teeth.

The Hero stepped back, aghast, and at that moment the ghoul seized her and drove its claws into her neck. Then it took a great bite out of her breast. By the time the Hero had recovered himself and put a silver bullet into the monster, she was dead.

Well, not un-dead, anyway, my dears, as the Hero said later.

10. Hero Me No Heroes

The Hero was not looking forward to the coming ordeal. His pretty assistant was still convalescing at her dear, white-haired old mother's gambling den in Soho, and he had to face a night alone at Copford Old Rectory. It was only the thought of his personal dignity and the Bishop's blank cheque that kept him from abandoning the haunted parsonage altogether. He walked reluctantly between melancholy yews along the drive to the front porch, thinking all the time gloomy thoughts about the legend of the evil old eighteenth century baronet who had been gruesomely done to death in the drawing-room by a pack of savage foxhounds. The Hero did rather wonder what the squire and his hounds were doing in the rectory, but he knew that the wicked man's ghost had haunted the house ever since, terrifying anyone who was bold or ignorant enough to stay there overnight.

He reached the porch, and was fumbling in his coat-pocket for the key that the Bishop had given him, when he was astonished to see the door slowly opening. The small hairs rose on the back of his neck, and he was on the point of fleeing when he observed that the door had not opened of itself, but by the agency of a small elderly man of melancholy appearance and formal garb.

"Heavens, my dear!" he exclaimed. "You did give me a start! My name is Hero — John W Hero, my dear, actually."

"Oh, yes," said the old man. "Please come in."

The Hero entered and was conducted to the drawing-room. He felt just a little put out that the Bishop had made no mention of a caretaker at the rectory. "I suppose you'll be going home soon, my dear," he observed.

"Oh, no," said the old man. "This is my home. I live here — if you can call it living."

A resident caretaker, thought the Hero. How strange, my dear! Maybe there's nothing to this ghost story after all. "I've come to investigate the haunting," he said aloud.

"Oh, yes," said the old man again. "Sit down and I'll get you a drink. Would you prefer port or sherry?"

"Sherry, please — sweet," said the Hero.

His host left the drawing-room, closing the door quietly behind him. He returned a few minutes later, carrying a tray with two glasses and a bottle. The Hero noted with alarm that the old man had neglected to open the door again before walking through it.

"But this is awful!" he cried. "Heavens, my dear! You — you must be the... My dear, you're the ghost of Copford Old Rectory!"

The old man set the down softly on a little table. "Oh, dear," he said. "I had hoped you wouldn't notice." He sat down opposite the Hero, who was now looking very pale indeed. "No," he said gently. "I'm not the ghost. Not THE GHOST, at any rate. I had the misfortune to encounter him back in 1873 and died of fright."

He took a half-hunter watch from his waistcoat pocket and glanced at it. "There are thirteen or fourteen of us around here somewhere," he added. "The old squire himself walks at midnight, you know — in ten minutes' time. Would you like to meet him?"

But the Hero was gone.

11. A Hero For All Seasons

"Ah, my dear!" said the Hero, as his pretty assistant walked brightly into the office. "So splendid to see you again. I've been wearing my fingers to the bone typing out these reports. And the amount of Tippex I've used! Carry on with them, will you, my dear?"

"I trust you're feeling better," he added, as an afterthought.

The telephone rang. The girl typed a final letter on to the report for the Bishop on Copford Old Rectory (the Hero recommended the services of a demolition company in which, coincidentally, he had shares) and picked up the receiver. "Mr Hero's office," she said politely. "Mm... Yes, sir... Are they disturbing you?... I see... Very good, sir... Would you like to speak to him?... No?... Very good. Goodbye, sir."

She replaced the receiver. "A gentleman from Tiptree Parish Council," she told the Hero. "He says that a coven of witches seems to be holding nightly sabbats on the Heath. Or they might be satanists; he's not sure. At any rate, they're stopping the local residents from getting a good night's sleep."

The Hero was not sure that he fancied shooing witches off Tiptree Heath. He'd had several late nights recently, what with ghosts and ghouls and wild parties at the Oddfellows' Hall. And witches...! He shuddered as he recalled Auntie Gutsache and her sister Old Mother Boatpound. The latter's son-in-law had rushed into his office, wild-eyed, shouting, "My wife's mother's an old witch!" And he was right. The Hero had had to live on grass and bran-mash for a week until the spell wore off.

Still, he thought, sighing, I suppose not all witches are like that. "All right, my dear," he said. "We'll go and see about them."

Maybe I'll get a paragraph in the *Weekly News*, he thought, hopefully.

"Michael Fish said the night would be warm and dry!" The Hero was cold and damp, and not in a good humour. His assistant did not reply. She too was cold and damp, and she was rather annoyed with her employer for hogging the travelling-rug.

"Oh, look!" she cried suddenly. "There they are — over there!"

The Hero looked, and sure enough he could see cowled figures, convening evilly in a little hollow around a glowing brazier. Strong lights hung from scaffolding, illuminating the awful scene. "Satanists," he said. "Devil-worshippers to a man!"

"Or woman," he added.

The investigators crept quietly from bush to bush, until they were within yards of the sinister, black-robed figures. Just as they arrived, the diabolists all rose to their feet, and one of them, a brawny, dark-featured man, grasped hold of a young woman — plainly a captive — whose hair was loose and whose dress was becomingly torn.

The Hero was horrified. "My dear!" he whispered agitatedly. "They're going to sacrifice her — to the Goat, you know! It happened just like this in a story I once read. Heavens, my dear, this is awful!"

At that moment a voice rang out above the gruesome cackling of the satanists and the shrieks of the unfortunate prisoner. "Cut! Cut!" it shouted. "Take that scene again. Great Scott, I just can't afford to waste film like this! That was totally unconvincing. Nobody would ever believe you were supposed to be a group of devil-worshippers! Now, this'll be the thirteenth take. Let's get it right this time."

The two investigators looked at each other.

"Okay," said the voice. "Lights ready? Cameras? Action!"

The Hero and his assistant crept quietly away.

12. One Man's Hero

"Not Tiptree again, my dear, surely?" said the Hero. He had not forgotten the embarrassment of his last assignment there.

"Yes, sir," said his assistant, firmly. "The way they tell it is like this. At five-forty yesterday morning a fisherman at Goldhanger Creek saw a great amorphous mass rise up out of the estuary and start to slurp its way inland. The man described it at looking like a gigantic amoeba, but without any nucleus, and it seemed to be moving in an intelligent manner."

The Hero was still not convinced. "Go on, my dear," he said, guardedly.

"Well, sir, at eight-twenty-five, the creature arrived in Tiptree and headed straight for the jam factory, where it proceeded to wrap itself around all the strawberries and strawberry jam it could find. After it had absorbed all this, it belched and went to sleep. Now it's just like a great big jelly that's set there on the factory floor, except that it quivers, slightly but regularly. Perhaps it's breathing. They daren't try to shift it, in case it wakes up and eats them. They daren't burn it, in case the factory catches fire. They're stuck, and they want our help.

"*Your* help!" she corrected herself, hurriedly.

They arrived at the factory to find that the thing had woken up and was stretching itself squelchily before going on the rampage again.

"No place for a lady, my dear," said the Hero, patronisingly. Entering the factory, he saw the thing stretching upwards, as if to have a look around. It was now a rich translucent red from all the fruit that it had ingested. Heavens, my dear! thought the Hero. Whatever have I let myself in for? Oh, why didn't I follow Quentin's advice and become a choreographer?

Hastily he pulled out his .38 Police Special and brandished it ineffectively. With it came an inscribed photograph of John Inman in full make-up as Mother Goose (*"To John — I'm free! Love, John"*) which fluttered limply to the floor. The thing reached out a curious pseudopod to look at it.

Suddenly and violently it contracted, drawing itself in, becoming once again like an enormous jelly. This time, however, once it had ceased to quiver, there was not even the slightest movement from it. It had died of fright at the sight of the photograph! Or at the sight of the Hero. It was dead, anyhow.

The Hero collected his fee and his assistant and returned to Chelmsford.

And the jam factory sold strawberry jelly for a month.

13. Hero Today, Gone Tomorrow

One quiet summer afternoon, a whole segment of Danbury Hill swung open like a door, and out strode a gigantic man-like figure, about sixty feet tall, carrying a huge cudgel and chanting mightily:

> "Fee Fi Fo Fum —
> Look out, world, 'cause here I come!"

It closed the closed the hill again, with an easy movement of its great hand. Then it strode off along the road westward, causing chaos among the traffic all the way.

And thus came Gyrth, the Ogre of Danbury Hill.

The Hero was awakened from his afternoon nap (he was still feeling rather delicate after a wine-and-cheese party the night before) by the sound of heavy footsteps crunching through Chelmsford. He decided that it must be that wretched cadet corps from the Grammar School off on one of their beastly field days, my dears. But he was wrong; it was Gyrth.

An hour later the Hero's sleep was disturbed again. The ogre had gone as far as Leaden Roding and then decided to turn back and head the other way, towards the coast.

At about five o'clock, the Hero's pretty assistant came into the room to wake him. "It's this ogre, sir," she said. "He came out of Danbury Hill early this afternoon, strode out to the Rodings and back, and then set off along the road past Maldon and out into the Blackwater Estuary. Now he's settled down on Osea Island and issued a mediaeval giant's version of UDI. The authorities want you to go and help them get rid of him."

The Hero went, of course. He was becoming a fatalist.

"About this ogre, my dear," said the Hero to his assistant. "Don't they go around eating people, and things like that?"

"So I'm told," said the girl.

"Has this Gyrth eaten anybody?"

"Not yet," she replied.

The Hero shivered. They were standing near the site of Stansgate Abbey, at a point on the south bank of the river, close to Steeple Creek. They could see the giant standing on the shore of Osea Island, about half a mile across the water. The Hero raised a megaphone to his mouth.

"Come on out, Gyrth!" he called. "We know you're in there!"

The giant grunted.

"Oh, do come off it, my dear!" said the Hero. "They're bringing cannon and grenades and all sorts of things. And you'll catch your death sleeping out all night!"

Gyrth bellowed back at him:

"Fee Fi Fo Fay —
Here I am, and here I stay!"

The Hero was worried. How on earth could he shift the ogre and collect his fee (the Hero's fee) without carrying out his threat of guns and bombs? He didn't want to hurt Gyrth, who had not actually killed anyone yet — and besides, in his profession a tame ogre would undoubtedly give him a certain cachet.

His thoughts were interrupted by a distant rumbling noise approaching from the west. It rapidly resolved itself into the sound of heavy footsteps. And Gyrth evidently knew what it was. He groaned:

> "Fee Fi Fo Fee —
> It's my old wife come after me!"

And a lady ogre, a few feet shorter than Gyrth, soon arrived on the scene. She strode purposefully out to the island and grabbed her errant husband by the left ear, roaring:

> "Fee Fi Fo Fee —
> You'll never get away from me!
> "Fee Fi Fo Fum —
> Off with me and home you come!"

She marched the humiliated ogre back to Danbury Hill, which took them in as mysteriously as it had let them out, and that was the last that the Hero saw of them.

The next day he gave his assistant fifty pounds and told her to take a fortnight off. He himself was going somewhere quiet for a rest. Transylvania, he thought.

Afterword

In his generous introduction to the Sarob edition of *A Ghostly Crew*, David Rowlands wrote: "I have to confess to a slight sadness that an earlier Johnson character, John W Hero — a psychic investigator who, in the manner of 'Harris Tweed', depends on an attractive female assistant to bale him out of difficulties — is not represented in these pages, but maybe in the next collection...?"

I've always had a fondness for the old fraud (JWH, I mean, not DGR — though I am fond of him, of course), and on re-reading these tales I felt that the jokes stood up pretty well. So —

If you don't like them, blame David Rowlands...

A BUTCHER'S DOZEN: TALES IN VERSE

I   **To His Masters**

A stone tower stands within a darkling place,
Girt round by ancient woods both drear and deep.
The people of that forest fear to sleep,
For night brings dangers no man cares to face.
Yet in the tower dwell those of other race —
Dreamers by their dreams both curst and blest —
Whose eyes unmoved, unwinking dare to rest
On things that lurk at Horror's very base.

Dark spirits! ye have dwelt within that tower,
With ancient rotting books your only friends,
In sorcery, since Time's first unformed hour.
In magick ye remain, until Time ends.
My Masters! Thanes of Ælfland, ghostly Lords:
Your arts still tell the beauties Death affords.

II   **Desideration**

I craved that relic from the ancient tomb:
For dark intent it would fulfil my need —
For sorcery, my life, my only creed,
The magic that would prove my final doom.
Some daemon's urgings led me there alone,
At midnight, when the sickly moon shone pale.
I sought the vault, deep in its gloomy vale,
And entered it, and raised the coffin stone.

The wizard's body lay there, undecayed —
Yet hideous in its livid, bloodless look.
His opened eyes turned on me, and he *spoke*:
Such words of power no mortal ever made.
I fled the vault, yet still those words I hear —
And I must kill myself, or die of fear.

III   Companionship

My journey was to Josefsbad, alone,
On foot, through ancient woods where shadows creep,
Past louring cliffs and chasms vast and deep.
The winter's winds fair cut me to the bone.
Then in the forest, near the end of day,
With horror I beheld a great wolf's tracks —
I had no weapon, neither knife nor axe —
And my numbed mind no longer knew the way.

A peasant came: he'd show me through the wood.
He led me down a gloomy, untrod road —
Then turned. His eyes with malice strangely glowed.
I fled (I know not how it was I could)
Fled — for I saw the being change its guise ...
The man became the wolf before my eyes.

IV   Residence

No one would go there after Jock West died,
Or rather, disappeared — for none could say
Whether the mangled corpse they'd found inside
Was old Jock or some other. Who would flay
A living man, bite off his nose and ears,
Scoop out his viscera? Atrocity,
The doctor called it; and in all his years
He'd never seen more dreadful butchery.

At last, when yet more folk had disappeared,
I visited the house — and found a door,
Stairs down — a stench — worse horror than I'd feared.
Sickened, I backed away — and with a roar
Jock sprang, enraged with hatred and alarm,
Still clutching a half-eaten human arm.

V   **Invocation**

"He'll answer us," the leader gravely said.
"It was a perfect sacrifice this time.
I killed the girl myself; it was sublime.
The God cannot refuse her heart and head."
Music, at first quite gentle, like a flute,
Stirred up strange feelings in my flesh and bone.
Glory and power, I thought, are ours alone.
I smell him — yea! Our sacrifice bears fruit.

We grew ecstatic as each man in turn
Was opened to the spirit of the Goat.
"*Iö Pan!*" the cry went up. One shrieked, "I burn!"
And fell upon the priest, and tore his throat.
We saw the hooves that crushed him, saw the glare
Of goatish eyes — Great Pan had heard our prayer.

VI   **Recognition**

What is this place? My memory's at fault.
A crypt, I think: sour-smelling, lightless, wet ...
I've been concussed. Why else should I forget
What brought me to this dark and noisome vault?
My eyes become accustomed to the gloom.
There, on the wall — what is that cryptic sign,
Abstract and meaningless, and yet malign?
This cold stone monument — is it a tomb?

It looks somehow familiar. Wait! I think
Vague memory stirs. My uncle brought me here.
He laid me on the tomb, and calmed my fear
By giving me a soothing draught to drink —
Then plunged the knife! My blood flowed like a tide.
Yes, I remember: *this is where I died.*

VII   Metamorphosis

    Toward the end, my cousin found a book
    That seemed to hint at dark, forbidden things.
    He turned the pages, and his fingers shook,
    While in his mind thoughts rose on demons' wings.
    One antique symbol fascinated him.
    Amid the unknown text, it seemed to be
    Complex, alluring, and yet subtly grim.
    If there were secrets, this must be the key.

    A focus for strange powers was what he sought.
    Reclusively, he drew back from his kin.
    We saw it and were sad, but little thought
    What evil his obsession had let in.
    Alarmed at last, we sought him — and we found
    A loathsome thing that crawled upon the ground.

VIII Discovery

    Lost on the moors, the girl with flaxen hair
    Came to a lonely farm beside a tarn.
    Cold, wet and frightened, miles from anywhere,
    She hoped that she might shelter in the barn.
    We went in search when she did not come home,
    But couldn't prove the truth of what we feared.
    A few yards from the lake, we found her comb —
    But that was all. Our friend had disappeared.

    We often wondered what the farmer knew;
    But he was surly, close and taciturn.
    Our friend had gone: that's all that we could learn —
    Until one day the farmer vanished too.
    They dragged the tarn, and found his body there —
    Not drowned, but strangled by long flaxen hair.

IX   Reverberation

"This is the Bell of Doom," the hermit said,
Stroking the time-worn bronze with taloned hand.
"'Twas cast and fashioned in an antique land
That at the last its voice should rouse the dead."
I laughed and left him, to pursue my way,
At length arriving at the city gate.
Corrupt and foul, the townsfolk tempted fate,
Debauched more vilely than a man could say.

Amid the foulness, sickened to my soul,
Deafened by bitter cries of pain and lust,
I turned away, in weary, sad disgust .
Then, distantly, I heard the great bell toll —
And, as I saw the rank air shake and blur,
Beneath my feet the dead began to stir.

X   Paranoia

Born to a life of privilege and wealth,
From infancy he was afraid of dreams.
He'd wake himself, so piercing were his screams,
And sheer exhaustion undermined his health.
Awake, he could not quite explain his fright.
He thought some entity, malign and vague,
Something as foul and constant as the plague,
Was edging slowly closer, night by night.

Tired and afraid of life at last, he swore
That self-same day should see his final breath.
After such torment, he could welcome Death —
To rest in stillness, and to dream no more.
In pain he died, and heard amid his pain:
"I am your nightmare. Enter my domain ..."

XI Heredity

There long were rumours in the countryside
Of evil madness in my family's past.
Inheriting the house, I thought at last
To unearth what my fathers chose to hide.
I found the oldest coffin in the crypt,
That of one Leofric, a Saxon mage,
Son of a thane, respected in his age —
But from what mother's womb had he been ripped?

The priest and I removed the coffin lid,
And saw the corpse, preserved in fragrant oil.
My skin crawled, and I saw the priest recoil.
This was a monstrous thing, most wisely hid.
The world's mad, or I'm cursed! Here were the proofs —
I saw my forebear's horns and cloven hoofs ...

XII Offering

We found the print, cut from some ancient tome,
That seemed to show a pagan sacrifice.
We should have been suspicious of the price,
But wanted to examine it at home.
Upon a slab was bound some formless creature;
We studied it with nervous fascination,
And I, in awe of this obscene oblation,
Found I could distinguish each pale feature.

But as the face upon that thing unknown
Became more certain to my fear-struck eye ,
My friend collapsed; I heard his bitter groan
And saw his body wither, shrink and die.
Too high the price! Too late to make amends —
The face of that sad victim was my friend's.

XIII To His Late Mistress

I love thee now; thy beauties move me yet —
Thy marble limbs, thy small and slender feet;
Thy face so pale and delicately sad,
With eyes whose lust might make a poet mad,
And lips like blood-drops, teeth with piercing gleam;
Thy slim white hands, far stronger than they seem;
Thy low, soft voice, with accent strange and sweet —
Perchance I loved thee ere we ever met.

My love for thee near rends me like some knife!
Yet thou lov'st me, as I on thee do dote:
Thou show'st it by thy warm and hungry kiss,
Thy strong and cruel embrace — and more than this:
Two small red scars that now adorn my throat,
Wherefrom thou hast my blood, my love, my life.

Afterword

Donald Wandrei may have been the first to write a series of fourteen-line stanzas (purists would deny that they are sonnets), each telling a nasty little story. H.P. Lovecraft was stimulated by Wandrei's *Sonnets for the Midnight Hours* to write his own *Fungi from Yuggoth*, which in turn have inspired various others, including Lin Carter's cycle *Dreams from R'lyeh*.

August Derleth published earlier versions of "To His Masters", "Desideration" and "To His Late Mistress". The last appeared as "To His Mistress, Dead and Darkly Return'd", under which clumsy title it was later reprinted in *The Vampire in Verse*, edited by Stephen Moore. Derleth also accepted "Companionship", but his magazine folded when he died, and it was eventually published in *Tales After Dark 2*.

The remaining verses are new, written for this book.

Acknowledgements

The contents of the first section, *"Things that Go Bump in the Night"*, were published in 2001 by Sarob Press, as *A Ghostly Crew: Tales from the Endeavour* with an introduction by David G Rowlands.

The Scarecrow was first published in *Ghosts and Scholars 6* (Runcorn: Rosemary Pardoe, 1984), and reprinted in *The Year's Best Horror Stories XIII* edited by Karl Edward Wagner (New York: DAW Books, 1985).

The Watchman was first published in *The Best of **Ghosts and Scholars*** (Uncasville, CT: Richard H. Fawcett, 1986).

The Interruptions was first published, as "The Dog", in *A Graven Image, and Other Essex Ghost Stories* (Runcorn: Rosemary Pardoe, 1985).

The Wall-Painting was first published in *Saints and Relics* (Runcorn: Rosemary Pardoe, 1983), and reprinted in *The Year's Best Horror Stories XII* edited by Karl Edward Wagner (New York: DAW Books, 1984) and *The Mammoth Book of Ghost Stories* edited by Richard Dalby (London: Robinson Books, 1990).

The Searchlight was first published in *A Graven Image, and Other Essex Ghost Stories* (Runcorn: Rosemary Pardoe, 1985).

The Taking was first published in *Deep Things out of Darkness* (Loughborough: Garrie Hall, 1987), and reprinted in a revised version in *Tales of Witchcraft* edited by Richard Dalby (London: Michael O'Mara, 1991).

The Melodrama was first published in *Ghosts and Scholars 10* (Chester: Rosemary Pardoe, 1988).

The Prize was first published in *Ghosts and Scholars 11* (Chester: Rosemary Pardoe, 1989).

The Breakdown was first published in *Deep Things out of Darkness* (Loughborough: Garrie Hall, 1987).

The Pool was first published in *Picatrix* (Ruislip: Chico Kidd, 1992).

The Clues was first published in *Spectral Tales 2* (Upper Montclair, NJ: Robert M. Price, 1989).

The Night Before Christmas was first published in *Chillers for Christmas* edited by Richard Dalby (London: Michael O'Mara, 1989).

The Soldier was first published in *Mystery for Christmas* edited by Richard Dalby (London: Michael O'Mara, 1990) and reprinted in *The Year's Best Horror Stories XIX* edited by Karl Edward Wagner (New York: DAW Books, 1991).

The Souvenir was first published in *All Hallows 6* (Chester: The Ghost Story Society, 1994).

Sweet Chiming Bells was first published in *Shivers for Christmas* edited by Richard Dalby (London: Michael O'Mara, 1995).

Aliah Warden was first published in *The Count Dracula Fan Club Annual: H.P. Lovecraft Special Issue* (New York: Dracula Unlimited, 1985) and reprinted in *The New Lovecraft Circle* edited by Robert M. Price (Minneapolis: Fedogan & Bremer, 1996).

The Dreaming City was first published in *Deep Things out of Darkness* (Loughborough: Garrie Hall, 1987), and reprinted in *The Antarktos Cycle* edited by Robert M Price (Oakland, CA: Chaosium, 1999).

Custos Sanctorum was first published in *Deep Things out of Darkness* (Loughborough: Garrie Hall, 1987) and reprinted in *The Innsmouth Cycle* edited by Robert M. Price (Oakland, CA: Chaosium, 1998)

Ishtaol was first published in *Deep Things out of Darkness* (Loughborough: Garrie Hall, 1987).

From the Desert was first published in *Dark Dreams 3* (Liverpool: David Cowperthwaite & Jeff Dempsey, 1985).

The Fool's Tale has not been published before.

The Man Who Inherited the World has not been published before.

In Memoriam was first published in *Rehearsals for Oblivion, Act I: Tales of the King in Yellow* edited by Peter A Worthy (Lake Orion, MI, USA: Dimensions Press, 2006)

On Dead Gods was first published in *The Count Dracula Fan Club Annual: H.P. Lovecraft Special Issue* (New York: Dracula Unlimited, 1985), and reprinted in *Cthulhu Codex* 11 (1997).

The Serpent's Tooth was first published under the title "As Our Rarer Monsters Are" in *Dark Dreams 5* (Liverpool: David Cowperthwaite & Jeff Dempsey, 1987).

Enigma was first published in *Deep Things out of Darkness* (Loughborough: Garrie Hall, 1987).

Desideratum has not been published before.

Love, Death and the Maiden was first published, as "Mädelein", in *The Mammoth Book of Ghost Stories 2* edited by Richard Dalby (London: Robinson Books, 1991), and reprinted under the present title in *Best New Horror 3* edited by Stephen Jones and Ramsey Campbell (London: Robinson Books, 1992).

Oddities Investigated. Earlier versions of three or four of John W Hero's exploits appeared in now untraceable issues of *The Chelmsfordian*, *Zimri* and *The Count Dracula Fan Club News-Journal*. A privately printed booklet containing all the stories was issued for some of Mr Hero's friends in 1984.

A Butcher's Dozen. An earlier version of "To His Masters" was published, as "To My Masters", in *The Arkham Collector 10* (Sauk City, WI: Arkham House, Summer 1971); an earlier version of "Desideration" was published, as "The Relic", in *The Arkham Collector 9* (Spring 1971); an earlier version of "To His Late Mistress" was published, as "To His Mistress, Dead and Darkly Return'd", in *The Arkham Collector 8* (Winter 1971), and reprinted under that title in *The Vampire in Verse* edited by Stephen Moore (New York: Dracula Press, 1985); an earlier version of "Companionship" was published, as "The Traveller's Tale", in *Tales after Dark 2* (Loughborough: Garrie Hall, 1986). The remaining verses have not been published before.

Also from MX Publishing

Close To Holmes

A Look at the Connections Between Historical London, Sherlock Holmes and Sir Arthur Conan Doyle.

Eliminate The Impossible

An Examination of the World of Sherlock Holmes on Page and Screen.

The Norwood Author

Arthur Conan Doyle and the Norwood Years (1891 - 1894) – Winner of the 2011 Howlett Literary Award (Sherlock Holmes book of the year)

www.mxpublishing.com

Also From MX Publishing

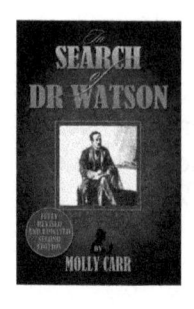

In Search of Dr Watson

Wonderful biography of Dr. Watson from expert Molly Carr – 2nd edition fully updated.

Arthur Conan Doyle, Sherlock Holmes and Devon

A Complete Tour Guide and Companion.

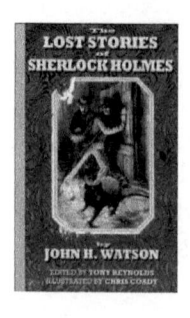

The Lost Stories of Sherlock Holmes

Eight more stories from the pen of John H Watson – compiled by Tony Reynolds.

www.mxpublishing.com

Also From MX Publishing

Watsons Afghan Adventure

Fascinating biography of Watson's time in Afghanistan from US Army veteran Kieran McMullen.

Shadowfall

Sherlock Holmes, ancient relics and demons and mystic characters. A supernatural Holmes pastiche.

Official Papers of The Hound of The Baskervilles

Very unusual collection of the original police papers from The Hound case.

www.mxpublishing.com

Also From MX Publishing

The Sign of Fear

The first adventure of the 'female Sherlock Holmes'. A delightful fun adventure with your favourite supporting Holmes characters.

A Study in Crimson

The second adventure of the 'female Sherlock Holmes' with a host of sub-plots and new characters joining Watson and Fanshaw

The Chronology of Arthur Conan Doyle

The definitive chronology used by historians and libraries worldwide.

www.mxpublishing.com

Also From MX Publishing

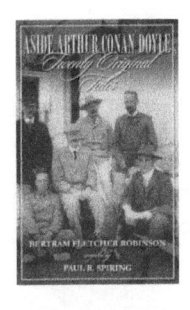

Aside Arthur Conan Doyle

A collection of twenty stories from ACD's close friend Bertram Fletcher Robinson.

Bertram Fletcher Robinson

The comprehensive biography of the assistant plot producer of The Hound of The Baskervilles

Wheels of Anarchy

Reprint and introduction to Max Pemberton's thriller from 100 years ago. One of the first spy thrillers of its kind.

www.mxpublishing.com

Also From MX Publishing

Bobbles and Plum

Four playlets from PG Wodehouse 'lost' for over 100 years – found and reprinted with an excellent commentary

The World of Vanity Fair

A specialist full-colour reproduction of key articles from Bertram Fletcher Robinson containing of colour caricatures from the early 1900s.

Tras Las He huellas de Arthur Conan Doyle (in Spanish)

Un viaje ilustrado por Devon.

www.mxpublishing.com

Also From MX Publishing

The Outstanding Mysteries of Sherlock Holmes

With thirteen Homes stories and illustrations Kelly re-creates the gas-lit, fog-enshrouded world of Victorian London

Rendezvous at The Populaire

Sherlock Holmes has retired, injured from an encounter with Moriarty. He's tempted out of retirement for an epic battle with the Phantom of the opera.

Baker Street Beat

An eclectic collection of articles, essays, radio plays and 'general scribblings' about Sherlock Holmes from Dr.Dan Andriacco.

www.mxpublishing.com

Also From MX Publishing

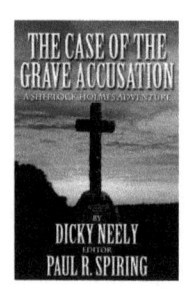

The Case of The Grave Accusation

The creator of Sherlock Holmes has been accused of murder. Only Holmes and Watson can stop the destruction of the Holmes legacy.

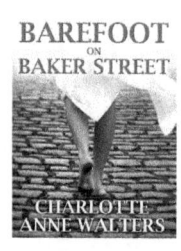

Barefoot on Baker Street

Epic novel of the life of a Victorian workhouse orphan featuring Sherlock Holmes and Moriarty.

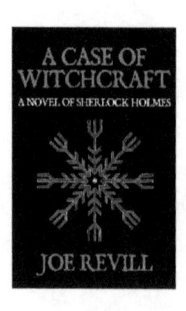

Case of Witchcraft

A tale of witchcraft in the Northern Isles, in which some long-concealed secrets are revealed including about the Great Detective himself.

www.mxpublishing.com

Also From MX Publishing

The Affair In Transylvania

Holmes and Watson tackle Dracula in deepest Transylvania in this stunning adaptation by film director Gerry O'Hara

The London of Sherlock Holmes

400 locations including GPS co-ordinates that enable Google Street view of the locations around London in all the Homes stories

I Will Find The Answer

Sequel to Rendezvous At The Populaire, Holmes and Watson tackle Dr.Jekyll.

www.mxpublishing.com

Also From MX Publishing

The Case of The Russian Chessboard

Short novel covering the dark world of Russian espionage sees Holmes and Watson on the world stage facing dark and complex enemies.

An Entirely New Country

Covers Arthur Conan Doyle's years at Undershaw where he wrote Hound of The Baskervilles. Foreword by Mark Gatiss (BBC's Sherlock).

Shadowblood

Sequel to Shadowfall, Holmes and Watson tackle blood magic, the vilest form of sorcery.

www.mxpublishing.com

Lightning Source UK Ltd.
Milton Keynes UK
UKHW021313021222
413271UK00009B/35